THE LAST

MW01538618

A Novel By
V. L. Hoyt

Illustrations by Tom Pomatti

To: Luc
WELCOME TO THE CRUSADE!

12/19/10

"The Last Crusaders," by V.L. Hoyt. ISBN 978-1-60264-418-2 (softcover); 978-1-60264-419-9 (hardcover).

Published 2010 by Virtualbookworm.com Publishing Inc., P.O. Box 9949, College Station, TX 77842, US. ©2010, V.L. Hoyt. All rights reserved. No part of this publication may be reproduced, stored in a retrieval system, or transmitted in any form or by any means, electronic, mechanical, recording or otherwise, without the prior written permission of V.L. Hoyt.

Manufactured in the United States of America.

Thanks and Acknowledgments

What a journey it has been in writing and publishing "The Last Crusaders" – what an adventure! And so many people accompanied me on that journey in such varied ways. So, although I have tried to make this an exhaustive list, it may well be that – like so many Oscar acceptance speeches – I have inadvertently omitted some names. If so, I apologize and assure you that there was no intent to snub.

First and foremost, my husband, Tom Paccioretti, the love of my life, who never let up on my getting this to print.

To Jenifer Catalano – my writing partner of many years – who can make me laugh like no other, and who always provides the best critiques (and muffins!)

To Pamela Lane – my writing coach and editor – who is fabulous in everything she does.

To Michelle Bauman – my long-time job sharing partner and life coach – whose support and encouragement I relied upon most heavily.

To my mom, Louise Porter Bowers, and my sister, Patricia Hoyt Maher – for being the best mom and sister anyone could hope for.

To my bros, Peter, Stephen and Norman.

To Greg Huebner and (Karen) Leigh Chapman – friends extraordinaire! Thanks, Leigh, for catching those last pesky typos and incorrect Brit & Irish slang!

To Laurie Pesce, my "twin" and PR guru, who was instrumental in getting this in such amazing shape for publishing.

To Tom Pomatti, the illustrious illustrator.

To friends who read my book in its various versions and whose encouragement kept me going – Victoria Katchis, Zada Clark, Judy Kramer, Gretchen Goetz, Stephanie Caprielian, Susanne Jett, Michael Rosenfeld, John Shulman, Steven Ritz Barr, Jennifer Casey and Tom Rogers.

To Kate McMains, who edited my book early on and had wonderful suggestions.

To Monique Raphael High, who encouraged me over a decade ago to pursue my writing.

And to the 2009-2010 Oakwood School 5th Grade Book Club: my first and foremost fans, who loved the manuscript, gave me wonderful suggestions on making it even better, and asked for my first autographs! That Wednesday in April 2010 when I met with you will always be one of the highlights of my life. Thank you to their exceptional teachers – Judy and Jen – and to you **amazing** readers! Keep reading!

And a final shout-out to Alex Bauman, who got the ball rolling with the Oakwood School by reading my manuscript, loving it so much he wrote a book report on it, and whose enthusiasm got the manuscript selected as a Book Club choice by the 5th Grade. You are **the** guy, Alex!

Table of Contents

Chapter One

Reality Bites

Elaine "the Mink" LaCroix stood before what she called "the biggest henhouse" of her cat burglar career – Kinkakuji, the Temple of the Golden Pavilion in Kyoto, Japan. The full moon shone through the cherry trees, creating a bizarre pattern of daggers on the ground. She shimmied up the nearest tree. The blossoms gave off a perfume so heavy it seemed to cling to her hair and skin. Flaring her nostrils, she sprang to the top railing of the ten-foot black fence, teetering for only a second before regaining her balance.

"The Mink always lands upright," she muttered to herself.

She lowered her body over the fence. The silver ring on her right hand burned briefly, but intensely. Slashing her arm on one of the iron finials, she screeched, *"Mère de Dieu!"* and collapsed upon the mossy ground. She gingerly examined the gash on the inside of her forearm. "The Mink can take the pain," she whispered. Whipping out a pink handkerchief with "the Mink" embroidered in red, she held it to the gash and looked away. "The Mink hates blood." It was the tiniest of whimpers. She rose and ran from the shadows of the cherry trees to the wooden wall of the first floor of the temple, her left arm tight against her chest.

The ring burned again – longer and hotter.

"Yaaah!" Elaine struggled to tear it off her finger. But the ring felt two sizes too small. She made one last wrench, then froze. A growling came from her right — a guttural gnarling, like a cross between a lion and wolf.

Elaine flattened her body against the smooth timber, then raised her nose in the air and sniffed as if she were, in fact, a mink. The creature — whatever it was — smelled wild and ancient. Fear raced down her scalp and across her arms in tingling waves. The predator had become the prey. But the Mink knew fear and did not let it paralyze her. Swiftly, silently, she fled to her left toward the lake. The crunching of leaves and crackling of twigs came faster from behind. "Steady, little Mink, steady. Not much farther. There!"

The wall broke away to her right, forming a small alcove. Blessed with keen night vision, the Mink reached for what most others would have missed — a squat door with lock and handle. "Patience, patience." She pulled an intricate pin from her leather pouch and inserted it in the lock. The snarling rose in intensity, joined suddenly by a second growling, this one at a higher pitch.

The hairs rose on the back of her neck as she caught the last of the tumblers and twisted the iron handle. The door swung inward, Elaine along with it. She caught only a glimpse of the beast as it thundered into the alcove, froth flying from its jaws. It had two yellow eyes and one green one above them in the center of its forehead that glowed with an unearthly light. She slammed the door and turned the lock. The sickening thud of flesh and bone against foot-thick wood sent a shockwave that almost knocked Elaine to the floor. Then, a squeal of pain, a whimpering, a soft pawing at the door. Finally, silence.

The sinister warlock stood on a cliff, arms high above his head, white limbs unfurling like albino serpents from within the depths of his crimson robes. His hands offered the copper scarab to the dark heavens — while below the weary knight and his faithful steed awaited their gruesome fate.

"Damn! Do I use the endomorphic travel ring or blast the sucker with the laserscopic sword?" Fifteen-year-old Lucas Moreno talked to himself, never taking his eyes from the computer screen. "The scarab makes this guy immune to laserscopy. Gotta go with the travel ring." His fingers flew over the keyboard.

Out of the darkened sky came crashing thunder, scorching lightning and...the gentle gurgling of a small stream. A crescent moon hung with the soft white stars in the night sky. No more warlock.

"Friggin' great!" he shouted. A golden retriever sat up and barked.

"Sorry, Shadow." Lucas knelt and absently ruffled the dog's head and chest fur. "Course, now the ring's juice is gone, and I'm stuck until I find another endomorphic power source. Where the hell am I, anyway?"

Lucas hadn't been in that level of the game before. He shrugged. "Any place is better than the Penumbran Deserts. And being out of juice beats the heck out of being torched by lightning." Lucas pressed more keys. "Time to scope out the place."

The knight dismounted and tethered his horse to a cherry tree in blossom. He stared through the bars of a ten-foot iron fence, topped with wicked-sharp finials. Inside stood a three-story wooden structure, the third story smaller than the first two, and the two top stories covered in gold, each with a black sloping roof. It sat at the edge of a lake, surrounded by pines and cherry trees.

"Companac, Sir Lucas?" asked a computerized voice. The soft masculine voice reminded Lucas of the slither of a snake. Freaked him out a little. He didn't trust it.

Companac. Compass, map, and almanac. What dweeb thought up that name? Lucas shook his head and said, "No," then took another bite of a half-eaten apple.

The words "Buddhist Temple, Japan" appeared on the computer screen, followed seconds later by a red flashing light and siren.

"Some kind of warning. Oh, man!" Lucas pounded the desk.

Shadow's cold nose nudged his hand. He scratched behind the dog's ears, never taking his eyes from the monitor.

Dozens of strange symbols flickered on the screen. Lucas leaned back in the swivel chair, arms crossed. *This friggin' bites.* He tossed the apple core into the metal trashcan where it landed with a clang.

"Okay, okay, I know we're in Japan, and me with no friggin' lingual decoder badge."

Lucas sat up in his chair. "I'm going in." He leaned over the keyboard, shoulders hunched, rapidly pressing the directional keys to animate his computerized alter ego.

The knight climbed the cherry tree, balanced on the fence, and jumped. The horse whinnied. The knight crossed through the trees and ran to the temple, edging along the wooden wall toward the lake. Suddenly, a low snarling sounded. The knight stopped. A high-pitched shriek followed.

Shadow howled.

"There's gotta be a door somewhere. Come on, man!" Lucas urged the knight on.

The knight began to run. The snarling and shrieking grew louder.

Shadow whined and tried to crawl under the desk.

"What's going on in there, Lucas?" After a knock, the door flew open. Sandra Moreno entered holding a pile of folded clothes. "What's wrong with Shadow?"

Sandra placed the clothes on Lucas's bed, smoothing the comforter. "Turn it down, please. Did you tell Rocky and Jason about your birthday present and invite them to the Dallas-Washington playoff game?"

Lucas sat hunched over the keyboard, nose almost touching the computer screen.

"Lucas? Do you hear me? Lucas?" Sandra stood with her hands on her hips.

He turned. "What? I'll put the clothes away later, Mom." He swiveled back to the computer.

"Lucas Moreno," said Sandra, "you look at me this minute."

"But Mom!" Lucas glanced over his shoulder. "I'm in the middle of –"

"Another computer game? I've told you how I feel about this, Lucas. Between those games, track and band practice, it's a wonder –"

The computer emitted a loud, agonizing scream. Lucas jerked his head.

The knight lay on the ground. Rather, pieces of the knight lay on the ground – an arm here, a leg there. The horse was gone.

"An agonizing defeat," whispered the computer. "Better luck next time, Sir Lucas."

"Damn it!" shouted Lucas.

"Lucas!"

"Sorry, Mom. But I was *this* close!" He held his thumb and index finger an inch apart, then swiveled back to the computer.

Sandra warned, "Don't even think about starting another game. Your father should be home soon, and I need some help with dinner." At the bedroom door, she turned, smiled and, with a curtsy, said, "Sir Lucas."

"Comical, Mom. Real comical."

After she left, Lucas leaned down and stroked Shadow, who was still cowering under the desk. "It's okay, boy. It's only a game." He stared at the torn, bloody knight-parts, which were slowly disappearing from the screen. "Some wicked kinda game."

Elaine exhaled with relief and pushed away from the door with her good arm. She swallowed, forcing back bile. But the coppery taste of fear remained. Breathing quietly, she let her eyes adjust to what little light there was. "Now, to play the thief."

The Sacred Room of the Eye was down a long corridor to her left, just before the main temple. The Mink crept swiftly along the hallway, pausing now and then to cock her head and listen. Was that the low murmur of distant growls? Raising her nose, she sniffed – nothing but the resin scent of pine and oil from the polished floors. "Safe inside the henhouse, little Mink."

Down the hall a few yards she stopped, pulled chunky black glasses from her bag and put them on. Six beams of violet light, spaced a foot apart and running horizontally across the massive iron door, sprang to life. "Clever." Smiling, she pulled something else from the pouch – a thin, cylindrical metal object – and ran it up one side of the doorframe, then down the other. The violet lights vanished. "Not clever enough." Seconds later, she toggled the lock pin until the tumblers gave way. Stepping into a small chamber not much wider than the door she gasped.

It sat on a pedestal of gold and onyx, surrounded by gold bars, like a caged bird. "*Sacre mere de Dieu,*" she whispered. An oval of bright green jade, as big as a man's fist, blazed from behind the golden prison, beckoning. The Eye of Buddha. Mesmerized by the dazzling jewel, Elaine didn't notice the steady, soft steps padding up the hallway or the measured breathing of her attacker. Her hand stretched to caress the golden cage.

A black-clad arm grasped her shoulder and pinched.

The Mink slumped to the ground.

Elaine's assailant heaved her body under one arm and closed the door behind him with a loud CLANG! He slogged down the corridor to another door, Elaine's feet dragging. Stepping into the main temple, he tossed her at the feet of his master. Two monstrous beasts, each with a glowing green eye in the middle of its forehead, whined and paced back and forth.

The beast master turned. He was dressed entirely in black, but for a brilliant purple cape that contrasted sharply with his alabaster skin and piercing blue-green eyes.

"Excellent, Shotoku, excellent. She will be a welcome addition to our little dungeon." With a twist of a smile, Mordred reached for Elaine LaCroix.

Like a vulture clawing the flesh from its prey, the white bony hand plucked the glowing ring from the fallen crusader.

———

Half a world away, Merlin shuddered and opened his eyes. "It was not meant to be, little Mink," he whispered, then closed his eyes and drifted back to the sleep of the enchanted.

Chapter Two

The Penumbran Deserts

There had been a terrible accident. Sandra Moreno exited the glass doors of the ICU in San Antonio's University Hospital into the waiting area. Lucas could tell his mother was seriously upset: Her eyes were red and swollen, and her lips quivered. She hugged Lucas's two sisters and reached up to ruffle his hair. When she tried to talk, her voice seemed squeezed. "Your father needs his rest." Lucas frowned. Not good news. She touched his forearm. "He's asking for you. Bay 333. On the right."

Me? Why me? Lucas turned toward the glass doors.

"No more than a few minutes, Sweetie. Try not to tire him."

Lucas nodded. As he entered the ICU, he heard his grandmother say, "What did the doctors say? When can I see him? How –" The glass doors shut behind him, cutting her off.

Lucas walked hesitantly down the muted yellow and green tiled hallway, keenly aware of the constant blip, blip, blip of heart monitors and the gentle whoosh, whoosh of breathing machines. The soothingly lit corridor was empty. He took deep breaths, determined not to cry in front of his father. He knew the accident had been bad. Falling cranes on construction sites always killed people on the news. He just never imagined it would be his father pinned under tons of metal. *Those accidents aren't supposed to happen to architects!* He stopped short. 333. Taking another deep breath, Lucas walked into the bay and pulled open the first curtain on the right. It

7

felt like he'd caught the high jump bar and landed full force on his gut, and couldn't breathe.

His dad lay on a hospital bed, covered in bandages tinged with blood, with tubes everywhere, and a gray-green oxygen mask hiding his face. Lucas took a deep breath, then gagged. Almost worse than the sight of his father was the stale, sickly air surrounding him – like rotting meat that no amount of Lysol could conceal. His dad opened his eyes.

Tomás Moreno stared at Lucas for a few long moments through his swollen, blood-red eyes...and managed a weak smile. Lucas pasted on a false grin, wishing his dad had *not* asked for him. But he knew he was his dad's favorite. He used to tell Lucas, "You look so much like your great-grandpa, Tony." Lucas loved to hear his dad's stories about spending the summers on Anthony Moreno's ranch in the hill country north of San Antonio, loved to hear his dad say, "You are the picture of your great-grandpa. Same black hair and eyes. So lean and wiry. And so impatient!" His dad would laugh. "Pacing about like a caged wolf-cub. Just like he did!"

But Lucas didn't pace now. He stood rooted, waiting.

Tomás sighed and struggled to lift the oxygen mask from his face, then winced and dropped his bandaged right arm. He spoke in a raspy voice, and Lucas could barely make out the word, "Mask."

Lucas fought off the urge to vomit and forced himself to his father's bedside. He grimaced as he removed the oxygen mask, fearful of disconnecting wires or tubing.

"Box. Silver ring." The words came out in a ragged whisper, then his father began coughing in long, deep spasms. Lucas quickly placed the oxygen mask back over his dad's mouth, debated pushing the red emergency button next to the headboard, and sighed with relief when the coughing subsided and his dad breathed easier. Tomás indicated with his right hand for Lucas to take the mask again. Lucas slowly removed it. Tomás clasped his son's hand, but his grip was weak.

"Suitcase." His dad spoke in a halting whisper. "Maybe...only...fairy tale." Pause. "Give...to you." Shallow breath. "Find...out. For...your son."

Box? Silver ring? What is he talking about? Lucas opened his mouth to ask when his dad raised his hand and tenderly stroked

Lucas's cheek. It felt like bones raking across Lucas's skin. Cold shivers rippled down his spine.

Tomás let his arm fall back against the mattress and closed his eyes, whispering, "Sandra." Lucas gently re-arranged the mask and turned to leave. His dad murmured, "Love you...Lucas."

Filtered through the oxygen mask, the words took on an eerie quality, as if spoken from somewhere far, far away. Lucas closed his eyes to stave off his sudden dizziness and saw himself running down a long winding hallway, screaming, "Dad, don't go! Don't leave me!"

"Lucas?"

Lucas opened his eyes and stared at his dad. And knew. Somehow, he knew. He would never see his father again.

"I love you, too, Dad." Lucas hoped his words could reach him. That his father could take them with him to...wherever. Now heedless of the tears streaming down his face, he closed the curtain.

Chapter Three

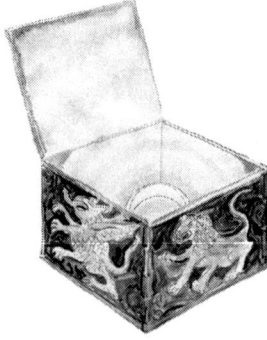

Hanging On

Lucas lay on his bed, arms propped behind his head on two pillows. Shadow lay at his feet, or rather, *on* his feet. Lucas didn't mind. The golden retriever's fur kept him warm. He still wore his track team sweat shorts and tank top – the Churchill Chargers – that he'd slept in the night before. He looked at the alarm clock – 10:00 A.M. on a Saturday morning. Rocky, Jason and the other guys would be at the track meet. Lucas sighed.

A knock sounded and his mom opened the door. "Hey, sleepyhead, time to rise and shine." She pulled open the wooden blinds on the two windows overlooking the backyard. The winter-spring sunlight poured into the room, little dust-bunnies swirling in the rays.

Lucas turned away from the windows, shielding his eyes from the glare. "Jesus Christ, Mom!"

"You know I don't like that talk." She slapped him lightly on his butt. "It's a beautiful day. Why don't you call Rocky or Jason?"

"They're at track," Lucas mumbled, a pillow over his face. He breathed in the faint scent of jasmine. His mom insisted on adding a few drops of the perfume to the wash for all their linens and towels.

He felt Shadow leap from the bed. "You could always join them," his mom said. "Coach Mallory called again. You can come back anytime you like."

Lucas raised the pillow from his face. "What's the use? It's all bullcrap."

His mom frowned, her back stiffening. "Watch your language. I don't want to have to tell you again."

Lucas placed the pillow back over his face. "Sorry," he mumbled through the down. "I just don't see the point."

"I know, honey." His mom's voice softened. "And I know it's only been six weeks since...." Her voice trailed off.

The funeral, Lucas thought, *only six weeks since his funeral.* He felt his eyes burning from unshed tears.

He heard his mom sigh before saying, "But we can't just lie around or watch TV all day, as much as we might want to. Life goes on."

Lucas clutched the pillow hard to his face and mumbled, "In a few minutes."

His mom sighed again, then said, "Come on, Shadow. Breakfast." Lucas peeked from behind the pillow. The retriever followed her out the door, tail wagging.

"Bullcrap!" Lucas sat up and threw his pillow across the room, knocking over a picture of him and his dad at a track meet. Grumbling, he got up from bed to retrieve the fallen photo. His grinning dad stood next to him, one arm around Lucas's shoulders. That had been the day Lucas set the regional high jump record. Placing the frame photo side down on the desk next to his flute case, he picked up another photo.

Father and son stood behind an architectural model of a YMCA building. Lucas had helped build the model – the building itself was one of his dad's *pro bono* projects. When Lucas had asked why his dad was designing the project for free, Tomás had said, "It's not just me. Lots of companies and individuals are donating time and money. Together, we can make a difference in these kids' lives. And they can make a difference in the world."

Lucas shook his head in disgust. *What difference does it make now?* "It's all a bunch of crap," he told the room.

Lucas sighed and set the YMCA photo face down, then felt something wet and sticky on his free hand. "Hey!" He turned to see Shadow grinning at him, tongue hanging. Lucas made a face and wiped the combination of dog drool and kibble bits onto his shorts. He knelt by the retriever – who had become Lucas's constant companion – and hugged him.

But Shadow was only a dog, not his dad.

Out of the corner of his eye, Lucas saw a silver ring glittering on the floor near the window. He walked over, bent down and picked it up – only a pop-top from a soda can. *Funny*, he thought, tossing the metal circle into the trashcan, *I could have sworn it was a silver ring*. He froze, his hand still in mid-throw. *The silver ring!*

Lucas walked through his parents' bedroom to the closet. His mother still hadn't packed away any of his dad's clothes. *It still smells like him.* He held the sleeve of his dad's favorite sport coat to his face and breathed in. Honking back tears, he walked to the back corner. There it was: his dad's worn, leather suitcase.

Lucas searched it, finally finding a rosewood box in a zippered side section. He studied it for a minute, rubbing his hands over the carvings of strange animals and birds. Inside was a silver ring with weird writing engraved inside and two pieces of paper: one a slip, yellowed with age with cursive lettering which read,

Merlin, Knights of Round Table, Quest, Dream

and the second, a folded sheet of stationery with "LUCAS" written on it. Lucas fingered the ring as he unfolded the sheet and read it.

"Lucas, *mi hijo*, this is our legacy, your legacy. This ring was given to me by my father, and to him by his father, and to him by his father – back to the time of King Arthur. We are descended from one of the Knights of the Round Table, Don Vasquez of Spain. Legend has it this ring was forged by Merlin to aid Don Vasquez in a great crusade. But he failed and gave the ring to his son. And so it has been handed down from father to son for generations. That's all I know. I think it's time we found out more. On a family vacation in England this summer. You and I will research the books on King Arthur and Merlin. And Don Vasquez. We'll have our *own* great crusade. Happy Birthday, Lucas."

Some birthday – Lucas shoved the suitcase back on the shelf – a week later, his dad was gone. And he had charged Lucas with "finding out" about the ring. Lucas hugged the box and silver ring to his chest. *I can do that, Dad. I can do that.*

———

That night, with Shadow resting at his feet, Lucas sat in front of his computer staring at the slip of paper on which he'd printed the writing from the ring. *Runes* were what they were called, an alphabet of medieval Anglo-Saxons. In surfing for information on runes, he stumbled on a chat room for English History and joined the conversation by posting the question, "Can anyone translate these?" and scanned the runes into the computer:

ᛒᛗ ᚠᚥ ᚹᚾᛏ
ᚹᛁᛞ ᛞᚾ ᚱᛗᛜ

He signed his query "*L.M.*" and logged off, then wrestled with Shadow, laughing at the dog's attempts to escape by licking Lucas's mouth and nose. He realized he hadn't laughed like that in a long time. It felt good.

———

Lucas rushed home from school instead of hanging with his friends the next two days and signed into the website, only to be disappointed when he found no response to his ring-rune inquiry. On the third day, he grabbed Shadow's leash, and the two visited Tomás' grave. Lucas liked the cemetery. It had only been six weeks since his dad died, but he felt closer to him there.

The only other person at the cemetery was a very old woman placing flowers on a grave not far from his father's. Lucas had seen her before – the widow Martinez. He waved.

"Hello, Lucas. I see your mother brought roses again." Mrs. Martinez grimaced as she straightened up, rubbing her hands over her lower back. "How I would love to have her green thumb."

As Shadow sniffed around Tomás' headstone, a strong wind gusted suddenly, blowing petals off the flowers. Lucas shivered from the cold and pulled his sweatshirt over his head. That's when Shadow began growling – a deep guttural sound that made all the hairs on Lucas's arms tingle. He popped his head through the sweatshirt to see Mrs. Martinez hobbling away. The place seemed deserted. Then, he noticed a black limousine in the middle of the cemetery.

Not unusual to see a limousine at a graveyard. But this limo seemed different; it gleamed as if it had just been polished, and the windows sparkled with the sun glinting off them. Lucas looked straight up – at a sky overcast with dark clouds. He looked back at the limo – shining as if there were a blazing sun. It sat idling in an area of open graves, but there was no one around, no funeral service in progress.

Shadow's growls turned to whimpers, and he pawed Lucas's pant leg. Lucas knelt and stroked Shadow's head. "What's up with you?"

Just then, the rear window on the passenger side of the limo rolled down. A very white, bony hand pointed at Lucas, beckoning him. As if in a trance, Lucas started for the limousine. Shadow gave a ferocious howl and leaped at Lucas, sending him sprawling onto his father's grave, scraping his palms and ripping the left knee of his jeans. He held his stinging palms around his bleeding knee and yelled, "Jeez, Shadow! What the...." The rest of the sentence died in his throat. Shadow's hair stood straight out in a ripple down his entire back, and his lips pulled away from his teeth in the scariest snarl Lucas had ever seen.

Lucas jumped up and called for Shadow to follow. As he raced across the cemetery, the powerful revving of an engine made him glance back. Just then, the black limo shot forward, speeding toward him. Lucas turned and ran as if he were breaking the world record 100-meter dash, ran so hard that his lungs began to burn. But the limo was gaining on him. Yards before the cemetery entrance, Shadow flew past him, barking madly. Lucas could see people turn to see what the commotion was all about, could see some react with horror, hear others scream. As he reached the entrance, he could smell the acrid fumes of the hell-bent limo, and then he was catapulted across the blacktop!

As he flew through the air, he heard a dog's painful yowling. He landed on patchy grass, scraping his elbows, the wind knocked out of him. He turned over, wheezing, only to see the limo screech away. And then he saw Shadow, yards away, lying on his side, mewling.

"Shadow!" Lucas ran to him, pushing aside the man and woman who knelt next to the injured Golden. He cradled the dog's head in his lap, crying, "Shadow," over and over, until his throat swelled and tears ran down his cheeks.

"We've got to get him to a vet, quickly." An older man with salt-and-pepper hair, dressed in a suit and bolo tie, placed a firm hand on Lucas' shoulder. "Put him in my car. There's an emergency vet just down the road. You two, help us get him into the back."

It was only when the man whispered, "I've had dogs hit by cars, son, and all was well. He'll be fine so long as we get him to the vet *now*," that Lucas allowed others to lift Shadow into the rear compartment of the gray-suited man's Lexus station wagon.

"Go ahead, son." The older man gestured with his arm toward Shadow. "Crawl up next to him and keep him calm."

Lucas wiped the tears from his face and blew his nose on the sleeve of his shirt, then slid next to Shadow, careful not to nudge the dog. As he laid his head next to the Golden's, the dog mewled and licked Lucas' face. He let the tears begin again as he petted the dog and whispered, "You'll be all right, boy. Everything'll be fine."

It was only then that Lucas heard the animated chattering outside the car. He saw at least ten or more people crowded around the cemetery entrance, gesturing and pointing to Lucas. One young woman turned to a much older one and shouted into her ear, "I said, the dog saved that boy from being run down! Just leaped in front of the car, it did!"

"It won't be long, son." The older man shut his door and put the car in gear. "What's your dog's name?"

"Shadow." Lucas wiped his nose on his sleeve. "Hurry. Please."

"You keep Shadow calm and let me handle the rest."

Lucas didn't respond until he heard a police siren and glimpsed a flashing light...coming from their car! He leaned over the backseat and saw all the cars ahead of them pulling to the side of the street. *We're gonna make it!* He shouted over the noise, "Thanks, Mister!"

The man gave a thumbs-up, and Lucas nestled next to Shadow, who was trembling – whether from pain or the siren, Lucas didn't know. He stroked his red-gold fur and murmured, "You're gonna make it, boy."

When the car came to a stop and the siren and lights went out, Lucas pushed himself up to find them in a No Parking zone outside an emergency veterinarian.

"Stay here, I'll get someone." The man hustled through the automatic doors.

Not even a minute later, a man and woman dressed in blue scrubs had transferred Shadow to a stretcher and rolled him inside the facility to an operating room. They allowed Lucas to stay with Shadow through the examination and administering of the anesthesia. Once the dog was under, a female tech escorted him back to the waiting room, where the gray-suited man sat reading "Dog Fancy" magazine.

He rose to greet Lucas, holding out his hand, "Bill Barton."

Lucas grasped his hand and said, "Lucas Moreno. Thank you so much, Mr.—"

"You handled it well, Lucas," Bill interrupted as he gripped Lucas' shoulder. "Now, you need to give your mom and dad a call."

———

After a subdued family dinner that night and vegging in front of the television, Lucas popped into the kitchen for a snack and found his mom standing with palms on the sink, her shoulders shaking with sobs. Lucas went to her and put an arm around her shoulder. "It's okay, Mom. It'll be okay."

She rested her head on his chest, then sniffed, and took a deep breath. "I couldn't have taken it if you were..." She plucked a tissue from a pink metal container on the countertop and blew her nose.

"But I'm not. I'm fine, and Shadow's gonna be fine." Lucas opened the fridge and grabbed a root beer. "And Agent Barton'll get that bastard in the limo."

"Lucas!"

He gave her an exasperated look. "C'mon, Mom."

Smiling, she relented. "Just not in front of the girls." She glanced at the wall clock. "It's after ten, you should be getting to bed, sweetie. Are you sure you're okay?"

He nodded. "I've taken worse tumbles in the high jump." He swigged from the root beer bottle and then said, "Mom?"

She finished hanging the damp dishtowels on the oven handle. "Yes, sweetie?"

"Um," he hesitated.

His mom stared at him. "What is it, Lucas?"

"I'm sorry about the vet bill. I know it's gonna be a lot, but I have some money saved—"

"Don't you dare think that, Lucas Moreno!" She went to him and took his face in her hands. "Shadow's family. And he saved your life, today." She kissed him on the forehead, then released him. "You take your own advice. It's all going to be fine. Now off to bed. I'm exhausted."

Back in his room, Lucas got ready for sleep, but when he lay down on the bed, he was still wide-awake. He thought about calling Jason or Rocky, just to talk about the creepy guy who tried to run him down, but he wasn't up to talking about Shadow yet. He knew his dog – his *heroic* dog – was going to be just fine, but even thinking of saying Shadow had almost been killed choked him up. And, truth be told, Lucas got the heebie-jeebies when he closed his eyes and pictured that white, bony hand beckoning him from the gleaming black limo. Shoot, Lucas had shivered when he described the guy to Agent Barton – the nice older guy in the gray suit – who turned out to be head of the San Antonio FBI office.

Lucas got up and went to his dresser. Cool business card. Agent Barton had even written his personal cell number on the back, urging Lucas to "Call anytime, day or night, if you remember anything more. We'll get this guy, Lucas." Lucas smiled as he fingered the card.

He wanted to tell someone, and he knew he'd get an *awesome* reaction from his two best friends – like "slammin', man!" or "no way, dude!" Reconsidering, he picked up his cell phone to text Jason, then noticed the wooden ring box and went to his computer instead. A Morgan Dunmoore had provided a translation to his ring-rune inquiry:

Be as one with the ring.

The rest of the message surprised Lucas. Apparently, Dunmoore had received another request for the same translation. What's more, he was asking to see Lucas's ring.

But I never mentioned having a ring. He frowned. "And what does 'be as one with the ring' mean?"

Lucas placed the ring on his ring finger. Nothing.

On his pinkie. Nothing.

"It's too big," he sighed, placing it back in the rosewood box.

But he took the ring to bed that night, slipping it on and off his fingers. Nothing. He was about to give up when he placed it on his right index finger. Suddenly, he couldn't get it off. The ring *fit*. His heart began to hammer in his chest. He waited – for what seemed an hour – but nothing happened. Tossing and turning with disappointment, Lucas finally dropped off to sleep.

And dreamed.

Chapter Four

Don Vasquez

Lucas stood in a small clearing in the middle of a towering forest. A cold mist hovered over the ground, and a sighing sort of sound swept through the pines – half-wind, half-human – followed by the clippity-clop, clippity-clop of horse's hooves. But the sound echoed around and through the trees so that Lucas couldn't make out where it came from. A weird tingling began at the top of his head and shot through his body and out his feet. Suddenly, a flash of green burst through the mist at the south end of the forest.

A knight on a chestnut stallion galloped toward Lucas. The rider had jet-black hair, a goatee, and wore a green silk cape over his suit of armor. A matching green silk blanket was under his saddle. The knight reined in his horse only feet from Lucas and surveyed him with pale blue eyes. Finally, he dismounted and bowed.

"I am Don Vasquez *de* León, an emissary of Merlin. I have long awaited you. But my wait may have been too long. So much time has passed since I began the quest."

Lucas started to interrupt, but Don Vasquez placed a hand on Lucas's shoulder and a finger to his own lips. "You have many questions, but we do not have much time. Listen carefully and watch closely, for I promise that all you need to know will be revealed."

Vasquez mounted his steed and pulled Lucas up behind him. Lucas wrapped his arms tightly around the knight's chain-mail waist and hung on for his life as he bounced on the galloping animal out of the forest to open countryside.

A short time later, they entered another, smaller forest. Vasquez slowed the horse to a walk. "I served King Arthur as a knight of the Round Table. That was a time of many wondrous adventures and crusades. The last was the greatest – the crusade to end the domination of evil. And it was Merlin who ordered it."

"Merlin was real?" asked Lucas.

The knight gave a deep chuckle. "As real as I."

Yeah, like that helps, thought Lucas, but he had no time to argue, for Vasquez continued his story.

"Merlin was the King's sorcerer and closest advisor. One night, he assembled the twenty-four original Knights of the Round Table." Vasquez turned his head and gave Lucas a wink. "I was one." He clucked the horse on at a faster pace. "Merlin told us the time had come to send us on our grandest journey, but he feared many would not return. We were to split up into groups and seek three holy objects."

"Relics?" asked Lucas.

The knight nodded. "The Holy Grail, the Hands of Allah, and the Eye of Buddha."

Lucas whistled. He knew all about the Grail. *But what are the other ones?* Before he could ask, Vasquez halted the horse on the shore of an immense lake.

"We were to return with them to this spot." Whitecaps had begun to form on the lake from the rising wind. Vasquez dismounted, then helped Lucas down from the huge horse.

"I failed the quest. As did other knights and their descendants. Now, my ring has passed to you, Don Moreno, and so has the quest."

He called me Don Moreno! thought Lucas, and he couldn't help feeling a slight pride.

"If you do not succeed, there may not be the chance for your children or grandchildren to complete the crusade. Know that the journey is fraught with dangers – more than you might imagine."

The small smile faded from Lucas's lips.

"But also know that the journey's end is more magnificent than you can conceive." The knight placed a hand on Lucas's shoulder. "Finally, know that doing nothing, failing to undertake the journey, will bring about more danger than you will want to know. I bid you luck and farewell."

The lake was now a sea of frenzied whitecaps, heralding a storm. Vasquez turned to mount his horse, but Lucas grabbed his gloved hand. "Don Vasquez! Where am I? Where do I begin? What do I do? I'm only fifteen, I don't even have my learner's permit yet!"

"*Mi hijo*. My son." Vasquez caressed Lucas's face. "Where are you?" The knight cocked his head. "Where do you think you are? Has our time in history been forgotten so soon?"

He tossed his cape from his shoulder. "Where do you begin?" Vasquez pointed to the great oak tree by the shore of the lake. "Here, where Merlin was imprisoned."

"What are you to do?" The knight placed one hand on his steed's neck and smiled. "Begin at the beginning. You are only fifteen, but you believed, Lucas. And you must keep believing." Vasquez mounted his horse. "Join the crusade."

Rider and horse raced away. Lucas yelled, "No! Stop! I don't want the ring!" but the wind swallowed the words. As the storm began to pelt him with huge drops of rain, he twisted the ring off his finger and...

Awoke in his bed, drenched with sweat, the ring clutched in the palm of his hand.

———————

A week later, Lucas sat at a long polished table in the Winston Churchill High School library. Jason and Rocky's ribbing about Lucas being Spanish "royalty" had gotten to him, and he was even more determined to unravel the mysteries of the ring. And Shadow was almost back to his old doggy self – no lasting repercussions from the "incident." Lucas refused to call it an "accident" because he knew damn well the limo creep had hoped to kill, had *tried* to kill, Lucas. So, there he sat, reading another book on Arthurian legend, this one by Professor Morgan Dunmoore – his Internet connection. He was so deep into the book that the librarian's sudden appearance at his side startled him.

"Here are two good books on Spanish History, Lucas," said a pleasant black woman who wore too much perfume. "I especially like the one by John Crow."

"Thanks, Mrs. Grayson." Lucas opened the Crow book, *Spain, The Root and the Flower.*

Several hours later, dusk began to seep through the library windows, forming shadow-figures in the corners. No one but Lucas remained in the reading hall. After much research, he had finally located the Don Vasquez of his dream – Lorenzo Vasquez, born in 913 A.D. to the wealthy Vasquez family of León, in what is now Northern Spain. Vasquez left León to join one of the many crusades, returning from time to time to see his relatives. After being wounded and taken prisoner in Northern Africa, Vasquez managed to escape and return to León, where he died at his family's house.

"He must have had the ring then," Lucas mused out loud, absent-mindedly twisting the ring on his finger.

He felt a breeze and looked up to see mist rising from the floor. Glancing around the reading hall, he pushed back from the table and walked over to the floor vents. He placed his hands through the mist onto the vent plates – nothing seemed to be coming from there.

"Siiiigghh."

Lucas jerked his head around at the sound – half-wind, half-human. But he was alone. A familiar tingling began at the top of his head and shot through his body. A shimmery figure strode out of the mist – Don Vasquez!

The knight wore the same green silk cape over the same suit of mail armor, and his pale blue eyes still seemed to pierce through Lucas's mind, as if Vasquez could read his thoughts.

"*Mi hijo.* You have learned much to speed you on your way. But the Dark Powers know about you. You must go to the ancient oak by the lake where Merlin was enchanted. *Now.*"

Although spooked by the phantom knight, Lucas couldn't help blurting out, "Why are you doing this to me? I don't understand. I don't know where Merlin was enchanted in England, and how would I get there? And what are these *Dark Powers*?" As the words left his mouth, Lucas felt dizzy. "The cemetery," he whispered. "Were the Dark Powers in the limo?"

"I come because you have been called, Lucas." Vasquez placed his hands on Lucas's shoulders and gently squeezed. His touch felt human. "You will understand more when you journey to England. All I can tell you is what needs to be done – by *you* – in order to save this world, your world, from the Dark Powers. Yes, they were the ones who tried to run you down, who hurt your dog. Because you have done nothing since that time, they may believe their tactics worked, that you are not a threat to them. But you must be prepared. For at some point, even if you do nothing, the ring itself will call to them, and they *will* come."

Lucas felt the dizziness wash over him again, but Vasquez continued. "Young people throughout history have performed great deeds. Joan of Arc was seventeen when she led France to victory. King Arthur himself was only fifteen when he ascended to the throne. And you *will* find a way to England, because you must. Know that there are good forces at work, to guide and assist you."

The ghost-knight opened the Dunmoore book. "Destiny has been thrust upon you, Lucas. You can choose to ignore the ring and continue your life as a boy, or you can embrace the quest and begin life as a man. Either way, the decision you make affects the entire world. I will try to be there when you need me, but I cannot promise it. I respond only to a summons from Merlin. And the ring has a will of *its* own."

Vasquez abruptly turned and strode back into the misty carrel. Lucas hesitated only seconds before running after him, but the knight had vanished. Lucas ran headlong into the librarian, causing her to drop the armful of books she had been shelving.

"I'm sorry, Mrs. Grayson. I didn't see you. I was looking for someone..." Lucas looked around, but the mist had disappeared. "...but I guess he's gone." *And how stupid do I sound?*

The librarian knelt to gather the scattered books from the floor. "These things happen. Maybe if you hurry, you can still catch your friend."

I must be the only one who can see Don Vasquez, he thought. *No way for Mrs. Grayson to have missed him otherwise.* Lucas slowly returned to his table and gathered his books and notepad. He closed the Dunmoore book. *Wait. What's that?* A photo of a lake with an old, gnarly oak tree. *The place where Don Vasquez took me in my dream!* Lucas read the caption:

Lake Windermere in Cumbria, England.
Believed to be where the sorcerer Merlin was imprisoned
by the enchantress Vivienne.

"The place where Merlin was imprisoned!" He checked out the book and ran home, the ring clutched close to his heart.

Chapter Five

The Internet Connection

Lucas had no time to dwell on Don Vasquez or his warnings when he got home. He stopped on the front porch to check the mail. Sorting through the various bills, letters and advertisements, he stopped and examined a letter under the porch light. It was addressed to an "Elaine LaCroix" in Paris, France, and was stamped with a big, red pointing finger and the words, "Return to Sender." What startled Lucas was that his *father* had sent it. That was his handwriting. Lucas could barely make out the postmark – ten days before his father died.

Who is she? Why was Dad writing to her? Lucas had never heard his father or mother mention an Elaine LaCroix.

He stuffed the letter into his jeans and opened the front door.

Pandemonium erupted. His mother almost bowled him over as she exited the house, shouting to eleven-year-old Christina to, "Watch your sister!" When she turned to see him standing there, she screamed, "Lucas!" and threw her arms around him. He felt her tears on his bare neck, felt them soak through his shirt.

Christina shouted from the entryway, "Lucas!" And little Caridad, the seven-year-old who adored her brother, ran out the front door and wrapped herself around his legs, hiccupping between sobs.

"What's going on?" Lucas tried to push his mother away, tried to pry Cari off him so he could walk, but neither one would let go. "Mom, calm down, calm down." Finally, his mother looked up at him and wiped the tears from her face. Lucas said, "What's wrong? You all are acting *loco*."

"Oh, Lucas."

His mom started to sob again, but Lucas grabbed her shoulders in a firm grasp. "Nuh-uh, don't do that. Tell me. Cari, let go." He managed to gather his sister in his arms, where she clung fiercely to him, her head nestled in the crook of his neck.

"It's all over the news!" Christina hopped back and forth on her legs as she wiped her nose on her shirtsleeve. "We thought you were–" She resumed crying.

"What? Thought I was what?"

His mom stroked his cheek and whispered, "Dead. We thought you were dead." She choked out the last word, then sniffled and smiled. "But you're here." She sniffled again.

"Dead?" exclaimed Lucas, gaping. "Why would you think—"

The telephone rang. "Inside, inside." His mom grabbed him by the hand and tugged him through the doorway. Cari refused to be put down. His mom slipped off her coat as she answered the phone. "Hello?"

Silence.

"No, Mary, he's right here! Just got home! I'll call you later." She hung up and looked at Lucas. "You need to see this. The den." She grabbed his hand again, as if she couldn't bear to have him out of her grasp.

That's when Lucas noticed that the dining table was set and food sat barely touched on three plates, growing cold. He allowed his mom to pull him to the den, to the television. On the screen, a building was in flames, surrounded by smoke, spectators, police cars with flashing lights and several bright yellow fire engines. Sirens wailed, flames crackled, and people screamed.

"That isn't—" began Lucas.

"Yes, the YMCA," answered his mom.

Lucas stared. "*Our* YMCA? Dad's building! How—"

"It started in the pool locker room right after..." His mom paused and honked back tears. "...lifeguard training."

Lucas felt the same dizziness from the library creep into his brain and fog his thoughts.

His mom touched his shoulder and whispered, "I thought you were there. I thought you—"

"I blew it off. I was studying at the library." He looked from his mom to the television then back to his mom. Frowning, he asked, "But why did you think I was—" And he finally got it. He shook his head as he stared into his mom's eyes. "No, that can't be, please say no one was..." He wouldn't finish the sentence.

Water welled in his mom's eyes and she nodded. "Two. That they know of."

Having the wind knocked out of you by a bad fall in the high jump didn't hurt as much as the news that two people – probably guys he knew – had been killed in a fire. That someone had torched his dad's building, had murdered people. That *he* could have been burnt to a crisp.

"Sit down, sweetie." His mom led him to the overstuffed chair and tried to take Cari from him.

"No!"

The little girl held on, and Lucas let her sit in his lap, let the awful news sink down to the pit of his stomach. Finally, Cari relaxed her grip on him and asked, "Will Daddy's building be okay?"

Lucas fought off the fear that licked at his mind, fought off his light-headedness and gently squeezed her hand. "Yeah, it'll be okay. The firemen'll save it, right, Mom?"

"Of course, sweetie." Sandra sat on the chair arm and smoothed Cari's hair, then caressed his cheek.

He saw that his mom knew, too. There was no way they would save Tomás Moreno's YMCA. Not only had people died, another bit of his father had died. Lucas felt as if he would hurl any moment, and he rocked his sister to stave off the sickening feeling.

His mom rose and turned off the television, then put her arm around Christina. "How about we forget good nutrition and have ice cream sundaes for dinner at Baskin Robbins?"

The girls squealed with delight, the fire forgotten for a time. Lucas shook his head. "I can't."

His mom nodded. "I'll bring back a pint of Rocky Road."

Lucas smoothed out the letter for the fifth time, as if de-wrinkling it would somehow decipher it. His father had written,

Dear Ms. LaCroix:

I received your letter yesterday and am quite intrigued, to say the least. Yes, I do have a silver ring that I am told comes from the time of King Arthur. And yes, I did have an ancestor named Anthony Moreno – more affectionately known as Grandpa Tony – but he passed away some years ago. No, I have never had any "vision" of Tony or any other ancestor.

My family and I have plans to visit England this summer – in part so that my son and I can investigate the legend of the ring. Perhaps you would be able to meet with us? I am quite curious as to how you know these things about the ring and my family. Would you kindly elaborate in future correspondence?

Sincerely yours,
Tomás Moreno

P.S. Your cryptic reference to "danger" piques my interest further. And, no, I have not sensed anyone "tailing" me. I am mystified as to why you would ask and can only assume there is some connection with the ring? I am hopeful you will explain in your next letter.

It still made no sense to Lucas. "How can she know about Grandpa Tony?" he said to Shadow. "And what kind of vision are they talking about? Seeing Don Vasquez?" He sighed and stroked the dog's golden fur. "And this 'danger' she warns dad about, it's gotta be the Dark Powers, right?" Shadow thumped his tail. "If only I could find her letter to dad." But he'd already searched through his father's desk – no letter from Elaine LaCroix.

"This thing with the ring keeps getting weirder and weirder."

He left Shadow dozing contentedly on his bed, logged onto his computer and hit the English History website. He found two messages directed to him – L.M. – both from Dunmoore, who was eager to look at the ring with the runes. *Very strongly request that you advise whether you have the ring in your possession. Urge you to respond as soon as you receive this communication.* Lucas thought, *This guy's a dweeb.* He opened the second message.

I assume, with hope, that the reason for your not responding to my previous messages is that you have been out of the country or engaged in other pursuits such that you have had neither the time nor opportunity to join in our English History dialogue. Please contact me at the University where I lecture at 011 44 18 65 726 871 to discuss arranging a meeting, either in England or where you reside, so that I may see the ring (again, I assume that you indeed possess this object) and any other material you might have connected with it. I will gladly pay all costs associated with your traveling to London, if necessary. Time is of the essence. Morgan Dunmoore.

Lucas re-read the message, stopping at the line, *I will gladly pay all costs associated with your traveling to London, if necessary.* Was this guy kidding? Then Lucas remembered what Don Vasquez had said in the library about there being "good forces" out there to help. Maybe this Dunmoore was one of the good guys?

Lucas began to type a response but stopped after the first few words. Another message to L.M. had just been posted:

Ring boy. We are glad to see you have not joined the English History dialogue in some time. If you consider taking up certain offers of assistance with travel arrangements, we urge you to refuse such offers and cease all contact with certain individuals. A CEMETERY can be a very frightening place. Though perhaps not as <u>scorching</u> as a YMCA?

Dark Powers! a voice in his head shouted. Lucas snatched his fingers from the keyboard as if they had been burned. Quickly turning off the computer, he huddled on his bed next to the retriever. "How do they know so much about me? Why do they want me...dead?"

Shadow only licked his hand.

"What if Dunmoore's one of them? What if it's a trick to get me to England and get the ring?" Lucas got up from his bed and crossed to his dresser. He took down the wooden ring box and, sitting Indian-leg fashion on his bed, studied it.

The rosewood box had animals carved on each side. On one side he recognized a griffin, a mythological animal whose front part looked like an eagle and back part looked like a lion, but with a long, snaky tail. On the backside was a phoenix arising out of flames. The other side had a carving of a crane with long legs and a sharp bill. And a lion stood on the front of the box. Lucas had researched and found that the griffin stood as guardian of the roads to salvation. The phoenix symbolized destruction and re-creation. The crane was a symbol for justice and diligence, while the standing lion was part of King Arthur's coat-of-arms.

On top of the box were carvings of a goblet, open hands holding a crescent moon and five-pointed star on a square with a chain, and what looked like a large eye. Having spent many hours studying the box, Lucas felt fairly confident that the carvings represented the Holy Grail, Hands of Allah, and Eye of Buddha. From his Sunday School classes, Lucas knew that the Holy Grail was the chalice, or cup, that Jesus used at the Last Supper. Lucas suspected that the Hands of Allah was a pendant or medallion. He had no idea about the Eye of Buddha.

Lucas opened the box and took out the piece of paper wrapped around the ring. Lucas had memorized the ornate script:

Merlin, Knights of Round Table, Quest, Dream

He still didn't know who had written it.

His mother knocked on his open door. "I would think you'd be ready for bed by now. Can't you sleep, sweetie?"

Lucas shook his head. "My mind just starts to race." He put the paper and ring back in the box, then pulled out the paper again as a thought struck him. "Mom, do you know whose writing this is?"

His mother examined the scrap. "It looks very much like your great-grandfather Tony's writing. He had beautiful penmanship, and he loved stories about King Arthur. Now, try to get some sleep." She kissed him on both cheeks. "I love you so very much."

"Ditto."

His mom blew him a kiss before closing his bedroom door.

Lucas crossed to his dresser and wondered out loud, "Did great-grandpa Tony dream of Don Vasquez and the quest? Or did he just write down what *his* dad had told him about the ring? And how did this Elaine LaCroix know about him?" Whatever the answers, Lucas knew now that the knight had spoken the truth. It had not been simply a dream, but the beginning of something – something big. And Lucas was not sure he wanted to be a part of it. Not with the Dark Powers involved. He glanced at the computer and shivered.

Lying down on the bed with his arm around Shadow, he noticed the photos of him and his dad were smiling back at him again. His mom must have straightened them. He rose from the bed and crossed the room to the one at his dad's office. There was the YMCA model. He remembered the flames licking at the walls and windows, the blue and yellow and red paint bubbling and peeling. *That was ours, damn it!* He replaced the photo and looked at his computer. "I don't know what to do," he whispered to Shadow, who thumped his tail. Lucas fingered the ring box on his dresser. *Do I even have a choice?*

Chapter Six

K

The Ring of Nightmares

Lucas wore the ring to bed that night, hoping Don Vasquez would appear. Instead, he dreamed of armies massing in some foreign country – speaking something that sounded like Russian – attacking small villages, killing old men, women and children. He saw drug lords ordering guerrillas to overthrow a government. They spoke Spanish, but not Texas Spanish – it was a different accent. He saw hate-filled white men with small, hard eyes and stockpiles of guns. Americans. He watched them blow up a building or something in Washington, D.C. – flames and smoke poured from the rubble, and sirens and screams drowned out all other sound.

Lucas awoke the next morning with a pounding headache. He stumbled into the bathroom and splashed water on his face. The mirror reflected his blood-shot eyes and the silver ring. He twisted the ring off his finger, stuffed it in its box and slammed the lid. "You're no help. Neither is Don Vasquez." That's when he heard his mother cry out.

He rushed downstairs to find her sitting at the kitchen counter in front of the tiny television set – hands across her mouth, eyes wide.

"What happened, Mom? What's wrong?"

She turned to him, tears in her eyes. "Someone blew up the Lincoln Memorial. There were so many people inside. Tourists, school children."

Lucas watched the live news reports: Dozens of bodies covered in tarps lay next to columns of once-white marble, now blackened. A charred hand protruded from under one of the tarps. The statue of Abraham Lincoln was in pieces, and three firemen cradled Lincoln's marble head. It looked like the president had been decapitated. *It's almost like he's been assassinated all over again,* thought Lucas. "Who did it?"

"They don't know." His mom wiped tears from her face. "Maybe a paramilitary group, like the Oklahoma City bombing."

"No!" The word came out in a strangled whisper. *That's why it looks so familiar. I dreamed this!* But it was not the dream Lucas had requested. *What had Vasquez said in the library?* The ring has a will of its own.

Lucas squeezed his mother's shoulder. "I gotta get to school. You okay?" His mother only half-nodded, never taking her gaze from the television screen.

In his bedroom, he looked at the YMCA photo, then took the ring box from his dresser. "I get it," Lucas told the ring. "You gave me these dreams. To show me just how bad the Dark Powers are. Because you want me to go to England."

The ring glowed.

A green-tinged glow, like his mother's emerald earrings.

Lucas dropped the box on the floor. The ring rolled to the doorway. The glow faded. Lucas gingerly picked up the ring and held it in his left palm. "You want me to go to England, don't you?" he whispered.

It glowed again.

"And if I don't go?"

The glow faded.

"The Dark Powers will grow stronger?"

It glowed a third time.

"Until they destroy the world?"

The emerald green glow turned brighter and deeper.

"Then...I guess I have to go."

The ring glowed so brightly Lucas had to shade his eyes.

He replaced the ring and box on the dresser, turned on his computer, and scrolled through the English History dialogue, stopping at Dunmoore's last message and copying the telephone number, then scrolling down to the "ring boy" message. Ignoring his pounding heart, he typed *DARK POWERS BE DAMNED*, hit "Send," and logged off, then hoisted his "Chargers" backpack.

His message eerily reappeared on the dark computer screen in a pulsing neon green. He wiped the beads of sweat from his forehead and opened the ring box.

And the ring glowed.

———

It was lunch break when Lucas jogged down to the football field and under the bleachers, away from two seniors necking. He had borrowed Rocky's cell phone to call Dunmoore. London was six hours ahead of San Antonio time, so it was a little past six P.M. there. Lucas doubted Dunmoore would still be at the University, but he didn't know how else to contact him. He knew he couldn't use the Internet anymore, not with the Dark Powers monitoring it, which meant they might have tapped his home phone, maybe even his cell.

"Bet you bastards didn't think of this," he said aloud, then punched in the number.

His stomach rumbled from hunger. On the fourth ring, Lucas was about to hang up and head to the cafeteria to stuff his face when a male voice answered, "Hullo."

"Professor Dunmoore? It's Lucas Moreno."

The voice on the other end said, "Who?"

Right, I never gave him my name. "L.M., about the ring."

"Ah! Lucas Moreno, is it? From Texas? Pleased to meet you. I am *so* glad you rang!" It all came out rather quickly, in a clipped British accent.

"How do you know I live in Texas?"

"You used a regional user group – SWCOM – did you not? That meant you had to live in the southwestern part of the U.S. From there, I simply had to use certain...ah...connections to try to locate you. Unfortunately, I could ascertain only that you lived in Texas. That is why I was so desperate for you to contact me."

Lucas considered Dunmoore's response; it sounded likely enough. "Okay, so now what? You said you would pay for me to travel to England. Are you serious?"

"Yes, but only if you bring the ring. You have the ring, don't you?"

Lucas pulled his ear away from the phone, frowning. *This guy's too eager to get his hands on the ring.*

"Hullo? Are you there?"

"I have the ring." Lucas paused before asking, "How do you even know about it?"

Dunmoore didn't miss a beat. "Because of your inquiry on the Internet, of course."

Like a bright neon light, "WARNING" flashed through Lucas's brain. "I didn't say anything about a ring. Only if anyone knew what the runes were. What gives?"

"The runes themselves mention a ring," Dunmoore replied. "Moreover, I previously informed you that yours was the *second* inquiry into that translation. The first individual mentioned the writing was an inscription from a silver ring."

Lucas rubbed his free hand on his jeans. The "WARNING" light in his head flickered weakly, then went out. "All right," he said as he exhaled. "But you're willing to pay lots of money for me to come to England. There has to be more you're not letting on."

For the first time there was a long pause on the other side of the Atlantic. Finally, Dunmoore answered. "Are you calling from a land line?"

"No, why?"

"They may be able to track your cell call as well," said Dunmoore, "so we haven't much time."

"*They?*" asked Lucas. "The Dark Powers? You know about them?" Lucas felt his head begin to spin. He leaned against a bleacher stanchion.

"I know about them." Dunmoore's voice sounded weary. "And I imagine they know about me. Which is why I am desperate to see the ring and learn about its powers. Will you come to England or shall I come there?"

Lucas could hardly hear Dunmoore for the pounding of his heart in his ears. He took several deep breaths, then croaked out, "I have to come to England. I'll need some time to figure things out. When to come, where —"

"You must come now! Before it is too late."

"I don't have to do anything!" Lucas snapped out of his daze. "I'm fifteen, and my mom isn't going to let me go to England to meet a stranger. So I can't let her...know about it. Get it?"

"*Fifteen?* I see, I see," Dunmoore stammered. "I daresay that does change things a bit. Do you have a passport? When is the soonest you can come?"

"I'm thinking next week, during Spring Break. Passport's no problem. My dad took me to Argentina once." Lucas smiled at the memory, feeling wistful. And alone. He wished his dad were there to help him.

"Done, then. You'll come to England sometime next week. Call me the minute you know what day you can get away. I shall send you a ticket."

"You can't mail it to my house. And you can't do an e-ticket because, you know, the Dark Powers." Lucas paused to think. "Can I just pick up the ticket at the airport?"

"Let me know your flight number and I'll arrange everything. I'll meet your flight at the baggage claim at Heathrow Airport. And be careful, Luke. Be very careful."

"Ditto. And it's *Lucas*." He hung up the phone and checked his watch. Only ten minutes before class. "Damn. Looks like it's the vending machines for lunch."

As he jogged back, he couldn't stifle a big grin. He knew it was crazy, he knew it was dangerous, but all he could think about was having an adventure in England!

Chapter Seven

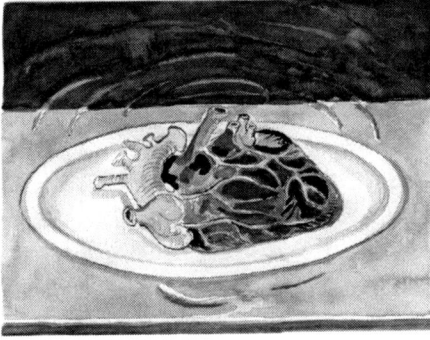

The Fortress of Shadows

Six ebony marble towers rose from the coal-black castle that sat atop the mountain. In the bright light of day, the polished stone towers shone like beacons of wickedness. The largest tower – the keep – faced directly south and bore upon its dark stone a coiled serpent of blood-red marble. The castle had few openings for light and air; its inhabitants were bathed in perpetual shadow.

Within was Mordred, the human spider, spinning his web of evil. The darkest of all the Dark Powers, he was the result of a deceitful union between the sorceress Morgan Le Fay and the unsuspecting King Arthur.

Mordred, the bastard heir to Camelot, was still young and handsome, although his skin was so pale one almost seemed to see the blood pump beneath it, and he wore his auburn hair long and flowing. From beneath his brows shone one blue and one green eye, sparkling with intelligence, cunning and malice. He sat on an onyx throne surrounded by his evil minions.

The pungent scent of incense permeated the room, causing the eyes of those who stood before their master to water. The men and women were dressed uniformly in black. One man, only slightly younger and slightly less pale than his master, trembled, his head bowed.

"So, Kretan, you have returned. What say you?"

"M'lord." The trembling Kretan knelt on a silk carpet of stitched black and red serpents. "I was unable...He has the ring...But he knows nothing. He does nothing."

Mordred twisted an ivory ring on his left pinkie and smiled.

"He knows nothing? He does nothing?"

"Yes, M'lord." Kretan offered a tentative smile in return.

"Rattar, the file."

A short, plump man with slicked back hair and handlebar mustache scurried to the throne and placed a red folder in Mordred's outstretched hand, then backed quickly away, twittering nervously. Mordred selected a piece of paper and read portions of it aloud. "Lucas Moreno. Descendant of Don Vasquez." He spat out the name with a sneering distaste. "Deciphered runes. Internet. Professor Morgan Dunmoore?" Mordred looked at Rattar and smiled. "How delightful." He returned to the paper. "Reservations to London." He stared at Kretan. "Knows nothing? Does nothing?"

"B-b-but M'lord, I tried...The cemetery...The fire...The –"

"Failures, every one. Tsk. Tsk. Kretan, we expected more of you."

"But he's only a boy! He poses no threat."

Mordred's eyes narrowed. "No threat?" He looked at the piece of paper. "DARK POWERS BE DAMNED!" Mordred stood and flung the folder across the room. Rattar scurried after it.

"Please, M'lord," Kretan pleaded. "Another chance, I beg you! I will not fail."

The others in the room, save one, backed up until they were several paces behind Kretan, their glances darting between the kneeling man and their glowering master. Mordred looked to the tall, slender man who stood next to Kretan. "What say you, General Vassalar?"

The man smiled, revealing two pointed, gold canines, which had earned him the nickname, Vassalar the Vampire. "I think he shall not disappoint, M'lord." He spoke with a slight Russian accent.

Exhaling with relief, Kretan craned his neck. "Thank you, General."

Vassalar nodded and backed into the flickering shadows cast by the candlelit sconces of black marble, intertwined serpents that lined the stone walls.

Mordred made a clicking sound with his tongue and a pinching movement with his hand. "Nailom."

A tall, muscular woman stepped from the others and spun Kretan around. She raised her right hand, plunged her ten-inch metal fingernails into his chest, and ripped out his heart.

Kretan took one last look at his bloody, beating heart in the palm of the Amazon warrior and collapsed. Crimson liquid flowed from beneath his body to cover the carpet-serpents.

With a triumphant smile, Nailom held high the heart, steaming in the cold air, then slapped it onto a gold plate and offered it to Mordred. Rattar bustled forward and presented a golden knife and fork with a slight flourish.

"Just a small bite," said Mordred.

The tittering Rattar sliced a small piece of heart for his master, who chewed, swallowed and licked his lips.

"Most excellent. You were correct, Vassalar. Kretan did not disappoint." Mordred wiped his mouth with his sleeve and surveyed the room. "Now, who will go to Texas?"

Chapter Eight

W

The Beginning of Deceit

Lucas's school band was going on a weeklong field trip, first to the Florida Everglades, then to Disney World to perform during Spring Break. He hadn't planned on going, in fact, he'd pulled out after his dad died, but it would provide the perfect cover for his trip to England. And he knew his mom would go crazy with joy over his change of mind; she'd been upset when he told her he wasn't going. He just had to figure out the rest of the lies he was going to have to tell so that his mom thought he was with the band. The band already thought he was staying with his family.

"Mom, I'm home!" Lucas called out as he entered the house. "Hey Shadow!" Lucas rassled with the golden retriever who had bounded to the door to greet him.

His mom came out from the kitchen, wiping her hands on her apron. She gave him a big hug – smelling of flour, butter and chocolate. "How was school, sweetie?"

"It's school, Mom, what do you think? Hey..." He sniffed and headed to the kitchen. "What smells so great?"

"I'm baking a pie for dessert. Chocolate pecan, your favorite."

"Because?" Lucas raised one eyebrow.

"Oh stop." She swatted him lightly on the shoulder. "Because I wanted to. Because I love you, despite your being a pain at times."

Lucas grinned, then said, "Do you love me so much you'll let me go with the band to Disney World?"

"Oh, Lucas!" His mom hugged him. "I'm so glad you changed your mind. Your grandmother will be, too." She took a piece of paper and check off the dining room table and handed both to him. "It gets even better." She smiled.

"Five hundred dollars! Slammin'!" Lucas stared at the check. "Why would Grandma send me this much money?"

"She wants her very talented grandson to play the flute at Disney World. It was to be a bribe." She smiled. "I won't let on you'd already changed your mind." She hugged him again. "I will miss you at Easter though...in Los Angeles."

"Huh?"

"Along with the check for you, Grandma sent plane tickets for the rest of us to visit."

Lucas tilted his head at his mom. "You're going to fly to Los Angeles to spend a week with *Grandma*?" Lucas knew he sounded surprised. And he was. Mom had never liked Grandma Moreno.

Christina skipped into the dining room and said, "Grandma's taking us to Magic Mountain. You'll be stuck in Disney World – it's s-o-o-o tired." She gave a smirk that only a fifth-grader could give. "Maybe you'll fall into the Everglades and get chomped by a crocodile!"

"You won't be eaten by a crocodile, will you, Lucas?" Cari's voice trembled as she trailed her sister.

Lucas pretended to catch her nose between his thumb and fingers. "No, Cari, I won't even be near crocodiles, don't worry." He turned to Christina and whispered, "They're alligators, pinhead, and watch it or you'll be the one who ends up being chomped!"

"Mom!" whined Christina.

Sandra Moreno only shook her head and returned to the kitchen. "If I don't get this pie out the of oven, there will be no dessert to chomp!"

———————

After dinner, Lucas took his turn clearing the table and loading the dishwasher. Before going to bed, he checked on his mom. "When are you guys going to Grandma's?"

His mother laid the book she had been reading on her lap. "Saturday morning, 7:00. When does your flight to Florida leave?"

"8:30 A.M." *What incredible timing* that *is*, Lucas thought. With his mom already gone, he wouldn't have to figure out how to make it appear he was going with the band to Florida and, instead, board a plane to England.

"Maybe you should stay the night at Rocky's and have his parents take you to the airport?"

"No!"

His mother's eyebrows raised. "Are you and Rocky having a fight?"

"No, it's just that...." Lucas paused. "I'd rather see you guys off at the airport."

"I don't like the idea of your waiting at the airport by yourself."

"C'mon, Mom. I'd only have to hang around about half an hour before Rocky and the rest of the band got there. It's not like someone's gonna abduct me." *Yeah, right, and the cemetery and YMCA are only **coincidences.***

Sandra Moreno smiled. "All right. I'd love to have you put us on the plane. It was something your dad always did." She gave him a soft, sad smile.

Lucas bent down and kissed his mom on the cheek. "I miss him, too."

Up in his bedroom, Lucas set his alarm for one A.M. to call Dunmoore. Lucas had confirmed on the computer that there was space available on British Airways Flight 337, from San Antonio to London, with a stop in Dallas to pick up the bulk of the transatlantic passengers.

At the alarm's muffled buzzing – Lucas had placed it under his pillow so his mom wouldn't hear it – he called Dunmoore from Jason's cell phone. He'd secretly snatched it during track practice.

"Hullo, Luke, m'boy," chirped Dunmoore. "I hope you have good news for me?"

"I have all the flight information."

After confirming the arrangements, Dunmoore said, "Don't contact me by Internet or telephone again unless it's urgent."

Duh, Lucas thought. Aloud, he said, "Right." But Lucas didn't tell him that he had already spent hours on the Internet checking *Dunmoore* out. So far, everything about the guy seemed cool – renowned authority on King Arthur, esteemed Oxford professor, author of numerous books. Still, Lucas was nervous. "Appearances can be deceiving," his dad used to say.

Before hanging up, Dunmore cautioned, "You must be extremely careful, Luke."

"Yeah, you too. And it's Lucas!" He thought he heard Dunmoore chuckle before he hung up. "Butthead," Lucas said into the dead phone. "And he's supposed to be one of the good guys?"

Chapter Nine

Lucas on His Own

Lucas didn't feel much like a good guy himself with all the lies he was telling, but he could see no way around it. He woke at 4:30 Saturday morning – D-Day. He was traveling pretty light – jeans, sneakers, T-shirts and sweaters in his duffel bag. He wore jeans, a polo shirt, sweatshirt and hiking boots. He carried his "Chargers" backpack and his dad's leather bomber jacket – from when he had been a Navy pilot. Lucas liked the feel of the worn leather and the musky smell of the jacket. It reminded him of his dad.

So did the worn, brown leather hat with the rattlesnake band and two dried rattles around the brim. It was like the one Harrison Ford wore in the *Indiana Jones* movies – Lucas's dad's favorites. His dad had even named Lucas after the producer, George Lucas. Lucas knew it was corny, but he liked the feel of the hat and how it looked on him – now that it fit him. And the rattles were from two snakes his dad had killed when Lucas was only five. They had accidentally stumbled across the rattlers at Great-Grandpa Tony's ranch. To this day, Lucas hated snakes – same as Indiana Jones. But damn if he didn't like the hat.

That left the silver ring. Lucas wasn't stoked about getting visions at who-knew-what times, so wearing it was out. In the end, he had decided to wear it on a silver chain around his neck. The chain had once belonged to Great-Grandpa, Tony – the one fascinated by King Arthur and Camelot. Lucas figured that was another good omen – like the jacket and hat.

Shadow lay on Lucas's bed, staring at him with mournful eyes. Lucas was convinced the dog knew he was leaving. When Lucas packed, Shadow retreated to Lucas's bed, refusing to play or even eat. Lucas kneeled on the floor and took the dog's head in his hands. "I'm only gone for a week, boy. And you're right next-door at the Camden's. Swimming in their pool, getting spoiled rotten." Lucas kissed the dog on the snout and grabbed his knapsack.

In it, he had packed a framed picture of his family and the returned letter from his dad to Elaine LaCroix. He figured Dunmoore might know who she was. Candy bars and gum, his passport, and the ring box completed the main pack. He picked up the Swiss army knife and checked all the blades, including the scissors and corkscrew, then placed it in the outer pocket of his suitcase. He would have preferred carrying it in his knapsack, but he knew there was no way it would get by Security. "Crappy substitute for a gun," he muttered.

He still couldn't believe his mom had gotten rid of his dad's service revolver. When he'd asked her where she kept it, she went nuclear – from interrogating him about being a gangbanger to lecturing him about guns and violence. Turns out she'd given it to his Uncle Jimmy. Lucas had never handled a gun, still....

"Lucas, the taxi's here!"

He hefted his bags and went down the stairs and out to the porch, followed by Shadow. His sisters already stood by the taxi, squabbling over the front seat. Mrs. Camden was coming up the walk to get Shadow.

His mom put the key in the lock, then stopped and stared at Lucas. "Aren't you forgetting something?"

He felt his face flush. "Wh-what do you mean?"

"Your flute? Or is this an 'air flute' performance?"

"Doh!" Lucas slapped his forehead. "I'll be right back!" He ran to his room and grabbed the flute case from his bedroom closet. When he got back to the front porch, his mother and bags were in the taxi, and Shadow sat next to Mrs. Camden at the end of the drive.

Lucas hugged the retriever. "See you soon, boy." Shadow whined. Lucas turned away, a lump in his throat.

"Let's go!" yelled Christina.

And with a grinding of gears, followed by the driver's "so sorry I am, yes," in a thick Indian accent, the white-and-red taxi lurched away from the curb.

At the airport they ate breakfast, his sisters chattering away in their excitement. Lucas mostly moved the food around on his plate. His stomach wasn't up to eggs and bacon. They waited only ten minutes at the gate before the boarding call for the flight to Los Angeles was announced.

His mom said, "Take care of yourself, Sweetie. Play well and have fun. And don't get chomped!" She gave him a long hug. "I'll see you in a week, okay?" At the gate, she turned. "You have Grandma's number, don't you?" Lucas nodded. His mother waved. "Call collect if you need anything. I love you."

Lucas felt a sudden tightening in his throat and stinging in his eyes as his family disappeared down the ramp. He was on his own.

When he arrived at the British Airways ticket counter, he was relieved to find that a ticket in his name was there. He checked in with a cute blonde agent, but even her easy chatter couldn't lighten his spirits. After passport control, Lucas waited at the gate for the boarding announcement, tapping his feet and gnawing his fingernails. He began to watch people, imagining each one to be an agent of the Dark Powers. *Chill, man.*

He headed to the rest room to splash water on his face. A man in a dark coat, hat and sunglasses entered right before he did. Just as Lucas reached the entrance to the rest room, he felt a hot stab in his chest. He dropped his flute and knapsack and leaned back against the wall, digging frantically under his sweatshirt and polo shirt. Finally, he pulled out the ring. It glowed red-hot! A hand grabbed his shoulder. Lucas gave a startled yelp and pulled away.

A British Airways flight attendant stared at him, concern evident in her hazel eyes and puckered brow. "Are you okay, hon?" She spoke in a soft Texas drawl. "Do you need to sit down?"

"Damn, you scared me!"

"Talk about a scare, hon. I come out of the ladies' room and see you damn near fling yourself into the wall. You looked like you'd just been bucked off a bronc."

The ring cooled down. Lucas tried to nonchalantly put it back inside his sweatshirt. "I'm fine, thanks." The attendant stared at him. She had long blond hair, worn in a bun, with small, sparkly bobby pins throughout. Her large eyes still reflected concern, but also doubt.

What? Does she think I'm a runaway? That's all he needed – getting turned in before he even got on the plane. He could feel the sweat on his forehead and palms. The little voice in his head popped up. *Tell her something. Anything.* "I'm waiting for a flight to London. Meeting relatives at Heathrow. I just need to use the rest room." The ring glowed red hot. "Jesus!" Lucas pawed at his shirt.

"London? *I'm* working that flight. Why don't you come with me and we'll try to get you pre-boarded? You can use the rest room on the plane." The ring cooled immediately.

The words "gift horse" and "mouth" flitted through his head as Lucas hefted his knapsack and flute case and allowed the attendant – Karen, from her nametag – to put her hand through his arm. She was about his height – five-eight – with long legs. *Really nice long legs.*

Once on board, Karen introduced Lucas to the rest of the flight crew, then got him settled. "I'll be right back, hon."

Lucas reclined in his seat and took out the ring. "What the hell is going on?" The ring just sat there. "You are becoming a royal pain in the butt."

Karen returned minutes later. "Would you like to fly in first class, hon? We got heaps of empty seats this flight. Normally, we can't let y'all come up to the first class cabin, but the flight crew and I agreed that I don't have enough passengers to keep me busy. So, we have recruited *you!*" Karen took down the flute case from the overhead compartment. "Maybe you can entertain us all later." There was that toothy grin again. "Come on, hon, grab your rattler hat and follow me."

Karen pointed to the window seat in the first row. "That's so I can keep an eye on you." Karen winked and pointed to her "jump seat" directly across from him.

For the first time that day, Lucas smiled. "Thanks, Karen, thanks a lot." He extended a hand.

"That's much better." She took his hand. "You ought to smile more often, hon."

Thirty minutes later, the plane idled on the runway. As it lifted off, Lucas stared out the window at the landscape, feeling lost...and homesick. The ring began to warm up. Lucas took it from inside his sweatshirt and held it in his palm. It gave off a gentle warmth this time, comforting, calming. "Here we go," Lucas whispered.

And the ring glowed.

Chapter Ten

Shadow Figures

Flickering candles sent shadow fingers crawling up the walls and across the mahogany dining table, inlaid with rubies and diamonds in the shape of two intertwined serpents. At the end of the forty-foot table sat Mordred, dwarfed by an armchair of matching mahogany nearly six feet in height. The table held platters of barbecued goat, roast rack of lamb, steaming beef kidneys, and assorted cheeses.

Mordred tore the last of the barbecued goat strip from a hindquarter and flung it over his shoulder. Two massive Rottweilers, Cerb and Berus, leapt from their perches to snatch the remains. Their guttural snarling and snapping ceased with one word from their master – "*Heil.*" They slunk back to Mordred's chair, one on either side.

"*Gut.*" After a quick slap to the head of the beasts, he tossed each a beef kidney. Their chomping and gulping made him smile until a sudden tingling in his left pinkie distracted him. He licked his fingers and twisted the ivory ring around and around, muttering something in Gaelic. "Rattar!" he roared.

The plump manservant with the slicked down handlebar mustache scuttled from the shadows behind his master and stood to his left, next to a growling hound. A swift kick from Mordred turned Cerb's growl to a whimper.

"M'lord?"

"What hear we from Texas?"

Rattar frowned. "Nothing, M'lord."

"Nothing?" Mordred drummed his fingers. "Any news from Hugin or Munin?"

The two sneaky Slavs were the eyes and ears of their dark leader, slinking like shadows through the outer world and reporting back on the mayhem and misfortune wrought by agents of the Dark Powers.

"A faxth juth in, M'lord." Rattar spoke eagerly, his words marked by an unfortunate lisp, "From Hugin."

"Well, bring it here, man!" Mordred pounded the table. Berus rose, growling. Cerb cautiously raised his head and sniffed.

"Yeth, M'lord." Rattar waddled out, returning less than a minute later, breathing heavily, a single sheet of paper in hand.

Mordred snatched it and read while sucking on rack of lamb. A minute later, he closed his eyes and let the lamb drop to his plate. After letting the dogs lick his greasy fingers, he wiped them on his shirt and said, "Bacchus has let us down, Rattar. You know we don't take kindly to that."

"No, M'lord. I mean, yeth, M'lord. I mean..." Rattar twisted the ends of his mustache.

Mordred held up a hand. "And all over a *boy*." He heaved a great sigh. "Tell Hugin to be done with Bacchus."

"How, M'lord?" Rattar's eyes glittered with anticipation.

Mordred opened his eyes, pushed back from the table and stood. He snapped his fingers, and the dogs scrabbled to attention. "He lost the boy. He loses his head." Turning on his heel, Mordred departed, flanked by the hounds.

"Exthellent, M'lord. Mosth exthellent!" Rattar rubbed his hands together, bowed to the empty chair, then scurried to the communications room to do his master's bidding.

Chapter Eleven

The Ring Returns Home

Nine hours of flying gave Lucas too much time to worry. Fortunately, Karen kept him entertained for most of the flight. He had to admit that first class was a pretty fine place to be! The meals were great: Spinach salad and lobster for lunch – he'd only eaten lobster twice in his life – and some fancy meat dish called *osso bucco* for dinner. Fresh-baked chocolate chip cookies and hot fudge sundaes with whipped cream and walnuts were dessert. And Lucas's seat reclined flat so he could stretch out and sleep. When he got bored watching movies or playing video games on his personal console –*Rocky and Jason would go nuts over this!* – he talked to Karen.

Karen had been born in London, but her parents had moved to Texas when she was a baby. She had gobs of relatives in Great Britain and two weeks of vacation after this flight. The first she planned to spend in England, then she was off to Cairo, where a friend of hers was working on an archaeological dig. She was excited about seeing the pyramids and the Sphinx.

Karen said if Lucas got bored with his relatives, he could call her and she'd show him around London. She scribbled her cousins' number on a cocktail napkin. Lucas doubted he would get a chance to call, but at least he'd have a fallback if things took a really strange turn.

Maybe she's the strange turn, Lucas. There it was, that annoying little voice again. Lucas had noticed it a lot since finding the ring –

always questioning Lucas's gut feelings about people. Like Dunmoore. *Shut up*, he told the voice. *The ring isn't warning me about Karen. And she's had more than enough chances to...do something if she wanted.* Lucas put his palm to his chest, over the ring. *On a crowded plane?* asked the voice. *How much could she do? And you don't know that much about how the ring —*

Lucas cranked the volume up on his headset. The music of Smashing Pumpkins drowned out the intruding whisper.

———

Several hours later, Karen gently roused Lucas. "Buckle up, hon. We're almost there."

Stretching and yawning, Lucas looked out the window at London below. It looked like any other big city lit up at night, but his heart began to beat a little faster. As the plane began its descent into Heathrow Airport, Lucas again took the ring from inside his sweatshirt and held it in his palm. He found the same comforting warmth. The pilot made a smooth landing and taxied to a stop at the terminal. And the ring glowed. *Home.*

Karen turned to Lucas. "Hon, why don't you wait until everyone else gets off? We can go to baggage claim together."

Any other time, Lucas would have jumped at the chance to spend even more time with this beautiful woman, but he didn't want to blow his cover. It certainly wouldn't look good if he couldn't even tell who his "Uncle Morgan" was. *And it would look even worse if she jumps you and steals the ring.* The voice startled him. All he could think to say was, "Karen, I'd love to, except...I really don't want to keep my relatives waiting, what with how late it is."

For the first time the entire flight, Karen's smile disappeared. "Oh. Whatever." She turned away to help another passenger on with a coat.

Lucas hung his head. *How can I be such a jerk? She helps me in the airport, gets me into first class, keeps me entertained the entire flight, and offers to take me around London. And I can't wait to walk with her to the terminal?*

It's better this way, Lucas. Less risky.

How he began to hate that voice. He told it, *yeah, well if risk is what you're afraid of, the train stops here. Get the hell off.* Then, he tapped Karen on the shoulder. "Karen, I really *would* like to walk with you to baggage claim. I mean, what's another twenty minutes?" Karen turned, not smiling. Lucas added in a pleading voice, "Can I wait for you? P-l-e-e-a-a-s-e?"

Finally, she gave him her megawatt smile. "What the hey. Yes, you can tag along."

Lucas knew he was beaming as he sat back in his seat and waited for the last passengers to leave, until it hit him that he better find a way out of this mess. On the way to baggage claim, an idea came to him, but Dunmoore had better catch on quick if it was going to work.

At passport control, they separated – Karen had a British passport. "I'll meet you in baggage claim, hon."

Lucas got into the shorter of the two lines for non-European Union passengers, and the ring immediately grew hot. *What's up?* He checked around. No one seemed strange, or out of place. Then, he noticed the passport control agent for his line. The tall man was thin and wiry and quite pale. Lucas knew England didn't get much sun, but he didn't think that was the poor guy's problem. It was the shock of red-orange hair that really caught Lucas's attention. The man reminded Lucas of an albino Ronald McDonald. As the line moved forward, Lucas realized the agent was looking at *him* – ignoring the people whose passports he was supposed to be examining. The ring grew uncomfortably hot.

He whispered, "Do you want me to switch lines?" The ring cooled just a bit. *Good enough for me.* He retreated to the back of the longest visitor queue. The ring cooled drastically. Lucas risked a glance at Albino Ronald, then turned quickly from the fierce scowl he received. He felt the familiar fluttering of fear in his chest. Lucas checked out the new passport agent. That man seemed involved in his work, not noticing Lucas or anyone else not immediately in front of him. *Come on, come on.* Lucas tapped his foot and forced himself to ignore the albino.

When he reached the booth, Lucas handed over his passport.

"How long do you plan to stay in England?" the agent inquired.

"A week, sir. I'm visiting relatives."

The agent checked something off on a sheet of paper. "Where will you be staying?"

Lucas pulled his address book out of his knapsack and read off Dunmoore's. The agent nodded, checked another box and stamped Lucas's passport. "All set to go. Have a good visit."

As he headed to the baggage claim area, Lucas saw that the redheaded albino again was staring at him, his back to the foreign visitors, one of whom began talking loudly. Lucas wiped his sweaty palms on his jeans and turned to find Karen waiting.

They retrieved their bags and stood in yet another line for customs. "You on a turnaround or spending a little time in England, Karen?" the customs' agent inquired.

"I'm on holiday, Nigel. Visiting the landed gentry cousins in Bath. Play your cards right, and I'll let you take me out for a night on the town. Your wife won't mind?"

"Not bloody likely," laughed the agent as he motioned Karen through without checking a piece of her luggage. Then he turned to Lucas, all congeniality gone. "Open the bag, please."

Lucas glanced back at passport control and saw the albino heading his way. The loud, ignored visitor began shouting and shaking his fist. Beginning to panic, Lucas thought, *Will he try to kill me? Do I run?*

"Where are my manners?" Karen stepped in and placed her arm around Lucas's shoulder. "Nigel, meet Lucas Moreno, a friend of mine who is staying with relatives in London for a week. Lucas, meet Nigel Banner, the best customs man in the business!"

Nigel eyed Lucas. "First time in England?"

Lucas swallowed the bile of fear that had lodged in the back of this throat. *Think. Say something.* Putting on what he hoped was a "puppy-love" expression, Lucas looked longingly at Karen. "Yes, sir. I only wish I could stay with Karen instead of my relatives."

Nigel chuckled, telling him to pass on and warning, "She's a heartbreaker, lad."

Practically trotting out of customs, Lucas risked a glance back. Nigel had intercepted the passport agent, along with two men in military uniforms with automatic weapons. Lucas exhaled the breath he'd been holding and wiped the sweat from his brow.

As they entered the main greeting room, Karen waved to an older couple across the terminal. "Erica! Richard! Over here." She turned to Lucas. "Where are your relatives, hon?"

Before Lucas could even look around, he heard, "Lucas Moreno! Luke, m'boy! How are you?" A man in his early fifties, with dark brown hair, graying at the temples, came toward them. He wore gray flannel slacks, a maroon pullover sweater and a khaki raincoat. He was what Lucas's mother would call "ruggedly handsome," with gray eyes, and Lucas could tell he was fit and muscular beneath his clothes. That surprised Lucas, who had been expecting a more professorial type – reed-thin with thick, owlish glasses and a pipe.

Lucas gave a hug to a very surprised Dunmoore and whispered, "Play along. I'll explain later." He turned to Karen. "This is my Uncle Morgan. He's married to my mom's sister, Aunt Jane. But I don't see her?" Lucas looked around the terminal.

Dunmoore gave an "Ahh!" and shook Karen's hand warmly. "A pleasure to meet you. Luke should travel to London more often!"

Karen smiled.

Lucas scowled.

Dunmoore said, "Janie would have been here, Luke, but she has a bit of a cold and I didn't want it to turn nasty while you were here."

By this time, Karen's genuine aunt and uncle had made it through the throng of passengers. Karen said, "Well, it looks like it's time to go, Lucas. Or is it *Luke*?" She hugged him. "Thanks for keeping me company on the flight. Make sure you call me if you get a free day, hon."

"I will. Thanks for everything, Karen." He would miss her. *I told you she was the real thing*, he told his inner voice. *Sometimes, you just gotta go with your gut.* But the little voice stayed mute.

Dunmoore asked, "Everything set to go?"

"Yeah. Glad you recognized me so quickly."

Dunmoore patted Lucas's school knapsack. "Hard to miss a San Antonio Charger in London. Shall we be off?"

Lucas took one more look at the lit, crowded terminal, then stepped out into the damp, frigid air of England.

Chapter Twelve

Meet Professor Dunmoore

Reality hit hard as Lucas left the warm terminal. He was in a foreign land with a total stranger. *I hope I don't end up on the front page as the latest victim of some Oxford maniac.* The thought made him hug his knapsack, his hand resting on the pocket with the Swiss army knife that he had stashed there after getting his luggage. When they reached Dunmoore's car – an old Austin Healy roadster, British racing green – Lucas's uneasiness vanished.

"Great car!" he exclaimed. "What is it? A '60 Sprite?"

Dunmoore's eyebrows raised. "You know your cars."

"My dad was into cars. We were working on restoring a '65 Mustang Convertible before he died."

Dunmoore was obviously taken aback. "When did your father die?" He put Lucas's bag and flute case into the trunk of the car.

"A couple months ago."

"I'm sorry, Luke, er, Lucas." Dunmoore closed the Austin's trunk and opened the front door on the left side of the car.

"It's weird getting into the passenger seat on this side," Lucas said.

"You get used to it after a bit." Starting the Austin, Dunmoore began the small talk — What was Lucas's house like? What was Lucas's family like? Fascinating hat, is there a story there? — which lasted the thirty-minute drive to Oxford. Dunmoore pulled off the road at a small sign reading "Le Manoir aux Quat' Saisons," and drove down a long tree-lined drive, parking the Austin in front of a large brick fortress.

"You live in a castle, Professor? With a name?"

Before Dunmoore could reply, a valet opened his door saying, "Good evening, sir. Checking in?"

"My young friend is. I'll be no more than five minutes."

"Very good, sir." The valet — dressed in crisp black pants, vest and jacket, with bleach-white shirt — rounded the Austin and opened Lucas's door.

Lucas stayed seated, his knapsack on his lap, and said quietly to the valet, "Just a minute, okay?"

The valet nodded and said, "Very good, sir," then returned to the entrance of the "castle."

Dunmoore poked his head around the open trunk of the Austin. "Is there a problem, Luke?"

"I don't get it. I don't have much money and this place looks expensive."

Dunmoore's head disappeared again. His words came out muffled. "Not to worry. I told you I would cover all expenses."

Sweat had begun to bead on Lucas's forehead, and his armpits felt damp. "I still don't get it."

Dunmoore slammed the trunk lid and hefted the duffel bag and flute case. "I thought you might be more comfortable for your first few days if you were staying at a hotel instead of a stranger's home. I know I would." Dunmoore started toward the hotel, calling without looking back, "Of course, if you'd prefer to stay in the parking lot..."

Lucas got out of the Austin.

The hotel's lobby was huge, furnished with twinkling chandeliers, fireplaces with roaring fires, plush oriental carpets, leather chairs and couches, beautiful oil paintings, dark wood tables and gleaming brass. He heard Dunmoore say, "Mason, Lawrence, but I'll be paying for the room," and hurried to the front desk, where Dunmoore was handing a credit card to the clerk.

"Lawrence Mason?" Lucas whispered. He frowned before adding, "Dweeb name. And do I *look* like a Lawrence Mason?"

Dunmoore simply grinned and gave him a quick wink.

Several minutes later, they were following the bellhop out the doors of the elevator and down a soft carpet of green and blue spirals to room 333.

"Here we are, sirs." The bellhop inserted the cardkey, turned on the entrance lights and carried Lucas's bags into the room. After giving a mini-tour of the room, the bellhop handed Lucas the cardkey, thanked Dunmoore for the tip and left.

Lucas looked around the room. It was ginormous! Two queen-size beds and a small sitting area with a fireplace. A huge bathroom with a whirlpool tub. Lucas called out, "It says the shower is also a steam bath! Can you believe it?" As Lucas came out of the bathroom, he said, "You sure you can afford this place? *My* teachers couldn't."

Dunmoore laughed – a good, solid laugh, not fake. *He's got my dad's laugh.* Lucas felt his shoulders relax a little. He hadn't realized he'd been so tense.

Dunmoore said, "A university professor makes a bit more than a primary school teacher. But most wouldn't be putting up guests on a regular basis at this hotel. My father left quite a sizable estate when he died. I live quite comfortably on that and my salary."

"When did your father die?"

Dunmoore tapped the rose-gold Rolex watch on his wrist, then held it to his ear. As he wound the stem, he finally replied, "Many, many years ago, when I was sixteen." He looked up. "Let's leave that for tomorrow, shall we? It's past one A.M., and I imagine you must be somewhat exhausted. Why don't I ring you up about nine?"

"You mean the telephone, right?"

"I'll swing by after and take you to breakfast." Dunmoore opened the door. "We have many things to discuss."

"You haven't even asked about the ring," said Lucas. "Don't you want to see it? Isn't that why you brought me here?"

"I am quite anxious to see the ring," said Dunmoore as he turned. "But I can tell you are knackered, and I have waited all this time. Surely I can wait another night. Sleep well." He closed the door.

Lucas walked to the picture window and watched Dunmoore drive off. *That's pretty strange.* He pulled the ring from inside his sweatshirt. "He brings me all the way from Texas to see you, then doesn't even ask. I wonder if he was being considerate or if something else is going on?"

The ring did nothing.

"And he lost his dad at sixteen. I wonder if that's connected to this?"

The ring glimmered a little.

"Oh, man. I'm too beat to figure this out, now." He started to take the ring and chain from around his neck, then decided to wear it to bed.

He thought it would take some time to get to sleep. He was far from home, none of his family or friends knew where he was, and he didn't really know anyone in England. But the minute he laid his head on his pillow, he fell fast asleep. His last waking thought: *The ring will keep watch.*

———

Lucas awoke to a strange bird-like sound. Still groggy, he looked around for an alarm or clock radio or a bird – *something* that chirped. His glance fell on the telephone on about the fifth *cheep*.

He picked up the phone to be greeted by Dunmoore's cheery voice. "Hullo, did you sleep well?"

"What time is it?" Lucas yawned.

"Precisely nine o'clock. Pick you up out front in half an hour. Don't forget the ring, Luke."

"Lucas." He stretched his arms above his head and got out of bed. He surveyed the sky through the large picture window – a rainy, dreary morning. He would have liked nothing better than to crawl back into bed and sleep for another hour. "No chance of that with the Prof," he muttered to himself as he stumbled into the bathroom.

Twenty-five minutes later, he stood in front of the dresser. He put the ring box into his knapsack and picked up the ring and chain. "Ready to go, buddy?"

The ring did nothing.

Lucas sighed. "Someday, I'll figure you out." He put the chain around his neck and tucked it inside his sweater, but outside his T-shirt, because there was still a blister on his chest from the airport incident.

The Austin pulled up only a minute after Lucas got to the lobby, and he dashed to the passenger door, trying unsuccessfully not to get wet. "Hey, Professor. Nice weather you got here."

"April is the soggiest month of the year. I think perhaps we ought to purchase a raincoat for you. I don't think your leather jacket will hold up very well."

Lucas examined the water stains already forming on his jacket. "Yeah, you're probably right. But, hey, can we do it after breakfast? I'm starving."

"Right-o." Dunmoore put the Austin in gear and pulled out of the hotel driveway. "I've got just the place. Good food and not too loud."

Dunmoore parked outside a little café on a bustling street in Oxford. A minute later, a stocky redhead escorted them to a cracked, green leather booth in the far corner of the diner and handed them menus. Dunmoore asked for coffee.

Lucas put his hat on the bench next to him and studied the menu, his stomach growling from the smell of fried eggs and meats. "What's good here?"

"Not so different from home, what? I'm having fried eggs, bread and bacon."

"Sounds good to me." Lucas closed the menu.

When the waitress returned with coffee, Dunmoore ordered, then turned to Lucas. "Shall we get down to business, then?"

Lucas nodded and opened his knapsack. He handed the wooden box to Dunmoore.

"The ring box," Dunmoore said. "Yes, yes. The griffin, crane, phoenix and..." Dunmoore turned the box around in his hands, "...the crest of King Arthur."

"How did you know that?" Lucas stared with open mouth at this unexpected familiarity with his stuff. "Is the box described in one of your books on King Arthur?"

"All in good time, all in good time." Dunmoore smiled. "May I see the ring?"

Lucas slowly took the ring from beneath his sweater and the chain from around his neck. He handed them both to Dunmoore. "Be careful. Sometimes the ring burns."

"Burns? What do you mean?"

Lucas smiled. "All in good time."

Frowning, Dunmoore took the ring between his right thumb and forefinger. He stared at it. "Yes, yes," he murmured, then added something in a strange language.

"What's that?"

"Middle English for 'be at one with the ring.' Rather a strange tongue, yes?"

"Yeah," replied Lucas. "But it seems...right, somehow."

"I quite agree. Might I try on the ring?"

Lucas shrugged. "Sure." But he watched with a rising anticipation.

Dunmoore slipped the chain off the ring and placed the ring on his first finger – a tight fit. Lucas looked around the café for...he wasn't quite sure what – mist maybe? Don Vasquez appearing from nowhere?

Dunmoore must have noticed the odd behavior. "What is it?"

"Nothing." Lucas felt his cheeks grow warm. "You just never know with that ring."

Dunmoore admired the silver circle on his finger once more, then gave it back to Lucas. "Thank you."

"How do you know so much about the ring and the box?"

Dunmoore took a sip of coffee, then said, "Because I've seen them. I've held them. You see, my father had a set."

What? Lucas leaned forward, elbows on the table. "Your father has a ring? Then why did you want to see mine so badly?"

"My father *had* a ring. But now the ring, the box, and my father are gone." Dunmoore said these last few words softly, with just a hint of wistfulness. Lucas instantly recognized that emotion – it was the tone he used when he talked about his own dad.

The waitress returned. "Here ya go, gents." She placed the plates of food in front of them. "D'ya need anything else?"

"No, thank-you." When she left, Dunmoore said, "Go ahead and eat. I'll start with my story."

Lucas hesitated. "Uh, Prof?"

"Something wrong?"

"What's this?" Lucas poked his fork at what looked like an uncooked slab of meat and fat.

Dunmoore chuckled. "Bacon. Don't worry, it's cooked. And quite delicious."

Not like any bacon I've ever seen. Or eaten. A quick sniff of the fried eggs and bread started his stomach growling again. *What the heck. When in England.* He dug in, and Dunmoore began his tale.

Chapter Thirteen

Getting to Know You

"When I was ten years old, my father took me for a ride in the country. After several hours, we arrived on the shore of a vast lake in Cumbria, England."

"Lake Windermere!" Lucas almost choked on the bacon.

Dunmoore nodded. "My father said Merlin was imprisoned there, and he showed me a wooden box and a silver ring – exactly the same as yours." Dunmoore paused to take a sip of coffee and a bite of his eggs.

"He said the ring had been handed down to him from his father, and to his father from his father, and so on and so on, back to the time of King Arthur. And one day, he would be called to embark upon a great crusade to save the world, and he would depart from Lake Windermere."

"That's why Don Vasquez wants me to go there," said Lucas.

"Don Vasquez?" asked Dunmoore, and when Lucas shrugged, added, "All in good time. Yes, I understand. That is all my father told me, except to say nothing to my mother about the ring or the legend." Dunmoore stopped and stared into space, then swept his hand over his eyes.

Like he's wiping away some vision in his head, Lucas thought. He asked, "What happened? Did he go on this crusade?"

Dunmoore's father never mentioned the ring, the box or the quest again – until the night of Dunmoore's sixteenth birthday. His parents had permitted him to throw a big celebration, with beer and wine and girls. After the party, his father had stopped at Dunmoore's room and told him the time had come. The ring was calling him and he was answering its call. At the time, Dunmoore didn't recall the ring or the story.

"I was sixteen and knew everything. And my father was old and knew nothing." Dunmoore shook his head. "I remember saying, 'Well, Father, have a good time.' And that's when he hugged me. Tightly. He hadn't done that in a long time." Dunmoore gave Lucas a rueful smile. "Then he whispered, 'I do this for you, Morgan, so you will have many other birthdays' and kissed me on the forehead."

Dunmoore glanced at his watch, held it to his ear, then wound it. He said in a monotone voice, "I never saw him again."

Lucas stopped eating, his fork midway to his mouth, not knowing what to say.

Dunmoore looked up with a slight smile. "You're not even half-finished. And here I thought you were famished."

Lucas pushed the food around on his plate with his fork. "Your father went on the quest, didn't he?"

"Yes." Dunmoore leaned back in his chair and took a sip of coffee. "But he never returned."

His father had told his mother that he was going on a business trip. When a week went by without so much as a phone call, Dunmoore's mother grew frantic and called the plant manager, who told her that no one at his father's firm – plastics manufacturing – knew anything about any kind of trip.

That's when Dunmoore confessed to his mother what his father had told him about a box and a ring and a crusade. She immediately rang up the police, who discovered that Dunmoore's father had withdrawn a huge sum of money from his accounts and boarded a plane to Japan. Japanese officials had a record of his father entering Japan, but not leaving.

"We didn't hear from my father until almost a year later. I received a letter from him, dated six months earlier, posted from Morocco."

"Morocco!" exclaimed Lucas.

"He said he was attempting to elude the Dark Powers."

Lucas shivered and glanced quickly around the café. When he turned back to Dunmoore, he whispered, "Did he use those words? The Dark Powers?"

"It's all in the letter." Dunmoore took a package from the inside pocket of his raincoat, opened it and handed Lucas a yellow envelope and faded piece of paper, both encased in plastic covers. At Lucas's quizzical look, Dunmoore explained, "I knew at some point that I would reread that letter and envelope so much they would wear out."

Someone had written "Morgan Dunmoore" in ragged penmanship on the envelope. The postmark was from Rabat, Morocco. Lucas examined the letter: It was written in the same shabby script on what appeared to be stationery from a hotel, although he couldn't read the heading – it was in some foreign language, probably Arabic if it was really from Morocco. Lucas noticed a drawing on the bottom of the page: a pair of open hands, holding a crescent moon and five-pointed star, on a square pendant with a chain attached to it. "The Hands of Allah," Lucas whispered.

"I dare say so." Dunmoore swallowed a forkful of eggs. "Read it, Luke. It's in English."

The letter read:

My dearest Morgan,

I write with a heavy heart for I do not believe I shall ever see you or your dear mother again. I have failed in my quest. What is worse, I should not have failed, had I only taken more time to find the others. Now, the Dark Powers are very near and very real. And they grow stronger every day. <u>Do not underestimate them, Morgan.</u>

Remember Lake Windermere, where I showed you the wooden box and silver ring, and pointed out the great oak tree where Merlin was imprisoned? That is the beginning of the quest, Morgan. <u>Your quest.</u> The runes on the ring read, "Be at one with the ring." Place it on your right index finger, Morgan, and remember the dream. Sir

Lancelot will come to you and tell you what you need to know. We are direct descendants of Lancelot, and you must try to find other descendants of the Knights of the Round Table. The ring might be of help to you in that respect. Only with the others can the Dark Powers be vanquished.

Again, do not underestimate the Dark Powers. I did, and now I fear I will pay for that mistake with my life. I was woefully unprepared and failed in my attempt to obtain the Hands of Allah. Alas, I learned too late the necessity of other Crusaders. Find the others, Morgan.

A trusted ally – Jafar – has promised to send this letter and ring to you if I should not survive this night. The ring must not fall into the hands of the Dark Powers.

Tell your mother I am sorry to have caused her concern and grief. Tell her to remarry, for she is beautiful and bright and should not spend the rest of her years in mourning.

Love,
Father

Lucas handed the letter to Dunmoore. "What about the ring? You said you didn't have the ring."

Dunmoore replied, "I don't."

"But the letter says –"

"There was no ring."

"You think this Jafar guy stole it?"

Dunmoore shook his head. "Why would he have posted the letter at all? No, it remains a mystery. You can understand why I so badly wanted to see your ring." He took a sip of coffee. "Now, if you would be so kind as to tell me your story."

Lucas debated over how much to tell him. He didn't really know Dunmoore, and he didn't particularly like him – especially because he kept calling him "Luke" – but now he felt a connection with the odd Englishman. Here was another guy who'd lost his father as a teenager. And here was a guy who still felt that loss, even after all those years. Lucas knew that for sure. But the real reason Lucas decided to level with Dunmoore was the ring. The ring had not burned Lucas even once around Dunmoore. Lucas figured that meant Dunmoore was not one of the bad guys. *I have to trust somebody, don't I?*

Five minutes into his tale, Lucas noticed a rapt expression on Dunmoore's face. When Lucas related the part about the ring's glowing, Dunmoore put down his knife and fork – despite being only halfway through his breakfast – and never picked them up again. Lucas began to enjoy the storytelling. And to his amazement and relief, Dunmoore believed him.

When the tale was told, they sat in silence until Lucas couldn't stand it any longer. "That's it, Prof. That brings me up to this slab of bacon in this diner in Oxford. So say something, would you?"

Dunmoore took a sip of his coffee and made a face. He called to the waitress. Within seconds, he was pouring cream into fresh hot coffee. "You told me everything?"

Lucas nodded.

"And it all happened exactly the way you told me?"

Lucas nodded.

"You have no idea how fantastic this all sounds, and yet what a relief it all is. My father wasn't starkers." Dunmoore looked down at his hands around the cup of coffee. "And I'm not mental to have believed him all these years."

"And I'm not crazy, either," Lucas added.

Dunmoore looked up, his eyes opening wide, his eyebrows arched. "Ahhh. You've come all the way to England to meet me – a veritable stranger – and take on some kind of quest, as well as...certain individuals...all because of a ring and a dream." Dunmoore shook his head, then smiled. "The entire world could very well think you, and I, have both lost touch with reality, Luke. But the world would be wrong. We just have to prove it."

"Where do we start?"

"To quote your Don Vasquez: Begin at the beginning."

Lucas nodded. He and Dunmoore said at the same time, "Lake Windermere." And much to Lucas's delight and Dunmoore's astonishment, the ring glowed.

———

Lucas again sat on the left side of the Austin as Dunmoore sped down the motorway. He stared out the window, fascinated that everyone managed to drive on the left side of the road without any accidents. *And I think getting a learner's permit in Texas is gonna be hard!*

Dunmoore said, "We need to run several errands before heading out for Cumbria. Suitable rain gear for you. I need to pack a few things, make reservations at a local inn. Oh! And explain things to Joanna."

"Jesus!" Lucas reached for the now-burning ring on the chain around his neck as Dunmoore swerved and slammed on the brakes.

A black limousine had pulled right in front of them. Fortunately, the milk truck driver behind the Austin had been paying attention and had managed not to smash into them. Both Dunmoore and the milk driver waved their fists and cursed at the limo, which sped away.

Dunmoore turned to Lucas, "Are you all right?"

"Yeah, but Jesus."

"Quite. What caused you to yell right before that dratted limo almost rammed us?"

"It got hot all of a sudden." Lucas fingered his ring. "Now it seems fine. I wish this thing had come with directions." He shrugged. "Who's Joanna?"

"My fiancée."

"You never mentioned her before." *And I never ran across that little fact when I investigated you, Prof.* But he kept that to himself. "What are you going to tell her? Does she know about everything? The ring? The —"

"She knows very little," Dunmoore interrupted. "Nothing about the quest, though she is aware of my...how shall I put it?...<u>interest</u> in the rings, and in Arthurian legend in general. She would think me quite mad if I were to tell her everything." Dunmoore sighed. "Joanna is a colleague of mine at Oxford. She's a wonderful woman, but I do believe she'd try to have us <u>both</u> committed if I let on what we were planning to do."

"What are you going to tell her?"

"Some foreign exchange students are in town and I am taking them on a tour of King Arthur's England, to Cumbria and Lake Windermere."

Lucas whistled. "Not bad. But who are these students? Isn't she going to want to meet them?"

"I'll tell her I'm picking up one student in Oxford – you – and the rest are meeting me in Cumbria tomorrow. I find that if one sticks as close to the truth as possible, one has more credibility."

The Austin turned down the long, tree-lined drive to Le Manoir aux Quat' Saisons. In the daylight, Lucas could actually see parts of the vast grounds – twenty-seven acres according to the desk clerk – and the enormous stone building. *If this is what they call a country house, how big are the friggin' castles?*

Dunmoore pulled up to the entrance, waving the valet away. "I think I might have a raincoat that will fit you. That is, if you don't mind a hand-me-down from my prep school days."

"As long as it isn't weird or anything."

Dunmoore smiled. "It's a standard, London Fog issue. You won't stand out, I promise."

Like you'd have a clue, thought Lucas. He said, "What should I do?"

Dunmoore stroked his chin for a few moments. "Pack and check out of the hotel, then buy a journal and write down what you told me this morning. Everything. That way, we'll have a written record of our quest." Dunmoore handed some English currency to Lucas.

Lucas took the colorful bills, which looked like Monopoly money to him. "I'll hang in one of those leather chairs in front of the fireplace."

"Right-o," replied Dunmoore.

Lucas opened his door to get out of the car, but Dunmoore grabbed his hand. "Be careful. We didn't talk about the Dark Powers this morning, but we know they exist and, unfortunately, they know we exist. Trust the ring. I think it can recognize agents of the Dark Powers."

"I pretty much had that one figured out." Lucas nodded. "Remember the limo and the milk truck? We gotta keep a lookout for black limos."

Dunmoore released Lucas's hand. "I concur. But you must be doubly vigilant."

"What about you? You don't have a ring. You have to be more careful than me."

"Than I." Dunmoore ignored Lucas's rolling of his eyes. "It is precisely because I do *not* possess a ring that I have been left alone all these years."

"I hadn't thought about that." *Guess the Prof is pretty up on things, after all.* He got out of the Austin and watched as it sped away. He felt a few raindrops and looked up at dark clouds gathering overhead. Shivering, Lucas pulled his leather jacket more tightly around him and entered the hotel.

It took Lucas only minutes to pack and stash his bags at the front desk. He couldn't find a travel journal at the hotel store, but managed to finagle a pad of paper from the desk clerk, then curled up in a big, burgundy leather chair in front of one of the fireplaces. A fire was already roaring, keeping Lucas and two other guests nice and toasty. He only had to listen to the conversation of the other guests for a minute before he could place them as Americans from New York or New Jersey. The woman – wife, Lucas guessed, by the gaudy gold and diamond band – was complaining to the husband – "I told you the rates were low because of the crappy weather this time of year, but do you listen to me? <u>Nooo</u>."

Lucas quickly tired of the couple, when a waiter appeared with a tray of hot cocoa and scones and leaned close to him. "Could I set this down for you in front of the other fireplace, sir? A bit more private?" The waiter nodded his head toward the American couple, the wife still carping.

"Thanks." Lucas nearly vaulted from his chair. "I was wondering when to make my move."

Settled into his new, quieter location, Lucas wrote everything he could remember about the ring and his journey – in between gulps of liquid chocolate and bites of raisin scone. After about twenty minutes, he put down his pen and scoped out the lobby. Another couple had taken the obnoxious Americans' place. Lucas guessed they were from India, from the man's turban and the woman's sari, and their soft accented voices. A welcome change. He turned back to the fireplace and snuggled up in the chair. Still full from breakfast and warm from the cocoa, he felt sleepy. He yawned and stretched his arms. *Just a quick nap.*

The spot on his chest where the ring rested grew uncomfortably warm. Lucas held the ring – it was hot. He looked around the room. The Indian couple still conversed in low voices, the desk clerk spoke rapidly on the telephone, and the valet sat reading inside the front doors.

Lucas whispered to the ring, "What's going on?"

Nothing.

"I don't see anything. Or anyone."

Nothing.

"So, what gives?" Lucas started to put the ring back under his sweater, but it heated up, again. He stared at the silver circlet in frustration, then slipped it on his finger.

The ring cooled.

"Have it your way," Lucas grumbled. He settled back into the chair, cocked his hat down over his eyes – smiling at the raspy rattle – then drifted off to sleep.

...and dreamed.

Chapter Fourteen

Harrods

A neon glow illuminated the entire scene, like a lemon-lime Gatorade wash. Lucas and Dunmoore stood in a misty swirl in front of a cash register. Dunmoore carried a new raincoat over one arm. A young black boy exited the scene through revolving doors. Dressed in jeans and a too-long slicker, the boy was also enveloped in mist. Lucas heard the half-wind, half-human "siiigghh" and saw that the boy wore a silver ring on his right hand.

Lucas glanced at his ring, glowing dull red. He felt a tingling at the top of his head and, looking up, saw the boy outside on the curb, about to cross the street. A long black limousine headed down the street at the same time, picking up speed as it approached the boy. Lucas screamed, "Watch out!" The boy turned toward Lucas, oblivious of the limo. Just as the car struck the boy, the rear passenger window rolled down and a white bony hand pointed to Lucas.

Lucas woke in the leather chair in the lobby of the hotel; a scream stuck in the back of his throat. Taking ragged breaths, he wiped the sweat from his forehead, then looked around. The Indian couple was gone, and a group of elderly tourists were emerging from the elevator, headed for the valet. Lucas fastened the chain and ring around his neck. "Heat up all you like."

He finished writing almost an hour later, dutifully recording every event surrounding the ring – except for his disturbing nightmare. In the light of day, in front of a fire, with the hustle and bustle of people all around him, the vision had already dimmed to an unpleasant dream. He felt a strong hand grasp his shoulder and gave a small gasp.

"Sorry," said Dunmoore. "Didn't mean to frighten you."

"You didn't. I was just getting up." But the words came out way too fast. Lucas could tell by Dunmoore's smile that he didn't believe him. "How'd things go?"

"Rather well, all things considered." Dunmoore sat on the ottoman. "Joanna didn't ask many questions, but she would like to meet you." Dunmoore averted his glance. "She's in the car."

I don't believe it – he's blushing! Lucas grinned.

Dunmoore hastily added, "I saw no harm in simply introducing you. Please don't bring up the ring."

"Let me grab my stuff. How long will it take to get to Lake Windermere?"

"It's 350 kilometers – roughly 250 miles – from London to the lake. About an hour from Oxford to London. So, I'd say between five and six hours."

"Is London on the way? Cool!" *Maybe I'll get to see Big Ben and Buckingham Palace, after all.*

Dunmoore coughed into his hand. "No, but I'd forgotten I'd promised to take Joanna to Harrods in Knightsbridge and then have dinner with her parents in Kensington. She's letting me off the hook on dinner, but rather insistent on her shopping. Something about a dress and social function."

"Harrods?"

"You've never heard of Harrods? It's a venerated institution, established in–" Dunmoore checked himself and smiled. "It's a department store. Whilst there, we can get you a raincoat. I couldn't locate any of my old ones. So, two birds and all."

Outside, the rain had taken a break. Weak sunlight fell in shafts through several narrow openings in the cloud cover. Lucas stopped and turned his face to the sky. Closing his eyes, he took a deep breath and felt his spirits rise at the sharp, fresh scent of spring after a storm. What had his mother always said? *Spring is God's way of getting us through winter. A chance to start anew.*

"Luke?"

Lucas opened his eyes. Dunmoore stood next to a black Range Rover, where an attractive woman with red hair sat in the front passenger seat. Lucas trotted to the car.

Dunmoore said, "Joanna Richards, meet Luke, er, Lucas Moreno. Lucas, Joanna."

Joanna extended her hand and smiled. "Very pleased to meet you, Lucas. Morgan has told me *nothing* about you."

Lucas took her hand. "The Prof speaks very highly of you, Ms. Richards."

"The *Prof*, is it?" Joanna glanced at Dunmoore, who scowled.

"All us exchange students call him that." Lucas grinned.

With a grunt, Dunmoore got into the car and put the Range Rover in gear. During the drive to London, Joanna politely questioned Lucas. Where was he from? Had he been to England before? What family was he staying with in London? Lucas answered without hesitation: Texas. Never been to England, but hoped to come again. Staying with the Chapmans in Bath. Lucas mentally high-fived himself when he remembered Karen's last name and the town her cousins lived in.

While Joanna grilled him, Lucas closely observed *her*. Her smile revealed perfectly straight white teeth. She had a husky voice and made Lucas feel like he was the only person in the world when she spoke to him. Her hair was the color of autumn leaves at their darkest red. She dressed well and didn't wear a ton of jewelry – just earrings, a gold engagement ring with a big emerald, and a small ivory ring on her pinkie. The only thing Lucas found disturbing were her eyes. They were a dark hazel, more brown than green, but the color wasn't the problem. Lucas just didn't sense any warmth in them.

An hour later, Dunmoore pulled into a parking space on Brompton Road across from Harrods. A mob of traffic and shoppers greeted them. Lucas stared at the department store, struggling to remember something that seemed to be on the tip of his brain, just out of reach.

Dunmoore turned to him. "Shall we?" They crossed the street, Dunmoore holding Joanna's hand. Once inside the store, Dunmoore and Lucas headed for Menswear. They were to meet Joanna at the front of the store in half an hour. After trying on various raincoats, Lucas selected one. While waiting to purchase the coat, Lucas suddenly gasped, then whispered to Dunmoore.

"In the hotel, while waiting for you, my ring began to burn and only cooled when I placed it on my finger. I dozed off and had the strangest dream. It happened here. In Harrods."

When Lucas finished relating his nightmare, Dunmoore had reached the register and handed his credit card to the cashier. He turned to Lucas, his brow furrowed. "The ring is trying to tell us – you – something."

At that moment, Lucas spied the back of a young black boy dressed in jeans and a too-long slicker. No mist enveloped the boy this time, but he wore the silver ring. "That's him, Prof." The boy was just exiting the revolving front doors. "I'm going after him!"

Dunmoore signed the credit card slip. Grabbing the coat, he told the cashier he didn't need a bag and hurried off after Lucas.

The black boy now stood on the steps outside the store. While trying to catch up to him, Lucas and Dunmoore almost collided with Joanna.

"No time to explain, darling. We need to go now."

A security guard arrived as Joanna placed a hand on Dunmoore's arm. "It's a handsome coat, Morgan. Is Lucas going to wear it out?"

The guard immediately grabbed Dunmoore's arm. "Do you have a receipt, sir?"

Lucas glanced through the glass doors. The boy had stepped down from the curb into the street. Lucas looked up the street toward Hyde Park and saw the black limo.

Dunmoore struggled to get the receipt out of his coat pocket to show the guard.

Lucas said, "Come on, Prof!"

Joanna turned to Lucas and put her hand out. "What's wrong, Lucas?"

The ring on his neck chain blazed with a searing intensity. Lucas dodged Joanna's grasp, dashed out the doors and yelled to the boy. The boy stopped mid-street and looked questioningly at

Lucas. The black limo sped down Brompton Road. People began to shout.

Instinct and adrenaline surged inside Lucas, and he raced into the street and tackled the boy, catapulting both of them to safety on the opposite sidewalk. Lucas craned his head to see around the crowd that was gathering. The limo stopped at the corner. The rear passenger window rolled down and a man stuck out his head, then ducked quickly back into the limo as Lucas looked his way.

It was the redheaded albino from passport control!

Chapter Fifteen

D

Des and Destiny

Lucas felt the pounding of his heart in his chest and ears, drowning out all other sounds. Light-headed, he turned his attention to the boy. A large bearded man grasped Lucas's arm and asked if he was "'urt?" Lucas shook his head. He figured the boy was unhurt, too, although he recognized fear in his wide eyes and ashen face.

The boy pushed himself up from the ground, murmuring something about having to get home. Shaking off his wooziness, Lucas grabbed the boy's hand. "The ring, the ring." The boy jerked his hand away and protectively covered the ring. Lucas got up and took his ring from beneath his sweater.

The boy's big, brown eyes opened even wider. He stared, unblinking behind his thick tortoise shell glasses. "You, too?" He had an accent Lucas couldn't figure out.

Dunmoore managed to push through the crowd. "Are you all right, *Son?*" He took Lucas's arm.

"Yes, *Dad.* Can we go now. I think *Jason* wants to go home." *The poor kid's gotta be freaking out.* Lucas clutched "Jason's" arm and whispered, "Go along with this so we can go somewhere and talk."

The boy looked a sight: His blue jeans were scraped, the front of his white shirt was stained with black from the impact with the wet pavement, and his glasses were comically tilted.

Dunmoore leaned over the two boys. "If we don't leave now, the constabulary is sure to arrive and ask questions."

"Jason" snapped back to reality. "N-n-no police."

Dunmoore turned to the now-large crowd. "Thank you for your concern, but my son and his friend seem to be fine. I'm going to take them home, now. Please make room for us to pass." People began to disperse.

Suddenly, a female voice called out. "Don't you want to wait for the police, guv? That man woulda kilt your boy."

"She's right, mister," boomed a man.

"Woulda killed them boys, he woulda," another voice rang out.

"Leave it to the bobbies!" called others.

The crowd blocked Dunmoore and the boys' escape. Lucas tugged Dunmoore's coat sleeve and whispered, "We gotta get out of here."

"Right-o." Dunmoore addressed the crowd again. "Did any of you see the license plate on the car?" Murmurs shot through the on-lookers. No one had caught the numbers.

Dunmoore said, "Nor did I. That being the case, I don't see how the police are going to do anything about it at this moment. But rest assured that I will request the authorities post notices about the incident so people who may have seen something will call in. The boys are rather shaken, so I ask again, may we please get to our car?"

This time, the crowd parted, though grudgingly, it seemed to Lucas. *They were probably hoping there'd be more blood and guts.*

As Dunmoore put the Range Rover in gear, Joanna tapped on the passenger side window, a tightlipped smile on her face. Dunmoore rolled down the window. "Darling! I'm terribly sorry!" Lucas clambered into the back seat with the boy, and Joanna settled in the front. They pulled out of the parking space just as a police car careened down the street, lights blinking and siren screaming. The Range Rover passed the police car and took the next left.

Several minutes later, Dunmoore parked on a small side street and turned to the boy. "Where are you staying? We need to go and gather your things before we head to Cumbria."

The boy stared out the window for a few more moments, then slowly turned to Dunmoore. "Grosvenor House in Hyde Park, not far from here."

"I know the place. Right-o, off we go." Dunmoore turned onto the main road.

Joanna said, "What do you mean, 'off we go'? And who is this young man?"

"Jason. Carpenter. Jason Carpenter," Lucas said. Lucas turned to the boy and nodded, arching his brows. *God, I hope he gets it.*

Dunmoore cleared his throat. "Jason is one of my exchange students. I recognized him leaving Harrods, which is why I was in such a rush to exit the store."

"But isn't he the one nearly run down?"

"The car didn't come close to hitting him, Joanna," Lucas said.

Joanna narrowed her eyes. "Then why did you tear out of Harrods like a banshee?"

Her stare unnerved Lucas, and he stammered, "The Prof and I were supposed to pick Jason up at his hotel this afternoon and meet up with the other kids in Cumbria, but the Prof forgot where Jason was staying." Lucas gave Dunmoore what he hoped was an accusatory look.

Dunmoore said in a sheepish voice, "I'm afraid Luke is right. Awfully sorry about that, Jason. Joanna has to remind me where my keys are most mornings." Dunmoore grinned at her.

She frowned, then gave the boy a sympathetic smile. "Are you sure you're not hurt, Jason? I rather think we ought to report the incident to the police."

Lucas watched the boy and held his breath, crossing both sets of fingers.

The boy looked at Dunmoore, then Lucas, then Lucas's ring. Finally, he looked at Joanna and smiled. "I'm fine, thank you. It wasn't the car, it was my own fault."

Another frown from Joanna.

"Luke startled me when he came running and shouting out of Harrods. I tripped in a pothole and hit the pavement." The boy looked at the asphalt on his shirt. "My clothes took the worst of it."

Lucas exhaled deeply, then realized Dunmoore had also.

Joanna glanced sharply at both of them. "We really should call his parents, Morgan."

"No! I-I wouldn't want to worry them. You see, they live in Morocco."

"Morocco?" Joanna's eyebrows arched.

"I attend Eton. Rather than return home for Spring holiday, we thought the Prof's –," he looked at Lucas, "– field trip would be the ideal alternative."

"It certainly will be, I promise you that." Dunmoore gave a hearty toot-toot on the horn. "And we can be on our way just as soon as we get your things and check you out of your hotel."

Joanna said, "The Grosvenor House is a favorite of mine. What room do you have?"

"777, overlooking the park."

"How lovely!" exclaimed Joanna. "Although it's much prettier when there's no rain or fog. Perhaps we can have tea, Morgan?"

"Darling, I'd rather we drop you off at your parents' first." Dunmoore looked at his watch, then fiddled with the winding stem as he said, "We must be on our way or we're going to be even further behind schedule. I'd rather not have my other students cooling their heels in Cumbria." He cocked his head toward his fiancée. "Do you mind terribly?"

Joanna gave Dunmoore a small pout. "I would love to see the lobby again and have tea." She heaved a theatrical sigh, then smiled. "I'll let you make it up to me another time."

Fifteen minutes later, Dunmoore turned the car into a driveway. "The family manse."

Joanna's parents' home was a Victorian style house in the Kensington area of London. Lucas easily pictured the two Oxford professors lounging on an antique sofa in front of a huge marble fireplace, reading the Sunday newspaper. *Probably doing the crossword puzzle. In ink.*

Joanna gave Dunmoore a lingering kiss and exited the Range Rover. Lucas climbed from the back seat into the front.

"Have a good trip, gentlemen." Joanna waved as they backed out of the driveway.

Dunmoore tooted the horn and called out, "Love to George and Martha!"

For the first few minutes of the ride to Grosvenor House, no one said much of anything. Lucas stared out the window the entire time, twirling the ring about on its chain. Finally, he looked at the boy and Dunmoore. The boy was staring out his window and twisting the ring around his finger. Lucas half expected...something...to materialize in the car, and he clutched his ring. He ran his hands along the scrapes on his jacket sleeves, where he had slid on the street after tackling the boy.

Dunmoore glanced at Lucas. "Battle scars. You've a tale to tell the others at school."

A voice came from the back seat. "They don't look much like battle scars on a slicker."

Lucas turned. The boy was small, and his big, light brown eyes seemed huge through his enormous tortoise shell glasses. His voice was surprisingly deep. *I would have pegged him as twelve, if that, except for that voice.*

"And how are you, really?" Dunmoore asked.

"I'm okay. But I'd like to get my hands on those bastards in the limo." The boy clenched his hands into fists.

Lucas asked, "What's your real name?"

"Desmondo Jafar Moboto. Des."

"What?" Dunmoore's eyebrows arched in surprise. "Desmondo *Jafar* Moboto?"

"Yes, sir," replied Des. "Is something wrong?"

Realizing Dunmoore had spooked the boy, Lucas said, "No, it's just...it's a long story."

Dunmoore added, "And one we will get to, I promise you. Where are my manners? I'm Morgan Dunmoore, and this is Luke Moreno."

"*Lucas*. Are you really from Morocco?" asked Lucas.

"Yes. And I really do attend Eton. And I'm really into computers."

"Wow! Morocco." Lucas whistled. "But you speak English so well."

"My family believes English is the language of finance and business and, to be successful, one has to master that language. I'm fluent in English, Arabic and French."

"Is your family still in Morocco?" asked Dunmoore.

"Yes." Des's voice came out soft, sad. "They think I'm with the family of a friend from boarding school, skiing over the holidays in Switzerland."

"And the friend's family think you changed your mind and are with your family in Morocco, right?" asked Lucas.

"How did you know?" Des asked.

"Same story, different locations."

"If they ever find out..." Des shook his head.

"Grounded for life," Lucas said, thinking about his mom.

"Not to change a depressing subject," said Dunmoore, "but how about telling us your story, Des?"

Des began his tale – leaning forward so he could be heard over the slap, slap of the wipers and the thrumming of the rain on the car roof.

"My father died almost a year ago," Des said. "I was home on leave from Eton because of my father's accident."

"Accident?" Dunmoore looked in the rearview mirror at Des, his brow furrowed.

"Hit-and-run. The police never caught the driver."

"A black limo?" Lucas asked. His palms suddenly felt sweaty and his heart beat faster.

Des nodded and said slowly, "I never thought about it before."

Lucas shuddered. *Those guys are all over the place. All over the _world_.*

"I managed to get to his hospital room only hours before he died. He told me he had left something for me, and I wasn't to open it until my fourteenth birthday. He made me promise."

Lucas saw a tear trickle down Des's face. He realized he had tears in his own eyes. After wiping them away with the sleeve of his coat, Lucas glanced at Dunmoore. Dunmoore stared straight ahead, seeming to concentrate on driving in the pouring rain.

Des blew his nose, then said, "On my birthday this year, I went to the safety deposit box and found something wrapped in brown paper and tied with string."

"Inside was a box and a ring, yes?" Dunmoore asked.

"And the box was carved? Like this?" Lucas rummaged in his knapsack and presented the ring box to Des.

Des took it as if it were glass and would shatter at the slightest touch. He whispered, "You have the same box."

"My dad left it to me, along with the ring." Lucas took the ring from the chain around his neck and laid it on top of the box.

Des looked at the inscription, then carefully slid Lucas's ring on his first finger, where it nestled against *his* silver ring. "They're one and the same, aren't they?"

Dunmoore asked, "Who was your ancestor from the Knights of the Round Table, Des?"

"My ancestor?"

"The one who appeared to you in your dream?"

"Mine is Don Lorenzo Vasquez, from Spain," said Lucas. "The Prof's is Sir Lancelot."

Des looked at the two rings once more. He handed Lucas's ring back, but continued to caress the rosewood box as he talked.

"I showed my mother the box and ring and asked if she knew anything about them, but she was just as mystified. I was going to research the inscription when I returned to school for Spring term. But while flipping through family photo albums with Kinisha and Molly — my sisters — I noticed that in two of the pictures, my grandfather was wearing a silver ring on his first finger. I couldn't tell if it was the same ring, but it certainly looked like it. That night, I put the ring on my first finger, just to see. And it...tingled."

"Tingled?" Lucas asked.

"I thought I was imagining it, but now I don't think so."

Lucas asked, "Did it ever glow?"

Des shook his head. "I wore the ring to bed and had the strangest dream. I was standing in a clearing in a forest with mist all around. Out of the mist rode a man on horseback. A dark man, dressed in armor with a fur coat, without sleeves, worn over the armor. I'd seen outfits like that in books on the Mongol invasions of Northern Europe, the ninth or tenth century."

"That sounds several centuries too late," Dunmoore commented.

Des looked at Lucas, who shrugged and said, "What can I say? He's a professor."

Des pushed his glasses back up on the bridge of his nose. "The man called me by name and told me to get behind him on his horse. We rode until we came to the shore of a large lake."

Lucas said, "And there was this huge, gnarled oak tree, right?"

"Don't tell me you had the same dream, too!"

Lucas turned to Dunmoore. "Lake Windermere!"

"This just gets weirder and weirder." Des readjusted his seatbelt and leaned forward again. Except for the different ancestral knight, his dream mirrored Lucas's. No one in Des's family had a clue as to what the dream meant until he mentioned it to his grandmother.

"One night, Grandmother came to my room and told me we were direct descendants from a knight of the Round Table, Modetta

Khan. When I showed her the box and ring, she started crying. She said the ring was one my grandfather used to wear. And Grandfather had told her of the exact same dream many, many years ago."

Lucas thought back to the slip of paper he had found with the ring: "Merlin, Knights of Round Table, Quest, Dream." *Someone in my family had that dream. I'm sure of it.* Des's talking brought him out of his thoughts.

"...the days of King Arthur. He kept a journal, which Grandmother started to read after his death. It scared her so much, she never gave it to my father, even though Grandfather had asked her to. That night, she handed me the journal and asked me to be very careful."

"Why did she give it to you?" Lucas asked.

"She had a nightmare. In it, most of the world was at war, and many of her relatives were killed. And right before she woke up, she saw me, wearing the silver ring, with three other young people and one old, old man, in long blue robes, who turned and pointed to her. He said, 'Without Desmondo, you have no hope.'"

"Merlin!" Lucas exclaimed.

"It may be, it just may be," said Dunmoore. "What happened next, Des?"

"I discovered the man in my dreams was my great, great, great, something, grandfather – Modetta Khan – an ancestor of Chinghis Khan, founder of the Mongol dynasty, the greatest empire ever. It stretched from the China Sea to Persia and from the Indian Ocean to Siberia!"

Des punctuated his words with big hand gestures, then pushed his glasses back up on his nose. The boy's excitement at being the descendant of such a great warrior made Lucas grin. Who would have guessed this small boy with the big round glasses had such a military ancestry?

"While Modetta Khan did not control even a tenth of Chinghis' empire, he certainly was a figure to be reckoned with, especially by China." Des paused. "I guess I'm getting sidetracked." He gave a shy smile to Lucas. "Anyway, Modetta Khan traveled to England to join the other Knights of the Round Table. And here I am."

"And here you are," said Dunmoore. "I have one question: Do you have the journal?"

"Back in my hotel room."

"Let's get it and get going to Lake Windermere," said Lucas.

"Now, you must tell me your stories," insisted Des.

Dunmoore smiled. "Go ahead, Luke."

"It's Lucas." He spoke as if it were now a ritual between him and Dunmoore. Then he turned to Des and spun his tale.

Chapter Sixteen

The Hotel Affair

"You see now why I was so surprised to hear that your name is Desmondo *Jafar* Moboto, from Morocco," Dunmoore concluded his story. "I think your grandfather and my father were...allied...in some way."

Des nodded and twisted his ring. "I think they did know each other. My grandfather mentions him in his journal."

When Dunmoore stopped the Rover in front of the hotel's two-story white and green marble entryway, Des hopped out. "It should only take me about ten minutes to pack."

"I think it best if we go with you," said Dunmoore. "Safety in numbers."

When they reached the lobby doors, Dunmoore said he'd forgotten something. Lucas and Des waited inside the lobby until Dunmoore returned – his raincoat over his arm – then took the elevator to the top floor. At the door to Des's room, both boys yelped at the burning of their rings. Dunmoore dropped his raincoat to reveal a handgun equipped with a silencer and motioned the boys to stand to one side of the door.

"Your cardkey, Des," Dunmoore whispered.

Lucas said, "Jesus, Prof, where'd you get the heat?"

"Stay here until I call you. If you hear shots, take the stairs down to the lobby and get the constabulary. Des, did you leave any lights on in the room?"

"A couple. Why?"

Dunmoore pointed to the gap under the door. It was dark. Dunmoore pried the cover off the hallway light nearest the room and unscrewed the light bulb. He did the same with the next three lights, shrouding the hallway. "Stay down!" he hissed, then entered the room, crouching low. The door closed behind him. Lucas heard several crashes, glass breaking and what sounded like muffled shots. Then a cry of pain, another muffled shot, and more glass breaking.

The boys raced to the stairwell and paused.

Seconds later, Dunmoore called out, "All clear!"

Lucas tore back up the hallway, looked about the room and gave a low whistle. Chairs and tables were overturned, a lamp was broken, and one of the glass balcony doors was smashed.

"We heard shots." Lucas eyed Dunmoore's revolver.

"I hit the intruder. He escaped by shattering the balcony door and climbing down the fire escape. I didn't want to risk further attention by engaging him as he fled. Moreover, I have always had a distaste for shooting people in the back."

"How often have you had to do that?" Lucas asked. *Not in the normal day of any teachers I know. There's something up with the Prof.*

"A discussion better saved for later. When we are safely away from here." Dunmoore turned to Des. "Make sure everything is still here and start packing. Luke and I will try to clean up as much as possible." He paused. "Lord knows how we'll explain this mess."

Des called from the closet, "Grandfather's journal is still here."

Dunmoore turned from gathering shards of glass. "You can read it aloud in the car."

Five minutes later, Des had finished packing and stood near the door with a brown suede satchel and suitcase in hand. Dunmoore left a note on the writing table, asking that the bill for the damage be sent to him. They left the hotel room, letting the door slam behind them.

———————

"Why don't you read us those parts of your grandfather's journal dealing with the quest?" Dunmoore suggested.

Des read for about five minutes, ending with "All seemed lost that night...." He looked up. "Then there's all these pages ripped out." He held up a torn journal. "This is the last entry."

October 31, 1954. Through our correspondence, it is clear that Dr. Habib remains greatly perplexed about Alfred's death and how we came to sustain our injuries in Egypt. For my part, I am loath to enter into any further conversations about what occurred that fateful night. I am still greatly saddened by my friend's death and, if the truth be known, still terrified by what we witnessed.

I have torn from my journal the pages detailing the events in Egypt and sent them to Dr. Habib. I cautioned him against attempting to explore the mystery by himself, especially since he does not possess a ring. But, in light of his recent news about becoming a father, I do not believe my warning was necessary. Perhaps my journal will help satisfy some of his curiosity, in any event. For my part, I cannot lie to myself. I had hoped to continue the crusade, begun so long ago by my ancestors. But since my return to Morocco and the news that my own wife is pregnant with our first child, I know I cannot. I no longer have the enthusiasm.

And I now have great fear and much more to lose. I am to be a father! Such a joyous occasion. Such a tremendous responsibility. I cannot forsake my wife, or my child-to-be, at this time. If that is deemed cowardice, so be it. Perhaps when my child is older, I can again take up the mantle of responsibility for the world. For now, I can only pray for a safe and happy childhood for my son or daughter. And for Morgan, son of my dear friend, Alfred Dunmoore. The will of Allah be done.

The Prof's dad! Lucas turned to Dunmoore, who wore an expression of shock and disbelief. *It's like he thought maybe his dad would turn up alive. After like forty years?*

Des asked, "So, Alfred Dunmoore *is* your father?"

Dunmoore only nodded, but his knuckles whitened as he tightened his grip on the steering wheel.

You gotta hold it together, Prof, thought Lucas. *I think this is just the beginning of some nasty news.* He said aloud, "Sorry about your dad. At least now, you know. Even though we don't know anything about where he was killed. If only we had the missing journal pages."

Dunmoore took a deep breath and flexed his fingers, first the left hand, then the right. "Jafar's journal does help solve part of the mystery: It always puzzled me that my father's letter was postmarked from Morocco, but written in Egypt."

"How do you know it was written in Egypt? His letter doesn't mention Egypt." Lucas closed his eyes and strained to remember the letter, but all he saw was faded ink on yellowed paper in plastic wrap.

"No, but the stationery is from Cairo General Hospital."

"No way!" Lucas exclaimed.

"I believe the requisite response is, 'Yes, way'?" Dunmoore smiled. "I had the stationery translated by one of my colleagues in the foreign languages department. And now Jafar's journal confirms that my father died in Egypt."

Des said, "True. But we still don't know where."

"But a Dr. Habib would, wouldn't he, Prof?" asked Lucas. His heart began to beat faster. Things were coming together.

"My precise thoughts," answered Dunmoore.

Lucas asked, "But what happened to the ring? Did your grandfather keep it?"

"What do you mean?" exclaimed Des, adding in an indignant tone, "My grandfather was not a thief!"

"No one said he was." Dunmoore spoke in a gentle tone. "But when I received the letter long ago, there was no ring."

Des crossed his arms. "I do not believe Grandfather kept the ring. He *had* a ring."

Dunmoore said, "My guess is someone else took it."

"The Dark Powers?" asked Lucas. He remembered the white bony hand in the cemetery. And the redheaded albino at Harrods. His growing excitement abated, like a balloon deflating.

"It seems the most likely explanation," said Dunmoore.

"But why send the letter?" asked Lucas. "Wouldn't they want to keep you in the dark?"

"Perhaps they have a nasty sense of humor? What good is the letter by itself? They knew I could do nothing without the ring. That I had no way of avenging my father's death. I imagine they had quite the chuckle over that." Dunmoore clenched his hands into fists.

"I hate them." Lucas clenched his hands into fists. *I really, really hate them.*

"I, too." Des imitated the others, hands now clenched.

And for the briefest of moments, Lucas thought he saw the silver sheen of his ring grow dull and tarnished. He rubbed his eyes and stared at his ring. *Still silver. I'm just giving myself the creeps.* But he wondered.

Back at the Grosvenor House, a dark figure stood in a telephone booth on the corner, one arm tied with a tourniquet, coat sleeve stained with blood. He placed a call, grimacing with pain at the effort it took to lift his wounded arm. When the call was connected, the figure said, "They are on their way. I could not prevent it." He replaced the receiver, then hailed a taxicab. As he ducked into the car, his hood fell down, revealing pale white skin, a shock of red-orange hair, and pinkish eyes without a hint of humanity.

Chapter Seventeen

A Mink in Time

She giggled as her father bounced her up and down on one knee while singing a silly ditty about "This is the way the ladies ride, clippity-clop, clippity-clop, this is the way the ladies ride, clippity, clippity-clop." She loved when he got to the way the "outlaws" ride – "gallop, gallop, and off!" – when he'd throw her in the air and catch her as she squealed with delight.

She winced at the pain that shot through her face when she actually squealed and struggled to open her eyes, only to fall back into a troubled sleep.

The pain she felt in the next dream was only emotional, but it caused her to weep, and tears soaked her pillow. She clasped her *Maman's* hand and gazed at the polished casket as men grunted while lowering it into the open grave. Her beloved Papa was gone. How could he leave her? She twisted the silver ring on her finger – the one her father had given her just days before her thirteenth birthday – remembering the fairy tale he told: about being direct descendants of *Chevalier* Griflet, one of the original knights of King Arthur's Round Table; about the wizard Merlin making magical silver rings and sending Chevalier Griflet and the other knights on a great quest. "Little Mink," her father had said as he gently pushed a dark lock of hair off her face, "you are destined for greatness. Never forget."

But she didn't want greatness, she wanted her Papa! She kicked at the casket now settled in the rich soil, kicked at the white roses the mourners had dropped on the wood, and kicked off the thin blanket covering her in her sleep. Shivered. It was so cold. Reaching for the soiled wool blanket, she tried to open her eyes; she didn't *want* these dreams, but something pulled her back into slumber.

This was more to her liking. She stood on the balcony of a mansion in the South of France, tight against the smooth plaster, hidden from the lights trained on the back lawn and gardens. The tinkling of champagne glasses and the chatter and laughter of guests rose from the courtyard below. But Elaine LaCroix tilted her head to catch sounds from the room off the balcony of the third floor. Yes, there it was, the flushing of a toilet, the splashing of a bidet, followed by a pattering of footsteps across the marble floor. Then, the room was bathed in darkness.

Elaine jimmied the glass doors, slid one open and crept into the room, drawing the curtains behind her. Flipping on her laser penlight – a top-of-the-line flashlight that could not be seen from outside unless one happened to have night-vision goggles – she surveyed the room, then smiled and hurried to the oil painting on the opposite wall. She slid her finger up the side of the painting and clicked the toggle switch, which swung the painting open on its side, like a bathroom cabinet. There was the safe, her meticulous research having paid off again. Ear tight against the cold metal, she turned the knob, stopping as each correct click of the combination fell into place. Then the moment of triumph when the safe door opened to reveal an array of jewels, packets of money and bearer bonds.

Her stepfather had taught her well. Elaine LaCroix – known to the public and law enforcement only as "The Mink" – shoved the cache into her large black handbag, put everything in the room to order, then slipped into the master bath and emerged dressed in an exquisite black and gold cocktail dress with mink wrap. She sauntered down the hallway and glided down the curving marble staircase to rejoin the party. Europe's foremost cat burglar had struck again.

A smug grin. And yet more pain. Why could she not wake up? What was happening?

She stood in a clearing in a towering forest with a cold mist hugging the hard ground, heard the eerie sighing of the wind-man, felt the strange tingling at her scalp and braced herself for the electrical surge, but it didn't come. And where was the familiar clippity-clop of horse hooves? Where was Chevalier Griflet? It hadn't been a fairy tale; the knight was real. She'd met him in a dream, learned about the Quest. How she had to find the others. She'd found one – Tomás Moreno – and written to him. But he'd never written back. Just as she thought. You could only count on yourself. And look what she'd done by herself – located the Eye of Buddha. *Wait. She had located the jewel, hadn't she?*

"Yes, Little Mink."

She swiveled, tried to find the source of the voice. *Was that...?*

"Yes, it is I."

A hand shot to her throat as a small gasp escaped it. In front of her, in the base of a huge, gnarled oak tree, was the image of an old, old man, with bent nose and long white beard, shaggy white brows and piercing blue eyes. "Merlin? *Incroyable!*"

"Not so incredible, I think," said the voice. A gravelly yet dignified voice. With power behind it.

And danger? she wondered.

"Not from me, Elaine LaCroix," said the wizard. "But you *are* in grave peril."

"No, no, I am good, as you can see." She twirled to show off her fine form.

"Ah, Little Mink," said Merlin, his voice soft and sad.

She felt a fluttering of fear – like a moth beating its wings against a light – and shook her head emphatically. "Where is Chevalier Griflet? And his magnificent steed?"

"Sir Griflet can only appear to one who bears the ring."

"But I *have* it!" She waved her right hand in the air, then gaped at the ringless forefinger. Her thoughts roiled as if in a windstorm, until she could only whimper, "How?"

"The others, *Mademoiselle* LaCroix. You were to seek the others."

"I did, *Monsieur* Merlin!"

"And the Eye of Buddha was not for *you*." The sorcerer's tone turned harsh. "Self-imposed isolation and greed have been your undoing."

Her fear now saturated with sorrow, Elaine asked in a small, small voice, "What will become of me?"

Merlin's expression softened to that of a loving parent, his tone kind and forgiving. "The others are making their way. We must have faith. Do not give up hope, Little Mink."

As the wizard's visage faded into bark, Elaine LaCroix cried out, "Do not leave me, Merlin!"

And woke to find herself on a burlap mattress stuffed with straw, surrounded by steel bars. The concrete floor sent shivers up her legs, but she only snatched them back to the mattress at the skittering of the roaches across her feet. Staring at her ringless hand, she raised it to her face and winced. Her cheek was bruised and her eye swollen almost shut. A woman's screams – *Chinese?* – made her shudder, and she wrapped the two scratchy blankets around her, lay on her pillow, and cried herself back to dreamless sleep.

Chapter Eighteen

H

Of Thieves and Princesses

Lucas drummed his fingers on the dashboard in time with the windshield wipers. "I've been thinking, Prof," he said. "What about the other ring?"

"Other ring?" asked Dunmoore. He glanced at Lucas's fingers. "Would you mind?"

"What? Oh." Lucas ceased his drumming. "You know. The other guy who asked you about the inscription? On the Internet?"

"Ah, yes. You mean the first inquiry. But it wasn't on the Internet. He wrote me a letter. It's in my briefcase. Des, would you have a look in the zipper pocket, please?"

Des handed a letter to Dunmoore. It had a return address from "Aran Islands, Ireland." "Aren't the Aran Islands on the West Coast of Ireland?" asked Des.

"Yes, off Galway. You'd have to cross all of Ireland and the Irish Sea to get to England." Dunmoore passed the letter to Lucas. "Would you read it aloud, please?"

Professor Morgan,

I heard about you from Mrs. Thornton, my teacher. She says you're an expert in English History, King Arthur and such, and you'd answer a couple questions. See, I got this silver ring with an

95

inscription in it. Mrs. Thornton said they're runes, but she can't translate them. Here they are:

ᛒᛖ ᚠᛉ ᚹᚾᛏ
ᚹᛁᚦ ᚦᚾ ᚱᛖᛜ

I was told that the ring came from Merlin. Mrs. Thornton doesn't believe that. She says Merlin was never real, but she thinks the ring is very old. Do you know what they say or not? You can get back to me through Mrs. Thornton.

Ryan C.

P.S. Do us both a favor and <u>don't tell anyone else about this letter!</u>

Lucas said, "This guy must know about the Dark Powers, don't you think? Why else would he say, 'don't tell anyone else about this letter'?"

"Where did he get the ring?" asked Des. "From his father, do you think?"

"I don't know," replied Dunmoore. "I never heard back from Ryan. When I finally connected with Mrs. Thornton, she said Ryan had run away."

"Run away!" Lucas heard Des echo his own exclamation.

Dunmoore tried to telephone Mrs. Thornton without success. And not knowing Ryan's last name, he simply sent a letter to "Ryan C., care of Mrs. Thornton" and waited for a response.

This guy tracks me down in Texas on the Net and he can't run down an Irish kid? Lucas thought, but he listened without comment to the rest of Dunmoore's story.

After a week, Dunmoore sent another letter explaining Ryan had not called and asking the teacher to contact him. Soon afterward, he heard from a very agitated Mrs. Thornton. She had given the letter to Ryan the day she received it. Several days later, Ryan disappeared, leaving his mother a note – something about it was time for him to leave, he was off on a great adventure, and maybe he'd come back some day. The entire island was in a bit of an uproar. Apparently, Casey – Ryan's last name – had financed his departure with some money taken from the school treasury. Dunmoore looked at Lucas and Des. "Our Mr. Casey is a thief."

"You don't think he's one of the Dark Powers, do you?" asked Des.

Lucas noticed Des twisting his ring back and forth. *He's scared. Not that he doesn't have good reason to be. But not from this Ryan Casey.* Out loud, Lucas said, "Nah, he's just a guy like us who found a ring and maybe had the same dream. But I'll bet he doesn't know squat about what he's getting himself into." Lucas stared out the window at the dwindling rain. *How do we find this Casey kid before he gets into deeper crap?*

Dunmoore said, "I think you've hit it squarely on the head, Luke. But I think our Mr. Casey is in a different league from you and Des. Mrs. Thornton was a bit of a gossip, and I had no problem getting the 'dirt' on Ryan. He trained one summer with the IRA, and his hero is the infamous Bobby Sands."

"That IRA guy who starved himself to death in prison?" asked Des.

"The one and only," Dunmoore answered, frowning. "Mrs. Thornton hinted that Ryan was a 'bit of a rebel,' and she was very concerned about his safety. I just hope we meet up with him before he gets himself into real trouble."

As the Range Rover rounded a curve, Dunmoore slammed on the brakes. "Hold on!"

A bus blocked their lane, its front off the road. Several passengers and the driver congregated near the rear of the bus, looking at the engine. Dunmoore carefully maneuvered around the disabled vehicle.

When they passed the front of the bus – which had a sign reading "Cumbria" – Lucas shouted, "Stop!"

Dunmoore parked on the shoulder. "What is it?"

Lucas held up his ring, now glowing a bright emerald shade. "Look!"

Des put his ring hand in Dunmoore's palm. "Feel it."

"My God, Des, it's tingling." Dunmoore turned to Lucas. "Is yours burning?"

"No, so I don't think there's any danger," replied Lucas. "But they're trying to tell us *something*." His eyes shone with excitement. "Maybe it has to do with the bus."

"Let's have a look. I'll engage the driver while you boys check out the passengers. If there is something, or someone, important here, I have an idea the rings will let you know."

Lucas scrambled out of the car, antsy to investigate. Des took his time, and when he closed the door, he was twisting his ring again – back and forth. *Scared again. I should be, too, I guess. But I'm not.* Lucas clasped his ring. "It's not hot, so, nothing to fear, right?"

Dunmoore answered, "Don't worry, boys. We do have some security with us." Dunmoore slipped his gun into his raincoat pocket and patted it.

The rain had let up, but the passengers along the road still stood under their umbrellas, a colorful mixture of blue, red, yellow and the occasional black or plaid. When the three Crusaders reached the back of the bus, Dunmoore tapped the driver on the shoulder.

"Excuse me, sir. We couldn't help but notice that you seemed to be having some trouble. I've done a fair share of mechanical work on my own cars and perhaps might be of assistance?"

The grateful driver took up Dunmoore's offer, mentioning something about "throwing a piston" and scooting away the other men gathered around the engine, craning to get a look. Dunmoore nodded to Des and Lucas, motioning with his head for them to start their search. Holding tightly to his ring, Lucas began to walk slowly past the passengers, Des at his heels.

The rings gave no signal whatsoever at the men at the back of the bus. As they made their way around the side, Lucas kept glancing down at his ring, then to Des's, hoping for some hint as to whom the mystery passenger might be. But the rings did nothing. When the boys reached the front of the bus, having passed all the riders without feeling the slightest warmth, glow or tingle, Lucas plopped to the wet grass.

Des took off his raincoat, spread it neatly on the ground, and sat in the middle of it. Noticing Lucas's smile, he said with a sheepish grin, "Already ruined one pair of jeans today."

Lucas said in an exasperated voice, "You just can't rely on these damn rings!"

"How are we supposed to find out if anyone else has one?" asked Des. "We can't simply ask people."

Lucas shook his head. "That would call way too much attention." He plucked a blade of grass and sucked on it. "You'd think these rings would recognize one another." He bolted upright, dropping the grass from his mouth. "That's it! *We* can recognize the ring!"

"But I thought we didn't want to ask people if they had a ring like ours?" Des's forehead creased in puzzlement.

"We'll pretend to find a ring and ask if anyone has lost it. And we'll watch for the reactions. I bet the person who has the ring will immediately look for it. What do you think?"

Des smiled broadly. "I think it's a grand idea!"

Lucas stood and pulled Des to his feet. They began to retrace their steps around the bus. Half-way around, Lucas bent over and pretended to pick up something from the ground. He held up his ring and called in a loud voice, "Hey, anyone lose a silver ring?" Several passengers turned and looked at the boys, shaking their heads.

Des grasped Lucas's forearm. "The Asian girl!"

Lucas spotted her just in time to see her drop a silver ring on a chain under her shirt. She was Japanese, about fifteen years old, maybe older. It was hard for Lucas to tell because she had on makeup. Lucas *could* tell that she was beautiful – long black hair to her waist, a full mouth and, most captivating of all, soft yellow eyes, like those of a cat. In her faded Levi jeans, black clogs, white guinea T-shirt and a short, black cardigan, unbuttoned, she was a babe. *Way finer than Candy Carson.* The head cheerleader at Lucas's school.

The girl stared at Lucas and Des, wide-eyed, then turned and jogged toward the back of the bus. Lucas noticed that the glances of most of the men – young and old – followed her. He turned to Des. "We've spooked her. You follow her, and I'll head her off the other way."

Lucas figured Des had done a good job, because the girl came flying around the bus, not looking where she was going. She ran smack into Lucas and opened her mouth to scream, or so he thought. He covered her mouth with his hand, showed her his ring and whispered, "Don't be afraid. We're also on our way to Lake Windermere. We are *not* the Dark Powers."

Lucas slowly took his hand from her mouth. The girl did not scream. Instead, she took Lucas's ring from his palm and looked at the inscription on the inside. She placed it in the palm of her left hand, then slowly took her ring from the chain around her neck and placed it next to Lucas's. Des walked up beside her and placed his ring in her palm. The three rings glowed a soft emerald color for a few seconds and then returned to their normal silver sheen. Lucas stared in wonder, then realized Des and the girl seemed equally mesmerized.

Lucas cleared his throat. "I'm Lucas Moreno, from Texas."

"I am Desmondo Moboto from Rabat, Morocco, but you can call me Des."

The girl was silent for a moment, then said, "Maya Hosokawa. Kyushu, Japan." Maya looked at Lucas. "Don't touch me like that ever again, *capisci*?" She tossed her head, swinging her blue-black hair off her face, and offered the boys their rings and her hand.

Dumbfounded, Lucas took her hand. Her skin felt deliciously smooth, but Lucas could feel the strength in her grip.

Dunmoore called, "Could one of you fetch the cell phone? It's in my briefcase."

"Prof, we need you for a moment," Lucas called back.

Dunmoore strode toward them. "What is it?"

"It's a who. Maya Hosokawa. She has the same ring." Lucas touched Maya's arm, then quickly withdrew it and waited for another withering stare. Maya only smiled. Lucas said, "This is Professor Dunmoore. He knows all about the rings and the quest. He's helping us get to Lake Windermere."

Dunmoore extended his hand. "Very pleased to meet you, Maya. Where are you from?"

"Takeo Onsen. It's a small city on the island of Kyushu, in southwestern Japan."

Dunmoore nodded. "Many great Samurai warriors came from Kyushu."

Maya's eyebrows arched and her eyes widened.

Lucas smiled. "The Prof knows way more than just the legends of King Arthur."

They heard the driver hollering. Dunmoore said, "We need to call the bus company to get a replacement. I can't repair the damage, and the bus radio isn't working." Des ran off to the Range Rover.

Dunmoore turned to Maya. "I know this is rather precipitous, but I think it would be wise if you rode with the three of us to Cumbria instead of waiting for a replacement bus. I get the sense that Des and Luke's rings alerted them to your presence not just because of your ring, but because they want to keep you safe from...how shall I put it? Any danger?"

Lucas explained, "He means the Dark Powers."

Maya shivered and rubbed her arms. In that slight gesture, Lucas guessed that the Asian princess had a vulnerable side after all. Maya must have sensed Lucas observing her, because she stood up straighter and flipped her hair off her shoulders with both hands.

She said, "I knew what he meant. I agree it would be safer traveling with you, Professor. I can protect you."

"Yeah, right, *poquita niña*," Lucas said. *Same ego as Candy Carson, that's for sure.*

Ignoring him, Maya spoke to Dunmoore. "It may not be so easy getting Mr. MacDougal to let me go with you. He feels responsible for my safety. He has three daughters of his own, and now two teenage granddaughters. He made me sit behind him the entire trip."

Des jogged up with the phone. Dunmoore said, "While I contact the bus company, why don't you three figure out a plausible explanation for Maya's joining us. I can see how the driver and other passengers might object to leaving a young woman in the care of three strangers."

Several minutes later, Mr. MacDougal relayed the news that a replacement bus would arrive in about an hour. Although the passengers were not pleased with the delay, only a few voiced complaints.

Dunmoore rejoined the teens and asked whether they had concocted a believable story.

"We took your advice, Prof, and came up with a story as close to the truth as possible," said Lucas. "Maya's one of the foreign exchange students in your group this week. On a tour of the legend and legacy of King Arthur."

"We're picking up other kids in Cumbria and setting out from there," Des said.

"I was taking the bus to Cumbria to meet them," added Maya.

Lucas said, "But seeing as the bus is broken down and we were on our way to Cumbria to meet Maya and the others –"

"You thought it only natural to take me the rest of the way," Maya interrupted.

"A very plausible story. Let's have a go at it." Dunmoore turned and headed back to the bus, the three teens close on his heels. Maya pushed her way to the front.

When they'd pitched their tale to the driver, "Mac" MacDougal, he scratched his chin and looked the group over. "I don't know, guv." He looked at Dunmoore. "Much as you seem proper and all, I'd hate if Miss Maya was to get hurt or something."

"Oh please, Mr. MacDougal," pleaded Maya. "I'll be perfectly safe with Professor Dunmoore. Look, I even have his book, with his picture." Maya opened her knapsack and took out the King Arthur book written by Dunmoore. The same book Lucas had been reading in the library when Don Vasquez appeared!

This can't all be coincidence, can it? Lucas checked his ring. Nothing.

Mac looked at Dunmoore's photo on the back cover. Glancing up at Dunmoore and back to the book, he said, "Yuh, that's him all right, though a bit younger then, eh, guv?" Mac chuckled as Dunmoore frowned. "Well, seeing as you really are a university professor, and seeing as Miss Maya seems to know you and all, I don't see no harm in it."

"Thank you, Mr. MacDougal." Maya gave him a peck on the cheek. Mac blushed. With that, Maya took off to fetch her luggage. Lucas followed.

As they climbed on the bus, Maya said, "You think I can't carry my own bag?"

"I don't know you well enough to know what you can and can't do."

"You think I might slip into the woods and head to Lake Windermere alone?"

"Just get your bag, Maya."

She hefted a large, black leather duffel bag – designer label – from the luggage rack above her seat and dropped it at Lucas's feet. "If you aren't going to leave me alone, you might as well make yourself useful." She skipped off the bus.

Lucas looked from the bag to the blue-black mane of hair whipping out the door. *Talk about your friggin' princess.* But he couldn't help a smile. *Way, way finer than Candy Carson.*

Dunmoore, Des and Maya had already settled into the Range Rover. Lucas tossed the black duffel into the rear of the car and got into the back seat. Maya had made a point of taking the front passenger seat. "From now on, princess, carry your own bag."

Des said with a puppy-dog smile, "I don't mind carrying your bag, Maya."

Maya stopped frowning at Lucas to smile warmly at Des. "At least one of you boys is a gentleman. Shall we be off?"

"Yeah, and you can tell us how you got here," Lucas said.

Maya said, "I'd rather hear your stories first. I don't know anything about you."

"Point well taken," Dunmoore said.

Maya turned and gave Lucas a small but very triumphant smile.

Lucas thought, *Ten minutes with this princess is nine minutes too much. How do I last a whole week?*

Dunmoore added, "I imagine you're feeling a bit overwhelmed by us."

Maya's smile turned to a frown. "Overwhelmed by you? Never."

Lucas grinned. "You're right, Maya. We already know each other. It's only fair that you'd want to be clued in, too. It's just that...we already know each other, you know? We're dying for a new story. It's your call."

Maya considered Lucas for a few long moments, then said, "I suppose it's only fair that, being the newcomer, I go first."

Well, isn't life just full of surprises, Lucas thought. *Wait, who said that? Karen. I'd love to see her reaction to this one.* Smiling at the thought, Lucas nodded and said, "That'd be great."

Maya offered Lucas a tentative smile – *of truce,* he thought. *But how long will it last?*

Chapter Nineteen

The Third Ring

"My father was a Nisei," Maya began.

"That means he was first-generation Japanese American, right?" Lucas asked.

Maya arched one eyebrow. "I'd always heard American kids learned nothing in school."

Lucas knew the haughty tone in her voice well. *She's got the snoots in common with Candy Carson, too.* He said aloud, "Don't believe everything you hear. *That's* what we learn."

Maya sniffed and turned to Dunmoore. "My father returned to Japan as a serviceman at the U.S. Air Force Base on Okinawa, where he met and married my mother. I was only a year old when he received orders to return to America. But he was killed in an accident only days before we were to leave Japan. I never really knew him."

She was silent for a moment, then tossed back her hair in what had become a familiar gesture to Lucas.

Maya's grandparents – her father's parents – returned from the U.S. to Japan and settled in Takeo Onsen with Maya and her mother. Last year, her grandfather grew very ill – a combination of years of smoking and exposure to radiation from the bombs dropped during World War II in Nagasaki, where he had lived before moving to America. During his last days in the hospital, Maya sat with him every day after school. "Just to be there for him when he was awake," she said, then grew quiet and stared out the car window.

I knew there had to be another side to this ice princess. Lucas remembered the last time he had seen his father in the hospital and shook his head to clear it of the painful memories. At the small, dry rattling, he removed his hat and held it on his lap, rubbing one of the rattles.

Maya continued. "One day, Grandfather gave me a wooden box with the silver ring in it. He told me I had an obligation to keep the box and ring safe until I had a son. He said we were descended from a great Samurai warrior – Shin'ichi – who had joined the Round Table."

"A Samurai knight in King Arthur's court?" Lucas asked.

"The Samurais were great warriors!" Maya turned to Lucas, her small chin jutting out, eyes slightly narrowed, as if taking great offense.

"Chill," Lucas said. "I didn't mean anything by it. Just never thought about it before."

Maya's eyes softened. "I didn't believe it at first myself."

Dunmoore said, "The premise of King Arthur's Round Table – 'might for right' – was an amazing one in that day and age. It attracted the attention of educated men far and wide. From Spain to Mongolia to Japan."

"That's what I learned," said Maya, who related the tale of her ancestral knight: Shin'ichi was a descendant of one of the greatest Samurais – Yorozu – and also the right-hand man of Tair no Masakado, a most infamous Samurai. When Masakado became a rebel warrior and proclaimed himself Emperor of Japan, Shin'ichi could no longer serve him. He left Japan to join the Round Table and was sent on a great undertaking. Maya warmed to her story. "According to legend, Shin'ichi was sent to a temple in Japan to retrieve the Eye of Buddha, but was attacked and killed by wild dogs."

Lucas grimaced. "What a way to go."

"Yes, but the alternative was not a – how would you say it? Picnic," said Maya. "The Samurai Code required Shin'ichi to commit suicide rather than be dishonored by failure."

"*Hari kari?*" asked Des.

"The sword through the gut thing?" asked Lucas.

Dunmoore said, "It's a highly revered ritual, but your rather graphic terms convey the essence of it."

Maya smiled. "Shin'ichi's aide escaped the dogs and returned the box and ring to our family. Where it has been passed down from generation to generation. That's all I know. Grandfather died two days later. Afterward, I discovered he'd written a book about Shin'ichi."

"That could prove quite enlightening," said Dunmoore. "Did you bring the book?"

"Yes. I've read it, but I didn't find any real clues. I also have Grandfather's papers – notes for his book. I haven't had the chance to go through them all."

Dunmoore said, "Perhaps I'll take a crack at them."

"They're mostly in Japanese," warned Maya.

Dunmoore smiled. "I know a bit of Japanese, though I am by no means fluent. That is one skill which still eludes me."

"Hey, that reminds me," said Lucas. "You never did tell us how you got so great with guns, Prof. What gives?"

Dunmoore frowned. "After Maya finishes her story."

"No way, Prof. You've put us off long enough, right Des?"

Des nodded. "You can give us the short version, if you'd prefer."

"I spent some years in the British Secret Service. No cracks about James Bond, what?"

"Impressive, Prof." Lucas grinned.

Des asked, "During the Cold War?"

"Short version. Now, may we please get back to Maya?"

"There isn't much left to tell," said Maya. "Grandfather gave me the ring for safekeeping. To pass on to a son. It figures the knights would be chauvinists." She gave a little "hmmph." "Grandfather told me he wished he had taken the ring seriously; maybe my father – his son – might not have died." Maya sighed. "How the ring would have prevented the accident is beyond me."

"An *automobile* accident?" asked Des, elbowing Lucas in the side in his scramble to lean into the front seat.

Rubbing his sore ribs, Lucas asked, "Was a black limousine involved?"

"How did you know?" Maya frowned.

Crap. Did they kill Maya's father, too? Then, another thought hit Lucas hard, sending a chill up his spine: *And what about my dad?*

Off the silence, Maya said, "What is it?" She looked frightened, her composed demeanor gone. "Please. You're worrying me. How did you know?"

Dunmoore placed a hand on Maya's shoulder. "Tell us about the accident."

Maya swallowed and explained that she had gone through family papers after her grandfather died. One was a newspaper article on her father's death. While returning home one night from work, he was hit by a car. The driver of the car never stopped. A neighbor witnessed the accident, but had only been able to identify the car – a black limousine – no license plate.

Another damn limo, Lucas thought. He caught Maya wince when she looked at him. He was pretty sure if he looked in a mirror, he'd see horror written all over his face.

Dunmoore said, "Des's father was killed in a hit and run accident by a driver in a black limousine. Des was almost run down himself by a black limousine. And –"

"– Don Vasquez confirmed that a black limo in a cemetery back home belonged to the Dark Powers," Lucas said.

"The Dark Powers," Maya whispered, then hugged herself.

She's scared, thought Lucas. *And you aren't?* asked his little voice.

Dunmoore said, "We can discuss that later. I want to know about *you*. Your part in this."

Maya stared at her hands in her lap, then talked about her dream of Shin'ichi. It quickly turned into a nightmare when the Samurai knight revealed visions of what would happen if she did not attempt the quest: Wars and riots, terrorist bombings and mass starvation, train derailments and, as if that wasn't enough horror, the gassing of a temple in Japan.

Dunmoore gasped. "You saw the Nara Tōdai-ji temple poisoning *before* it occurred?"

"I didn't remember it until it actually happened two days later."

"You mean where the supporters of that crazy religious guy shot nerve gas into a packed temple?" Lucas asked.

"Yes, that *crazy guy* was Shoko Asahara," said Maya. The leader of an apocalyptic cult called the Aum Shinrikyo. He was already in jail for the commuter subway poisoning. No one thought he posed any threat. They were wrong. "I tried to forget the dream. I was sc –" Maya paused. "I did not want to be involved. I tried to convince myself it was all a nightmare."

"I know the feeling," said Lucas. "After the first dream with Don Vasquez, I didn't put the ring on for a week. Who wants to deal with the fate of the world?"

Maya nodded. "I realized it wasn't just a nightmare when the temple gassing happened two days later. Mother and I were watching the news footage when I realized it was what I had dreamed. I became...upset." Maya blushed and looked down at her hands. "Before bed that night, I held the ring in the palm of my hand and said 'I need to go to England, don't I?' And then the strangest thing happened."

"The ring glowed!" Lucas interrupted excitedly.

Maya's jaw dropped. "How do you know all this?"

"Because the same thing happened to me!" Lucas grinned with excitement.

"How did you manage to get to England without your mother finding out?" asked Des.

Maya had received a scholarship to attend the summer semester at the London School of Economics, and was *supposed* to be attending a two-week pre-summer program to acquaint the foreign students with London.

"Wait a minute." Dunmoore stared at Maya. "Do you mean to say you were already planning to spend a summer in England even before you acquired the ring?"

"I thought it was only coincidence at the time. Now...I don't know if I can put it into the right words. But it seems as if there's some design to all this. The Japanese have a word for this. *Unmei.* A divine plan. That's how it feels."

"We call it *qadar,*" said Des.

"Fate, right?" asked Lucas.

"I prefer 'destiny' to 'fate', Luke," answered Dunmoore. "'Fate' implies an inevitable, and usually adverse, outcome. While 'destiny' also implies something which is foreordained, it most often suggests a noble course or great end."

Lucas said, "I'll take destiny over fate, Prof. I'm all for a great ending!"

Dunmoore held his Rolex to his ear, frowned and began to wind the stem. He met Lucas's gaze in the rearview mirror and asked, "Even if it should mean the end of us?"

Chapter Twenty

The Shadows Know

It was past midnight in the remote mountain region of Transylvania. But deep within the serpent castle, no one slumbered. Mordred was on the hunt.

When the last of the warriors strode into the cavernous throne room – his hair unkempt, eyes blurry from sleep – Rattar bustled to the throne and whispered in his master's ear, "All prethent, M'lord."

Mordred raised his head from his chest and opened his eyes. "Do forgive the timing of this meeting. We realize some of you only just arrived after an arduous journey." Mordred nodded toward the group, in particular the redheaded albino who, with the dark half-circles under his eyes and his bright red traveling cloak still around his shoulders, now resembled death in a clown suit. The albino bowed his head slightly in return.

"I thought Clodin screwed up?" the latecomer muttered to the colleague next to him, a slight Asian woman with green highlights in her jet-black hair.

She shrugged. "Clown still favorite." But her eyes narrowed.

"...the situation demands immediacy of action," Mordred was saying. "We have survived for hundreds upon hundreds of years. Is our demise to be at the hands of *children*?"

Angry muttering and shouts of "No, M'lord" spread through the assembly.

"Good, good." Mordred nodded and placed the fingers of his hands together in a pyramid. "As you know, success in our organization carries its own reward. And rank has its privilege, as we are sure Generals Zheng and Vassalar can attest."

The two generals stood front and center before the black throne. The huge Chinese Zheng, a good six and a half feet in height and 300 pounds in girth, stepped forward, bowed to Mordred, then turned and nodded to the others. The slender Vassalar followed suit. Their acts of cruelty and feats of deviousness were legendary. Vassalar's behind-the-scenes maneuvering had almost single-handedly brought about the 1990s Croatia-Serbia conflict.

"To aspire to a status such as theirs? Ah, a worthy goal, indeed." A slight nod, and the two generals returned to their places among the rank-and-file. "Alas," Mordred frowned, and the crowd tensed. "Not all succeed. Oh, one failure here or there can be overlooked. Two can be *counseled*. After all," he smiled, "we are hardly perfect." A slight tittering ran through the assembly. "But three?" He shook his head. "Three requires, nay, *demands* punishment."

The warriors tilted their heads slightly to the right to catch a glimpse of Clodin. A small, nervous smile twitched on the albino's face.

"Hugin," Mordred called.

A dark-haired man of medium height and slight build stepped from behind the great throne, a red folder in his hand. His appearance was ordinary, non-descript in every way, except for the lone streak of white hair he wore parted to the right. "M'lord?"

"The status of our young friends in England, if you would be so kind."

The informant faced the crowd and read from the folder in a monotone voice. "Moreno, Lucas, evades agent at Heathrow. Moreno rescues Moboto, Desmondo, from agent at Harrods. Dunmoore, Morgan, rescues Moreno and Moboto from agent at Grosvenor House." Closing the folder, he turned to the throne.

"And who *is* this agent who has failed three times?"

"Clodin, M'lord."

"Thank-you, Hugin."

The man unnoticed in a crowd slipped behind the throne, into the shadows. Mordred stared at the now solemn Clodin.

"M'lord?" Clodin's whole body jerked. He looked like a marionette clown.

"Do come closer, our dear Clodin. It's been so long. Let us have a look at you." Mordred motioned with his right hand.

But the albino stood still, rooted in growing terror. Suddenly, he was shoved violently from behind into the circle of light reflected by the flickering chandelier of black candles overhead. "M-m-m-lord?"

"What say you, Clodin? Our funny one, our clown? A new riddle? A joke perhaps?"

Clodin's lips moved but no sound escaped.

"No?" Mordred stroked the broad head of one of the dogs. "Well, never let it be said that we do not learn from those who serve us. *We* have a riddle for *you*."

Nearly every eyebrow in the crowd rose.

"What is orange and white and red all over?"

Clodin looked around the room with an expression of fear and confusion. He turned back to the throne and held out one hand in a plea for mercy, saying, "I don't...," He stopped at the sight of his red greatcoat. He stroked his coat, then raised one white, trembling hand to his frizzy orange hair. His questioning pink eyes met the brilliant blue-green ones of Mordred, who smiled and nodded. Clodin cleared his throat, swallowed and said, "M-m-me?"

Mordred laughed and clapped his hands. "Excellent, Clodin, excellent!"

The warriors glanced at each other, frowns of disapproval on some, open mouths of astonishment on others. Clodin's trembling lessened. He chanced a small chuckle.

"Now, *why* is it you, our funny clown?"

Clodin's forehead wrinkled. "Why, M'lord?"

"There is a reason behind every riddle, Clodin."

"Ah, yes." Clodin straightened, looking confident once more. He smiled and put his good hand to his face. "My skin is white." He touched his hair. "My hair is orange." He pulled his greatcoat open, revealing his injured arm, cradled in a sling. "My cloak is red."

"So close, Clodin. Come, take off the coat." Mordred clapped once. Rattar scurried to the albino, who slipped the coat off his shoulders into the milky hands of the plump little servant.

"Now, your skin is white, your hair is orange, and *you* dear Clodin..." Mordred clapped rapidly three times. From the shadows to the side of the throne room stepped two archers, who each let fly three arrows, all of which pierced the albino – in the head, the heart and elsewhere.

Clodin fell to the floor, blood spurting from six openings, soaking his clothes, face, hair.

"...are red all over."

The roaring of Mordred's laughter echoed throughout the fortress and into the cold, dark night.

Chapter Twenty-One

Around the Round Table

"Before we start out on this noble course, we need nourishment." With these words, Dunmoore pulled the Range Rover into the parking lot of a roadside pub advertising the 'Best Fish and Chips in the World.' "Let's see if they live up to their reputation, what?"

Lucas didn't know if the food was the best in the world, but he sure devoured his meal.

After they told their stories to Maya, she said, "I don't know what to say. A part of me wanted it to be *real*. Another part of me wanted...to not believe. To think it was only a dream and I was crazy to go along with it. But now, I can't go home. I have to see this through. And it's all quite..." Maya searched for the word.

"Scary?" suggested Lucas.

Maya glared at him. "No. It's *daunting*."

Lucas smiled. *She's scared, all right.*

Des said, "At least we're all together."

"Bravo, Des," said Dunmoore. "Remember what my father said? *Find the others.* Other descendants of the knights. We are stronger as a group than we could ever be alone."

Maya sighed. "Where do we go from here?"

"I've reserved two rooms at the Round Table Inn in Cumbria. If no other rooms are available, I propose Luke, Des and I share one room and Maya take the other."

Maya asked, "Are they adjoining rooms, Professor?"

"Feeling *daunted?*" Lucas grinned.

———

They arrived at the Inn around nine P.M. When Dunmoore returned from checking in with only two keys, he said, "There is no more room at the Inn." Lucas groaned. Dunmoore smiled. "Ours are a room apart. If you prefer, Maya, one of the boys could share your room?"

"Under the circumstances, I agree it might be best. What do you say, *boys?*" Maya tossed her blue-black mane, catching Lucas on the cheek.

Des looked down at the ground and mumbled something, while Lucas said, "*No problemo, muchacha.*"

"All settled then." Dunmoore gave out keys. "Lucas and Maya in 313, and Des and I in 309. I suggest we all get a good night's sleep and formulate a plan of action over breakfast."

At the elevators, Lucas said, "Hey, Prof, what about the guy in 311? Maybe he'd switch rooms with us?"

Dunmoore shrugged. "I suppose there's no harm in asking."

They trooped back to the front desk. "I understand another guest has reserved room 311," Dunmoore said to the desk clerk, "and we were wondering if it would be possible to switch one of our rooms with his? In order to have adjoining rooms, you see."

After checking the guest register, the clerk shook his head. "Sorry, sir. Young Mr. Sands has already checked in."

Back at the elevators, Lucas got another idea. "Wait up." He dashed to the front desk.

The clerk stood at the counter, filling out papers. "Excuse me, sir," Lucas said.

"Haven't made it up to the room, yet?" The clerk smiled.

"I was curious when you said it was *young* Mr. Sands. What did you mean?"

The clerk colored slightly. "I really shouldn't have said...well, I guess there's no harm in it. He looks to be about your age, although he certainly wants to give the impression of being older. A bit of the Sinn Féin in him, if you ask me." Lucas smiled and leaned over the counter. The clerk lowered his voice. "It's always a bit odd when we get a teenager staying here by himself. I wouldn't be surprised if his parents had no idea where he was. Or the bobbies."

Lucas glanced back at the elevators. Dunmoore was gesturing for him to come, while Maya stood with her arms crossed, tapping her foot. Lucas asked, "One last thing: Are you sure his name isn't Ryan Casey?"

The clerk checked the register again. "No, it's Sands. Casey Sands."

Hot damn! Lucas ran back to the others. "I'm getting that feeling, Prof." The elevator doors closed. "The guy in room 311 is about our age. And his name is Casey Sands."

Blank stares.

"Don't you get it?" asked Lucas. "Our age. *Casey* Sands. Ryan *Casey*. Bobby *Sands* – Ryan's hero. It's pretty damn close. And, he's here by himself."

"You could be onto something, my boy," said Dunmoore as the elevator doors opened at their floor. "Let's stow our luggage and then discuss what we ought to do about Mr. Sands."

They came to room 309 first. Dunmoore unlocked the door and held it open for Des, then turned to Lucas and Maya. "Don't bother unpacking."

Lucas and Maya continued to room 313 without a word. Inside, Maya toyed with the lock on the door connecting their room to 311. "Do you really think it might be him?"

"I just have that feeling, you know?" Lucas tossed his hat on the bed and opened the door to the hallway. But Maya was not behind him. "What's up?" he asked.

"My ring's hot."

Lucas realized his ring had begun to heat up. "Mine, too." He looked at the connecting door and said slowly, "Maybe I'm wrong. Maybe we *don't* want to know this kid next door."

Maya asked, "How many more of us are there?"

"Beats me."

"You two coming or what?" a voice called from the hallway, causing Lucas to jump. Des appeared in the open doorway.

Lucas said, "Jesus, Des! Don't go sneaking up on a guy like that."

Des grinned. "I would have knocked, but the door was open. And the Professor's getting impatient."

"Surprise, surprise," said Lucas. "Hey, Des, is your ring hot?"

Des's smile disappeared. He pushed his glasses back up on his nose and nodded glumly.

"We think it may have something to do with the boy in 311," said Maya.

Des twisted his ring back and forth. "We should get back to the Professor."

Seconds later, they entered Dunmoore's room. He sat on one of the double beds, finishing up a telephone conversation. "Yes, I'll be here tomorrow night. I'll ring you up around 10 o'clock tomorrow evening, say? Love." He looked at Lucas. "I said no unpacking."

"We weren't, *Dad*. We just got to talking."

Dunmoore muttered something under his breath before saying, "You may be right about Casey Sands being Ryan Casey, but I'll be damned if I know how to prove it. Any ideas?"

They sat quietly for a few minutes, until Des came up with the solution. "Why don't we ring up room 311 and ask for Ryan Casey? If he answers to the name, it must be him. And if not, if we're wrong, we won't have given away our names or location."

Dunmoore picked up the telephone and dialed, then asked in his most professorial voice, "Ryan Casey?" He put his hand over the mouthpiece of the telephone and whispered to the others, "It's him."

Lucas jumped up and stood next to Dunmoore, his ear near the receiver.

Dunmoore spoke into the phone again. "Ryan. This is Professor Dunmoore. You wrote me about the silver ring."

Lucas heard a tinny gasp from the earpiece. Then silence.

Dunmoore said, "Ryan? Are you there?"

The boy at the other end of the line asked in a soft voice, with just a hint of fear, "How did you find me?"

Lucas thought, *This kid's got to be thinking we're the Dark Powers.*

Dunmoore said, "Mostly luck, I think, but then again, maybe not luck so much as destiny. There are three others with rings, Ryan. They'd like to meet you."

"Three more rings?" the boy repeated.

"All teenagers, like yourself. Wouldn't you like to meet them?"

The boy paused and then, with what Lucas was sure was false bravado, replied, "Yeah, sure. Why the hell not? When and where do you want to meet?"

"What about now? Why don't you come to our room? We're next door in room 309."

The boy hesitated for a few seconds. "I'm not dressed. Gimme ten."

"Right-o." Dunmoore hung up the phone. "Mr. Casey will be here shortly."

"All right, Prof! Fist bump!" Lucas gleefully held up one fist and Dunmoore, chuckling, knocked knuckles with him.

Des stood in the doorway to the hall. "What's the matter?" asked Maya.

"I want to make sure Ryan doesn't run. He needs to see the ring." Des held up his hand, ring aglow.

"Slammin' idea." Lucas placed his ring on his finger and joined Des in the hallway.

Just as Maya crossed to the hallway, the door to room 311 opened, and a teenage boy exited, stopping at the sight of the others.

He looks like a jackrabbit caught in a coyote's path, thought Lucas.

Ryan's duffel bag hung over one shoulder, and he backpedaled into his hotel room, but Lucas reacted quickly by inserting his body between the door and jamb.

"We're Crusaders. See?" Lucas held up his right hand.

Des stuck his right hand through the opening next to Lucas's hand and repeated, "See?"

Maya followed suit, squeezing in front of Des and Lucas.

"Jaysus, Mary and Joseph!" cooed Ryan, then slowly raised his right hand and placed it next to theirs'. The four rings glowed brightly for a few seconds.

"May I suggest that formal introductions be made inside?"

Ryan looked at Dunmoore, who stood in the hallway. "Have at it." He turned and strode back into his room.

Fifteen-year-old Ryan Casey fit the part of an Irish youth to a tee. He stood 5'6" and was thin, with curly, dark red hair and brows, and a spray of freckles across the bridge of his nose. Lucas watched Ryan's piercing green eyes assess the group, lingering on Maya. *Yeah, the cool Asian chick in a slick, black leather jacket. You got taste, Casey.* Ryan wore the uniform of teens worldwide – Nikes, jeans, white T-shirt, a green hooded sweatshirt, zip-up style, and a faded Levi's denim jacket – but he wore it with brash confidence. He reached into the back pocket of his jeans, took out a pack of Camel unfiltered cigarettes, tamped one out and struck a match.

"This is a non-smoking room. Do you mind?" Maya asked in her best haughty princess manner. Lucas couldn't help but flinch every time that tone came into her voice.

Ryan gave her a sardonic smile – his right lip curling slightly – and lit the cigarette. He plopped onto a chair, stretched one arm behind his head and exhaled a stream of smoke in Maya's direction. "So, how did you find me?"

Maya muttered something in Japanese – *not complimentary, I'll bet,* thought Lucas – then scowled and turned her back on Ryan.

"Hey, *you* came looking for *me*. In the middle of the damn night, too." Ryan's eyes narrowed to slits, and he took a long drag on the Camel.

He doesn't trust us. Even with our having the rings. Lucas forced a grin. "Actually, we just kind of stumbled upon you."

Ryan appraised him with a look Lucas knew well – the ones he got from opposing runners as they stood next to each other on the track. *He's wondering if I'm competition. For what? The quest? It might not be so easy talking this guy into joining us.*

Dunmoore said, "Our apologies for waking you."

"I'm a light sleeper, mate. Kind of have to be with the Dark Powers about, you know." Ryan glanced at the others with a smug smile.

Des and Dunmoore were clearly surprised, as was Maya, although she attempted to hide it with an expression of disdain. Lucas maintained a calm demeanor. "Yeah, we know," he said.

Ryan narrowed his eyes again. "Is that right, mate?"

"Right-o," said Dunmoore, clearing his throat and tapping his Rolex.

From his fidgeting, Lucas knew Dunmoore was uncomfortable with the tension in the room. He also knew they were all dying to hear Ryan's story, but Ryan seemed to delight in being contrary. That sparked an idea. "My story's pretty fascinating, don't you think, Prof? It'll give everyone a reason to stay awake."

The others, save Ryan, blinked their eyes and stared. *Yeah, I can be as cocky as the next guy*, Lucas thought. *Let's just hope Casey takes the bait.*

"Not bloody likely," said Ryan. "My story won't put anyone in slumberland."

Lucas looked at Ryan, then nodded. "Go for it."

As Ryan began telling how he came to possess the ring, Lucas smiled at Dunmoore. Dunmoore put his right thumb and forefinger together in a circle.

"I found the ring in me grandda's things two months ago," Ryan began. "Actually, I found it in me great-grandma's trunk, but she died long before I was born. Grandda had packed all her stuff away. Said he didn't like to be reminded of her. Never forgave her for leaving the family when he was barely fifteen. He died two months ago."

Lucas asked, "How?"

"Lung cancer. He was a two-pack-a-day smoker since he was seventeen. Guess that's how I'll go, too." Ryan exhaled another stream of smoke. "You'll be dashed, eh, Princess?" Ryan grinned at Maya, who glared back.

Ryan crushed out the cigarette butt in an ashtray shaped like a castle. "After the funeral, I was going through the stuff in his attic. Found a trunk stashed way back in a corner of the attic, covered with cobwebs and spiders. It had a note on it – 'Margaret Anne' – that was me great-grandma's name. 'Grandma Maggie', me mom called her. At first, I thought the stuff was going to go to me three sisters. You know, dresses and other frilly crap. But then I saw this wooden box. Jaysus, Mary and Joseph! It was covered with carvings of crazy animals and symbols. But it was hot." Ryan's eyes grew wide.

He's as hooked as the rest of us, thought Lucas.

Des said, "Wait one minute, please?" Ryan lit another cigarette and frowned. Des unlocked the adjoining door to Room 309, then went out Ryan's door into the hallway. A minute later, the lock on the adjoining door clicked, and Des walked through, closing and locking the door behind him. He had his backpack slung over one shoulder and held in the palm of his hand the carved, rosewood box. "This was in your grandmother's things, right?"

Ryan dropped the burning cigarette, bolted up from his chair, and took the box from Des, slowly turning it around. "It's *exactly* like Grandma Maggie's." He handed it back, saying, "That was worth the interruption, little guy," then sat and leaned back in his chair again. Grinding the glowing cigarette in the ashtray, he said, "You know what was inside the box. The silver ring." He glanced at his ring, twisting it. "I also found a diary and a picture of a man and woman. Didn't notice it until later, but they both wore silver rings. The woman in the picture was me great-grandma. The man was *not* me great-grandda."

"Who was the man?" Lucas asked.

Ryan gave him a lingering look. "According to Grandma Maggie, he was Anthony Moreno, from Texas."

"What?" Lucas exclaimed. "Anthony *Moreno*? From *Texas*?"

Ryan smirked. "Wanna see the picture?" Dumbfounded, Lucas could only nod. Ryan reached for his backpack and unzipped it, taking out a leather-bound book. Inside the book was an envelope containing a very faded black-and-white photograph of a smiling man and woman. They stood in front of an army tent with a red cross on it. Snow blanketed the ground, and both the man and woman wore fur coats and hats. And on the first finger of their right hand, each wore a silver ring.

"Do you know the man, Luke?" Dunmoore asked.

Lucas looked up from the photo. "I'm pretty sure it's my great-grandpa Tony."

Ryan nodded. "When I heard your name, I figured, hell, you had to be related."

"Can I see the diary?" asked Lucas.

"Yeah," Ryan replied. But as Lucas reached for the diary, Ryan held it out of his grasp. "After I finish me story. When you read the diary, you'll see how Grandma Maggie inherited the ring." Ryan patted the leather book in his lap. "Even the warped dream she had."

Maya asked, "What knight from the Round Table appeared in her dream?"

"Sir Gawain. To cut to the chase, she ended up in England, at Lake Windermere. In the middle of World War II, and the bombing of London, me great-grandma is talking to Merlin." Ryan chuckled and shook his head. "When she returned to Ireland, she enlisted with the Red Cross in Finland."

"Why Finland?" Dunmoore asked.

"It's like, 1939, when the Russians invaded Finland. The Brits sent medical aid."

"That's right!" Lucas could barely contain himself. "Great-grandpa Tony was a pilot with the Red Cross in Finland!"

Maya rubbed her goose-bumped arms.

"Destiny, remember?" Dunmoore said.

"Destiny me arse. It's what the bloody Pope tells the poor to keep 'em down." Ryan scowled, then shrugged. "It's all in the diary. Grandma Maggie went to Finland, met this Moreno guy, and off they went to find the Holy Grail."

"Did they find it?" asked Lucas.

"Don't know. She never wrote about it in her diary. And she never made it back."

"What?" Maya now leaned forward in her chair, dropping all pretense of disinterest.

Ryan looked down at his ring. "She was killed in an automobile accident. In Russia."

"What kind of an automobile?" Lucas asked.

"What does it matter?" Ryan stood, frowning. "No one in the family got any of the details of how she died. The Russkies just shipped her back in a body bag. Bastards." He turned and glared out the window, his fists clenched.

When he turned back to the group, Lucas could see the hostility in his eyes, hear it in his voice. Ryan asked, "What the hell kind of car did you think it would be?"

Dunmoore answered. "It seems the Dark Powers are fond of using black limousines to eliminate any risk to their empire."

"Dry up!" Ryan exclaimed. His face paled, the freckles standing out in sharp contrast to his white skin. "There was this strange black limo at Grandda's funeral." As he spoke, he pulled a silver chain from inside his T-shirt and rubbed a small silver trinket that hung from it. It was a Celtic cross – with a circle around the part where the shaft and crossbar met. Ryan continued, "It was raining, but the limo was gleaming like the sun was out. Gave me the willies."

Lucas whispered, "That's *exactly* what happened to me."

Ryan and Lucas stared at one another. And in those few seconds, Lucas knew something akin to respect passed between them. They were alike in more ways than they imagined.

Chapter Twenty-Two

Intruders

Ryan's recollection of the gleaming limo at his grandda's funeral seemed to make all the rings blaze like burning coals. Then, there came movement in Dunmoore and Des's room. Dunmoore flicked off the overhead light and motioned for Ryan to douse the lamplight.

Lucas put his ear to the adjoining door. From the sounds of it, he figured at least two people were rummaging around inside. He froze when the handle to the door twisted. But the lock stopped the intruder from entering.

Dunmoore drew his gun.

Swift as a black cat on Halloween night, Lucas unlocked the door between Ryan's and his rooms, then slipped into the hallway. He pulled the red handle on the fire alarm and darted back into his room. *WHOOP! WHOOP! WHOOP!* sounded throughout the hotel. Slapping on his rattler hat, he grabbed his and Maya's bags and entered Ryan's room through the adjoining door.

The intruders in Des and Dunmoore's room began cursing, their "damns" soon mingling with other voices in the hall.

Dunmoore spoke in a quiet, yet urgent tone. "Here are my car keys, Luke. Take your bags and follow the group in the hall down the stairs to the exit. Get to the Rover. If I'm not there in five minutes, leave without me. Then, call my home number and let

Joanna know that something has gone wrong. Let her know where you are so I can reach you."

Lucas nodded and picked up his bag and backpack.

"Not so fast," said Ryan. "What the hell are *you* gonna do?"

Dunmoore smiled and held up his gun. "I'm going to get our bags. Now go. *Quickly.*"

Lucas stuck his head into the hallway. People in various stages of undress milled about, looking sleepy, many with hands over their ears to deaden the whooping siren. *No one weird.* He glanced at his ring. Dull red. Not as hot. He whispered to the others, "All clear."

Maya and Des ducked out the door and filtered into the line of people moving to the stairway exit. Lucas looked back at Ryan. The Irish teen shifted from foot to foot, one fist clenching and unclenching in time to his shifting. *Damn, he's gonna take off on us.*

Dunmoore hissed, "Ryan. I know you'd like to see this thing through by yourself. I know we can't stop you. But the people who killed your Grandma Maggie, and my father, will not hesitate to kill you. Or me. Or anyone else. We are much stronger as a group. Maybe together, we can succeed. Just hear us out. You can leave whenever you choose. I can't, and I won't, stand in your way. You have my word."

"Okay. For now." Ryan's fist unclenched. "But no promises."

Dunmoore repeated, "No promises."

Lucas and Ryan ran after the others.

Dunmoore locked the door after them, then approached the adjoining door to room 309. He unlocked it, slowly twisted the handle, then kicked it open and dove into the room, landing on the floor, and turning with his gun, ready to shoot. No one was there. He rose from the floor and grabbed his and Des's bags.

Heavy footsteps sounded in the hallway. Dunmoore locked the hallway door to room 309, went through the adjoining door into room 311 and locked the door behind him. He crossed to the window, opened it and climbed out onto the fire escape. His heart began to hammer in his chest and beads of perspiration dotted his brow. "Just don't look down," he muttered.

Dunmoore's secret service career had ended because of his vertigo – his incapacitating fear of heights. And now, here he was on a flimsy metal platform, several stories above the ground.

His heart continued to pound, and his head began to sway from dizziness. *"Don't look down!"* he repeated. Focusing solely on the iron rungs of the ladder, he descended it rung by rung. He gripped the ladder so tightly that, by the last level, the railings had imprinted grooves in his skin.

He now stood only twelve feet above the ground. As he tossed the bags over the rail, he glanced up: A light appeared in room 311. He clicked the safety catch on his gun and climbed atop the rail. Sweat now poured from his face.

"Hey!" came a voice from above, accompanied by a gunshot.

Dunmoore leaped, hitting the wet grass and rolling with the impact. Another shot rang out, and clods of mud splattered his face. Far too close.

The gunman stepped onto the fire escape.

Dunmoore fired two shots above the man's head, forcing his attacker to dive back into the room. Dunmoore grabbed the bags and hurried away, staying in the shadows.

People congregated in the parking lot in bathrobes and slippers, trying to keep as warm as they could in the damp, cold night. Dunmoore headed for the Range Rover, where he could see Ryan in front, the others in the back seat. He trotted over to the car and stuffed the bags in the trunk. Without a word, Dunmoore got behind the wheel, put the Range Rover into gear and quickly exited the Round Table Inn. He shook his head, and a spray of water and mud splattered the car.

Lucas asked, "Hey, Prof, what's with the mud?"

Dunmoore rubbed the clay from his jaw and off his coat sleeves. "Everyone all right?"

"I'm glad you weren't hurt, Professor," said Maya in a low voice, "But how did the Dark...how did they know we were there?"

Dunmoore ran a hand through his hair. "Sheer luck? Some nefarious means? I've no clue."

"The desk clerk?" Lucas suggested.

"Perhaps." Dunmoore said. "Luke, that was very quick thinking on your part to pull the fire alarm. You may have saved all our lives."

Des cheered, "Hear, hear!"

"Not bad for an American," Ryan muttered.

Maya said with a smile, "There may be hope for you, yet, Moreno."

Lucas blushed. "It was the ring that warned us."

"Thank God for that," Dunmoore said. "Now, we must find new lodging."

"Anywhere, so long as I can curl up in a big chair in front of a cozy fire and sleep." Maya stretched her arms above her head.

Just like a cat, thought Lucas. *Beautiful, sensual, dangerous.*

"Maybe the Dark Powers have connections with the credit card company. You charged the rooms, didn't you, Prof?" Ryan's voice took on an accusatory tone. "Jaysus. Every little wanker in Belfast knows you don't use your own credit cards or your real name!"

Maya said, "Leave the Professor alone. And you should talk. Like we weren't able to figure out that *Casey Sands* was *Ryan Casey?*"

Lucas smiled at her defense of Dunmoore. *A mother cat, with claws.*

"No, Ryan's right," said Dunmoore. "I'm afraid credit cards are now a luxury. Unless we're careful, they could prove our undoing. I'll withdraw money from the bank tomorrow."

"Maybe we can camp out at Lake Windermere?" suggested Lucas.

"We don't have any camping gear," Des said.

"And it's freezing outside," said Maya.

Ryan sneered, "An ice princess like you ought to be used to the cold."

"The Spensers' cabin, that's it!" Dunmoore hit his forehead with the palm of his hand. "Family friends have a cabin at Lake Windermere. My father and I stayed there the time he told me about the ring."

"All right, mate!" Ryan said. "Now you're thinking."

Dunmoore smiled. "It's about ten miles from here. I don't think the Spensers will be there, but if they are, I don't think they'll mind us bunking down for the night. All that's left is for me to remember how to get there. I was here two years ago for their sixtieth anniversary."

Ryan first spotted the sign for Merlin's Way. Turning left, they followed the road up a hill and down around a curve. Forest surrounded them.

Then, Dunmoore exclaimed "Aha!" and turned the car onto a narrow dirt road, guarded on either side by small stone lions.

Less than a minute later, Dunmoore parked in front of a large stone cabin. It was an A-frame house, with large windows, a chimney and a long front porch. No lights shone outside or inside the cabin. "I don't believe anyone is at home," Dunmoore said. "They usually leave the outdoor lanterns lit."

Lucas got out of the car and looked around. In the very dark but clear night, with the moon almost full, thousands of stars dotted the night skies, making it easy for them to find their way up the path.

"Let's get in out of the cold, shall we?" Dunmoore headed toward the front porch.

"Are we going to have to break in?" asked Lucas.

"No." Dunmoore stopped in front of a statue of a frog. He turned the frog over, pushed on a lump on its bottom and extracted a key from an opening. "The Spensers have been hiding a key there ever since I was a young lad." He inserted the key in the front lock and opened the door. The light switch by the right side of the doorway lit several wall sconces.

Dunmoore started a blazing fire in the main room, while the teens rounded up what they could find in the pantry and refrigerator for a bedtime snack. After they had settled in the main room, Ryan completed his tale between bites of peanut butter and red currant jelly sandwich.

"Except for Grandma Maggie's journal, ain't much more to tell. Me Ma said she remembered Great-Grandda flying over to Russia to bring back Grandma Maggie's body." Ryan swallowed a huge bite of sandwich. "The Russkies had confiscated her things, and Great-Grandda had to fight to get them back. I don't know why he bothered, though. I don't think anyone in the family ever read the journal before I found it. And Grandda never spoke about it or her."

"How sad to have your mother leave when you are only fifteen and never come back."

Ryan glared at Des. "No worse than your father leaving when you're only ten."

Whoa, what's this now? Lucas swallowed a toasted marshmallow too quickly, burning the roof of his mouth. As he gulped water, he contemplated why Ryan was so touchy.

Dunmoore asked Ryan, "After you found the journal and ring, you contacted me?"

"And all I got was 'be at one with the ring,' or something gacky like that. No offense, Prof, but that was gammy. Then, I remembered the picture – you know, Maggie and Tony in front of that Red Cross tent? I put the ring on and bingo! I had the dream."

"So, you borrowed some money from school and set out for Lake Windermere."

Ryan stared hard at Dunmoore. "No. I *stole* money to finance this trip. Who ratted? Mrs. Thornton?"

"Your family is worried, Ryan." Dunmoore spoke gently.

"You don't know them." Ryan scowled. "After the dream, I knew what Grandma Maggie had written was true, and that my having the ring could be a problem for my family." Ryan quickly added, "Even though they don't mean that much to me." He shrugged. "I had to skip town fast, which meant I needed cash. Anyone want to make a case out of it?" Ryan set his jaw at this, daring the others to take him on.

"Speaking of Grandma Maggie, can we read her journal?" Lucas asked.

Ryan pulled the battered red leather journal from his pack and opened it. "*I'll* read it."

Lucas felt his ring begin to tingle – a pleasant vibration. He took it from around the chain on his neck and placed it on his ring finger, then closed his eyes. Ryan's voice became that of the narrator of a movie. And Lucas saw Grandma Maggie's life unfold in living color on the movie screen in his mind.

Chapter Twenty-Three

Maggie

Twenty-year-old Margaret Anne Ryan stood on the oil-slick deck of the ferry bound for Calais, France. Her hands gripped the iron railing, and she closed her eyes as the wind gusted, whipping the ocean spray onto the deck and its occupants. She had always loved the ocean – the smell of brine and fish, the "caws!" of the gulls, the never-ending, undulating motion of the waves. But April was not the ideal month for travel by boat across the English Channel. All around her, men in drab uniforms were groaning and retching from nausea.

When Maggie opened her eyes, she saw one young man whose face was so seasick-green in color it nearly matched the faded olive combat gear he wore. Maggie shook the wetness from her strawberry blond curls and got down to business. She assisted the American soldier below decks to a cot in the cramped dispensary and, soon thereafter, the soldier was sleeping with the aid of a powerful anti-nausea medication.

Maggie wrote in her journal that night:

April 23, 1917 Arrived in France to find Patrick. The ferry ride was bitter cold, and people could not fathom why I was traveling <u>to</u> France, when everyone is trying to get <u>out</u> of France, away from the war. How can I let my brother spend his birthday in a field hospital alone?

Three days later, a newly arrived battalion of British soldiers said their farewells to "Nurse Maggie," after depositing her outside Ypres, Belgium. The black clouds that had been her travel companions for the past six hours burst just as she slugged through the last of the mud to the entrance of the field hospital. The constant *rat-a-tat-tats* of machine guns, solitary *bursts* of rifle fire, and the *BOOM-BOOM* of canons from not far off made Maggie jittery. Inside the huge, brown tent, the din of the downpour on canvas made it difficult for conversation. A combination of shouting and pantomiming finally did the trick, and the medic pointed to a cot halfway down the length of the tent on the left.

There he was: Patrick Michael Ryan, only twenty-two years old, with an oozing wound on his right thigh and a bandage around his head. Maggie caught her breath at the sight of her beloved brother writhing in agony on the tattered, barely standing cot. With his swollen, bruised face and constant grimace of pain, Maggie almost didn't recognize him. He had once been so handsome, so lively, so young.

Maggie blinked back the tears and set her bag on the ground. She sniffled only twice as she prepared the needle, then put on a big grin as she swabbed Pat's arm, right above the inside of his elbow. "Happy Birthday, Pat."

Pat's eyelids cracked open and he stared, then raised an eyebrow. "Maggie?" It came out in a croaky whisper.

"Shhh." Maggie expertly and painlessly plunged the needle into his vein. "This will help you sleep." She stroked his cheek. "Sleep, Pat, dearest."

With a soft "ah," Patrick slipped off to a morphine dreamland.

Maggie knelt beside her brother, stroking his cheek and crooning the Irish lullaby their mother had always sang to them.

"Hey! What're you doing? Redhead!"

Maggie stood and wiped away her tears. She placed the needle and empty morphine vial back in her rucksack, picked up her small suitcase, and went to explain herself.

Her journal entry that night betrayed her fears and hopes:

April 26, 1917 He has a serious infection, and they might have to amputate his right leg. But he's finally sleeping. Thank god for Dr. Callahan and his stash of morphine! I really don't know how

Pat has managed to stand the pain. Maybe things are not as bad as I think. Maybe my coming will bring new hope.

"Happy Birthday, dear Patrick! Happy Birthday to you!"

From the whistles, hoots and cheers, Maggie wouldn't have believed she was in an army infirmary with mighty sick soldiers. But their bandaged wounds, amputated limbs, and the pain and desperation in their eyes betrayed the falseness of their chatter. They were putting on a show for one of their own. And Maggie had to laugh at the sight of her brother wearing all his presents at once: two scarves, two hats, a sweater, vest and gloves! The gift Maggie had brought was the one that brought the tears to his eyes, the one he wouldn't let the others see: that sweet, sweet morphine.

She wrote that night:

April 27, 1917 It was good to see him laugh. But it was over too quickly. Pat made me write down which soldiers should get which clothes if he should die. And told me I was to decide who got the morphine.

Maggie spent the next day at her brother's side, leaving only to grab a cold sandwich and coffee and confer with the surgeon. It had to be done. They'd remove his now-gangrenous right leg, just above the thigh, tomorrow mid-morning. It wasn't until ten o'clock that night, after a dog-tired Maggie administered the evening's morphine and turned to retire, that Pat placed his hand on hers and said, "Not yet."

In between shuddering breaths and moments of nodding off, Pat told Maggie about when he was ten. When Grandda Michael had given him a rosewood box, covered with carvings and, inside, a silver ring. Grandda told Pat that Merlin had forged the ring to be used by only the bravest of knights, and that the Ryans were direct descendants of Sir Gawain, one of the original knights of Arthur's Round Table.

Patrick's breathing steadied, and his eyes stayed closed. Maggie rose to leave when Pat said in a whisper, "Take them, Maggie. You are the bravest person I know."

Maggie sat on the ground and held his hand. And cried.

She didn't write in her journal until the following night:

April 29, 1917 Patrick did not survive the operation. I gave his presents to his friends and the morphine to the medic who has taken care of each of these men, these boys, as if they were all beloved brothers. Who can be so evil that young men have to die such horrible deaths so far from home and loved ones? How I want those responsible to suffer so!

———————

Maggie tugged at her curls as she flipped through yet another dusty tome on English Genealogy. Her cheeks had hollowed slightly and her eyes had lost some of their youthful spark in the two years since Patrick's death. But she was still a beauty with her golden-red curls, sprinkling of freckles and hazel eyes.

She closed the book in exasperation, then sneezed from the dust particles. As she rummaged in her purse for a handkerchief, the dowager librarian appeared, a stern look on her sour puss.

"Miss Ryan, I would think you, of all people, would have better things to do than waste time over some silly family tree."

Taken aback, Maggie could only stutter, "I-I-" before the guardian of books continued.

"Ireland, nay, all of Europe is still recovering from the war, and nurses such as yourself are in great demand." The woman stood with pursed lips, hands clasped and resting on her ample abdomen. "Good day, Miss Ryan."

That night, Maggie wrote:

March 1, 1919 I have not cared to write since Pat's death. So many deaths. 400,000 men and boys lost their lives in the Battle of Passchendaele. Only now have I made some peace with it. I found the box and ring where Pat told me they would be. And I've put them in my hope chest. There, they shall stay. For now.

———————

"For now" had turned into twenty years. It was 1939, and a second world war had taken the first one's place. Maggie had married, borne four children and continued to practice as a county nurse. She rediscovered the box and ring in her hope chest while preparing for her youngest daughter's wedding. Delighted, Maggie wore the ring to bed and received a visit from her dream-knight, Sir Gawain, who set her upon the path to Merlin. When Maggie awoke, she passed the whole thing off as a "lovely" dream. Until a week later, when Gawain again visited her in her sleep. After chastising Maggie for her inaction, the knight revealed the monstrous acts of Hitler to come: the bombing of England, the gassing of millions of concentration camp prisoners. And only Maggie had the chance to put an end to such evil. It was then that Maggie believed.

———————

Maggie's youngest daughter was passing the stuffed marrow squash to fifteen-year-old Patrick when Maggie tapped a spoon on her crystal water glass and announced, "We are descended from Sir Gawain, a knight of the Round Table." At the open-mouthed stares of her family, Maggie proceeded to tell them about the box, the ring and her brother Patrick, about the dreams and Sir Gawain.

Maggie's husband laughed the loudest. He chucked her under her chin and said, "Good on ya, Maggie, me darlin'."

Maggie's sudden *thwap!* of her hands on the table silenced the giggles. She stood and scrutinized each of her children. When she set her gaze upon her husband, she said in a soft tone, "Do I look to be joking? 'Tis not a laughing matter. We are all of us in great danger, unless something is done."

One of those long, awkward silences followed Maggie's taking her seat. The children exchanged worried glances with each other and their father, until her husband cleared his throat. "You've been putting in too many hours, Margaret Anne. Between your nursing and taking care of the family, and tending to Annie's wedding plans, it's no wonder you're having these dreams. You need a right vacation, lass." He nodded and grinned. "You go visit your sister Louise in Dublin. What say you, Maggie?"

Maggie dabbed her mouth with her napkin and smiled at her husband. "Lovely."

She wrote in her journal that night:
October 25, 1939 Oh, but not to Dublin. I have other plans for my week's vacation.

Maggie wiped the sweat from her face and tied the blue-and-white bandana around her head like a gypsy. She pushed herself up from the grass with a slight groan, then smiled and murmured, "You're not that old, lass." Although, at the age of forty-two and after four babies, she thought she deserved a little self-pity. She was resigned to traversing the lake's circumference in its entirety – eleven miles. But after only two hours into it, she began to realize the monumental task she had set for herself: Even if she found the oak tree, how would she know it? How would she contact Merlin?

She hefted her rucksack filled with water, apples and sandwiches and wiped away the tears of disappointment. Suddenly, a heavy mist engulfed her, and she heard the thundering of horse's hooves. A gallant Sir Gawain swooped her up and set her behind him on his gray stallion, depositing her several minutes later in front of an ancient oak tree at the side of the lake. Maggie hadn't trusted herself to speak the entire exhilarating gallop.

"Fair Margaret, you must trust in yourself and the ring." Gawain's courtly smile dissolved into a warning. "You no longer have the luxury of questioning your task or yourself. To turn from the quest will be as dangerous as embarking upon it. Trust the ring."

With a *"Heeyaat!"*, horse and rider whirled and disappeared into the mist.

Maggie looked at the enormous, weathered oak tree with both wonder and trepidation. She took a step toward it. And the ring began to glow! With each step, the ring grew ever brighter until, at the very foot of the oak, the brightness was almost unbearable. When the glow slowly began to fade, she heard a voice. And a face appeared *in* the tree, in its very bark.

It was the face of an old, old man, with long white hair and beard, and piercing blue eyes. And the voice. Ancient but powerful. It reminded Maggie of majestic mountains.

"Margaret Anne Ryan," commanded the voice.

Maggie quaked. Her tongue felt large and heavy. She could only nod.

"You are a true believer and bearer of the ring. Will you undertake the quest? Will you go forth on this last of crusades? Will you do battle against the powers of darkness?"

She swallowed and managed to whisper in a voice aquiver, "I will do as you ask, but I am not a warrior. I am only a mother, a nurse. If that will do, if that is who you need, then I am at your service."

"Your courage and faith brought you this far – that is the heart of a great warrior." A glimmer of a smile formed on the old wizard's lips for but a second. "Do not believe you are at my service, or you are whom I need. Your world needs you, Margaret; you are in the service of your world."

***

Safe in her cozy room at the inn that night, Maggie recorded in her journal everything she could remember of what the sorcerer revealed...and commanded:

October 31, 1939 The Holy Grail! In a cathedral in Russia! Oh, Merlin. I know what you expect of me. If only I could find the others. But I do not have time. I must begin tonight. My only consolation is that I may find others along the way. Merlin hinted at such a prospect. I pray he is right.

***

Over her family's vehement objections, Maggie volunteered for Red Cross duty in Finland, less than 300 miles from Novgorod, Russia, wherein stood a cathedral that housed the Holy Grail. She arrived in Mikkeli, Finland, near the Karelian Isthmus, in mid-December 1939, to be greeted by the horrors of yet another war. The teeth-jarring explosions, ear-splitting whine of missiles, and acrid smell of fire and blood wakened long-buried memories of Patrick.

Mikkeli was 150 miles from Leningrad, only another 100 miles to Novgorod. But it might as well have been 10,000. Maggie found she had to call on all her internal resources simply to cope with the bitter cold and the massive injuries of the soldiers she had promised to care for. But she did not question herself or her task.

She wrote in her journal the night of her arrival:

December 15, 1939 I shall find the Holy Grail. And I shall return it to Lake Windermere. I shall find a way. But for now, I shall be content to save these soldiers' lives, or make their deaths more comfortable. Strangely, for now, it is enough.

An unexpected ray of hope and light arrived on Christmas Day. Though Maggie was exhausted after an arduous day of tending to the wounds of battle, she allowed herself a Christmas indulgence and raised a martini glass at the makeshift "Officers Club" in celebration of the Finns' victory at Suomussalmi.

Jane, a taciturn nurse from Scotland, nudged Maggie with her elbow, and tilted her head discreetly. Maggie glanced at the next table to find her gaze locked with that of a handsome "flyboy." With black hair, cocoa-brown eyes, and skin the color of golden sugar, Maggie found it hard to look away.

"Lad's been eying you since you walked in, Mags."

Maggie blushed and turned back to Jane. "I'm sure it's not like that." She twisted her wedding band.

"Might I join you two ladies?" He was clearly an American, but with a soft drawing of his vowels.

Maggie shook her head, not trusting herself to speak, and not wanting to look at him because she knew she was blushing an even deeper shade of crimson.

He placed his right hand next to hers so that his pinkie grazed her thumb. Maggie shivered from the physical contact. Then gasped. The man was wearing the silver ring!

"Everything all right, Mags?"

Maggie felt the weight of Jane's hand on her forearm, and she gave her friend a smile. "I'm fine. Would you mind?" She inclined her head toward the man and bit her lower lip.

"What? Oh, of course not." Jane stood and tipped her glass at the stranger. "Merry Christmas."

"Anthony Moreno, from Texas. Tony." He sat down and smiled. "Mags?"

She grinned. "Margaret Casey. Maggie."

"Ireland is it?"

She liked his voice. Strong, masculine, kind.

Maggie examined his ring; Tony examined hers. They were identical, down to the very runes. Before Maggie could ask all the questions she was aching to ask, Tony explained why he was in Finland. He was a pilot with the RAF.

"How odd," remarked Maggie. "An American flying with the RAF?"

"I could no longer stand the fact that my country refused to assist our allies against Hitler and Mussolini." He gave her a cocky grin. "The RAF welcomed me with open arms."

"But why did you volunteer for this Red Cross mission?"

Tony gave her an odd look, a mixture of frown and surprise, then said softly, "Because of the quest. It begins here."

And they talked late into that night. And the next.

And Maggie wrote in her journal:

December 26, 1939 We don't know what to expect or what to bring or what to do. Fortunately, the rings provide invaluable assistance in directing us to the right path. In less than a month, we will be on leave for six days. It should be enough time to smuggle ourselves into Russia and smuggle the Grail out. It will have to be.

No longer alone, Maggie and Tony made plans for their assault on the Novgorod cathedral. In late January 1940, they stole behind enemy lines and found fortune with the Gagarins, owners of a small inn, The Hissing Monkey. The Gagarins concealed the two Crusaders' presence from the authorities and assisted them in obtaining supplies.

Before slipping into the eerily quiet night to tackle whatever lay in the cathedral, Maggie made a final entry in her journal:

January 22, 1940 Had we lived at another time, had we not had our families? It is almost midnight, and Tony should be at the door any minute. I must go. Should I not return safely, let this be a testament to my life, my desires and dreams, and my devotion to not only my family, to not only Tony, but to the world and the good that lies therein. To whoever reads this, please don't let my death – if that is what is to be tonight – be in vain. Let my children and grandchildren and great-grandchildren know what needs to be accomplished, what tasks need to be completed. Seek out the other Crusaders. Seek out Merlin. Seek out the Quest.

———————

Maya clutched one hand to her heart as she studied the old photograph of Maggie and Tony. Lucas – surprised to see her eyes glistening with unshed tears – rested his hand briefly on hers. She rewarded him with a broad smile. *God, she's beautiful when she smiles.*

"I'd think a poor Mick nurse and Spic pilot would be unworthy of your highness's consideration." Ryan exhaled a stream of cigarette smoke at Maya.

Maya laid the photo in her lap, narrowed her eyes and faced Ryan, her body tense but poised. "A common thief such as yourself is beneath even my contempt." She smiled – a hard, tight smile. "But Maggie and Tony were beautiful, brave, intelligent and resourceful. For that, they deserve my respect."

Ryan crushed out his cigarette. "And what do you deserve, Princess?" His wiry body seemed tightly coiled around his anger, although his voice was soft and seductive.

It's like watching a panther tangle with a rattlesnake, Lucas thought.

"I think we all deserve some much-needed sleep." Dunmoore stood.

Lucas jumped up and grabbed his hat, rubbing the dried rattles. "I'm all over that, Prof. I'm beat." He noticed that Des darted anxious glances at Maya and Ryan.

The two adversaries continued to stare at each other – Maya expressionless, Ryan smiling. Dunmoore touched Maya on the shoulder, but looked at Ryan as he said, "You two can finish this just as easily tomorrow."

Maya gave a tightlipped smile to Dunmoore. "Goodnight." She placed the photo on the table and turned from the living room.

Ryan tamped out another cigarette and lit it, leaning back in the armchair with his stockinged feet on the table.

As the others headed for their respective bedrooms, Dunmoore exclaimed, "Drats!"

Lucas turned at the top of the stairs. "What's the matter, Prof?"

"The Spensers still don't have a telephone in this place. I must call Joanna and let her know where we are."

Lucas's ring began to heat up.

"I'll fetch my cell phone from the car." Dunmoore snatched the key ring and called out, "Be back in a minute." As he unlocked the door, a loud thud sounded outside. "What the...?" He rested his hand on the doorknob.

Lucas stared at his ring – hotter and now burnt-orange in color. He heard Maya exclaim, "Ouch!"

Ryan followed with "Bloody ring!"

Des simply stared at Lucas with wide eyes and trembling lower lip.

Lucas felt as scared as Des looked, and he called down the stairs, "Prof! Don't go out there!"

Chapter Twenty-Four

What Dreams Await

Dunmoore took his hand from the front doorknob.

"Our rings are burning. Maybe there's someone out there or," Lucas's voice dropped to a whisper, "in here."

Dunmoore nodded and retrieved his handgun from his raincoat. "We'll check out the house." With Dunmoore in the lead, they searched all the rooms, upstairs and down, re-locked the outside doors and re-bolted the windows tight. Then, they gathered in the living room.

"Everything seems to be in order," said Dunmoore. "But I thought I heard something thud just as I was headed to the car."

"My ring isn't hot anymore. What about yours?" Lucas turned to the others.

Ryan said, "Cold as a corpse. Weird, ain't it?"

"While I take exception to your simile," said Dunmoore, "I agree it is very odd, indeed. I suggest we get some sleep."

Still wired from all the action of the day and in a stranger's bed, Lucas didn't think he'd be able to fall asleep for a while, but the moment he closed his eyes, he fell into a full dream state.

He opened his eyes to find himself on the banks of Lake Windermere, in front of Merlin's tree. Not far away stood a grove of weeping willows. The same mist shimmered on the lake and wafted through the surrounding forest.

Lucas heard the strange sighing – half-wind, half-human – and searched the treetops, feeling the familiar tingling begin at the top of his head. He braced for the slight current to race through his body and shivered as it did, leaving him, as always, energized. The rapid *clip-clop* of horse hooves made him whip around.

Don Vasquez galloped from the willow tree cluster and, for a moment, Lucas wasn't sure whether the knight was going to knock him down or whisk him up behind him. The knight brought his steed to a hard stop only feet from Lucas.

"*Mi hijo*, you are near to completing the first part of your journey," said Vasquez from astride his red-brown stallion. He leaned toward Lucas. "More than ever, you must be on constant guard. Already, you have been unwittingly betrayed."

"What?" Lucas pulled at an ear, as if he had gone slightly deaf.

Vasquez merely gazed at him.

"That's impossible." Lucas shook his head. "No one knows we're here. No one knows..." Lucas stopped. *It can't be.*

The knight tilted his head and raised an eyebrow.

"Are you saying I can't trust the others?" Lucas heard the anguish in his own voice. Felt the cold chill of desperation in his chest. *Don't say it, don't say it,* he silently pleaded.

With a soft *chucking*, Vasquez urged the horse to Lucas's side. Lucas could feel the steed's breath on his cheek. He slowly lifted his hand and patted the horse's smooth neck.

"The Dark Powers have *yet* to turn any Crusader." Vasquez placed a gloved hand on Lucas's shoulder. "But only a fool would underestimate them. You do so at grave peril. For yourself and the quest."

Lucas frowned. "So, I *can* trust the others?"

Vasquez picked up the horse's reins. "Trust in the ring, *mi hijo*. Heed its warnings." With one sharp whistle, the knight and stallion raced away, to be swallowed up by the mist.

Lucas didn't even bother to try to follow or call after them. He simply stared at the silver ring upon his finger.

——— ——

When Lucas woke, he wrote down the details of the strange dream until his growling stomach urged him downstairs in search of sustenance. Fifteen minutes later, Ryan joined him in the kitchen. Having already devoured two slices of toast, Lucas offered a buttered slice to Ryan and popped another slice in the toaster. Ryan found orange juice in the freezer and filled up the sink with hot water to defrost the can. A few minutes later, Des appeared, rubbing his eyes and yawning. The boys went about the business of getting breakfast in companionable silence. Until Maya entered.

She wore jeans, a white T-shirt and a black and green argyle cardigan, socks but no shoes. Her long, black hair hung in a braid. *Beautiful*, Lucas thought. *Beats Candy Carson hands down.* He called out at the same time as Des, "Good morning, Maya."

"Sleep well, Princess?" asked Ryan with a smirk.

Maya frowned. "No, Little Thief, I did not sleep well. I had a very disturbing dream."

"Me, too," Ryan mumbled, toast in his mouth. "Gawain showed up with a warning."

Des's eyes widened. "So did Modetta Khan!"

"I bet we all had the same dream," Lucas said. "I wrote mine down." He pulled the small spiral notebook from his back pocket and read from it, finishing with, "So, you guys have the same dream?"

"Pretty much," replied Ryan. "I asked Gawain who the scum traitor was."

Maya arched her eyebrows. "Impressive, Little Thief."

Why didn't I think to ask Don Vasquez that? Lucas mentally kicked himself.

"Yeah, well Princess, he wouldn't tell me. Told me he didn't know, that he wasn't privy to everything." Ryan sighed. "Sucks, don't it?"

"It sucks big time," said Maya. Lucas and the other boys stared. She stood with hands on hips. "Tell me it doesn't!"

Laughing, Lucas said, "We still don't know who the traitor is."

"I spent an hour trying to figure it out." Des sighed.

"Not me. I came down to eat." Ryan put another slice of bread in the toaster. He looked up at the others. "Cut me some slack! I can't think on a empty stomach."

"I know the feeling precisely," said Dunmoore as he strolled into the kitchen.

After hearing about their dreams, Dunmoore stroked his chin and said, "Perhaps Merlin will know." He chuckled. "Any chance your dreams told us where to find his tree?"

"It's near a grove of weeping willows."

Dunmoore stared at Lucas.

Ryan asked, "Can't be too hard to find, right?"

"Let us hope," said Dunmoore, still staring at Lucas. "Otherwise, it will take us several days to walk the shoreline of Lake Windermere."

The Crusaders went about the business of dressing and preparing for the day. The last ones in the kitchen were Dunmoore and Lucas. Lucas said, "It gives me the creeps to think someone we know could be a rat."

Dunmoore put his arm around Lucas's shoulders. "I'm sure we'll discover who it is."

"But what if..." Lucas hesitated. "What if it's someone...we like?"

Dunmoore sighed. "When you get to be my age, you realize that life goes on even after what may at first appear to be a major setback. Now, more than ever, we have reason to defeat these Dark Powers. Because of my father, Grandma Maggie, perhaps Des's and Maya's fathers. And now, perhaps, because of someone close to one of us." He clenched his fists and narrowed his eyes. "I want revenge."

These last words sent shivers scurrying up and down Lucas's spine. His ring burned briefly, then went still.

———————

The frog's butt swallowed the house key whole. Dunmoore replaced the rock frog on the slate walk, and they loaded into the Range Rover. When they stopped at a local grocery store in the small lakeside village of Bowness-on-Windermere, Dunmoore asked the proprietor if he knew the location of a grove of willow trees around the lake. The proprietor did not, but an assistant did, marking the route on a local map of the area.

Just as they were leaving, Des exclaimed, "Allah!" The others turned to find him reading the *London Times*. He pointed to a headline: "Bus Goes Over Cliff – Killing All Aboard." Des said softly, "Maya's bus."

The proprietor shook his head. "Fifty-six passengers and the driver, MacDougal. Knew Mac going on twenty years, now. Damn shame."

"How did it happen?" asked Dunmoore.

"Don't know. Scotland Yard's investigating now. Bloody terrorists, I'll wager."

"There were children on that bus." Maya's face paled, and she trembled as the words came out in a soft whisper. "Mr. MacDougal had grandchildren my age."

God, she looks like she's going to faint, thought Lucas. He took a step toward her.

The proprietor said, "Little tykes. Wouldn't put it past the IRA. Damn the lot of 'em."

Lucas glanced at Ryan, who stared out the glass doors, fists clenching and unclenching.

A still ashen-faced Maya made it to the Range Rover. They rode to the lake in silence, broken every so often by Des asking, "Are you okay, Maya?"

The third time, Maya snapped, "Enough already, Des!"

Lucas couldn't help but smile with relief. *Back to her old self.*

Dunmoore parked the Range Rover in a campground area. Hoisting their backpacks, they began the hike to what they hoped was the grove.

Fifteen minutes into the hike, Lucas heard Maya say in a soft voice, "I'm sorry, Des. I just don't want to think about it. All those people. Those children. Mr. MacDougal."

Des said, "I'm just glad it wasn't you."

"Me, too," called Lucas over his shoulder.

When he heard Des exclaim, "Maya, your ring!" he turned. Maya's ring glowed emerald green. Lucas looked at his ring. Same radiance. He called for Ryan and Dunmoore to stop.

Lucas couldn't help but feel satisfaction at Dunmoore and Ryan's gapes. Four glimmering, green rings. Suddenly, a thick mist descended, cold and damp, and a keening kind of sighing swept through the forest. Lucas braced for the tingling in his head.

The four teens put their right hands together. The intensity of the rings' color seemed to deepen. The prickling hit Lucas's scalp at the same time Maya whispered, "It's like they're connecting to one another."

Dunmoore said, "It certainly seems as if they are more vital together than apart."

"That is one of the most important lessons you will take away from this meeting with Merlin. Remember it always, Professor Dunmoore."

In unison, the group turned and gasped. Vasquez, Khan, Shin'ichi and Gawain stood together, their horses on leads behind them.

The knights were dressed exactly as they had appeared to the Crusaders in their dreams. They wore the native garb of the warriors of their respective countries – Spain, Mongolia, Japan, England – with the sole exception of a red lion, symbolizing King Arthur, displayed prominently on silk worn by the knights over their armor chest plates.

"Do not be afraid, Crusaders. Permit me the introductions. I am Don Vasquez, of León, ancestor to Lucas Moreno." Vasquez bowed, then motioned for Lucas to do the same.

Feeling as awkward as when he had had his first dance lesson, Lucas bowed from his waist, holding one hand behind his back as Vasquez had done, but with the other hand on his hat to keep it from slipping off.

"Modetta Khan, of Mongolia, ancestor of Desmondo Moboto." Khan also bowed to the Crusaders, followed by Des.

"Shin'ichi, of Japan, proud ancestor of Maya Hosokawa." Shin'ichi bowed in Maya's direction. Maya bowed low in return, causing Shin'ichi to grin with pride.

Gawain stepped in front of the Samurai knight and gave a courtly bow. "Sir Gawain, original knight of the Round Table, loyal to King Arthur and England, and proud ancestor of Master Ryan Casey."

Vasquez chuckled. "Gawain, your pomposity is a reliable constant through the centuries."

Ryan attempted to imitate the stately bow of Gawain. "Ryan Casey, of Ireland, proud descendant of the great Sir Gawain of the Round Table of King Arthur."

Vasquez nodded to Gawain. "Clearly, he is your heir."

Lucas cleared his throat.

"What is it, *mi hijo?*" asked Vasquez.

"Aren't you forgetting someone?" Lucas pointed to an unusually quiet Dunmoore.

"Ah yes," replied Vasquez, "please forgive us, Professor. Unfortunately, Lancelot could not accompany us because you are not in possession of the ring."

"Wh- wh-" Dunmoore cleared his throat. "Why is it that I am able to see you if I do not possess a ring?"

Shin'ichi replied, "You are a true descendant of one of the original twenty-four knights. And you are accompanied by other descendants who possess the rings."

"One not a true descendant would not be able to see or hear us," Gawain added.

Lucas looked at Vasquez. "So that's why the librarian didn't see you, even though you walked right past – I mean *through* – her."

Khan said in a gruff tone, "My fellow knights forget why we have been summoned." Khan nimbly mounted his black steed, bent down and held out his hand toward Des. "Give me your arms, *Sidi* Moboto."

Des looked at Lucas, trepidation evident in his wide eyes and wrinkled nose. Lucas nodded. Des took Khan's outstretched arm and wound up behind the knight on his horse.

Vasquez said, "While Khan's manner may be abrupt, he is right. Merlin will answer your questions. Or choose not to. Don Moreno?" Vasquez sat astride his chestnut horse and reached down to Lucas. Meanwhile, Shin'ichi had pulled Maya onto his white steed, while Ryan sat behind Gawain on his gray stallion.

Lucas whispered to Vasquez, "What about the Prof? We can't just leave him."

Vasquez whistled. A chocolate brown mare trotted out of the mist. Vasquez said to a wide-eyed Dunmoore, "While Lancelot could not appear, he sent his steed, Lluagor, to speed you on your way."

With a mighty "*Heeyat!*", Khan and his horse vanished into the mist. Shin'ichi and Gawain swiftly followed and disappeared from sight.

Dunmoore took the reins from Vasquez and mounted Lluagor. "Don Vasquez?"

The knight turned and smiled. "Lluagor knows the way. Trust her." He slapped his and Dunmoore's horse with his reins and they soon went the way of the others.

Minutes later, the knights halted their steeds and helped the Crusaders dismount.

Once again, a heavy mist surrounded them, and Lucas could hear the faint sighing of the wind-person and feel the tingling in his scalp. They stood in a clearing on the shore of the lake, in front of a huge, gnarled oak tree – Merlin's prison. Squinting, Lucas could barely see across the clearing. But he noticed the grove of weeping willows.

Vasquez said, "We must leave you now."

"How will we contact Merlin?" asked Lucas.

"This is not our quest," replied Vasquez. "We are but messengers of Merlin. Remember all I have told you, *mi hijo*. Trust in the ring."

"In the ring," echoed the other knights. With their ringless right hands held high, the phantom-knights galloped into the mist.

The Crusaders looked at each other, then to their rings, still glowing green. Sounding more tentative than Lucas had imagined possible, Dunmoore suggested that they put their rings together again.

They glowed a brighter green. The mist cleared in front of the oak tree, and an image of a man appeared. He looked exactly as Grandma Maggie had described him in her journal – long white hair and beard and piercing blue eyes. But when he spoke, it was with a voice as wise and kind as Lucas had ever heard, recalling memories of his father reading to him when he was a small boy. "Who summons Merlin?"

Lucas felt a gentle elbow in his ribs. He raised his eyebrows at Maya, then answered. "We do. Sir."

"And you are true believers and true bearers of the rings?"

They replied, "Yes, sir," except for Dunmoore, who said in a shaky voice, "I am a true believer, but I do not possess Lancelot's ring."

"Will you go forth on this quest? Will you undertake this last of crusades? Will you do battle against the powers of darkness?"

Ryan said, "Damn! Right out of Grandma Maggie's journal!"

"You are correct, Master Casey," said the wizard. "Margaret Anne Ryan was a true believer and bearer of the ring. She was also courageous in the face of daunting evil. You would do best to emulate her and follow her footsteps, away from the path you now tread."

Lucas felt a bit queasy at Merlin's reproach and glanced at Ryan. Ryan's eyes had narrowed and his fists were clenched at his side. *This guy's not the one to take on.* Lucas squared his shoulders, breathed deeply and took two steps forward. "I'll go forth on the quest. And I'll battle the Dark Powers, if that is what you ask. But, I don't know what I have to offer."

Merlin said nothing.

Des stepped forward. "I, too, will go forth on this crusade and battle the forces of darkness. I join with Lucas." Des stood next to Lucas and held out his hand.

Lucas grinned and grabbed Des's hand.

Maya stepped up and stood tall. "I freely choose to undertake this quest. I will do as Shin'ichi did. I will stand strong with the others." She stepped to Lucas's other side and took his hand, not looking at him. But she returned the gentle pressure of his squeeze.

Ryan sauntered forward and stood as tall as his five-foot-six height allowed, all bravado even now.

Lucas shook his head. *What is it Mom always said about guys like that? Strutting cocks. That's Ryan, for sure.*

"I would never dis me Grandma Maggie. I'll go on your damn crusade. And I'll go up against the Dark Powers. But not for you." Ryan pointed his thumb back over his shoulder toward the others. "And not for them. I'll do it for me. And Grandma Maggie. I'll follow *her* path." Ryan stepped next to Des. Des looked at Ryan, nodded his head, and put out his hand. Ryan hesitated for a second, then took Des's hand.

Finally, came Dunmoore's turn. "If you will allow it, I would undertake this crusade, to battle the powers of evil and avenge my father." Dunmoore glanced at the Crusaders and back to Merlin. "I would willingly assist my young friends on this quest." He took Maya's hand.

Merlin nodded and opened his arms toward them. "You have shown yourselves to be true believers. And warriors. But do not believe you are in my service or that you do my bidding. Or," Merlin gave a stern look at Ryan, "that you do the bidding of anyone else. You are in the service of mankind, as am I. But I am imprisoned, as I knew I very might be. Which is why I fashioned the rings. And which is why I wait, century upon century, for the true believers and bearers of the rings. Only by defeating the Dark Powers will the world be set free. And I gravely fear that your failure on this quest could mean the end of freedom. For all mankind."

Lucas couldn't contain himself any longer. He dropped Des and Maya's hands and rocked from foot to foot, hands clenched. "But *how* do we defeat the Dark Powers? Why do we need to find the Holy Grail and other stuff? And *how* do we find them?"

The others said nothing. Lucas could see them darting glances from Merlin to him then back to the shimmery wizard. Merlin was also silent, his gaze firmly fixed on Lucas. Although his heart pounded at the sorcerer's unrelenting stare, Lucas kept eye contact.

Finally, Merlin spoke. "The questions to which you seek answers are valid ones. Questions which would have been answered in due course. Although your heart is true, Master Moreno, you should learn to curb your impatience. Lest it be your undoing."

Lucas exhaled and nodded. "Yes, Sir. It's just that we have come such a long way and have had no answers. Only puzzles to solve. I'm sick and tired of it. Sir."

Merlin said, "There will be still further riddles for you to solve. For defeat of the Dark Powers lies also in the *journey*, not simply the end. What you have learned thus far, and what you will learn along the way, are as important as what I tell you today, if not more so. But I shall tell you what I can."

Chapter Twenty-Five

A History Lesson

"Many centuries ago," began Merlin, "there were many religions, with different gods and beliefs. And the people were, for the most part, content to go about the business of practicing their religions and letting others practice theirs in peace. This spirit of religious harmony was exemplified by the maintenance of three sacred relics here at Lake Windermere – the Holy Grail, The Hands of Allah, and the Eye of Buddha. They were the symbols of three great religions of the time, Christianity, Islam and Buddhism.

"But the forces of evil were not pleased. Harmony kept hatred and corruption at bay, which did not suit their purposes at all. For the Dark Powers to reign, there must be constant conflict and bloodshed between people. Thus, the powers of darkness conceived a most diabolical plan.

"In the ninth century, they descended upon Lake Windermere, killed the keepers of the relics, and separated the relics to the furthest corners of the globe. People no longer practiced religious tolerance, but set upon each other with hatred. A darkness settled over the world."

Lucas flinched. He could see that the other Crusaders were also shaken. Des's brow wrinkled, and Maya stood with arms crossed, tight against her chest. Even Ryan frowned.

Merlin offered a comforting smile. "There were still periods of light and hope. The reign of King Arthur was one of those times. Camelot was founded upon the concept of peace and tolerance. 'Might for Right.' And the knights of Camelot came from all over the world, from different religions, and yet peacefully coexisted.

"It was during this time that I received a heavenly vision. I was entrusted with sending warriors – emissaries of the gods – to retrieve the relics and join them together again at Lake Windermere. I crafted twenty-four magic rings, one for each of knight of the Round Table, and set them on their greatest crusade. Those that were unsuccessful were to pass the ring – and its quest – to the next generation." He sighed. "None succeeded in reuniting the three relics.

"Many a knight came close to retrieving a relic, and some actually attained one, only to be killed before they could find sanctuary here at Lake Windermere. The relics remain separated, guarded by agents of the Dark Powers." Merlin's image hovered silently, a look of despair upon his aged, lined face.

"Who is their leader, sir?" Lucas asked.

"Mordred."

"*Mordred?*" Dunmoore's mouth dropped. "But King Arthur slew his bastard son on Salisbury Plain, near Stonehenge, after receiving his own fatal blow."

Merlin shook his head and sighed. "Were that only true, Professor Dunmoore. It appeared Mordred had been run clean through by Arthur's spear, but no one could have known that Mordred had attained immortality."

"Immortality?"

Merlin sighed again. "During the final crusade, Mordred plotted with his mother, Morgan Le Fay, a most powerful and wicked sorceress and my life-long nemesis. She crafted a spell over the relics: So long as they remain separated, the leader of the Dark Powers shall remain immortal. Should the relics be reunited, the leader shall perish."

The thought of such evil being *immortal* sent a shiver down Lucas's spine.

Merlin continued. "Mordred embarked upon his own crusade. He departed Camelot with his strongest allies, defeated the then-tribunal of the Dark Powers, and became immortal. He has ruled from his godforsaken fortress ever since, bent on destroying every ringbearer and capturing the rings."

"Why doesn't he just destroy the relics?" asked Lucas. "Wouldn't that keep them separated for eternity?"

"The answer has eluded me for centuries, Master Moreno. It has something to do with the rings, but I know not the connection."

"Where's this Mordred guy's fortress?" asked Ryan.

"Remote and inaccessible – and where you shall not venture, Master Casey." Merlin narrowed his eyes. "Certain death awaits those who enter the Fortress of Shadows. The relics are not there, so you need not concern yourself with Mordred's whereabouts. You are charged only with retrieving the relics and returning them to Lake Windermere."

He turned to Lucas. "Now then, Master Moreno, you know *what* the relics are and *why* you must obtain them. And you have information as to where they are located, is that not so?"

Ryan said, "I'm betting the grail's in some cathedral in Novgorod. It was in 1940."

"A fortunate wager, Master Casey. Yes, the Holy Grail still resides in that cathedral. None of the three relics has been moved in this century. Or so I am informed."

Lucas noticed Maya's frown at the wizard's praise of Ryan. She said, "Then, the Eye of Buddha should be in a temple in Japan, where Shin'ichi was killed."

"Very good, Mistress Hosokawa," said Merlin. "And The Hands of Allah?"

Des blurted out, "According to Grandfather's journal and the letter from the Professor's father, it must be in Egypt."

Merlin smiled. "You have paid attention to your family histories. That should serve you well in your quest."

"But which cathedral?" asked Ryan. "What temple? And where the hell in Egypt?"

"All good questions, Master Casey. All of which you must answer yourselves, on your journey, for I know not the answers."

Lucas's mind whirled. "Sir, are you saying we have to go to Russia, Egypt and Japan?"

Maya said, "I don't have enough money for that!"

"If the princess here can't afford it, no way I can." Ryan shrugged. "Unless you can direct us to buried treasure or a bank we can rob."

All Des said was, "School begins in a week's time!"

"I can cover all of our expenses," offered Dunmoore, "although I doubt we will be able to conclude this quest in a month, much less a week. But, even when we ascertain the location of the relics, how do we retrieve them?"

"Your generosity is admirable, Professor Dunmoore, but there is a means of travel to these destinations conserving both time and resources." Merlin smiled at the anticipation on their faces. "Recall that the relics, united, are a force for good. Separated, they do not easily withstand evil. I fashioned the rings from the same principle. When united, the rings are far more powerful than when separated. When I dispatched the original knights on the quest, I cautioned them to travel in no less than groups of three. When together, the force of the rings is subject to the ring-bearers' will, which must also be as one."

Lucas voiced his thoughts. "You mean, if we put our rings together, they will do what we tell them to do?"

"Within limits, Master Moreno. But you have correctly interpreted my statements."

Eyes wide, Maya asked, "We could tell the rings we want to go to the temple in Japan and the rings would take us there?"

"But you must be specific as to *which* temple, and where in Japan, Mistress Hosokawa."

"Bleedin' deadly!" exclaimed Ryan.

Merlin's stare made even rebel Ryan bow his head and clutch his Celtic cross.

"One more thing," said the wizard. "The directions, if you will, must be in Middle English, the language from the time of their creation." Merlin looked to Dunmoore. "Do I presume correctly that this is not a problem?"

Lucas could see everyone was as excited about this magical possibility as he was, except Dunmoore, who stood stroking his chin. *Oh man, here we go with some professorial question.*

Dunmoore answered, "Yes, I speak Middle English. But Sir, if you would indulge me. From all I have read and researched, King Arthur lived in the fifth century A.D., not the tenth."

Merlin looked at Dunmoore but said nothing.

Dunmoore continued in a faltering voice, "Sir John Rhys, R. G. Collingwood, Geoffrey Ashe, David Day and a slew of others, all put King Arthur's reign in the fifth century."

"While I am no *expert* in these matters," Merlin replied with a slight twinkle in his faded blue eyes, "I do know of what I speak. Sir Rhys and the others who suggest that Arthur was merely the heroic cavalry general Arturius in the fifth century are wrong. King Arthur ruled his England in the tenth century, A.D., from his castle in Carlisle, here in Cumbria. Perhaps a new book is needed?"

Dunmoore simply shook his head.

It's as if he just learned the Earth is flat, thought Lucas.

Merlin added, "As for how you will retrieve the relics and bring them here, once again, that is something you must decipher for yourselves. Remember the power of the rings and the purpose behind them." Merlin's image began to fade.

Maya said, "Wait, sir! One more question, please!"

Merlin's voice grew faint. "Time lessens."

"You said that agents of the Dark Powers guard the relics. How will we know them? How will we defeat them?"

To Lucas, Merlin's voice sounded like a faint echo in a faraway chasm, like when he had yelled into the Grand Canyon on a family road trip. He could barely make out the wizard's parting words.

"You will know them. And you *must* defeat them. Trust the rings. Trust yourselves. Go forth true believers. And may the gods go forth with you." His image dissolved into nothing.

The heavy mist vanished almost as suddenly, and Lucas found himself in front of a huge oak tree across from a grove of weeping willows, on a sunny spring day. He broke the stunned silence. "Where to first, guys? Russia, Egypt, or Japan? Prof?"

"Forgive me. I am still reeling from how centuries of writers about King Arthur could be so wrong!" Dunmoore wiped his hands over his eyes then looked at Lucas and the others. "You have a difficult decision to make. You must deal with the dark agents who guard the relics, without knowing who those agents are. And I may not be able to accompany you."

All the teens protested, Lucas the loudest. "You aren't planning to abandon us now, are you, Prof?"

"I would never abandon the quest, Luke," Dunmoore said, fixing Lucas with a stern gaze. "But I do not possess a ring. Merlin did not say someone without a ring could be transported with the others."

Lucas felt his cheeks flush. "Sorry, Prof. It's just not fair. You're a part of us."

"And you're the only bloke who knows this Middle English crap," said Ryan.

Dunmoore smiled. "I wouldn't worry quite yet. Let's have a go at it, shall we?"

"How about after lunch?" suggested Ryan. "Dealing with knights and wizards leaves me starving!"

While they ate, they decided their course of action. They would first travel to Novgorod, in Russia, find the cathedral and retrieve the Holy Grail. As Dunmoore pointed out, "At least, we know the Holy Grail resides somewhere in Novgorod. How many cathedrals can there be?"

But before setting off for Russia, they conducted several experiments in the travel-use of the rings. They selected the weeping willow grove as the trial destination for Lucas, Des and Ryan – over Maya's vehement protest of sexism. The three boys placed their ring hands on top of each other and said in unison what Dunmoore had taught them in Middle English: "Rings, take us to the weeping willow grove on the shore of Lake Windermere, near Merlin's oak tree." Instantly, they disappeared. No mist, no smoke, nothing. They simply vanished.

Lucas felt as if he were in a canyon with wind whipping all around. When the windstorm passed, he opened his eyes and gasped. He and the boys stood in the weeping willow grove! He looked across the meadow to Merlin's oak. Maya and Dunmoore waved and shouted. Lucas waved back. Then he put his hand on top of Des and Ryan's and, together, they chanted the Middle English words Dunmoore had made them memorize. *Whoosh.* Lucas stood next to Maya and Dunmoore again!

"Powerful!" Ryan's green eyes radiated excitement.

Lucas felt the same incredible high. *It's like Star Trek come to life! But without the tractor beams.* He exchanged whoops of glee and fist-bumps with Des and Ryan.

"Whoa!" Dunmoore's own eyes glittered with the thrill of seeing it happen. "On to the next experiment. We shall all travel to the weeping willow grove. I will put my hand on the bottom of yours and, remember, tell the rings to take you – *and me* – to the grove."

And so it came to be that they learned the ways of the rings. They could travel in no less than a group of three. They traveled instantaneously, but in the present. Only a Crusader with his (or her) ancestral ring could be part of the necessary group of three – Dunmoore's attempt at borrowing another Crusader's ring failed. And, thus, they planned what Ryan dubbed "the taking of the Holy Grail."

They drove back to the Spenser cabin, where they changed into suitable clothing for an April in Russia. Dunmoore left a brief phone message for Joanna and a note for the Spensers. Maya acted as Dunmoore's secretary – an arrangement she also protested as sexist, but accepted with a toss of her shiny tresses – and made a reservation for Suite 333 of the Beresta Palace Hotel, in the northeast part of Novgorod, on the Volkhov River. Then, they returned – via ring-travel – to Merlin's oak, an auspicious location from which to depart.

They stood in a circle as before, placed their ring hands on top of one another and repeated the traveling spell.

Lucas closed his eyes as a strong gust of wind embraced him. The scene from *The Wizard of Oz* flashed in his mind – the one with Dorothy's house twirling inside the tornado funnel. *Just no witches or flying monkeys, please,* he silently prayed.

Then, all was still.

Chapter Twenty-Six

Rings of Bondage

The sharp click of heels upon stone echoed down the corridors as Mordred strode through the fortress. Rattar hastened after him, palmtop and stylus in hand, stopping every few minutes to mop his brow and catch his breath. A snowstorm raged outside, lowering the temperature inside the castle, but beads of sweat continued to dribble down the lumpish man's face.

"Rattar!" Mordred bellowed, by now many yards ahead of his manservant.

"Coming...M'lord...coming," Rattar wheezed, his head down, striving to pump his stumpy legs faster.

The dark lord halted at the top of a great stone staircase, dimly lit by sconces in the shape of intertwined snakes placed at intervals down the curving stairwell. "Rattar!"

Now only feet from his master, Rattar raised his head to answer and tripped over a huge rat hiding in the shadows. The rat went squealing one way while the servant fell headlong the other, palmtop and stylus flying from his hands.

"Th-thorry, M'lord." Rattar scrambled to his knees to retrieve the items, flinching at the sight of the stylus on one of Mordred's black, steel-toed boots. Grimacing, Rattar grasped the black computer pen and pushed himself clumsily to his feet. Spying the palmtop in the middle of the corridor, he gave Mordred a quick smile and bent over. A sharp kick in the behind sent him sprawling. "Uhnf," he groaned as he hit the stone floor.

Mordred chuckled.

Rattar grabbed the small computer and lumbered to his feet.

"How many in the dungeon?"

"Four, M'lord."

"Only four? It's hardly worth having a dungeon for a mere four." Mordred sighed with mock concern, then gave a deliberate smile. "On the bright side, it appears as if we soon can expect more guests." He started down the steps. "Get General Zheng down here. And bring the faxes from Hugin and Munin. We'll be with our pets."

Rattar scribbled furiously on the palmtop.

"One more thing, Rattar."

The servant looked up, hand halted in mid-air.

"The caviar shipment?"

"Yethterday, M'lord. Beluga, ath you ordered."

"Excellent, most excellent. Bring a jar." He thudded down the stairs, long hair flowing behind him.

Rattar headed to the communications room, this time at a leisurely pace. He pulled from his coat a small cellular telephone. "General Zheng? M'lord would like you to join him immediately at the lagoon." Rattar deleted an item from the palmtop. "Communicationth room," he muttered to himself, picking up the pace just a bit.

In the depths of the fortress, Mordred forged through the dungeon's narrow passages, breathing deeply of the dank, moldy air. Most of the rats scampered away. The few reckless enough to stand their ground received brutal kicks. Cells lined both sides of the passageway. Constructed of stone on three sides and bars facing the corridor, each contained two mattresses – straw encased in dirty burlap – two scratchy wool blankets, a metal bucket for human waste and two wooden buckets, one for water, one for food. Metal rings hung at various intervals and heights around the cell, to which prisoners could be chained if Mordred so desired.

A high-tech office occupied the middle of one row of the stark, medieval cells. Three of the office's stone walls were insulated with beautiful tapestries; the fourth contained a glass door. Persian carpets covered the floor, and an electric heater and air conditioner provided additional warmth or cooling. Fluorescent lights hung from the ceiling. The office came equipped with a desk, chairs, couch, television and audio system for comfort, and a fax machine, computer and phones for efficiency of operations.

Mordred entered with a dramatic flourish of his cape. "Intaki."

The small brown man turned from the wide-screen television set. He gave a toothy smile and stood up. "M'lord."

Mordred glanced at the documentary – scenes of fire engulfing acres of rain forest in South America. "Nostalgic are we, Intaki?"

The jailor, originally from a tribe along the Amazon, was eager to return to his homeland. Intaki sneered, "I could do more damage than that in half a day."

"We are sure you could, Intaki. In time, in time. Now, who are our guests this week?"

Intaki handed Mordred a clipboard with four dossiers, then recited from memory. "Charles Garudin, French. Kidnapped banker, but family won't pay ransom. Meng Ti Chen, Chinese. One of the leaders of student revolt in Beijing. Carlos Golembe, Columbia. Ran competing cocaine smuggling operation. Elaine LaCroix, South of France, cat burglar."

"Ah yes, our little Crusader. No, we're not done with the Mink quite yet." Mordred rubbed his chin. "As for the other dignitaries, let us see. Chen? No, she might come in useful someday, after we've...ah, reprogrammed her. Golembe? Possible, possible." He shook his head. "No, we'll need his body shipped back in pieces as a warning to others. And once our pets start feeding, there's no stopping them." He handed back the clipboard. "Garudin. If his family and government don't care about him, why should we?"

A rap sounded on the door. The shadow of General Zheng took up most of the tinted glass door. He stuck in his enormous head. "You asked for me, M'lord?"

"We've selected lunch for our pets. Join us for the festivities."

"Of course, M'lord." But the Chinese giant sounded hesitant.

"You know where to bring the prisoner, Intaki." Mordred strode down the passageway, Zheng at his heels.

In one of the cells they passed, a young Chinese woman lay on a mattress. She was filthy: Her hair was matted, skin streaked with dirt and blood, and feet and hands bruised from beatings. When she saw them pass, she crawled to the bars and began screaming in Chinese.

"What is she blabbering on about, Zheng?"

"Same as always, M'lord. First, we are gutter pigs for whom she wishes nothing but a painful death. Then she apologizes and pleads for mercy."

"Gutter pigs? We thought a graduate student from China's premiere university would have a bit more imagination. Tsk, tsk. The youth of today."

Several cells over, Elaine LaCroix lay on a burlap and straw mattress. She sported bruises on her face and chest – large yellowish-purple stains – and cuts scabbed over many times.

Mordred stopped. He twirled the ring he wore on a silver chain around his neck and called softly into the cell. "Little Mink."

Elaine opened her eyes. Her gaze fell immediately on the ring. As if hypnotized, she rose and limped to where her tormentor stood. She stretched a hand toward the twirling silver.

Mordred chuckled and slid away from the cell, just out of reach. "Perhaps later, little Mink, if you are nice to us." Mordred darted forward and shot out a hand to caress the battered face.

Elaine shuddered and backed away.

Without taking his gaze off the prisoner, Mordred said to Zheng, "Have her bathed and fed."

The farther down the passageway they went, the warmer it became. The cellblocks ended and the corridor took a sharp left. The hallway opened up to a massive cavern. Taking up most of the space was a tropical lagoon, heated by a small nuclear reactor located a third of the way down the mountain.

"Ah, sweet pets, come to us!" Mordred shouted, snapping his fingers.

From a small island in the middle of the lagoon came several splashes and five huge crocodiles. The prehistoric-looking creatures – three black, two white – swam through the water and tried to climb the fifteen feet of bank to where a grinning Mordred stood. The massive Zheng cringed several paces behind his master, ready to run at the sight of a toothy snout above the bank.

"Hello, darlings. Are you hungry?"

The enormous reptiles snapped their jaws at Mordred's voice.

"The prisoner, M'lord." Intaki came from behind, forcing a handcuffed man to his knees.

Mordred gave a mock bow. "Ah! Monsieur Garudin. So nice of you to join us for lunch."

"Monsieur Mordred, I beg of you! My family will pay! Mercy, please!" Tears streamed down the banker's black-and-blue eyes, bruised cheek and cracked lips.

"Ah, but you see, our dear Garudin, you are but payment enough. Our pets have not had delicacies in such a long time."

At the sight of the snapping crocodiles, the prisoner began screaming hysterically. One swift blow to the head from Intaki's baton knocked him senseless.

"Uncuff him before you roll him in, Intaki. We don't want metal to upset their delicate tummies."

As Intaki bent to unlock the cuffs, Rattar scurried in, papers in his right hand, a tray of caviar in his left. "Your caviar and faxthes, M'lord."

Mordred dipped the horn and onyx spoon into the glass and silver container and sucked down the small black fish eggs. "Exquisite." He picked up the three faxes. Just as Intaki rolled the unconscious prisoner onto the precipice, Mordred murmured, "What have we here? Stop!"

Intaki knelt beside the body on the edge of the embankment. "M'lord?"

"It appears as if the Garudins care for our dear Charles after all. They have paid the ransom." He shook his head and sighed. "Get him cleaned up and ready for release, Intaki."

The grumbling jailor put his hands under Garudin's armpits and began to drag the unconscious man back down the corridor.

"*What is this?*" screamed Mordred. He waved a fax at Zheng. "*What is this?*"

A trembling Zheng read the fax aloud. "Dunmoore, Moreno and Moboto escaped from Inn. Unable to locate Casey."

"Fools! Incompetents! *Idiots!*"

"But M'lord, it does report that the girl is dead."

"Does it now? And what *else* does it say about the girl, General?"

"Bus over cliff...all passengers dead...ring..." Zheng gulped and looked at Mordred. "Ring not yet recovered."

"Ring not yet recovered," repeated Mordred as he paced. "Ring not yet recovered." He stopped in front of Zheng and screamed, "WE NEED THAT RING, YOU MORON!" He slapped the huge man's head with the fax, then lowered his voice. "And do you know *why* we need that ring?"

Zheng nodded and opened his mouth to speak, only to be cut off.

"We'll tell you why. Merlin created the rings *before* our dear mother was able to conjure the immortality spell. Which means we cannot destroy the relics and cement our immortality for all time until we have destroyed all twenty-four rings." He began to pace the edge of the lagoon. "*Damn* Merlin. *Damn* those Crusaders. *DAMN THOSE RINGS!*" Grabbing the caviar server, he heaved it into the lagoon. The crocodiles left the bank to investigate the splash.

"We're holding you responsible, General. Get us those rings."

Zheng nodded furiously while backing away from the lagoon. Mordred reached for the caviar. Rattar flinched. Mordred looked from the empty tray to the lagoon. The crocodiles were slowly paddling back his way. He looked to the corridor. "Intaki! Return with the prisoner."

Smiling, the little man lifted the prisoner onto his small shoulders like a rolled-up carpet and jogged to his master. "M'lord?" he panted.

"Dump him in the lagoon."

"B-b-but the ranthom ith paid, M'lord," said Rattar in a small, small voice. "What do I tell the family?"

"They were too late."

Intaki dropped the Frenchman to the ground and rolled him over the cliff. The water must have brought him to his senses because, right before he was pulled under by the first of the five hungry reptiles, he began screaming.

"Such beautiful creatures." Mordred's smile grew with each splash, snap and gurgle.

Five minutes later, the feeding frenzy was over. Floating remnants of clothes and shoes were all that remained of the banker. As Mordred turned to leave, he called, "Rattar?"

"M'lord?"

"We'll keep the ransom, of course." His peals of laughter echoed through the dungeon.

Chapter Twenty-Seven

The Russian Crusade

Dunmoore broke from the wind tunnel first and headed for an ornately carved desk with gold flake trim. He picked up a folder, turned and smiled broadly. "According to this Guest Information packet, we are in Room 333 of the Beresta Palace Hotel in Novgorod, Russia!"

Lucas and the others burst into cheers.

Dunmoore left the room to check in, returning fifteen minutes later looking disgusted. He tossed papers onto a coffee table, his nose as wrinkled as if he smelled ten-week old rotten eggs. There were three brochures and a map, all in English. Each of the brochures had the name of a different cathedral on it.

Des asked, "There are *three* cathedrals in Novgorod?"

"More. But only these three claim to have possession of the legendary Holy Grail."

"Three Holy Grails?" said Ryan. "No fecking way!"

Dunmoore sank into a fluffy armchair. "I share your sentiment, Ryan, if not your unrestrained use of profanity."

Lucas held one of the brochures in his hand, open to a picture of a gleaming gold chalice embedded with jewels. "How do we know which one's the right one?"

"That's what we have to figure out, oh brilliant one." Maya preened as she perched on the arm of Dunmoore's chair.

The Professor gave a huge sigh. "I've no idea how to discern the true Grail from amongst the three."

So they brainstormed, trying to come up with a way to divine the right Grail. A grumbling Ryan was the first to give up. "The damn Grail might not even be here."

"It's here," Lucas said with conviction. "So we might as well go see these Grails and find out where they're located. Once we figure out which one's the right one, at least we'll know the layout in the cathedral."

They decided to split up to check out the three cathedrals and rendezvous back at the hotel in two hours. They did not want to risk alerting any agents of the Dark Powers to their presence, and they were uncertain whether the rings would give them away, so one of them would have to stay in the hotel room to guard the rings. The four teens picked straws to see who would stay behind: Des. He pretended to pout, but Lucas could tell from his laughing eyes that he bore no grudge.

The others hoisted their backpacks. Ryan took off for the Church of Our Savior-at-Ilino, on *ulitsa* (street) Ilyina, south of their hotel. Lucas headed for the Trinity Church, on *ulitsa* Dukhovskaya, almost directly across the Volkhov River from the hotel. Maya and Dunmoore tackled the Cathedral of St. Sophia, Novgorod's centerpiece, located in the Kremlin across the river – part park, part tourist attraction, and part archive.

Dunmoore cautioned, "Try not to attract attention. We do not have visa papers, nor do we want to risk exposing ourselves to...." He did not have to finish the sentence.

Silently, and grimly, they went their separate ways.

Ryan started off jauntily down the streets of the city, laid out in a spiderweb, the center of which was the Kremlin. The Church was only blocks from the hotel, and Ryan took advantage of his "alone time" to indulge in cigarettes and try to blow smoke rings in the brisk breeze.

Ignoring Dunmoore's warning to keep a low profile, Ryan delighted in the attention his cigarettes received: It seemed everyone from panhandlers (which were few) to businessmen and housewives (plenty) was hooked on nicotine and not shy about shagging a smoke from a stranger. Only when a policeman – in a black wool uniform and coat with red epaulets – stopped in mid-conversation with a liquor shop owner to stare at Ryan did the Irish teen's cockiness deflate.

Ryan ground his cigarette butt in the street with his heel, pulled up the collar of his leather coat, and stuffed his hands in his pockets, then hurried down the street and out of sight. He turned at the next corner, glancing over his shoulder to see if the cop was in pursuit, and bumped into a group of chattering Japanese tourists taking photos.

Ryan stared at the structure in front of him.

Built in the fourteenth century, the huge Church of Our Savior-at-Ilino still retained an odd charm, with graffiti-like ornamentation and lopsided gables. Ryan paid the small entrance fee and followed the Japanese tourists inside.

The church pamphlets boasted about the uniqueness of the interior Byzantine frescoes – some paintings on the wall – by a famous Greek artist, and lamented about the damage done by the Nazis. But what caught Ryan's eye was the shining gold and bejeweled chalice. The Holy Grail. *Worth a fortune, easy*, he thought. *No wonder the wiz wants it back*. And so he stood, mesmerized.

———

Three hours later, Ryan knocked on the door to Suite 333. "Crusader Casey reporting."

Dunmoore pulled him into the room. "You're late! We've been worried sick."

"You miss me, Princess?" Ryan gave Maya what Lucas's mom would have called a lewd grin.

"In your dreams, Neanderthal."

Lucas sensed another head-on collision between the panther and rattler. He jumped in with, "We voted you most likely to be arrested while trying to steal the Grail." He grinned at the Irish teen.

The others, even Dunmoore, broke into laughter. Ryan's face reddened in anger, and Lucas quickly added, "In all fairness, we also voted you most likely to succeed in stealing the Grail. So, hand it over." Still grinning, Lucas stuck out his hand.

Ryan's scowl faded. He slapped Lucas's hand. "I restrained meself. But I did get a good picture of it." He strolled into the living room and slumped onto the couch. "How about a drink? I'm dry as a virgin."

Lucas noticed the stunned look on Maya's face and said, "Save it for the locker room, Casey."

"Sorry. Just an expression me mates use." Ryan held his hands out to Maya in a peace gesture. "Truce?"

Maya shrugged. "Who said I was a virgin?"

This time, Lucas's jaw dropped.

Dunmoore said, "Now that we're all accounted for, shall we report on our activities?"

Ryan gulped a mouthful of soda, wiped his mouth with the back of his hand, and related his scouting of the Grail. The others' stories sounded identical. Each cathedral truly believed it held the Holy Grail. The prelate at the Trinity Church had told Lucas that many cathedrals in Russia laid claim to the relic.

"We're no closer to an answer than before we started," complained Maya, crossing her arms and frowning.

"Screw it. Let's just steal all three relics," Ryan suggested.

Dunmoore said, "We wouldn't have enough time to collect all three without the Dark Powers finding out. If we chose the wrong one, I doubt we'd get a second opportunity."

The Crusaders looked as despondent as Lucas felt, except for Des, whose smile seemed even bigger than usual. "What's up, Des?" asked Lucas. "You look like the cat who ate the canary."

"My, what big teeth you have, grandma," said Ryan. "What gives little guy?"

Des had used his time as "ring sentry" to re-read Grandma Maggie's journal. He remembered she had written about staying at an inn – The Hissing Monkey – with very helpful owners. Sleuthing on-line, Des discovered that the inn still existed, although the street name had changed in 1991, with the dismantling of the Soviet Union. Gregorivich Gagarin, the eldest son of Mikhail and Natasha, now managed the inn and lived there with his parents.

Lucas jumped from the couch and slapped the blushing Des on the back. The Crusaders hefted their backpacks once again and all headed for *ulitsa* Yakovleva and The Hissing Monkey.

They strode up the brick walk of the little inn just as the dark-red sun set. The blue shingles were peeling, and the white trim was in dire need of a new coat of paint, but Lucas could tell that the owners took pride in the place. The lawn was green and clipped, though muddy with the recent rains. And the huge porch running the length of the house was neat and clean, with two wooden benches on either side of the front doors. The sweet smell of night-blooming jasmine bushes filled the air, and the soft lights from inside gave off a welcoming glow. Dunmoore rang the bell.

They heard footsteps and a voice from inside. A big man with salt and pepper hair opened the front door and greeted them in Russian.

Dunmoore replied in broken Russian, "My Russian not good. You speak English?"

The man nodded, saying in perfect English, "How can I help you?"

"We would like to talk to the previous owners of your lovely *dacha*, if that is possible. We understand that Mikhail and Natasha still reside here."

The man's smile disappeared, and he eyed them with the same wary look Lucas had come to expect from Ryan. "My mother is not in any condition to receive visitors."

"Please." Dunmoore pointed to Ryan. "They knew this young man's grandmother, Maggie Ryan." He pointed to Lucas. "And this young man's grandfather, Tony Moreno. I assure you that we will only take a few moments of their time. It is a matter of some urgency."

The man scratched his head and stroked his burly stubble before saying, "I will ask my father if he remembers them." He opened the door. "Please, wait in the parlor."

The Crusaders followed him down the hallway to a large living room. A fire burned bright, beckoning them to warm their hands and faces. After the man left, the Crusaders wandered around the room. Ryan picked up a large, wooden doll from the mantle and examined it. When he took it apart, he found another, smaller wooden doll inside. And another one inside that, and so on and so on. Six dolls, all in diminishing sizes.

"Russian nesting dolls," said Maya from behind.

Startled, Ryan almost dropped the dolls.

"Hey, klutz," Maya giggled.

Ryan scowled. "Don't go sneaking up on me. You're lucky I didn't take you out."

The man re-entered the room, strode over to where they stood, took the nesting dolls from Ryan and replaced them on the mantle.

"My father does not know any Maggie or Tony," he said in a gruff voice. "You have the wrong place."

"Perhaps he would remember them if he saw a photograph?" Maya retrieved from her backpack the picture of Maggie and Tony in front of the Red Cross tent.

The man stood at the now open front door. "I told you, they do not know your grandparents."

What's this guy's problem?, Lucas wondered.

A voice called from upstairs. "Gregory, let me see picture." An old man hobbled down the stairs. He leaned heavily on the polished dark wood of the banister. His back was badly stooped, and a shock of white hair stood in tufts on his head, but his blue eyes sparkled with intelligence. When he reached the bottom riser, his son clasped his forearm and led him to the large overstuffed leather chair closest to the fire.

Gregory spoke in Russian to his father. Lucas did not understand, but he figured the son was not a happy guy.

The father smiled at the Crusaders and spoke in clear, accented, English. "My son, Gregorivich, scolds me for attempting stairs without assistance. As your Rodney Dangerfield says 'I get no respect.'"

Lucas guffawed at the reference to the classic American comic.

Gregory glared at him.

"He visit once. Long time ago." The old man waved a hand in the air and flashed a broad grin at Lucas. "Your grandparents stay here?"

Lucas replied, "My *great*-granddad, Tony Mor–"

"– and me great-grandma, Maggie. Yeah, they stayed here. During World War II."

The old man nodded at Ryan. "I am sorry, but the names do not –"

"Maybe this will help?" Maya handed him the photograph.

He held the photo almost to his nose and squinted. Suddenly, his face lit up with what Lucas hoped was recognition. "*Konéshno.* Maggie and Tony!"

Dunmoore slid a footstool over in front of the old man and sat, then introduced the group.

The old man said, "I am Mikhail. And you know my son."

Gregory nodded in acknowledgement, but remained standing in the living room, near the hallway. Watchful.

Mikhail studied the photo again. "It has been so long. Fifty years, no?"

Dunmoore nodded. "More. Which is why we need your help."

"Of course, I help. Maggie and Tony were wonderful couple. So much love."

Lucas glanced at Ryan, who raised his eyebrows in return.

"So tragic an end." The old man shook his head.

"You know what happened, then?" asked Dunmoore.

"We received letter from Tony. A shock to learn of beautiful Maggie's death." Mikhail looked at Ryan. "Your great-grandmother was beauty. Out *and* in." He touched his fist to his heart. "You understand?"

"Yeah," Ryan said, then added, "sir."

"Do you still have the letter, Mikhail? May we see it?" asked Dunmoore.

Mikhail sighed. "I do not know where letter is. Natasha put it somewhere."

"May we talk to Natasha?" Lucas asked. He had a funny feeling that something was not quite right.

"*Nyet.*" Gregory stepped into the room and spoke to his father in rapid Russian.

Mikhail looked at Lucas and shrugged. "Alzheimer's. Natasha is in another world now."

Lucas felt the smile fade from his lips.

"We never know when she be herself. When this happens, I ask her about letter."

"Another kick in the bollix," muttered Ryan. "We'll never find the right cathedral."

Mikhail touched Ryan's arm. "*Cathedral?*"

"The one Grandma Maggie and Tony went to knock...went to."

Mikhail's face erupted in a broad smile. "Perhaps I can help." He turned to Gregory and asked something in Russian. Gregory snorted and left, returning with a large leather-bound book. He placed it in his father's lap and returned to his post in the hallway.

Mikhail opened the book – a photo album. "We get photo of guests who stay here. This from 1940." Mikhail slowly scanned the photos on each page, finally stopping and jabbing a photo with a crooked finger. "Here. Maggie and Tony. At cathedral."

Lucas leaned over the back of the oversized leather chair for a glimpse. Though yellowed with age, and its corners curling somewhat, the photograph still quite clearly depicted Maggie and Tony, arms around each other, standing in front of a cathedral with a dragon draped around the top-most spire.

Maya said, "That's the Cathedral of St. Sophia!"

"What if this isn't the right one?" asked Des. "What if Maggie and Tony were also checking out the other cathedrals?"

"No, no," insisted Mikhail. "This is cathedral where Maggie was. . .taken." He took the photo from the book and gave it to Dunmoore. "Please to return it."

Dunmoore extended his hand to the old man. "We will take good care of it. We are so very grateful to you for all your assistance, Mikhail."

"*Das nova.* If not too impose, I ask most kindly for you to tell stories when you return?"

"Ahhemmph" grunted Gregory. He stood in the foyer entrance, the front door wide open. "It is time for my father's medication."

They said their good-byes to Mikhail. The last to leave, Lucas leaned down and whispered, "Take my son...please," in his best Rodney Dangerfield imitation.

Mikhail burst into laughter.

Lucas sped out the front door. He could *feel* Gregory's glare follow him down the path to the others.

"Now what?" asked Des.

"Gentlemen. And lovely lady." Dunmoore bowed to Maya. "We return to the hotel and make preparations for our assault on the cathedral of the one, the only, the true Holy Grail."

Maya took Dunmoore's bent arm. Trailed by the boys, they headed into the deepening night.

Chapter Twenty-Eight

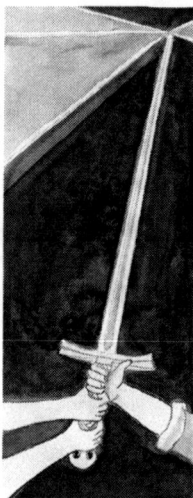

Dealing With Dragons

Back inside their hotel room, Lucas basked in the warmth of fire and friends as they put together the finishing touches to their "battle plan." Dunmoore and Maya reconstructed the layout of the cathedral of the dragon. They put in a quick ring-travel trip to an auto parts store for car batteries in England – sure to be deserted at that time of night – and Lucas held his breath as Dunmoore carefully, oh-so-gently, poured the acid from the containers into several small vials and stoppered them tightly.

The chalice rested in a steel case inside the cathedral. The plan was to open the case by using battery acid to burn through the locking mechanism. Des had seen the trick on a rerun of *MacGyver* one night while he was working on a Science paper at Eton. He had been captivated by it and confirmed with his chemistry teacher that it wasn't just Hollywood magic.

The cold, moonless night quickly dampened Lucas's enthusiasm. Outside, a dark sky greeted them, with only the light of the stars as guides. At the brick walk leading to the cathedral, they hit their first obstacle: a tall, spiked iron gate – locked.

"This bites!" said Ryan.

Des said in a soft voice, "We have the rings. Don't we just ask them to take us to the other side of the gate?"

Dunmoore clapped Des on the back. "Good thinking. We've all got to get into that mindset. And I think I can improve on your suggestion, Des. We'll have the rings take us *inside* the cathedral, directly to the Holy Grail. Keep the element of surprise on our side."

"The dragon is gone!" Maya pointed to the roof – a large central dome surrounded by twelve smaller, onion-shaped domes, representing the twelve Apostles. The stone dragon was missing. "I don't like this."

Dunmoore placed both hands on Maya's shoulders. Lucas saw her tremble, whether from cold or fear, he couldn't tell. Her yellow cat-eyes glowed. Dunmoore said, "There must be a rational explanation."

Maya looked from Dunmoore to the dome and back to Dunmoore. She took a deep breath. "Of course. It can't have flown down. Sorry. It's just...."

"Daunting," said Lucas. "But we have the rings, remember? If we get into trouble, we just wish ourselves back to Merlin's oak tree."

Dunmoore said, "All right, then, my fellow Crusaders, to the Holy Grail!"

The Crusaders gathered in a circle, stacked their hands together, and chanted the Middle English words to take them inside the cathedral. The wind picked up, and almost before Lucas could blink, he found himself staring at the inky blackness of the cathedral, lit only by the light of the heavens filtered through the stained glass domes.

Until they turned on their flashlights and found themselves in front of a large steel case – about ten feet high, six feet wide and four feet deep. Inside stood a simple and crudely crafted chalice of metal and wood. A purple velvet rope encircled the case. Dunmoore had warned them not to go beyond the rope, for he and Maya had learned that it not only kept visitors from getting too near the display case, but also delineated the boundaries of the laser alarm system.

Lucas thought he heard a ragged, hissing breathing, like a teakettle just starting to sing. His heart rate quickened.

A bit of the willies, kiddo? The small voice in Lucas's head had returned.

"Quickly, Des, the acid," Dunmoore whispered.

Lucas took a deep breath to calm his racing nerves. *What's that?* He peered into the shadows that surrounded them. He sniffed. It smelled like the remains of a bonfire, or cinders stirred up in a fireplace.

The small boy's hands shook as he carefully twisted the stopper on one of the vials. Des wore thick leather gloves as a precaution, although Lucas knew the acid would eat right through the material in seconds.

What the heck? Lucas felt the heavy movement in the air at the same time a strange fluttering shadow from above caught his attention.

Ohjeez-ohjeez-ohjeez! "A dragon!" shouted Lucas.

It was, indeed, the dragon from the dome – come to life.

The creature perched on the rafters. It was about fourteen feet long, encased in green and silver scales, except for its four huge feet, each of which had six long, spiked talons. Its wings looked like those of a pterodactyl – leathery and yet almost sheer, its bones clearly visible through the skin. When it took off from the rafters, its wingspan filled the main worship area of the cathedral. Its tail was nearly as long as its body, with sharp spikes at the end of it. And it had the nastiest urine-yellow eyes and teeth.

A lurching in Lucas's gut told him this was the real thing. No willies. No video game.

Dunmoore ran into the nearest aisle and fired his pistol at the attacking dragon until he had emptied the clip into it. The creature made terrible screeching noises and turned back to the rafters. In its swooping turn, the dragon spewed flames at Dunmoore, singeing him.

"Bloody hell!" Dunmoore yelled, clutching his smoking right arm. Ryan ran and knelt in front of the Professor, drawing a gun and assuming a shooter's pose.

Where did he get that? wondered Lucas.

It looked like the .38 caliber handgun from the Spenser cabin – a souvenir from Mr. Spenser's Army days. Ryan had eyed it with longing and argued for status as a second shooter, bragging about his summer training with the IRA. But the others had been unanimous in not wanting to arm the impulsive youth. *So much for majority wins*, thought Lucas.

Maya shrieked as the hideous winged creature headed for the ceiling, spitting fire while circling high above them.

Lucas scrambled with Maya and Des to the back of the cathedral. In their panic and confusion, they dropped their flashlights and then collided with a heavy object.

"Ow!" Lucas's left shoulder throbbed with pain. His hat skidded across the floor.

CRASH!

A glass case with a suit of armor and sword from a Russian Orthodox knight of the 11th century toppled over. The Crusaders narrowly avoided being sliced by the glass shards.

Lucas heard Dunmoore scream, "Watch out!" and turned to see the dragon dive-bomb from the rafters. Ryan shot the beast time and again. The monster's ghastly screams chilled Lucas, who covered his ears to muffle the gruesome sound.

As Ryan backed away, still shooting, he tripped over Dunmoore and went sprawling on his back, the handgun clattering across the marble floor. The dragon must have sensed an opportunity, for it did not retreat again, but swooped directly at Ryan and Dunmoore.

Lucas swallowed the metallic taste of fear in his mouth and looked around the room for some type of weapon. Des and Maya must have been doing the same, for all three reached almost as one for the sword from the shattered case.

As their right hands locked onto the sword's hilt, Lucas caught the green glowing of their rings. "Aim it at the dragon!" he shouted.

A bolt of neon-green lightning flew from the honed steel tip, zapping the creature in mid-flight. It fell to the floor with a horrible screech and tremendous THUD! Then, lay still.

"Holy Jeez," whispered Lucas. He stared at the sword, then looked to the fallen dragon. The three friends dropped the sword, where it landed with a CLANG! on the cold marble floor.

Dunmoore and Ryan limped to the back of the church. Lucas grabbed his hat and joined the others at the stand of the Grail. Though Dunmoore's clothes were burned, and he bore singe marks on his face and arms, he was okay. Ryan had only bruised his hip.

Dunmoore said, "No time to waste, I can hear sirens. The acid, Des."

Ryan shoved Des aside and aimed his gun. "Forget the acid, mate." Ryan blasted the lock to smithereens – setting off the alarm in the process – and the iron doors opened. Des grabbed the chalice. Amid sirens and shouts from outside, the group formed a circle.

Out of the corner of his eye, Lucas saw a glint of metal. "One sec!" He dashed to where the sword lay and gingerly grasped the gold hilt, encrusted with diamonds and rubies. The heft of the sword felt good.

"Lucas!" whispered Dunmoore, urgency in his voice.

Lucas scanned the area near the sword and spied the scabbard – it was ivory, with gold and silver inlay in delicate swirls, and yet more precious gems. "Got it!" Lucas slid the sword into the scabbard and ran back to the circle. Just as he thrust out his hand, the hairs on the back of Lucas's neck prickled, and his ring scorched his finger. He looked behind him. A scream locked in his throat. The dragon was still alive!

Despite the noise and terror that surrounded them, Lucas suddenly heard Don Vasquez. "Trust the ring, Lucas. Trust the powers of the ring."

Lucas shouted, "The Grail! Put your right hand on the Grail!" When they did, a brilliant green laser beam shot from the simple chalice and struck the scaly monster full on in the chest. It disappeared in steam and smoke, leaving only a horrible stench.

Heaving a great sigh of relief, Lucas put his right hand on top of Maya's in the circle. The front doors of the cathedral slammed opened, and black-clad men raced in, brandishing pistols and shouting in Russian.

Lucas saw a glint of light reflecting off a car parked outside. *But it's night! No moon.* He squinted. It was a gleaming black limo!

Fighting back panic, Lucas focused and repeated the traveling spell with the others. They disappeared in a gust of wind, reappearing seconds later at the base of Merlin's oak.

Before Lucas could breathe deeply of the crisp, Spring air, his ring turned a deep emerald green. A heavy mist fell, and the windman's sighing swept over him. Merlin's image appeared in the tree. "Well done, Crusaders, well done. You have the Holy Grail?"

Des held the relic aloft. "What should we do with it?"

"I shall take it for safekeeping," the wizard replied, holding out translucent limbs. The relic disappeared into his misty arms. "And what have you learned?" he inquired.

"Learned?" asked Lucas. *What's he talking about? We barely escaped alive.*

"The dragon," whispered Maya.

Ryan shouted, "There was a goddamn *dragon* at the cathedral! A manky, fire-breathing lizard. It almost killed us!"

Merlin sighed. "I had heard rumors of such guardians of the relics. The Dark Powers must have powerful magic indeed to create such a beast. How did you defeat it?"

"Me and the Prof shot it. At least I put some lead into its damn hide," said Ryan.

"A lot of good that did," said Maya. "If it wasn't for the sword. And the rings —"

"The rings! That's it!" said Lucas.

Merlin asked, "What of the rings, Master Moreno?"

"If three of us touch something with our rings, we can use it in a way we never could otherwise. Like that lightning bolt from the sword."

Dunmoore said, "Aah! The object becomes imbued with the power of the rings."

"Yes, Professor Dunmoore, that would appear to be the case."

"Why didn't you tell us this before? The Professor and Ryan could have been killed back there!" Des said, angrily.

Merlin turned his gaze on the slight teenager, and Lucas flinched in anticipation. But the wizard merely smiled. "I did not endow the rings with such magic, Master Moboto. I suspected that the rings might have more power than my traveling spell, but I was not certain until now. I know only what is reported back to me from my Crusaders. No Crusader, or should I say, no *three* Crusaders, had ever brought such news. It is the *journey*, Master Moboto."

Des bowed his head. "I'm sorry, sir. I didn't realize."

"Did you encounter any agent of the Dark Powers other than the dragon?" asked Merlin.

Lucas scowled as he said, "The black limo was there. I'm sure of it."

Merlin sighed. "They now know about you – that there are at least three of you – and they will be better prepared." The sorcerer shook his head in dismay. "Had the Dark Powers not been there, you would have had a head start on the next part of the quest. As it is, you may have to battle more than the guardian of the relic."

Lucas frowned at the crestfallen faces of his fellow Crusaders. *That ain't the way to motivate your team, Merlin,* he thought.

He caught the wizard staring at him before saying, "There is no need to dwell on what may or may not occur in the future. You succeeded where others failed, and you learned much about the powers of the rings. Knowledge that should serve you well. And," Merlin looked at each Crusader in turn, "you did not falter in your courage nor panic in the face of doom."

Lucas felt his spirits rise at this unexpected praise.

Merlin's image began to fade. He whispered, "Remember always – in unity, there is strength," then disappeared.

Chapter Twenty-Nine

B

Tony

The descending mist dampened their already flagging spirits. "Damn!" said Ryan. "I wanted to ask him more questions!"

"He does seem to come and go without regard to our needs," said Dunmoore.

Lucas added, "And I don't think he'll be back until we bring the next relic. "So what's it gonna be? Japan or Egypt?"

"Better to ask what guardian monster we go up against, isn't it?" asked Maya.

Ryan replied, "No way of knowing, Princess. I vote for Japan. I'd like to see more women like you."

Ryan's smirk did nothing more than amuse Lucas – *it's so junior high*, he thought – but he could see Maya was irritated.

Des said, "I would like to see Japan, also, Maya. Although I do not think there could be any woman more beautiful than you."

Ryan snickered. "The little guy's hot for you, Princess!"

Des blushed and looked at his feet.

"Can it, Ryan," said Lucas.

Maya added, "Shut up, you Irish imbecile," as she put her arm around Des's shoulder. "Thank you, Des."

Des gave her a joyful smile.

Maya said, "I don't think it's rash to want to know what we're up against before we choose. What if the next one is worse than a dragon?"

Dunmoore agreed. "Better to be forewarned and well prepared."

"You're just slinjing, Prof," said Ryan. "I say we vote on it. And Des and I vote for Japan." He leaned back against the oak tree and tamped out a cigarette.

Maya crossed her arms. "And the Professor and I vote for prudence in making a decision."

Ryan took a drag on his cigarette and said as he exhaled a stream of smoke, "Lucas, mate, looks like it's your call."

All eyes turned to Lucas. But he wasn't flustered. He'd done his share of refereeing disputes between his sisters. He said in what he hoped was a calm, firm voice, "You're right, Maya. We don't know what guardian we're dealing with in Japan or Egypt."

Maya put one hand on her hip and gave a triumphant smile to Ryan.

Lucas added, "But Ryan's got a point. We don't have time to argue. The Dark Powers are onto us now, and we don't want to give them a huge head start. *We* should surprise *them*, not the other way 'round. We may not know what the monster of the Japanese temple is, but at least we know we're looking for a temple. We don't know *what* we're looking for in Egypt."

Maya stood with her arms crossed, a pout on her face, then finally nodded. "What you say makes sense, Lucas." She sighed as she massaged the back of her neck. "But, I still have a bad feeling about this."

"Japan it is," declared Lucas. "But where in Japan?"

Dunmoore – whom Lucas suspected had deliberately allowed the teens to hash out the decision – replied, "I suggest we return to the Spenser cabin and make additional preparations, as we did before Novgorod."

"And have a bite to eat, right? I've a mouth on me!" Ryan said.

"You're always hungry," said Des.

Ryan's eyes twinkled. "Especially when I'm fighting fire-breathing dragons!"

In seconds, they stood again in the middle of the Spenser cabin. Dunmoore asked them to wait a moment before dispersing.

They sat quietly while Dunmoore cleared his throat. "Things have been rather...hectic recently, and I imagine they will be even more manic in the days to come. I'd like to offer a commendation and a suggestion. First, you all deserve tremendous praise. What you did in the cathedral was extremely courageous."

All but Ryan blushed.

"Thank God for the impulsiveness of youth." The Professor turned to Ryan. "Your taking that gun from the cabin – against our wishes – most likely saved my life. Without your aid, I might have been dragon fodder. Thank you."

Ryan began to redden.

"And you three," Dunmoore turned to the others. "Your quick thinking saved both Ryan and me. Thank you."

"You're welcome, Prof," Lucas said. "You would have done the same for us."

"I sincerely hope I will not have the opportunity to do so, Luke. But I thank you for your faith. Now, the suggestion. We have much research and brainstorming to do before we set off for Japan. Before we get that underway, I am of the opinion that we return to Novgorod and collect our things. And then return the photo to Mikhail Gagarin. I sense we shall not have the opportunity to do so if we wait much longer."

The last suggestion did not go over well. Ryan was hungry. Maya was tired. Even good-natured Des protested.

Lucas said, "Guys, guys. We have the rings, remember? We can travel to the hotel, grab our bags, hit The Hissing Monkey, return the photo and be back here in fifteen minutes flat. Even Ryan's stomach can wait fifteen minutes."

Within seconds, they stood in their suite at the Beresta Palace Hotel and, within minutes, Dunmoore had checked out, and they all stood again on the porch of the bed and breakfast. As Maya placed the photo of Maggie and Tony in a protected spot, a light came on.

The door slowly opened to reveal Mikhail, a finger to his lips. He motioned with his arms for them to enter, and they followed him into the living room, where he took his seat in the same leather chair. In the rocking chair across from him sat an old woman. Even though her face bore many wrinkles, her skin was a translucent pearl color, and her white hair was tied back in a long braid. Lucas could tell she had been quite a beauty in her day.

"Please, sit down," said Mikhail. "This is Natasha." Mikhail motioned to the woman. "Natasha, these are people I tell you about. Grandchildren of Maggie and Tony."

Natasha's purple eyes sparkled with warmth and intelligence. Lucas didn't know much about Alzheimer's, but Natasha looked lucid enough.

"Very pleased to meet you." Her voice was soft and deep, lulling as Lucas's mother's when she comforted him after a bad dream. "Mikhail has told how sorry we were to hear of Maggie's death. Which one of you—?"

"Ryan Casey." Ryan stepped forward and put his hand out. "Pleased to meet you."

Natasha took his hand and held it for a moment. "You have her hair and eyes." She turned to the others and focused on Lucas. "And you are very image of Tony."

Lucas extended his hand. "Lucas Moreno. It is an honor to meet you, Mrs. Gagarin."

"Please to call me Natasha. How is Tony? He still alive?"

"No, ma'am, uh, Natasha. He died before I was born."

Natasha sighed. "At least now he is with his beloved Maggie in heaven."

"Natasha remember where she put letter." Mikhail held a letter in his hands.

Dunmoore asked, "May I have the honors?" and took the unsealed envelope. Inside was a short note to Mikhail and Natasha and another envelope, sealed. Lucas noticed the quizzical look Dunmoore gave to Mikhail.

Dunmoore read the note out loud. It was dated March 3, 1940.

Dear Mikhail and Natasha,

I write with terrible news. My dearest Maggie is gone, killed by a hit-and-run limousine driver outside the Cathedral of St. Sophia on our last night together. I do not believe the driver will ever be brought to justice. He is one of *them*. I spent many days in a cell. I was not permitted any visitors, except for Maggie's husband, who came to claim her things. I tried to explain, but he would not listen. Through the help of the American Embassy, I secured my release, but was immediately deported. Obviously, I could not contact you.

I did not want to risk your being arrested. Please accept my apologies for any worry our absence caused you.

Enclosed is a copy of a letter to Maggie's heirs. Her husband has the original. It explains everything that happened that night. If you ever receive a visit from her family, please give it to them.

I do not know if you can imagine the depths of my despair over losing Maggie. It gives me some small comfort to know that we spent the most wondrous six days in your home. I hope that can be of some solace to you, also.

Thank you my friends.
Tony

Dunmoore picked up the sealed envelope. "You never opened it? Weren't you curious about what had happened to them?"

"Of course," Natasha replied, shrugging her shoulders. "But it not addressed to us."

Her explanation was so simple, and yet so amazing to Lucas. That these two people would have such profound respect for the privacy of people they had known only six days – even after more than sixty years – was inconceivable. At least it was in the world Lucas was used to.

"You satisfy our curiosity now?" asked Mikhail, a twinkle in his eye, a smile on his lips.

Lucas grinned. "How about it, Ryan? It may take more than fifteen minutes."

"Dry up, you gowl." Ryan nodded. "Go ahead, Prof."

Tony Moreno's letter described his and Maggie's assault upon the Cathedral on January 22, 1940. With only two Crusaders, Tony and Maggie were no match for the dragon – or the Dark Powers.

The letter ended with,

I have given Maggie's things to her husband. He would not listen to my story. To Maggie's story. So, I write this letter to you – Maggie's descendants. She would want you to join the Last Crusade.

As for me, I can't give you any advice. I don't even know whether I will tell my son about the ring and quest. But, then, Maggie's brother Patrick was right. Maggie was the bravest woman – person – I ever knew. She risked her life for mine inside the cathedral. She was willing to return. She wanted to save the world. She only succeeded in saving me. I loved her.

[Signed] Anthony V. Moreno

Silence filled the room, broken only by gentle sniffing. Lucas saw Natasha's eyes shining bright with tears, as were Maya's. Even hard-shelled Ryan snuffled and wiped his nose with the back of his hand.

"And you finish dragon off tonight?" asked Mikhail.

His question startled Lucas. "How did you guess?"

"Mikki sees all. They recruit him for KGB, but he refuse." Natasha spoke with pride.

"*Das nova.*" Mikhail dismissed his wife with the wave of his hand. "Do not listen to ravings of beautiful old woman."

Movement sounded upstairs.

"Gregory!" whispered Mikhail. "You go now or he never let Tasha and I forget how late we entertain foreign hoodlums!"

"Oh, Mikki," said Natasha, worry creasing her brow. "There is no time."

Lucas smiled broadly. "If you thought the dragon story was something, wait until you see this. We'll be gone before Gregory gets here."

Heavy footsteps started down the stairs. The Crusaders formed their circle and repeated the traveling spell.

Gregory stepped into the room, now occupied only by his wide-eyed parents. "What are you doing up so late? Who are you talking to?"

Mikhail and Natasha laughed.

Mikhail said, "Gregory, my son, if we tell, you never believe it!" And they laughed some more.

Gregory shook his head and grumbled his way back up the stairs.

Chapter Thirty

The Shadows Tremble

The sun rose over the Fortress of Shadows to a crisp, clear day. The blizzard had passed, blanketing the landscape in a snowy whiteness as far as the eye could see. But the serenity outside the castle was deceptive, for a storm brewed within.

"Rattar!" Mordred bellowed from the communications room.

"Here, M'lord!" Rattar cried, scuttling over. The massive communications room would have been the envy of NASA. Banks of computers lined one wall, large, flat-screen televisions lined another, and surveillance cameras occupied yet a third. The room buzzed with activity – from the computer geeks repairing glitches to the physicists devising new satellites. From this one room, Mordred could track his vast underworld empire with up-to-the-micro-second information. Despite the technological marvel of the place, Mordred preferred to conduct business in the candlelit throne room. The brightness of the communications room and its nearly constant hum of activity put him out of sorts.

"Has Munin arrived yet?"

"An hour ago, M'lord."

"We told you we wanted to see him immediately, did we not?"

Rattar nodded and covered his head with his hands.

"Imbecile!" Mordred whacked the manservant with a glove. "Have Munin join us in the throne room. *Now.*" He turned to his companion. "See what we put up with, Vassalar? Come, we require your counsel." Mordred strode from the room, followed swiftly and silently by the lean, olive-skinned Russian with the pointed gold canines.

Cerb and Berus rose from the floor of the throne room to greet their master. Mordred gave each Rottweiler a quick pat on the flat of the head, then yanked open the top drawer of a desk hidden in the recesses of the room. He pulled out two slabs of dried beef jerky and tossed them to the dogs. The black-and-tan beasts settled contentedly on the floor to gnaw on the treats.

Mordred sat on the throne and drummed his fingers on the polished stone arms. "We are concerned, Vassalar. Gravely concerned."

"I take it the ring has not been recovered?" Vassalar remained standing.

"No, damn it!" Pounding the chair arms with both fists, Mordred stood. The dogs raised their heads inquisitively, noses wrinkling, then went back to chewing. Mordred began to pace. "It is worse than that, Vassalar. Much worse."

"M'lord?"

Mordred stopped and whispered, "The Grail is gone."

"No!"

"We are afraid so. We were woken from sleep last night with the strangest feeling of loss. It was confirmed this morning, but details are still sketchy."

"Munin, M'lord." The rotund Rattar stood at the entrance to the throne room, a thin, shadowy figure looming over him.

"Munin! Come, come, be quick." Mordred motioned with his right hand.

The shadow glided into the room without a sound. Identical to his twin, Hugin – medium height, slight build, dark hair – he was ordinary and non-descript. Except for the lone streak of white hair he wore parted to the left. "M'lord?" A voice as soft as a cobra's slither.

"You have heard of the theft?"

"Yes, M'lord."

"How?"

"It appears there are *four* ringbearers."

"Four? How is this possible? The Professor has no ring. We destroyed it ourselves!" Mordred began pacing again, stopping in front of his informant. "*How?*"

"Forgive me, sire. Four ringbearers *and* the Professor."

"But the girl was killed," said Vassalar, keeping out of striking distance from the shadowy servant, whom Vassalar suspected might not be of Earth.

A thin smile split Munin's face for a mere second, then was swallowed whole. "The girl was in the cathedral. Along with Moreno, Moboto and Casey. *Four* ringbearers."

"Impossible." Mordred slumped onto the throne, muttering to himself. "And they are children, mere children." He looked at Munin. "Where are the agents responsible for this travesty?"

"Here, M'lord." Rattar bustled in again, leading a reluctant man of about 5'8" with severe acne, and a nose that looked like it had been broken more than once. The agent wore an expression of dread on his lopsided features, and he trembled as he bowed.

"Agent Winchell," Rattar announced, then stood aside to observe the festivities.

"We thought there were two agents, Munin?"

"Barnabus fled, M'lord. My brother reports he was last sighted in Chile."

"Winchell, is it?" Mordred turned to the agent. "Can you offer us any explanation for how the wretched girl managed to escape the bus crash? Or how the Irish bugger caught up with the others?"

Winchell replied in a strong, though stuttering, Cockney accent. "I watched the bus go down meself, guv, I mean, me lord. No one coulda got out alive. As fer the inn, they wasn't where we was told they'd be."

Mordred drummed his fingers on the throne's arms, a faint smile on his face.

Winchell added hastily, "But I can fix it, me lord. You needn't worry on that account."

Mordred's smile grew bigger. "Oh, we won't worry at all, Winchell." He nodded to Vassalar.

With an evil smile, Vassalar grabbed the confused Winchell and ripped out his throat with his teeth. Vassalar let the agent's body wilt to the floor, then smacked his lips and licked the blood from his fingers.

The two Rottweilers raised their snouts in the air and sniffed.

"Rattar. Dispose of this unsightly mess."

Rattar hurried from the shadows. "Yeth, M'lord. The lagoon?"

"Yes, yes. Be quick about it."

His face scrunched up in distaste, Rattar placed his plump hands under the dead agent's body and dragged him from the throne room, streaks of red trailing after them.

The two dogs rose and padded to the bloodstains, then turned to their Master, expectant. Mordred smiled and said, *"Zeit!"* And the beasts eagerly lapped up the bloody treat.

"Now, where were we? Ah yes. Munin, who is responsible for the agents?"

Munin looked from Mordred to Vassalar and back to Mordred. "M'lord?"

Vassalar coughed discreetly into his hand to hide his smile, then answered in a somber voice, "General Zheng, M'lord."

"Zheng? That grotesque, lumbering idiot! We want his head, Vassalar, do you hear?"

"M'lord, if I might, a word in General Zheng's defense?"

Mordred eyed the suave Vassalar. "You risk tempting our patience, General?"

Vassalar stood silent, head bowed.

Mordred waved a hand in the air. "Be brief."

"General Zheng has served the Dark Powers well, M'lord. He has his hand on the pulse of the Far East. I suggest that this is perhaps not the time to upset the delicate balance of powers in the region? I assure you Egypt is secure. And I have faith that General Zheng can guarantee Japan. Make an example of the two agents so that all will know your resolve. But allow General Zheng to shore up Japan as no one else can. Should he fail, I would be delighted to present his head on a golden platter." Vassalar bowed his head.

"Well said, Vassalar." Mordred turned to the informant. "Have Hugin pull the assassins nearest Chile. We want the eyes, ears, nose, tongue and fingers of the agent shipped here in a tidy little package for our darlings. Spare no expense. Spare no pain."

Munin bowed and slithered quietly out of the room.

Mordred turned to Vassalar. "Communicate with Zheng, omitting any reference to our earlier ill-will. We need not remind you how serious a situation this is?"

"No, M'lord."

Mordred nodded. "Good, good. Now, be off." After the general departed, Berus approached and sat at his master's feet, his head on Mordred's knee. As Mordred stroked the beast's fur, he whispered, "Merlin, Merlin. How very little rest you give us!"

Chapter Thirty-One

The New York Connection

Battling dragons not only made Ryan ravenous, it also made the others irritable and sleepy, or so it seemed to Lucas. Even he wasn't immune to the effect of being back in the Spenser cabin amid familiar surroundings. The bizarre circumstances of the cathedral began to diminish in impact. *It's like we were playing a video game and now it's over,* he thought. *And we got top score.* Lucas fell into the same routine as the others – eating, showering, napping. When everyone felt re-energized, they gathered to brainstorm their next move.

"The Eye of Buddha *has* to be in a temple in Nara," insisted Maya. "Shin'ichi was killed there. He had to be trying to recapture the Eye. Unfortunately," she sighed, "Nara has as many temples as Novgorod has cathedrals."

"I take it your grandfather never said *which* temple became Shin'ichi's murder scene?" asked Dunmoore.

Maya shook her head, and the Crusaders continued to research the book and notes of her grandfather. It was a slow task, for many of the papers were written in Japanese, which only Maya and Dunmoore could translate.

Impatience led to more irritability until Des piped up, "I think I can locate the temple."

"God, I hope so," said Lucas. *'Cause I'm about ready to rip these papers to shreds.*

Des held up a newspaper clipping. "This is from the New York Times about a meeting of the New York Samurai Society. Maya's grandfather was the main speaker that night, talking about Shin'ichi. It was clipped to this letter, which is mostly in English."

Des scanned the letter. "Maya's grandfather corresponded with a regent of the New York City Public Library named Akira Tanaka, who was also interested in Samurai lore. "

"My grandfather included a note to an Akira Tanaka in his book, thanking him for his assistance!" Maya flipped to the acknowledgment page.

Des had discovered that most of Akira's letters recited facts on Shin'ichi and Samurai society in general. One of the letters read: "You mentioned once, long ago (at that sake-tasting affair), that you had a most frightening experience in the town where Shin'ichi died. Would you please tell me more, old friend?"

"What town?" asked Ryan.

Des answered, "It doesn't say. And I can't find any response from Maya's grandfather. Did he keep any notes of such an experience, Maya?"

"No. I've gone through all his Japanese papers. There was no mention of Grandfather being in Nara. Or even in nearby Kyoto."

"Where does that leave us?" asked Lucas.

"Nowhere, mate. And with the Dark Powers on our tails," said Ryan. "Bleedin' deadly find, little guy," he added in his typically sarcastic voice.

Des shook his head vigorously. His glasses slid down his nose. "We must find Akira Tanaka. Maya's grandfather probably told him the name of the town."

"Good thinking, Des," Lucas said. Des smiled and pushed his glasses back up.

Ryan asked, "But how do we locate this Tanaka guy?"

"Simple." Maya smiled. "Des gets on his little computer and surfs the net!"

191

Lucas and the others gathered around Des as he accessed the Internet. Fifteen minutes later, Des found Akira Tanaka — or, rather, Tanaka's *obituary*.

"A dead bloke." Ryan scowled. "We never get any damn breaks!"

Maya slumped on the couch and nodded in agreement.

"Whoa, you downers," said Lucas. "It says that Tanaka's papers are on permanent loan to the Library. Doesn't that normally include correspondence, Prof?"

"I think you may have something there," replied Dunmoore.

The Crusaders quickly prepared for a side trip to New York City. They would wait until midnight New York time before traveling directly to the Japanese section of the library.

At five in the morning England time, Lucas and the others stood in a circle and chanted the traveling spell. In seconds, shelves of books surrounded them.

"What a rush!" exclaimed Ryan. "I just love that shite."

"We're in a place of academia, Casey." Maya frowned. "If you stay real quiet, you might manage to absorb some proper language."

Lucas knew well the grin Ryan gave Maya, and he braced himself for the sarcasm headed her way — probably rife with profanity.

Instead, Ryan said, "You talking literary osmosis, Princess?"

Maya gave Ryan a look of genuine surprise.

"I know what it means, too. Don't judge a book by its cover." Ryan strutted away.

Maya looked at Lucas. He shrugged and smiled. She sniffed and tossed her hair, then joined Des and Dunmoore, who were already searching for Tanaka's papers.

Fifteen minutes later, Ryan appeared from one of the far carrels carrying a heavy cardboard box, covered in an elegant gold and green Japanese script. "Akira Tanaka's life, for your reading pleasure, Princess." He set the box down on a sturdy table in front of Maya.

Another fifteen minutes elapsed. Maya waved several pages of rice paper, covered in Japanese script and crowed delightedly, "Here's Grandfather's response!"

I have declined your repeated requests for the story of my experience in Nara. Now that my son is gone, and I am entering the twilight of my years, I believe I will find some peace in telling another soul. Of those I could tell, you, dear friend, will accept what I say and not think less of me. When I was 30, my father gave me a silver ring, along with a carved rosewood box and a letter, originally written by Shin'ichi. My father did not believe a word of the legend contained in the letter. He told me it was simply a family tradition; one that I should continue with my son. At first, I did not believe the legend either. I was interested only in the history of Shin'ichi, especially after confirming I was truly descended from the great Samurai warrior. I became obsessed with Shin'ichi and how he died. Obsessed with finding the temple where the wild dogs killed him.

I cannot say now whether it was fate or chance, but on my 35th birthday, I found the temple. I happened to have the ring with me that day, although for the life of me, I do not remember putting it in my jacket, and certainly not putting it on.

Let me digress. My dear wife had planned an excursion to Nara for my birthday. She knew about my devotion to all things Shin'ichi. She used the excuse of visiting distant relatives, who resided on the outskirts of Nara. But I knew better.

I was taking an early morning stroll, as was my custom, when I passed by the Kinkakuji Temple. I noticed two enormous *shishi* temple dogs guarding the entrance.

Des asked, "What are *shishi* temple dogs?"

"Fierce looking dogs – or lions – made out of various things – gold, marble, stone – the guardians of the sacred temples," said Maya.

Lucas jerked up as his mind did a mental "click." "*Guardians.* Wild dogs. Oh jeez."

Maya stared at Lucas, eyes wide. She echoed softly, "Oh, jeez," then continued reading.

Both were crafted of stone. And there was a third eye – painted green – on the forehead of each dog. I started up the path to the temple to get a closer look when I felt a burning in my jacket pocket. It felt as if my hand had been struck by lightning. I found the ring on the first finger of my right hand. I looked up and saw one of the temple dogs begin to move.

Maya's voice became softer, but more insistent.

It looked as if it were shaking its hind legs to get life into them. Then I looked at the other dog and saw *it* begin to move. And growl. A growl that turned my blood to ice and my skin to marble. A growl from the very depths of hell.

Maya paused and looked at her audience, her gaze lingering on Lucas.

Lucas mouthed, "Oh, jeez," and pushed his shirtsleeves up. *Christ, it's hot in here*, he thought. *Only in your mind*, the little voice said. He'd thought he'd gotten rid of that voice. *Go away, back to sleep, whatever*, he silently growled at it. *Let's just get to the worst of it.*

Maya read again.

I rubbed my eyes and shook my head to clear them of this vision, and the ring shocked me again, bringing me out of my daze. Looking at the dogs, I saw one had almost completely come to life, all but the left foreleg. I am not ashamed to admit it, dear friend, but I took off running and did not stop until I was safely in the arms of my wife.

I took off the ring, put it in the box, and emigrated to America with my wife, who was most confused at this sudden change of circumstance, as you might imagine. She delivered to me a child a year later. A son. No, I never gave him the ring. And, now, there is no chance to do so.

"That's it as far as Nara goes." Maya dropped the letter onto the table.

Dunmoore stroked his chin. "We know the Kinkakuji temple houses the Eye of Buddha."

"And what the guardians of the temple are," added Des, twisting his ring yet again.

Ryan said, "So, Shin'ichi gets ripped to bloody pieces by stone temple dogs. Gruesome way to go."

"Maybe we should go to Egypt after all," suggested Maya.

Lucas heard the tiny note of fear in her voice. It surprised him. What surprised him more was a sudden rush of adrenaline and an overpowering feeling of protectiveness. Like when he'd stared down a huge Doberman that had gone after Shadow.

"Who knows what awaits us in Egypt," Dunmoore said. "Better the devil we know."

As if in response to talk of demons, a mist rose from the polished wood floor, the wind-man sighed, and Lucas felt the familiar eerie tingling in his scalp. He looked over his shoulder. "Oh, jeez."

Two huge lions swiftly but quietly padded down the main aisle toward the Crusaders.

"Into the circle," shouted Dunmoore. "Quickly! The traveling spell."

But Des was too far away. Lucas saw the boy's face freeze in fear as he ran toward the others. Lucas stretched out his arm to yank him in, but just as he encircled Des's wrist, one of the lions leapt from a great distance, knocking the boy out of Lucas's grasp. With a great cry, Ryan grabbed his gun from his knapsack and took aim on the first lion.

A gravelly voice said, "No, Boy, we mean you no harm." The second lion sat on his haunches, his front right paw held up, pad-side out.

"Are you all right, Boy?" The first lion asked Des, nudging him gently with his nose.

Des looked up from the floor at the huge lion's face, only inches from his. He grinned.

Get that. He's not afraid of them, Lucas thought. *It must be okay. I think.*

"I'm fine, thank you." Des called to Ryan, "I'm okay. Don't shoot."

Ryan did not fire, but neither did he relinquish his shooter's stance.

The first lion now sat next to the second. They were enormous! Sitting, their heads towered over the six-foot tall Dunmoore. The first lion had bright copper penny eyes and a caramel-colored coat. The second one had a honey-colored fur and eyes the color of roasted coffee beans. Around their necks dangled a gold medallion on a purple-and-gold-striped ribbon.

Lucas asked, "Who are you?"

"I am Patience," the first lion replied. "And this is Fortitude." The second lion bowed his massive head. "We are the guardians of the Library."

"Wait. You are the two *stone* lions at the entrance to the Library?" asked Dunmoore.

"That is correct," replied Fortitude.

Maya said, "But you aren't stone at all. You're flesh and blood. And fur."

"That is also correct, Girl," said Patience. "The magic in your rings brought us to this state, as they were meant to do."

This can't be, Lucas thought. *Can it?* Aloud, he said, "Are you saying that these rings were *designed* to bring you to life?"

Both lions nodded.

"But how can that be?" asked Lucas. "Merlin made these rings in the 10th century. You're not more than a century old, are you?"

Fortitude said, "Very perceptive, Boy. But it is the *magic* in the rings which brings us to this state. Magic that always has existed and always will exist."

Patience added, "But we have not been exposed to such magic for many years."

"Why has the magic brought you to life now?" asked Des.

"To assist you," Fortitude answered.

Patience explained. "We – the lions – represent King Arthur."

Lucas nodded. *King Arthur's coat-of-arms has a lion, right. But what* – His thoughts were interrupted by the lion's deep voice.

"We are on the side of all who work for King Arthur or Merlin."

Fortitude turned to Lucas. "Take the ribbon from around my neck, Boy."

Though apprehensive, Lucas did so, the lion assisting him by bending low to the ground so that Lucas could get his arms around the beast's massive head. As he felt hot breath upon his neck, he realized his entire head – heck, his entire *body* – would fit inside the lion's mouth. Despite the goosebumps now covering his arms, he collected Patience's ribbon next.

"Place both around your neck, Boy," said Patience.

Lucas did as he was told, pausing to rub his fingers over the shiny round medallions, which were the size of his palm and bore a standing lion on one side and a sword on the other. Grinning, he raised his head. "They're really light!"

Fortitude said, "These have the power to protect you. Now, listen to our counsel."

"In addition to the rings," explained Patience, "you must have patience and fortitude to complete your quest. Call upon them when you are at your weakest, and you will prevail."

Lucas said, "I don't understand. What do you mean? How–?"

But the lions had already turned and were making their way back through the library. Patience called over his shoulder. "Patience. It will be revealed."

The other said, "Fortitude. It will stay with you."

And then they disappeared.

"I don't understand this at all," said Maya.

"No osmosis on this one, Princess," Ryan agreed.

"They sure were brill, though, weren't they?" Des grinned broadly, his eyes gleaming.

Lucas stroked the medallions once more, then laughed and put his arm around Des. "Yeah, they were pretty damn brill!"

Chapter Thirty-Two

The Temple Scout

The magical encounter with the lions sent Lucas's spirit soaring. Using the ribbons as "It," Lucas began an impromptu game of library tag that sent the other teens running in several different directions. Even Ryan joined in. Lucas imagined that they looked to all the world like four kids enjoying life. *Not Earth's last hope for salvation.* The grim thought flitted through his head for only a second before Maya – as It – executed a flying leap in his direction behind the Southeast Asia aisle. Lucas ducked, but not quickly enough to avoid being tagged.

All four teens whisper-shrieked with glee – until Dunmoore's reminder that "Japan and the temple dogs beckon" grounded them. Thinking and muttering variations of "spoilsport," Lucas and the others reluctantly prepared for what Ryan dubbed, the "Asian assault." *Ryan's got the knack for naming paramilitary operations,* Lucas thought. *And the Prof for ruining a perfectly good venting party.*

Having reserved a suite at the Edo-San in Nara, a *ryokan*, the Crusaders appeared in seconds in the large Japanese cottage with thatched roof. Graceful pines and pale pink cherry blossom trees scented the bracing air around the cottage. A doe and her dappled fawn quietly munched on green tree leaves. They were but two of the thousand miniature deer which inhabited the Nara Koen Park and roamed freely around the various temples and hotels.

On Maya's advice they had packed lightly and appropriately for April in southern Japan, where the daily temperature hovered around 65°F. Because they were in Maya's homeland, they all agreed she should act as lead scout for their next reconnaissance. They did not agree on a second scout. Everyone wanted to accompany Maya, even Dunmoore. Maya chose Ryan.

Maya quickly explained, "It would be unseemly for a girl...young woman...my age to be in the company of an older Englishman. Forgive me, Professor." She turned to Des and Lucas, "It is no secret that many of my fellow countrymen are xenophobic. Suspicious of foreigners. It could compromise the entire mission."

"You're saying carrot-top here blends more than I do?" Lucas asked.

Ryan grinned. "What can I say, mate? She wants me. It's a gift we Irish have."

"It's called blarney, Casey," said Maya. "And the Blarney Stone is *all* you'll ever be kissing." She turned back to Lucas. "We don't dare wear the rings near the temple for fear of bringing the stone guardians to life. Ryan is the only one of us besides the Professor who is trained in firearms."

So, Maya and Ryan donned hats and sunglasses and set out for the Kinkakuji Temple in western Nara, leaving Lucas, Des and Dunmoore to strategize or, as Dunmoore so aptly put it, "anxiously await their return." The Professor stood and stretched. "I'm rather worn. I think I'll catch forty winks or so. Wake me when they return, won't you?"

Five minutes later, Lucas taped a note on the bedroom door and whispered, "Let's hit it."

Des looked up from a hotel brochure, his brow furrowed. "Hit what?"

"I don't trust those two together, do you?"

Des gaped, then said with a shake of his head, "No telling what Ryan might do."

Lucas added, "And Maya's a little too self-confident for me. I think we better tag along. But first," Lucas removed the beribboned medallions from around his neck and stowed them and his and Des's rings with the other rings. He grinned at Des. "Let's do it."

As Maya and Ryan wended through the ancient city, Lucas and Des discreetly followed, disguised in baseball caps, sunglasses and raincoats. Fortunately, neither group encountered anything out of the ordinary as they made their way to the temple. Two stone *shishi* dogs still stood guard at the temple's entrance. Seated, their heads came to Maya's shoulders. And each had a green eye painted in the middle of its forehead, just as Maya's grandfather had described.

Maya and Ryan joined a tour group led by one of the temple docents. The docent explained to the gathered tourists – Des and Lucas having linked up at the back of the group – that the dogs had been the guardians of the temple since the early ninth century, although Kinkakuji Temple itself had originally been built in the sixth century, as a home for Prince Shotoku's mother.

"The ninth century? Right around the time the relics were stolen by the Dark Powers," Des whispered to Lucas.

Lucas nodded. He had been slightly nervous approaching the statues, but the stone dogs did not come to life. Leaving their rings at the hotel had been a good call once again.

Inside the temple, Maya acted as interpreter for Ryan, introducing him to the temple docents as a foreign student staying with her family for the summer session. Ryan greeted the docents in Japanese, saying, *"Konnichi-wa, doo utsukushii otera"* (good day, what a beautiful temple), as Maya had taught him.

Lucas had a hard time not snickering over the sound of Japanese spoken in a thick Irish brogue. He also delighted in Ryan's efforts at bowing, noting that Des was having an equally difficult time not bursting into laughter. Maya had explained at the hotel that in Japan it was traditional, nay *expected*, to bow upon meeting someone. The more respectable or high-ranking the person, the deeper the bow to acknowledge the other's position. While Maya had to slap Ryan on the arm to remind him to bow upon first entering the temple, he caught on quickly, bowing deeply and appropriately to the various docents. It worked, for the docents seemed pleased with Ryan's efforts and took great pains guiding Ryan and Maya around the temple.

At the conclusion of the tour, neither Lucas nor Des had seen the relic nor read any literature about it. Lucas stood behind a bamboo partition and strained to overhear Maya and Ryan's conversation. Maya had just broached the subject to a docent when Ryan whispered, "Something's up with those two guys in black. They're watching us, trying to overhear our conversation."

Lucas peered around the partition as Maya casually glanced over her shoulder. Two men stood nearby, watching. Dressed all in black, they each wore off-white rings on the little fingers of their left hands. Maya quickly thanked the temple docents and took Ryan's elbow, escorting him around the public areas at a leisurely pace. Lucas and Des kept up, and kept out of sight.

But Lucas didn't trust the two men in black. "Des, we gotta split up, or those two guys will be taking an interest in us next. You stay with this group, and I'll wander around with that one." He pointed to a group of four middle-aged white couples, overweight and in sneakers – the standard give-away of an American tourist. "We'll both keep an eye on Maya and Ryan."

Within minutes, the two men in black seemed to have given up interest in any of the Crusaders and were studying a newly arrived group of school children, instead. Maya and Ryan perched near the group of Americans admiring a painting, not noticing Lucas in his baseball cap and sunglasses. Maya commented to Ryan in a voice loud enough for the Americans to overhear – but not the suspicious guys in black – "The temple is magnificent. But I'm so disappointed that no one has mentioned the Eye of Buddha."

The Americans, with the exception of Lucas, looked over with interest. Lucas simply listened and smiled with approval when Ryan took the cue.

"Eye of Buddha?"

Maya said, "A famous relic. It's supposedly worth a fortune, and I'd always heard it was kept here. But now, I'm not so sure."

As if scripted, a man from the American tour group asked one of the docents about the Eye of Buddha only minutes later.

Though greatly surprised, the docent reluctantly admitted, "It is a relic of great value, both spiritually and monetarily. The priests of this temple are dedicated to its protection. Because of attempted thefts over the years, it is now kept in a private area."

"Bingo," Ryan whispered. They were standing not five feet from the Americans and the docent, almost directly behind Lucas.

"But we still don't know its location," Maya whispered back.

Lucas pulled his "Cowboys" cap lower on his head and turned slightly. Out of the corner of his eye, he saw a very old man — dressed in the orange robes of a priest — touch Ryan's left elbow. Ryan turned quickly, one fist raised, then stopped and lowered it to his side. The man spoke in a voice too low for Lucas to hear, but he saw Maya and Ryan exchange glances, then nod and follow the departing priest.

As Lucas turned, he almost bumped into the men in black. But they were now concentrating on the Americans. Lucas smiled. *Guess they overheard the questions about the Eye, too. Way to go, Maya.*

Lucas found Des and whispered, "Something's up, let's go."

They caught up with the others a minute later around the side of the temple. The old man leaned on Ryan's arm as he led them to a small gazebo, overlooking a pond and rock garden. Lucas and Des stood several yards away, hidden by towering bamboo. The priest asked Maya and Ryan, "So, you are curious about the Eye of Buddha?"

Ryan and Maya gaped.

"What do you mean?" said Ryan, recovering first. "What's a Buddha Eye?"

Nice try, thought Lucas, *but I don't think this guy's gonna buy it.*

The priest smiled. "You cannot deceive me so easily. I overheard you and the girl talking in the temple. A clever trick. And very wise not to ask the docents directly."

"Who are you?" asked Maya.

"A friend. One who would help you in your quest." The old man turned and looked over his shoulder at the bamboo grove where Lucas thought he and Des were well hidden. "Would help all four of you in your crusade."

Oh jeez, thought Lucas.

Maya said, "*Four* of us?"

"You two and your two friends there in the bamboo. Please, reveal yourselves."

Des frowned, his brow wrinkled with worry.

Lucas shrugged and said, "Red-handed. Come on." They stepped from the shadows of the bamboo.

"What are you two doing here?" said Maya, hands on her hip.

"Spying on us." Ryan's face reddened. "Stinking, slinking chancers!"

"How *dare* you –"

"So little time." The priest cut Maya off and beckoned to Des and Lucas. "Please."

Lucas and Des entered the gazebo. Maya and Ryan moved as far away from them as they could in the small enclosure.

"Good, good," said the priest, his bright green eyes aglow. "I have waited a long time to help ones such as you. As my father waited before me. And his father before him. We have always known the Eye did not belong here. Buddha is not pleased with its presence here."

"Who are you? What do you –," Lucas began, but the priest raised his hand and Lucas shut up.

"Listen and you will know where the Eye is kept. And what dangers await you. Do you know anything about the Eye of Buddha? Its great religious significance?"

Lucas and the others shook their heads.

The old man nodded. "Not much is known about the relic. But it is as significant to Buddhists as the Holy Grail and the Cloth of Turin are to Christians. In the sixth century, B.C., before Buddha departed from his lesser life on Earth, he commissioned a statue in his likeness made from the whitest of marbles. And in the center of his forehead he placed a third eye – made of the finest piece of jade in the world – which represents the soul. For only with the soul does an individual truly see others and the world around him. Not only is the Eye worth a fortune in worldly terms, but also it is of inestimable religious value, for Buddha is said to have endowed the Eye with absolute clarity of vision. He who possesses the Eye possesses the power to see into another's soul."

The old priest paused and closed his eyes.

Jeez, did he fall asleep? thought Lucas.

The priest opened his eyes and smiled directly at Lucas. "Patience, patience." He looked at the others. "The statue was placed in a great temple in India. Sometime later the Eye was taken from the statue, with Buddha's blessing, and placed in safekeeping in England with two other religious relics."

Ryan exclaimed, "The Holy Grail and The Hands of Allah!"

The priest nodded. "But centuries later, the three relics were stolen and separated. And the Eye ended up at this humble temple. For many centuries it was on display – until almost fifty years ago. I was a young man then, following in my father's and his father's footsteps as a priest. At that time, a man came near the temple and caused a great disruption. We took the Eye off display. It is now kept under lock and key in a small room on the west side of the temple. I have a map of its location."

"Fifty years ago?" Lucas asked. "That must have been your grandfather, Maya."

The old man took a map from inside his silk robe and laid it on his lap. He pointed to a small room marked with a green eye. "Here is the front of the temple. To get to the Eye, you must cross through the main room and out a side door to the back. It is the second room on the right as you follow the hallway. But it will not be an easy task for you to reclaim the Eye. The forces that brought the Eye to this temple are very powerful. They have convinced the priests that anyone attempting to steal the Eye must be killed. And they have provided the temple with great security."

Maya spoke in a grim voice, "Yes, we know the *shishi* temple dogs come to life."

The old man waved his hand in a dismissive gesture.

It's like he expected us to know this, Lucas thought.

The priest warned, "But that is not the only obstacle you must overcome. Two mighty ninjas also guard the Eye. Well-trained in the arts of death, they will prove formidable foes."

"Why are you telling us this?" asked Ryan. "What gives? Don't you want to keep the Eye here if it's so important to you?"

"I greatly desire that the Eye remain here," said the priest with a small sigh. "But Buddha does not. Buddha created the Eye to bring truth and enlightenment to the world, not the darkness that has descended. When the Eye is returned to its designated place, Buddha's will shall be done. And I sense that time has come."

"What do you suggest we do, sir?" asked Des, having finally stopped twisting his ring.

"We finish our night services at 10:00, and there is only one ninja on guard until 10:30. That is your best time to come. I am responsible for securing the temple doors after the other priests have left. I cannot leave the main doors unlocked because the ninja checks them every night. But there is a small door on the left side which I will leave open and pray to Buddha that the ninja neglects his duty."

Lucas said, "Please don't do anything that would raise suspicion, sir. We have another way of getting into the temple."

"Locks are not a problem for us."

The old man raised his snow-white eyebrows at Maya.

Finally, something's surprised him, Lucas thought.

The priest said, "As you prefer. I will spend the rest of the evening after services praying to Buddha for your success."

The old man slowly rose from the bench. Lucas could almost hear the man's bones creak, and he grimaced in sympathy.

The priest smiled at Lucas. "Simply the discomforts of old age." He turned to the others. "Return the way you came. I shall go the opposite. Be sure to leave a donation."

Both Maya and Ryan bowed deeply. Des followed suit. Lucas was the last – he gave an awkward bow. Curiously, the priest bowed deeply to them.

Maya kissed the old man's left cheek and said, "Thank you, Father."

The smiling priest hobbled down the steps.

The teens turned to leave, stopping when they heard the old man whisper, "Do not forget Buddha. Call on Him to assist you in time of need. Your quest is an honorable one, and Buddha always assists those engaged in virtuous endeavors." Then he was gone, hidden by the tall, spiked bamboo growing along the path.

"All right, slinkers, let's go," barked Ryan as he started down the steps.

Lucas said, "Not so fast. We don't want those guys back there putting two and two together. We came in pairs, we leave in pairs. Maya and Ryan should return to the temple. Des and I will cut out from here."

"He's got a point," said Maya. "Let's go." With a toss of her hair, she left.

Ryan scowled and said, "Later, slinkers," then sauntered away.

When Des and Lucas arrived back at the *ryokan*, Lucas gave two raps, one rap, three raps on the cottage door. A falsetto voice called from inside. "Who is it?"

"Crusaders one and two," said Des, giving the code they had agreed upon in advance before Maya and Ryan had left for the temple.

Dunmoore opened the door and exhaled a sigh of relief. He tucked his pistol in the waistband of his slacks. "You've got some explaining to do. Where are the others?" He peered around the doorway.

Lucas said, "They should be along shortly. Where'd you pick up the girly voice, Prof?"

"Quite the wit, Luke. Now, would one of you like to tell me just what in the Queen's name you thought you were doing?"

"Why don't we wait for the others, Prof? I gotta to use the restroom," said Lucas.

"I'll get us something to drink." Des sped into the kitchen.

Five minutes later, Dunmoore had finally cornered Lucas and Des in the living room when another succession of raps sounded at the door. Dunmoore withdrew his pistol. "Who is it?" he asked in the same high voice.

"Crusaders one and two," replied Maya. She entered with Ryan and tried to sit down, but they were bombarded with questions from Dunmoore.

"Give us a bloody minute, mate!" Ryan turned to Maya. "Want something to drink?"

"Yes, thank you." She smiled.

"You two best of friends, now? The thief and the princess?" Lucas leaned against the couch with arms folded and what he hoped was a smirk on his face. *A smirk to hide your jealousy*, the little voice said. *Shove it*, he told the voice.

"Shove it," said Ryan, returning with two bottles of sparkling water. He handed one to Maya and took a seat next to her on the couch. "Go ahead, Maya, tell the Prof."

Maya did, finishing with, "That's pretty much it."

"Incredible!" exclaimed Dunmoore. "Who do you think the old man was? Do you think he can be trusted?"

"I don't know who he is, Professor," Maya replied, "but I believe him. I could feel the goodness in him."

Ryan nodded. "That mate was all right."

"I think so, too," said Des.

"What about you, Luke?" Dunmoore asked.

Lucas looked at his ring, then at Dunmoore. "Too bad I couldn't take the ring with me. I would have known for certain, then."

"Hard for a chancer to trust anyone, right?"

"That's enough, Ryan." Dunmoore spoke in a surprisingly harsh tone of voice, then turned to Lucas and asked gently, "What does your gut tell you?"

"I...*liked* him. I think we can trust him." Lucas sighed. "Don Vasquez said there would be good powers to help us out." He nodded at Dunmoore. "Like you."

"Yes, well, uh...," Dunmoore blushed. "That's enough for me." He rose from his seat. "If we expect to tackle the temple tonight, we best finish our preparations."

"I have a question," said Des. "What exactly is a ninja?"

Maya replied, "One trained in *ninjitsu* – in death and deception. Ninjas first offered their services as spies and assassins to the shoguns and daimyo lords, and sometimes to great Samurai families. Because they worked almost always at night and dressed completely in black, people believed they could make themselves invisible. But they did not have the same loyalty to their lord or shogun as the Samurai did. And there is no code for ninjas as there is for Samurai."

Des frowned and began twisting his ring. "I don't think I want to fight a ninja."

"Suck it up, guys, 'cause there ain't no getting around it," said Ryan.

Lucas added in a grim voice, "Let's just make sure we get *through* it."

Chapter Thirty-Three

Beasts of Battle

The specter of fierce warriors inspired the Crusaders to dress in traditional ninja garb – black cotton pants and top and black sneakers. Although Dunmoore felt foolish, he conceded that black was less conspicuous and that the clothing was more suitable for fighting...or fleeing.

"And it's free, Professor. Courtesy of the old five-finger discount." A grinning Ryan wriggled his fingers.

He's thrilled to be back in his element, Lucas thought.

Maya, Ryan and Des had used their rings to gain access to a store specializing in both traditional and contemporary "warrior" gear. Maya had explained that they couldn't risk using the Professor's credit cards.

"I hope we can steal the Eye of Buddha as easily as you stole our outfits," joked Lucas.

Des said, "Don't forget Maya's weapon."

Maya demonstrated the pair of *nunchaku* or nunchuks – two carved blocks of wood attached by a short length of chain. "They are quite effective. I learned to use them in *karate*, to supplement my *tae kwon do* training."

"I hope you will not need them tonight," Dunmoore said. "Or the sword."

Lucas said, "I hope so, too, Prof," as he clasped the sword from the cathedral. "But now that we know about the powers of the ring, it makes no sense to waste them."

It was 10:15. Hopefully the priests had cleared out of the temple after evening services. The Crusaders stood in a circle in the *ryokan* and repeated the traveling spell. The interior walls of the Kinkakuji temple materialized around them. Several electric sconces on the walls gave off a dim light, and moonlight filtered through the windows. Dunmoore left the circle first – pistol cocked – and surveyed the perimeter of the room. Upon his return, he whispered, "Quickly."

The priest had said that the room housing the Eye of Buddha was small, and even fitting three people inside would be a close call. Lucas, Des and Maya repeated the traveling spell Dunmoore had taught them. They reappeared in a tiny room barely the size of a broom closet and found a solitary solid gold case on an onyx stand – locked. Des wriggled out of his backpack and withdrew a gold fountain pen.

They knew that with the rings' power, an ordinary object became extraordinary. And in such cramped quarters, Lucas's sword would be too cumbersome. The three Crusaders put their ring hands on Dunmoore's pen and focused it on the lock. A green laser beam shot from the pen. The lock began to steam and sizzle until, with a loud click, the door swung open.

Maya gave a small, "Ooh."

Des grinned and whispered, "The pen *is* mightier than the sword."

Lucas simply stared with open mouth. The Eye of Buddha was a huge jade stone – almond-shaped – nestled on a stand of gold, lined with the blackest of velvets.

Suddenly, they heard shouting, then shots rang out.

"Grab it!" Lucas yelled.

Des struggled in the tight quarters to stash the relic in his rucksack.

"Back to the main room," Lucas ordered. He stuck his ring hand out. Des put his on top.

Maya kept her hand to her side. "We don't know where they are. What if we land on the ninja? Or the temple dog? Let's go to Merlin first and get rid of the Eye."

A scream.

Holy Jeez, that sounds like Ryan, thought Lucas. He shouted, "We don't have time!"

Des tried the door to the chamber. "It's locked."

"The pen!" Lucas said. With the pen-laser beam, they destroyed the lock and rushed down the hallway. Only to run smack into another locked door. Again, they used the pen to gain entrance to the main temple. Dunmoore stood over Ryan, who lay crumpled on the floor, moaning and cradling his bloodied left arm. Lucas heard a snort and turned. *Oh, jeez!*

One of the temple dogs come to life now circled Dunmoore and Ryan, ready to pounce. It was a huge beast, with a glowing green eye in the middle of its forehead and an enormous mouth with razor sharp teeth, blood dripping from them. Lucas raised the sword. Des and Maya placed their ring hands on his. A beam of light shot from the sword and felled the beast.

Dunmoore shouted, "Watch out behind you!"

A powerful man in black flew through the air, knocking them apart. Lucas struggled to his feet and went after the sword, which had gone clattering across the temple floor. He heard Vasquez' voice – "Duck *mi hijo!*" – and dove to the floor. A "starfish" blade screamed past his left ear. He heard Maya shout a battle cry in Japanese and saw her leap at the ninja, spinning her nunchuks.

The ninja turned to face the slight girl, a smile of pure evil on his face. He unleashed another blade, which Maya easily ducked, then another, and another. Maya managed to avoid them all.

"Yes, Maya!" Lucas cheered.

The ninja gave Lucas a venomous glare, then leaped at Maya in a classic karate kick. But Maya was too quick and dodged his attack, landing a blow to his crotch with her nunchuks.

The ninja screamed once, then collapsed. He writhed on the floor, moaning softly.

Lucas cringed. *Nice hit.*

By this time, Des had retrieved the sword and rushed over to Ryan and Dunmoore. Lucas joined them. Ryan was in agony, with a nasty gash on his arm.

Lucas knelt beside Ryan, "Grab hold of the sword."

Ryan kept his ring hand on his bleeding arm. "Let's get out of here!"

Des said, "We can't leave Maya!" a look of horror on his face.

"The ninja's done for. Maya can handle it until we come back!" Ryan insisted.

Maya screamed.

Lucas jumped to his feet. Maya lay on the floor, curled in a fetal position, the nunchuks beside her. The recovered ninja stood not far from her and sprang high in the air to inflict the final blow.

Ryan screamed "No!" and placed his hand on the sword.

In mid-leap, the ninja turned and smiled.

We'll wipe that damn smile from your face, thought Lucas.

The green beam knocked the ninja almost across the room, where he fell to the floor, motionless.

Des rushed to Maya's side. Before Lucas could move, he heard a low, menacing growl – one that a wolf makes before the kill – and the hairs on his entire body rose as one. A second temple dog slunk down the main aisle, yellow teeth bared. Lucas heard a second, fainter growl. The first temple dog began to rouse itself.

"The sword doesn't kill them!" Des shouted.

Lucas heard the panic in Des's voice. Then heard the old priest's calm voice in his head: *Remember Buddha. Pray to Buddha.* Lucas yelled, "The Eye. Use the Eye!"

Des rose from Maya's side and grabbed the Eye from his pack. But he was now separated from the others, and the first temple dog was headed his way, blocking the path. "What do I do?" he screamed.

"Hold still!" Dunmoore fired at the dog, but it barely flinched from the bullets and did not stray from its determined advance on the panicked Des and unconscious Maya.

Lucas heard another voice in his head – gravelly and majestic: *You must have patience and fortitude.*

Lucas spun around, searching for the library lions. *You've got to be kidding me?* The beasts' ribbons twirled around his neck, the medallions lightly slapping his chest. Lucas grabbed the gleaming gold discs and felt a surge of energy, a pulsing. *Their names. It's their names!*

The first temple dog was almost upon Des. Lucas could hear its rumbling growl, could see the saliva sliding from its curled lips. He held the medallions aloft and screamed, "Patience! Fortitude! Help us!"

In a blinding flash of light, the two lions appeared in the Temple and attacked the wild *shishi* dogs. The Temple's wooden foundation seemed to rock from the battle between the supernatural beasts. Fur, blood and spittle flew everywhere! Roars of fury and cries of pain echoed throughout the main worship area.

Patience – or was it Fortitude? – hit the first temple dog in the gut with its massive front paws and curling claws. The dog tumbled across the floor and thudded into a wall. Lucas could see four thin lines of red spring up on the beast's torso, where the lion's claws had sliced into it.

ROAR!

Lucas whipped his head around, and saw the other majestic lion shake the second temple dog from his shoulder. Blood poured from the tawny coat, and Lucas thought he saw muscle and bone exposed. He winced.

Although the wounded lion had flung the second temple dog from its back, the dog landed upright and now leaped onto the other lion, with an ear-splitting *GROWL!* Patience slashed the dog's snout and opened its mouth to rip into the now-whimpering dog's throat when the first dog sank its teeth into the lion's right haunch.

The lion's howl of distress sent shudders through Lucas. Fortitude sprang to Patience's aide, but the injured lion was limping badly. *We have to **do** something!* A hand grabbed his shoulder, and Lucas screamed! He swung his arm wildly and knocked his attacker to the floor. When he dropped down to throttle the ninja, he saw it was Des.

In the ensuing turmoil, Des had managed to rejoin Lucas and Ryan. Lucas grabbed Des by the shoulders and dragged him the few feet to where Ryan sat, cradling his arm and staring wide-eyed at the battle. "Hands on the Eye!" Lucas commanded.

They aimed the jade Eye at the dogs. This time, *two* brilliant green beams shot from the Eye, targeting the painted green eyes of the temple dogs. The dogs shrieked in agony, then disappeared in smoke, leaving behind the same stench as the dragon from the cathedral.

Lucas dropped the relic and raced to the lions. "You saved our lives!" He stopped in horror.

The majestic beasts' beautiful coats were streaked with blood and gore, their normally bright eyes were dim. Fortitude lay on his side, his breathing frightfully shallow.

"Your quick thinking saved your lives, Boy," responded an exhausted Patience, who stood on three wobbly legs, his right hind leg trembling in the air.

Des knelt by Fortitude's side. "You are hurt!" He stroked the honey-colored lion's matted fur.

Fortitude murmured between ragged breaths, "Our ribbons."

Patience bowed his head. Lucas placed one ribbon around the lion's massive head, then gently slid the other ribbon over Fortitude's mane. Lucas blinked, then grinned. Within seconds, the lions sat purring, their wounds completely healed – coats gleaming and eyes glistening.

"Those ribbons are brill!" exclaimed Des.

Lucas threw his arms around a now-unscarred Fortitude. "You're okay!" He could feel the lion's warm breath upon his shoulder, could hear its gentle purring. He released his grasp and grinned, then caressed the ribbon's medallion.

"Can we borrow these, again?"

Fortitude shook his head.

Lucas couldn't help the sinking feeling of dismay in his gut. "But what if we need you in the future? How will we call upon you?" He held tight to the smooth, gold circle.

"That is not for us to say," replied Patience. "Our task is complete."

Reluctantly, Lucas let go of the medallion and stepped away from the lion.

"Good-bye Crusaders," said Patience.

"And good luck," added Fortitude.

They disappeared in a flash of light. The Temple stood empty of lions and wild dogs, eerily quiet. *Too quiet*, thought Lucas.

Des gasped.

Lucas spun around, expecting more monsters or ninjas. *I knew we were gonna need those ribbons!* But they were alone.

"What is it?" asked Dunmoore. "What's wrong?"

Des squeaked out, "Maya."

"Maya!" When Lucas turned, he understood.

Maya was gone!

Chapter Thirty-Four

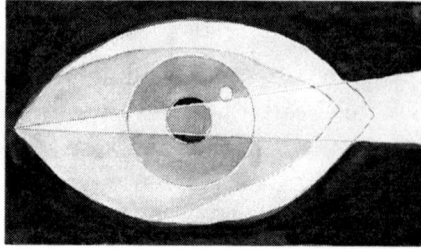

Lessons of The Temple

The foursome rushed over to where the fallen ninja still lay, breathing hard. *There are Maya's nunchuks. Where is she?* Lucas felt his heart pound in his chest as he looked wildly around the temple for a glimpse of Maya.

Muffled shouts sounded in the distance.

Dunmoore urged, "We must leave now."

"What about Maya?" asked Des, almost in tears. "We can't leave her!"

Dunmoore placed his hands on Des's shoulders and looked him squarely in the eyes. "We don't know where Maya is. And we are in no condition to fight any more agents of the Dark Powers. It takes three of you to use the Eye, and Ryan is hurt. Our being captured, or killed, will not help Maya. You see that, don't you?"

Des looked down, brushed tears from his eyes and nodded his head.

"What about the ninja?" Ryan asked.

His voice was soft and weak. *Not good,* thought Lucas. *Maya's vanished and Ryan's hurt. Not good at all.* Lucas made a decision. "He comes with us. We need to learn more about the Dark Powers. And where Maya is."

They held hands in a circle, the unconscious ninja's hand clasped in the middle.

"To the hotel, first," Lucas said.

"What? Why on Earth—" Dunmoore began.

"We can't bring an agent of the Dark Powers to Lake Windermere." Lucas spoke firmly.

Just then, a huge Asian man and a second ninja pounded into the room, not ten feet from them! But their battle cries fell on deaf ears because the Crusaders disappeared. General Zheng rubbed his eyes, looked around the temple, then fell to his knees, screaming in rage.

———————

The rustling of woodland creatures and whoops of night owls in Nara Koen ceased abruptly within seconds of their arrival back at the *ryokan*. So unnerving was the stillness that Dunmoore immediately broke from the circle and searched the suite. No intruders. They bound the ninja's hands behind his back and his legs around the bottom of a chair. Dunmoore then tended to Ryan's injuries.

The young Irish boy quietly groaned with pain while Dunmoore disinfected and bandaged his gashed arm.

"He needs a doctor," Lucas whispered to Dunmoore.

"As soon as we finish with our ninja friend here," Dunmoore replied grimly.

Ryan reclined on the couch. Lucas plumped pillows around him to try to ease his discomfort. The ninja regained consciousness, and Dunmoore began the interrogation. "Who are you and for whom do you work? Where have they taken Maya?"

The ninja moaned softly.

Lucas said, "Maybe he doesn't speak English?"

Dunmoore repeated his questions in Japanese. The ninja said nothing. He refused to even look at them.

"Ask him again," Des said, squirming in his seat.

But the ninja remained silent, staring into space. Suddenly, Dunmoore slapped the ninja hard across the face. "Do you understand this language, scum?"

Dunmoore's violent outburst shocked Lucas. The ninja spit out a torrent of Japanese – his tone venomous, eyes narrowed. Dunmoore shuddered once and looked away.

"What did he say?" Lucas asked.

"Something about surviving pain worse than we 'weak cowards' could ever inflict. Something about our slow, torturous deaths." Dunmoore struck the ninja across the face again, harder. Blood began to trickle from the ninja's mouth. "He shall see exactly what pain we are capable of inflicting." Dunmoore raised his hand a third time.

"No!" Des grabbed Dunmoore's arm. "We cannot do this. There must be another way."

"He's right, Prof," said Lucas. "We can't torture him."

"And you?" Dunmoore turned to Ryan. "You were almost killed in the Temple. And this piece of filth would have finished off Maya. Don't you want revenge?"

Lucas said, "That's not what the quest is about."

Dunmoore ignored Lucas. He stared at Ryan, waiting.

"Bloody right I want revenge," Ryan said, grimacing as his arm hit the side of the couch. "But not this way."

Dunmoore scowled. "Then you had better think of another way quickly, or we will simply have to leave him with his nasty secrets. Damn his soul to hell."

"*Soul.* That's it!"

"What are you going on about, Luke?" asked Dunmoore.

"The old priest told us about the Eye, that it's a kind of doorway to the soul," Lucas explained. "Why don't we use the Eye on him?"

The ninja trembled at the sight of the holy relic, averting his eyes. The three boys focused the piece of jade on the ninja while Dunmoore repeated the three questions. The ninja sat transfixed and answered the first two, as if in a trance. But his answers shocked Lucas and the others; even Dunmoore – the seasoned, undercover operative – paled at what they learned.

Each human agent of the Dark Powers wore the same ring on the pinkie of his left hand. An agent received the ring when he passed a most insidious initiation test into the society of the Dark Powers: killing a healthy baby and taking one of its ribs. For the ring was fashioned from the rib bone of the murdered infant. And it had to be an infant – an innocent – to signify one's loyalty to the Dark Powers, to their purity of evil.

The Dark Powers claimed more initiates each day...many, many more.

But of Maya's whereabouts, the ninja knew nothing.

Lucas almost spat at the vile murderer. "We should have let you beat the crap out of him, Prof."

"I'd enjoy doing it, Luke."

Lucas stared at Dunmoore. *He's serious. I don't think I like this part of the Prof.* He shook his head. "We should get back to Lake Windermere."

"What do we do with him?" Ryan pointed to the ninja and winced at the pain in his arm.

Dunmoore said, "We bloody well can't leave him here."

"I've got an idea," offered Des.

Within minutes, they had packed and checked out of the Edo-San and whirled back to Novgorod, Russia. There, in the Cathedral of St. Sophia, they left the ninja, still bound to the chair, a rag loosely stuffed in his mouth to muffle his curses.

As they formed the traveling circle to depart for Lake Windermere, Dunmoore stepped from the group and ripped the bone ring off the assassin's pinkie. He wrapped it in one of his handkerchiefs, secured it in his pocket and rejoined the circle. "One never knows." Then, they traveled to summon Merlin.

———————

It must be my imagination, Lucas thought when Merlin's apparition appeared on the old oak. *He seems...clearer...no, bigger? No.* Lucas shook away his thoughts and concentrated on the wizard's words.

"Well done, Crusaders." The Eye of Buddha vanished into Merlin's ghostly arms. "But something is amiss?"

Lucas said, "We need to get Ryan to a doctor."

"Maya's gone!" Des cried. "You have to do something!"

Merlin closed his eyes for a few moments. Finally, he nodded. "Even with only two of the relics...I feel it can be done. Master Casey, come forward."

"I'm fine."

Dunmoore placed his hands on Ryan's shoulders and pushed him forward. "Let him attend to your wounds, Ryan."

"No! I can take it. I want the pain."

Dunmoore said, "Don't be a bloody fool."

"You're no help to us with your arm like that," Lucas reminded him.

"I wasn't any help back there." Ryan spoke softly, his eyes to the ground.

What the hell is he talking about?, thought Lucas.

"Come forward, Master Casey." The wizard's tone of voice was one Lucas figured even Ryan couldn't disobey. And he didn't. When Ryan stood only inches from Merlin's apparition, the wizard stretched out his arms from the oak and placed a hand on either side of Ryan's head. He murmured an incantation, and a bright blue light emerged from his hands, bathing Ryan. After a minute, Merlin's arms melded back into the oak tree. The light faded.

"You've learned a powerful lesson, Master Casey. Although you hesitated for a moment, in the end you acted with courage and conviction. Margaret Anne Ryan would be proud."

Dunmoore unwrapped the bandage on Ryan's arm. The gash had healed completely.

Des said in a voice tinged with panic, "What about Maya? We have to find her. What if she's hurt?"

"I can do nothing about Mistress Hosokawa. Yet."

"But we can't just go on as if it didn't happen! As if she doesn't matter!"

Merlin responded in a gentle tone. "Master Moboto, do you not see that only by completing the quest will you have any chance of saving Mistress Hosokawa? She is still alive. Her ring is not destroyed. For I sense the rings. And my Crusaders."

Still alive? But for how much longer?, Lucas thought.

"When all three relics are reunited here at Lake Windermere," Merlin waved his arm toward the lake, "the Dark Powers will be destroyed. And they will have no power over Mistress Hosokawa. Her only hope now lies in your completing the quest. Will you do so?"

Des nodded but did not speak. Lucas could see the tears in his friend's eyes, and he put an arm around his shoulder and whispered, "We'll find her. No matter what."

Des replied through tears, "She was doing so well until...what happened?"

"I'm what happened," said Ryan. "I said we should just get out of there. That Maya could take care of herself until we came back. I never meant to *leave* her. It's just that damn dog...." He paused. "It was me."

Lucas could tell that Ryan was now struggling to hold back tears. *I know that feeling, man. No crying in front of other people, especially guys.* Still, Ryan's odd confession confused him. Lucas said, "Even if you had wanted to leave Maya, you couldn't control the ninja."

"Tell them, Master Casey. Impart the lesson."

Ryan stared at the sorcerer for a few long moments. Suddenly, the teen's hazel eyes lit up. "When I wanted to leave Maya at the Temple, I sapped our collective powers. I separated us. Just like the relics were separated. Right?"

"Yes, Master Casey. That is the lesson of the Temple. But in the end, you did not leave Maya. You overcame your pain and fear and stood strong with the others. And that is what saved her. Always remember, Master Casey, there is no valor without fear. A brave man knows what to fear, and it is only acting in the face of that fear that a man is truly courageous."

Ryan took a deep breath and turned to the others. "Will you forgive me?"

Perhaps more than anything else, this most unlikely of pleas stunned Lucas. For a moment, no one moved. Then, Lucas smiled and shrugged. "Nothing to forgive."

Merlin asked, "What other lessons have you learned, Crusaders?"

They looked at each other, clueless.

Dunmoore held his Rolex to his ear, frowning, and said as he wound it, "Something's been nibbling at me since we left that wretched creature in Novgorod, but I can't quite put my finger on it."

Then it dawned on Lucas. "The relics! The power of the rings. *Our* power. We're at our most powerful when we use the power of the rings on the relics! Remember at the Temple? We weren't able to stop the dogs with bullets, but the power of the Eye destroyed them. And remember back in the Cathedral?" Lucas could barely stand still, he was so excited. "Remember how not even the power of the sword was enough to slay the dragon? It took our using the Holy Grail!"

Des said with dawning comprehension, "And we got the ninja to talk only by using the Eye."

"What did he tell you?" asked Merlin.

Dunmoore repeated the ninja's hideous revelation.

Merlin heaved a great sigh. "Over my years of imprisonment, I heard rumors from time to time about the rings of the Dark Powers. Foolishly, even I did not believe them, did not believe man could be so monstrously wicked."

"But what about Hitler and the Nazis? Surely, that is enough to convince anyone of man's capability of extreme evil."

"Yes, Professor Dunmoore, you are correct. And if memory serves me well – which it unfortunately does – throughout the ages man has been susceptible to great depravity. The Spanish Inquisition, the Christians and the lions, are but two of thousands. It was foolish of me to hope the rumors of those rings were simply lies spread by the Dark Powers to enhance their reputation for maleficence. I had hoped, however, that my Crusaders would not uncover the truth."

"But isn't it better for us to know, sir?"

"Sometimes the truth, Master Moreno, can sap the energy and courage of even the bravest of men."

"No, sir. Nothing can stop me from finishing the quest and defeating the Dark Powers. Nothing." Lucas crossed his arms and stood up straighter.

"Hear, hear," said Dunmoore, placing his arm about Lucas's shoulders.

Des moved to the other side of Lucas and said quietly, "More than ever, I fight to save my family. And Maya."

Ryan joined last. "I will not abandon the quest or my...friends. Never again."

Merlin's image began to fade. "Very well, Crusaders. You now embark upon the last part of your journey. The Dark Powers are well aware of you now, and well will be prepared for your assault on The Hands of Allah. Do not forget the lessons. Do not forget what brought you together. Do not forget why those who went before you failed. All I can ask of you, all you can ask of yourselves, is to be true to the quest. I bid you Godspeed."

The wizard vanished.

Chapter Thirty-Five

Plans for Egypt

The mist once again began to uncurl itself from around the gnarled oak tree on the shore of the lake. The sighing wind-man fell silent.

"I wish the wiz wouldn't fade so quickly," Ryan complained.

"Yes," agreed Dunmoore. "Wishing us Godspeed is all well and good, but I would rather he had given us more advice on how to tackle this last part of the quest."

Lucas said, "Maybe he didn't have any advice, Prof. You know, lessons along the way."

"But he *knew* the lessons, mate. If he'd let us in on them before, I'd never have...Maya'd still be here." Ryan spoke in a bitter tone. "Just let me get me hands on those bastards."

I know the feeling. If they ever catch the guys who torched the YMCA..., but Lucas let the thought slip away.

Des argued, "He couldn't tell us. I think the lessons have to be learned by us, or we won't take it to heart."

"Still," said Dunmoore, "I am as weary of Merlin's riddles as Ryan."

Back at the Spenser place, they came up with ways to outsmart Mordred and his Dark Powers. First, they had to "borrow" someone's credit card; it wasn't safe to use Dunmoore's, and they were almost out of cash. They didn't have to buy plane tickets, but hotels usually required payment. So, Des, Ryan and Lucas traveled to the top floor of the Grosvenor House in London, where Lucas duplicated his immensely successful false fire alarm trick.

After observing the various guests evacuating their rooms – hands over ears to dull the blaring siren – Lucas pointed out a middle-aged couple exiting room 703. After the couple entered the stairwell, the boys traveled into the now-empty room and lifted a credit card from the husband's wallet, along with the man's passport, before disappearing from the room.

Lucas explained, "The Prof will have to check into the hotel, and they require passports, right? This guy, David Thompson, is the right age, height and coloring as the Prof." He showed the passport photo. "The Prof can say he now wears contacts, lost some weight, you know."

Dunmoore placed several calls. One to the Cairo Sheraton hotel, reserving a room in his new name with his Platinum American Express card. Dunmoore told the hotel that he would be arriving early the next morning on a business trip and needed to reserve a room for the previous night since the check-in time was noon. He explained he wanted to rest and refresh himself before a late morning meeting. The Sheraton assured him it had available rooms. Mr. Thompson was now registered in room 534.

Dunmoore next placed a call to Joanna, his fiancée, asking her to reserve four rooms for his group at Hadrian's Hotel in Carlisle. He lied that his credit cards had been stolen, and he could not get replacements soon enough. He also reported with great enthusiasm that they had stumbled upon a great mystery surrounding Merlin and were terribly excited about the prospect of spending two days exploring Hadrian's Wall and the surrounding region.

"She was frightfully upset at first," he told the boys, "because she had called the Round Table Inn and been informed that we had checked out several days ago! In my several messages to her, it seems I'd forgotten to mention that fact." He shook his head. "I'll have quite the time making it up to her."

Lucas said, "It's safer for her if she doesn't know where we are. Or where we've been."

"And if the Dark Powers are bugging your phone, maybe they'll go off on the wrong track, and we'll have more time to get The Hands of Allah," added Ryan.

"Let's just hope it *isn't* located in Carlisle, rather than Cairo," Des noted with a wry grin.

The third, and perhaps most important plan, involved recruiting a sympathetic stranger – a good force – to aid them in the last leg of their journey. As Dunmoore so bluntly put it, "Even if by sheer chance we manage to throw the Dark Powers off track with my call to Joanna, agents are certain to be watching for us in Egypt." They needed someone unconnected with them to find out the location of the relic. But who?

Family members and close friends were out – the Dark Powers knew too much about them. Dunmoore said, "The ideal candidate would also be somewhat familiar with Cairo, so as not to arouse suspicion."

Lucas wondered aloud, "Maybe she'd do it."

"Who?" asked Des.

"Karen, an airline stewardess I met on the plane from Texas. She's cool, on vacation, and no one would connect her to any of us. *And*, she mentioned she was going to Egypt next week to visit a friend who works there." Lucas turned to Dunmoore. "How many days have we been on the road?"

Dunmoore thought a moment. "Four days? Has it been only *four* days since I picked you up at Heathrow?"

"Feels like forever, doesn't it?" Lucas grinned. "Karen should still be with her cousins in Bath."

They decided then and there to audition Karen for an "Assistant Crusader" position.

Finally, the last and most dangerous idea to come out of the brainstorm session involved the use of the ninja's ring. If all else failed, if they could not locate The Hands of Allah on their own or with Karen's help, Dunmoore would place the ring on his finger and attempt to ascertain the exact whereabouts of the relic. "The ring's the key to *something*," said Dunmoore, silencing the teens' objections with a stern, "And my father was killed in Egypt. I must be permitted to avenge his death."

That decided, Lucas telephoned Karen and asked if she could meet with him and his "Uncle" Morgan that evening. A delighted

Karen suggested dinner at a pub around the corner from her cousins' house. Dunmoore knew the Bath area – his elderly aunt and uncle lived there – and knew of an abandoned lot to where the Crusaders could safely travel without arousing suspicion.

That evening, they formed their traveling circle and repeated the spell. Although the lot was abandoned, a homeless man was using it as his neighborhood bar. The dumbfounded man simply stared, midway through a swig from a bottle, the cheap wine running onto his lap.

Dunmoore took a five-pound note from his wallet and placed it on the ground beside the man, securing it with a stone. "Sorry to have frightened you, sir." He turned to the others. "The pub's about a block from here."

Lucas kept glancing back: The wino's rheumy eyes followed them across the lot to the street. Only then did he faint.

When they arrived at the pub, Lucas went in first to find Karen. She sat at the bar near the entrance, nursing a pint of Guinness. The burly bartender grabbed Lucas's arm. "Hold on there, mate," the bartender growled. "You don't look to be all of sixteen, much less legal."

"Peter!" Karen appeared at Lucas's side. "That isn't a very friendly way to treat one of my cousins from the States." Karen hugged Lucas. "You look wonderful, hon," she drawled. "Where's your uncle?"

Lucas said, "There's been a slight change of plan. Any place here where five of us could talk privately?"

Karen's eyes widened. "Five? I reckon that qualifies as a change in plan."

"It's really important. We...I need your help."

Karen nodded. "All right, hon, you asked for it, you got it. There's a back room. Go get your friends. Peter will show you the way." Karen turned and spoke to the bartender.

Lucas darted outside. Within seconds, the four Crusaders entered the pub and followed Peter's pointing arm. They found Karen in the back room, sipping her beer. Lucas knew she had to have been surprised to see two other teenagers, but she didn't let on. *Poker face. That's good*, thought Lucas.

Dunmoore gave her a hug. "It's a pleasure to see you again, Karen."

"Nice to see you, too, Morgan," Karen replied, her smile wide and toothy.

Lucas frowned at the smile.

What did you expect, buddy? He's rich, good-looking, knows stuff. Why wouldn't she go for him? It was that pestering little voice.

Just shut up, okay? Lucas thought. He could have sworn he heard the voice chuckle.

Lucas closed the door to the private dining room. "What we're about to tell you is pretty incredible. Unbelievable."

"A matter of great importance. To all mankind." Des wore his "solemn" face and began his now-ritualistic twisting of his ring.

Ryan said, "We got proof." He patted the three items he had brought along – Grandma Maggie's journal, Tony Moreno's letter, and the letter from Maya's grandfather to Akira Tanaka.

"All we ask of you is an open mind. A *very* open mind. Can you do that?" asked Dunmoore.

"Yes, Morgan." Her eyes twinkled with what Lucas thought of as amused puzzlement.

"It's going to take some time for us to explain all that has happened," Dunmoore said. "The less interruptions, the better. Why don't you begin, Luke?"

"It's *Lucas.*" *Especially with Karen.* Lucas sat next to her.

Except for a barmaid bringing beverages and dinner, there were no interruptions. By the time they reached the recapture of the Eye of Buddha, it had been almost two hours. Lucas concluded, "Now we're left with finding the Hands of Allah in Egypt. That's where you come in. If you're willing."

Karen stared at her hands twisting the napkin in her lap while the Crusaders waited in silence. Finally, she looked up at Lucas. "I must be out of my mind, hon, but I believe you. I don't see as how I have any other choice."

"Thank you!" said Des excitedly.

Dunmoore took Karen's hands in his. "You can see how happy, and relieved, you've made us. We can't thank you enough, but we don't have much time. We can finish our discussions at the cabin near Lake Windermere."

Karen withdrew her hands from his. "You mean you want me to go with y'all *now?*"

"We *need* you to go with us now," Dunmoore said.

"Hold on, folks. As I understand it, y'all want me to help you locate this relic somewhere in Egypt, is that right?"

Lucas answered, "You have a friend who works in Cairo."

"But if I'm to go to Egypt with y'all, I have to make certain arrangements. I need to let my relatives know I'll be leaving sooner than intended. I need to contact Richard – my archaeologist friend – and let him know I'm getting in sooner than expected. I need to make arrangements with the airline. I need to pack. I need –"

"I have a suggestion," Dunmoore interrupted. "Why don't you see for yourself? Come to Lake Windermere with us now, with the power of the rings, and then we can discuss what arrangements need to be made? What do you say?"

"Please, Karen," Lucas pleaded.

Ryan and Des chimed in, "*Please?*"

Karen shook her head, but she was smiling. "I must be crazy, but let's give it a go."

———————

They walked from the pub to the lot to find the homeless man gone. Dunmoore said, "I don't suppose we scared him terribly much. He had the wits about him to take the five pounds."

They formed their traveling circle, the boys said the spell in unison, and the group materialized in the living room of the Spenser cabin.

One glance and Karen collapsed into one of the big stuffed chairs. "Oh my lord."

"It takes a little getting used to at first," Des said softly, patting her hand.

Dunmoore appeared at her side a moment later with a glass of water. "Drink this."

She closed her eyes, took a few sips, then opened her eyes. "Anything stronger than water, Morgan? Scotch?"

Once Karen settled down with her scotch on the rocks, the Crusaders described their plan. After they traveled to the Cairo Sheraton, Karen would surprise her archaeologist friend with a telephone call, announcing her (impetuous) arrival in Cairo, and asking him to guide her around the city. She would first have to make a stop at the Cairo General Hospital, to look up an old friend of her father's, a Dr. Habib.

If Karen could locate Dr. Habib, she would try to arrange a meeting with him and the Crusaders. They hoped to obtain that part of Jafar Moboto's journal that he had mailed to Dr. Habib years ago – and which they believed contained the location of The Hands of Allah.

Of equal importance, Karen had to be on guard for agents of the Dark Powers – watching for the telltale pinkie ring of bone. They had told her about the Dark Powers, and she had examined the ninja's ring. Suitably horrified, Karen had expressed an even greater willingness to help them on their quest. She also had to try not to arouse any suspicion.

Karen smiled. "I play a very convincing dumb blond."

At midnight, the Crusaders and their recruit formed the traveling circle and said the spell. The whirlwind deposited them at the Sheraton Hotel in Cairo, Egypt, city of Pharaohs, pyramids and the Nile – and the last holy relic, or so they prayed.

Chapter Thirty-Six

Shadows of Selves

"AAAIIIEEEE!" The scream tumbled out of the young woman's broken teeth, over cracked, bloody lips, as the steam rose from her searing skin.

Intaki removed the red-hot poker from his victim's left shoulder. A coiled serpent was now branded into her flesh. The torturer hiccupped with glee. He tore a rag from around her waist and positioned the poker over her right thigh.

"*Arrête, imbecile!*" Elaine LaCroix screamed through the bars of the adjoining cell.

"Enough, Intaki. We don't want to kill our little guest." Mordred stroked his goatee as he looked from the torturer to the tortured, then to Elaine.

Intaki frowned. "Just one more brand, M'lord?" He pointed the hot poker at Elaine, who backed away quickly. "A cobra for the Mink?" He smiled a grotesque smile.

Elaine spat at him.

Mordred smiled. "Perhaps later, Intaki." He walked up to the newly branded prisoner and cupped her chin with his right hand. "Tsk, tsk, Miss Hosokawa. You are a sight."

Maya opened her left eye – the right one was swollen shut – and tried to speak, but no sound came out. A tear trickled down her face. Then she went limp.

Mordred let go of her chin. "Intaki! We do *not* want the brat to die on us. Yet. Off to the infirmary with her. Tell Dr. Hyde to prepare her for another round later today."

"Yes, M'lord." The guard freed Maya from the manacles and flung her over his shoulder like a sack of potatoes.

Mordred spoke softly to Elaine. "Little Mink. You risk our wrath for a mere child? We expected better from the slickest cat burglar in Europe."

Elaine cowered in the corner of the cell, her eyes avoiding his scorching gaze.

"How you disappoint us. But not for long now." The dark lord left the cell, humming and twirling a silver necklace with *two* silver rings attached.

Upstairs in the throne room, a congregation of warriors mingled, talking quietly. The two ninjas from the Temple stood by themselves, silent. All came to attention when Mordred entered. He sat upon the throne and waved his hand lazily in the air. "Yes, yes," – his signal for his soldiers to relax. "Rattar!"

The servant was already at his side. "M'lord?"

"Where are our generals?"

"Here, M'lord." Vassalar strode into the room, carrying a large object draped in a blood-red cloth.

Mordred chuckled. "General Vassalar, is that what we think it is?"

Vassalar returned a pointy gold smile. "As promised, M'lord." With a flourish, he flung the cloth to the floor and presented General Zheng's head on a golden platter – with an apple.

"Delightful, Vassalar! Most delightful." He clapped his hands in glee. "Please, present it to the assembly."

Vassalar turned to reveal the gift. A murmur of recognition ran through the crowd. More than a few warriors winced at the sight of the Chinese general's head, now collapsed and bloodied on the gleaming serving plate.

Mordred snapped his fingers in Rattar's direction. Rattar took the heavy platter from Vassalar and staggered from the throne room.

Mordred addressed the crowd. "With rank comes responsibility. Not all the fault lies with General Zheng." He turned to the two ninjas. "Sato?"

The shorter of the ninjas stepped forward, eyes wide, trying to maintain an impassive expression. He nodded to his dark master.

"Not only did you permit the Eye of Buddha to be stolen, but you ended up in a cathedral in the middle of Russia." Mordred clucked his tongue and shook his head. "Sato, Sato. Do you have any idea how much trouble you caused us? What an international incident this could have become? And, now we see your ring is gone. A sign that you are no longer one of us."

Sato screamed and ran for it, only to be speared through the chest by a large African warrior who stepped from the outer corridor at the last possible moment.

"Our darlings feast today. To the lagoon."

The warrior nodded and trotted away, the ninja's nearly lifeless body dangling from the spear.

"Tenshu."

The taller ninja walked slowly to the center of the throne room, shoulders drooping, head bowed, resigned to his fate. "M'lord."

"Are we to understand that the intruders at the Temple were gone before you were placed on duty by General Zheng?"

"Yes, M'lord." The ninja kept his head bowed.

"And are we to understand that you tracked down the treacherous priest, disposed of him, and captured the girl?"

"Yes, M'lord." He raised his head slightly.

"Well done, Tenshu, well done."

The ninja ventured a glance at the throne, his eyebrows raised, his voice questioning. "M'lord?"

"We only demand retribution where it is due. Your capture of the girl has brought us much joy." Mordred twirled the rings and chain. "In recognition of your success, we charge you with responsibility for the girl. Make sure she does not die until it is our pleasure."

"Yes, M'lord." Tenshu bowed deeply and joined the others.

"One last task. Miatsu?"

The slender Asian woman with the green highlights in her jet-black hair walked gracefully to the center of the room. She bowed deeply. "M'lord?"

"Vassalar, the pendant."

Now holding an ebony pearlized chest in his hands, Vassalar took from it a black and gold pendant in the shape of a quarter moon, strung from a piece of black rawhide. He handed the pendant to Mordred.

"Come to us, Miatsu."

The woman walked quickly to the foot of the throne.

"The photo, General."

Vassalar withdrew a photo of Maya from his pocket, placed it on a plate and held it under the pendant. Mordred raised the pendant over Miatsu's head and muttered an incantation in an almost forgotten Druid language. The photo burst into flames. When the last piece of the photo curled and turned to ash, Mordred circled the woman's head with the pendant three times, counter-clockwise. The pendant moon glowed blood red for a few seconds.

Mordred smiled. "Miatsu. Let them behold our power."

Miatsu slowly turned.

The audience gasped.

Before them stood Maya.

Chapter Thirty-Seven

Strange Reunions

If their prayers went unanswered, at least luck was with the Crusaders on their trip to Egypt – no hotel staff occupied the reserved suite when they arrived via wind funnel. Karen collapsed on a luxurious gold-and-ivory-striped chaise lounge. "I think it's going to take a little time to get used to this traveling by ring business."

"You have to admit, it's a blast," Lucas said.

Karen agreed. "It does come in handy."

"Yeah, but if every bloke had a ring, you'd be sacked." Ryan grinned.

Dunmoore held out his arm. "If you would be so kind, Mrs. Thompson, to accompany me down to the lobby to officially check in?"

"Why, I'd be delighted, Mr. Thompson."

When they returned to the suite, Karen received a call from her archaeological friend. Unfortunately, Richard was not available until the next day.

"The longer we wait, the worse it could get for Maya." Des was twisting his ring again.

If we don't find Maya soon, Des is gonna twist his damn ring down to the bone, thought Lucas.

Dunmoore said, "We can't risk the entire operation – or Maya – by all of our traipsing about Cairo in full view of the Dark Powers. And Karen cannot go unaccompanied."

"How about Des goes with?" Lucas suggested. "He speaks Arabic, French and English. He fits in. The Dark Powers won't be looking for a Moroccan kid with a blond American woman. And," Lucas grabbed his Ray Bans from his knapsack and put them over Des's thick black glasses, "dark sunglasses wrap it all up. Instant disguise."

"Maybe clip-ons?" Des joked, then turned to Dunmoore and Ryan. "I can do it."

Ryan shrugged. "The idea ain't half bad. I'm in, little guy."

"You gotta be okay with this, too." Lucas looked at Karen.

She smiled and said, "The idea ain't half bad."

Ten minutes later, the two left with Dunmoore's solemn warning to "be careful" ringing in their ears, and Jafar Moboto's journal and Alfred Dunmoore's letter securely stuffed into Karen's black handbag.

Lucas watched from the hotel room as Des and Karen hailed a cab to Cairo General. He held his hat in his hands, rubbing the dried rattles and murmuring a silent prayer for their safety.

———

It was only ten in the morning, and yet the temperature already felt oppressively stifling. The wind made them even more uncomfortable as it whipped about particles of sand and dirt, stinging their faces and hands. Once inside the taxi, Des said, "The weather is always unpredictable in April, the season of *khamsim*. Sandstorms."

Karen smiled and whispered, "Another plus to traveling by ring."

The broad streets of the city were crowded with pedestrians, bikes, automobiles, and the babble of humanity and honking of horns. Drivers careened from one stoplight to the next, from zero to sixty for one block, and then to a screeching halt. Karen stared at her lap for most of the ride, gripping Des's hand so tightly he had indentations from her fingers.

They made it safely to the hospital, notwithstanding the antics of the taxi driver, who made New York City cabbies look like little old ladies. At the hospital, they fought their way through the crowd to the harried receptionist and stood patiently in line.

"Dr. Habib?" the receptionist repeated, her fingers speeding over the computer keyboard. She didn't even look up as she said, "Orthopedics, Fourth Floor" in Egyptian, then called out, "Next!"

Des located the office by the brass nameplate, in both English and Arabic, "A. Habib, M.D., Orthopedics."

Karen took a deep breath, said, "Cross your fingers, hon. Here we go," and pushed open the door.

The receptionist was dressed in a stylish black-and-white polka-dot dress with sling-back heels. Her black hair seemed to glisten under the office lights, and she wore it in a neat French bun. She surveyed the two visitors with a slight frown and upturn of her nose.

Des said in Egyptian Arabic, "We would like to see Dr. Habib, please."

The receptionist gave a chilly smile. "The doctor is booked solid. He perhaps could see you..." She tapped the mouse and continued, "two weeks from tomorrow."

At Des's small "Oh" of dismay, the receptionist slid the glass window closed and returned her attention to her computer.

"Snooty witch," muttered Karen. She rapped sharply on the glass window.

The receptionist raised her eyebrows, sighed and slid open the window.

"Do you speak English?"

A reluctant nod from the receptionist.

"Good. It is urgent that we talk to Dr. Habib. Please tell him it has to do with an incident years ago, which resulted in a bizarre injury to a Jafar Moboto, and a perplexing death to an Alfred Dunmoore."

The woman frowned and started to shake her head, but Karen said firmly, "He'll know what I'm talking about, and I assure you, he will want to speak with us."

Five minutes later, Dr. Habib greeted Karen and Des with a warm smile and a ringless handshake. His eyes lingered on Karen, and he held her hand just a bit longer than good manners dictated. His dark brown eyes were flecked with amber and hinted at a keen intelligence and compassion. He spoke perfect English. "It is not every day that I receive a personal visit from such a lovely stranger, with such an intriguing message." He continued to appraise Karen, smiling broadly.

Karen found herself quite drawn to him, and then it dawned on her. "But you can't be Dr. Habib. You're too young!"

He chuckled. "I assure you, I am licensed to practice medicine. But I understand your confusion. I believe you are looking for my father, Dr. Ali Habib. I am Aba Ben Habib. Please, call me Ben."

"That would explain it." Karen nodded.

Des asked, "Does your father have an office here? Can we speak to him?"

Ben shook his head. "He retired many years ago. I took over his practice. Excuse my manners. Sit, please." He indicated the couch in a small sitting area in his office and took an adjoining chair. "I have heard of this *incident* and admit I am overcome with curiosity."

"We can't thank you enough, Dr. Habib...er...Ben," Karen said. She took the journal and letter from her purse and gave them to Ben – the journal open to the October 31, 1954 entry.

Karen and Des gave the doctor a few minutes of silence to read. When he finished, Ben returned them to Karen, who asked, "Curiosity satisfied?"

He smiled. "May I ask where you obtained these writings?"

"The journal is my grandfather's, Jafar Moboto," said Des. "He sent the torn out entry to your father. And the letter belongs to Morgan Dunmoore, who is –"

"There are many things we cannot tell you," interrupted Karen. "For our safety and yours, which is why our colleague, Morgan Dunmoore, did not accompany us."

"Curiouser and curiouser, said the cat," Ben quoted from Lewis Carroll's *Alice in Wonderland*. He looked at Karen, then Des. "How can I be of assistance?"

"We need the missing pages of my grandfather's journal."

Ben closed his eyes and placed the tips of his fingers together, forming a pyramid. After a few moments, he opened his eyes, looked at his watch and smiled. "Why don't I take you to see my father at his home?"

"That would be lovely, thank you." Karen said, rising from the couch.

"No, thank *you*. I imagine I will not have heard such an interesting tale in a long time."

"You can count on that," said a grinning Des.

The Habibs resided in one of the more affluent suburbs of Cairo, in a mansion with servants of all kinds – chauffeur, butler, cook, maids. Standing in the huge foyer, Karen and Des felt a sense of awe at the wealth surrounding them.

Ben had apparently seen such reactions before. "My parents are very down-to-earth people, despite the luxury in which they live. I think you'll like them very much."

The butler reappeared and led them to the drawing room. Dr. and Mrs. Habib rose from a love seat to greet them, hugging Ben and taking Karen and Des's hands.

"I cannot tell you what a pleasure it is to meet you," Dr. Ali Habib said to Karen. "And what a surprise it was to get the phone call from my son about your search." Dr. Habib then addressed Des. "Your grandfather was an amazing man. I am sorry to hear he passed away." He gestured to the cheese and fruit platter on the drawing room table, along with an assortment of beverages. "Please, do sit. Laila and I usually partake of a small appetizer before retiring to the dining room for lunch."

While they sampled the delicious fruits and cheeses – Ben explaining to Karen what the different foods were and feeding her bites from his fingers – the elder Dr. Habib related his small part in what occurred those many years ago. He produced a copy of Jafar Moboto's journal entry and gave it to Des, who read it aloud.

All seemed lost that night at the pyramids in Giza. The creature we were battling had all but cornered us. Both Alfred and I searched desperately for a way out when the creature turned the corner and spied us. With a loathsome hiss, it raised its entire, ghastly body and hurled itself down the narrow passageway, fangs bared. Alfred raised his revolver in a futile attempt to get one last shot off. The creature hit him full force in the chest, hurling him into me. As I was flung against the pyramid wall, I felt an incredibly sharp, burning pain in my right eye. I screamed in agony. As my left hand hit the side of the pyramid, a stone turned, and the side gave way. I tumbled down the stones, landing on a mound of straw, what seemed to be many feet below. A moment later, Alfred landed beside me. I forced myself to stop screaming – though my left eye burned with the heat of a thousand candles – but still I heard screams. I realized it was Alfred. Turning to him, I saw the grievous wounds on his chest. I tore my coat off, placed it over the wounds and tied it down, fashioning it into a very loose, though seemingly effective, tourniquet to stanch the blood flow. I prepared a similar bandage for my left eye.

Minutes later, I heard voices and footsteps. I searched for a weapon – both Alfred's and my revolvers were gone – anything to turn on my attackers. Three men turned the corner and stopped. I called to them, "Friend or foe?" The men seemed uneasy. One kept looking up at the top of the pyramid – perhaps to see the hideous creature? The tallest of the men finally answered, "Friend. Are you in need of help?" I cried out, "Yes. My friend is badly injured, and I am hurt. We need medical aid." The tall man spoke rapidly to the one who kept looking up at the pyramid. That one turned and ran. The remaining two began tending to our wounds. Very quickly thereafter, the third man returned with a motorized wagon, and Alfred and I were loaded onto it and taken from the pyramid. As we departed that godforsaken place, I looked up to see the creature's head sticking out from the place where the pyramid had opened up to drop us. I fainted dead away.

I woke an hour later in a hospital bed. At my rousing, a nurse came over, took my pulse and sent for the doctor. Moments later, a doctor appeared and informed me they had been unable to save my eye but, fortunately, the rest of my wounds had been superficial. I would live. I breathed a sigh of relief, then remembered Alfred. "What about my friend? Where is he? Will he be all right?" The doctor pointed to a bed near mine. Alfred's breathing was weak and ragged. "His wounds are very grave. I do not think he will survive. And he expended a great deal of strength the last hour writing a letter. I think you had better talk to him. We are simply trying to keep him comfortable until his...time."

The doctor helped me into a robe and escorted me to my friend's bedside. I touched his shoulder. "Alfred, it is I, Jafar. How are you?" Alfred opened his eyes – I could see death was not far – and whispered, "Jafar, my friend, we lost." I nodded. "Yes, but we escaped. We will be better prepared next time." Alfred tried vigorously to shake his head. The effort caused him to cough for some time. Finally, he opened his eyes again. "There will be no next time for me." What could I say? "Do not give up, old man," but my heart was not in it, and I knew that Alfred knew. He said, "I ask but one favor." "Anything, my friend," I assured him.

"Would you please ensure my son receives this letter, along with the ring?" Saying these last words, Alfred pointed to an envelope on the stand beside his bed and struggled to take the ring off his right hand. I stayed his hands and removed the silver ring. It glowed for an instant, then went dark. I picked up the letter and envelope from the nightstand. It was addressed to a "Morgan Dunmoore, Windsor, England." I placed the ring in the envelope and sealed it, then placed the envelope securely inside the robe I was wearing, patting the pocket. I leaned over Alfred. "He shall receive the ring and the letter, I give you my word." Alfred sighed and whispered, "Thank you, my friend." He closed his eyes, took one last belabored breath, and was gone.

The doctor – Habib was his name – appeared, took Alfred's pulse, and pulled the sheet over his head. He then assisted me back to bed. When he attempted to take the robe from me, I resisted. But, I was so tired! Dr. Habib stared at me. "May I ask you one question, please? Your friend did not die merely from the loss of blood, you know?" I looked up at him quizzically. "No," he continued, "he died from the poison in his system. Here is my question: Did the asp bite him before or after the wounds were inflicted?" I could only stare. Then, it dawned on me. Of course there would have been poison! I said, "The poison and wounds came at the same time. The asp inflicted those wounds." Dr. Habib drew his breath in sharply. "That is impossible!" he almost shouted. He lowered his voice. "That is impossible," he repeated. "There is no asp in existence that could inflict such wounds." "There is at the pyramids," I replied, then fell into a fitful sleep.

The silence in the Habibs' house mirrored the silence in the hospital those many years ago. Their amazement over Jafar Moboto's tale battled with their sadness over the death of Alfred Dunmoore. Finally, Des turned to the elder Dr. Habib. "Do you believe Grandfather?"

"Very much so. Now, I have a question to ask of you. Why are you so interested in what occurred many years ago to your grandfather?"

Des and Karen shot quick glances at each other. Des leaned over and whispered in her ear, "I think we can trust these people. I know Grandfather did."

Karen nodded and whispered back, "I like the Habibs. And there's not a pinky ring in sight. Go to it, hon."

Des turned to the elderly doctor and gave the Habibs a very abbreviated version of the tale of the rings. When he got to the part about Maya disappearing from the Kinkakuji Temple, Dr. Habib stood.

"Please, not another word."

He left, returning a minute later – Maya at his side.

Chapter Thirty-Eight

Uneasy Alliances

Des bounded from the couch, knocking a plate of olives to the floor. Rushing across the room, he gave Maya a big hug. Maya returned his hug just as fiercely. Karen and Ben sat on the couch, mouths agape. Laila Habib merely smiled.

After allowing them a moment, Dr. Habib tapped Des on the shoulder. "Might I suggest that Maya tell her story over our meal?"

During lunch, Maya explained how she came to be in Cairo and staying with the Habibs, beginning with her fight with the ninja in the Temple of the Dogs.

"The moment the ninja faced me, I felt Shin'ichi's presence and heard his voice. He told me when to duck to avoid the deadly stars, when to go left, when to strike with my nunchuks. I did not have to think at all. I simply cleared my mind of everything but Shin'ichi's voice."

"You were fantastic, Maya!"

Maya flashed Des a smile, then continued with her story of how her ring had burned horribly, Shin'ichi had fallen silent, and the ninja's kick had finally connected. Her ribs felt crushed and on fire. It was all she could do to remember to breathe, and she fainted. She awoke on a down mattress on the floor of a small room. Lavender incense burned. Her ribs were taped. The rice paper and bamboo doors slid open and the old priest from the Temple entered with a tray of miso soup, rice, and green tea.

The priest had watched everything from a secret hideaway, sneaking in during the commotion and rescuing Maya. He brought her to a friend's house in Kyoto, fearing the Dark Powers might search the Nara houses of the priests. Which they had. And he had helped Maya catch a flight to Cairo. Most curious of all was the reason he had given for risking so much.

"My name. 'Maya' is the name of Siddhartha Gautama's mother. Buddha's mom! He told me I could very well be a reincarnation of her and, of course, he could not allow Buddha's mother to perish." Maya smiled at the elder Habibs. "When I told Dr. and Mrs. Habib my story, they allowed me to stay with them."

"How were you able to locate my parents?" Ben asked.

"Internet. And I remembered a few things from your grandfather's journal, Des. A Dr. Habib from Cairo General Hospital."

"We were pleased to have Maya as a house guest," the elder Dr. Habib said. "Although disbelieving of her story at first, her silver ring immediately convinced me."

"Why was that?" asked Karen.

"Alfred Dunmoore and Jafar Moboto wore identical silver rings. Three such rings seemed far too much of a coincidence. That," Dr. Habib paused, "and what occurred when I attempted to investigate Alfred Dunmoore's death back in 1954."

After the mysterious death of Alfred Dunmoore, and Jafar Moboto's fantastical tale of the asp at the pyramid, Dr. Habib had begun to make inquiries. Two weeks later, he had received a visit from a man dressed all in black – overcoat, hat, shirt and tie, and dark sunglasses. The man had arrived unannounced at Dr. Habib's office at Cairo General, warning it would be best if the good doctor dropped his investigation into the death of Alfred Dunmoore and the ridiculous tale of a giant asp.

Dr. Habib had become incensed at the impudence of this stranger, until the man whispered in a voice as hard as steel, "It would be very unfortunate if something were to happen to your lovely wife, or the child she carries." The stranger departed, leaving a very shaken Dr. Habib.

For Ali and Laila Habib had only just found out that morning that Laila was pregnant with their daughter, Hadaar. They had not told anyone. Clearly, the dark stranger had illegal access to medical records and who knew what else. Ali could not afford to pursue the incident any further. He folded up Jafar's journal notes and filed them away.

———

"But I greatly regretted that decision." Dr. Habib looked at Maya. "And now I have a chance to atone. I will help you in any way I can."

"I throw my hat in the ring, also," said Ben, looking intently at Karen. "I would very much like to assist you in your quest."

Karen said, "That is very sweet of y'all, but you don't know everything. I think you were wise to drop the matter, Dr. Habib. Please, listen to the rest of Des's story."

Des reluctantly told his now-rapt audience about the interrogation of the ninja and the sordid tale of the bone pinkie rings. During his narrative, Laila paled dramatically. Dr. Habib rose and assisted his wife from the room.

When he returned, Karen said, "Please forgive us. We never meant to upset y'all. It just wouldn't be fair for us to accept your kind offers of help without letting you know what you would be up against."

"I am even more determined to help you," answered Ben, a grim smile on his face.

"Now, Ben," cautioned the elder Habib. "We have no experience or history on which to draw, unlike these young people."

"Karen has no history, either, Father." Ben turned to Karen and tilted his head.

"No ring, no knight in shining armor," replied Karen.

"You see, Father, it is not necessary that one have the ring or the legacy. What matters is that we must put an end to this evil."

His father shook his head. "This is not your decision to make alone. Your actions could put others in danger, and I am not referring only to your mother and myself. I am referring to your sister, Hadaar, and her family. Especially the new baby."

"Your father is right." Karen placed a gentle hand on Ben's arm.

Ben rose from the table. "If you will excuse us, we must speak in private." Ben pointed to the drawing room. "Father, will you come?" The elder Dr. Habib nodded and entered the drawing room, where Ben closed the doors.

Karen, Des and Maya looked at each other and at the closed doors, behind which they could hear murmuring and, occasionally, raised voices. Des put his hand on Maya's. "Are *you* okay with all this?"

Maya gave him an indulgent smile. "What about the others? Where are they?"

Karen replied, "At the hotel, waiting for us. We really ought to be getting back, or at least letting them know we're okay."

"I can take care of that," Ben said as he opened the doors to the drawing room. "I'll drive you to your hotel."

"What about your father?" Karen asked, craning her neck to see into the next room.

"He went to talk to my mother."

"Is he angry?" asked Des.

Ben shrugged. "He wishes things were not what they are, but he understands that wishing serves no useful purpose. If it were not for Hadaar's baby, he would join us. As it is, he will insist that Hadaar and her family stay here – in the compound – for the next few days. And he will hire additional security." Ben smiled. "He wishes us nothing but luck."

"That's the best wish I could hope for," said Des.

———

The two Crusaders and their recruits returned to the Cairo Sheraton, where a joyous reunion took place. Lucas couldn't help but notice that Ryan seemed the most affected by Maya's return. Which in turn seemed to irritate Maya. At his third apology, she said, "What is wrong with you, Casey?"

"You didn't tell her, Des?" Ryan asked.

"Tell me what?" Maya turned on Des.

Des said, "I thought that was best dealt with between you two."

"Will someone please explain?" Maya stood with arms crossed, tapping her foot.

Ryan repeated what he had told Merlin back at Lake Windermere. When he finished, he took Maya's hands and, in a voice full of emotion, whispered, "Please forgive me."

Maya did not whisper. She said loud enough for the others to hear, "You never meant to hurt me. How could you think I would be angry?"

Because you're the ice princess, thought Lucas. *I'd even be a little pissed off over being nearly exterminated by a ninja.*

Then, Ryan gave Maya a fierce hug, surprising Lucas. Even more astounding was Maya's hugging Ryan back, almost as tightly. Adversaries turned allies in the blink of an eye.

What is going on? Lucas felt utter bewilderment. *Jealous?* The little voice asked. *Maybe,* Lucas admitted, *but something more. She's different, somehow.* He pledged to the voice that he'd take his time with the "new" Maya.

The telephone rang. It was Richard.

"Who's Richard?" asked Ben.

"A friend of Karen's who's going to take her on a tour of the pyramids to locate The Hands of Allah," answered Des.

"Not any more." Karen hung up the phone. "Richard broke his ankle at the dig today. He won't be able to put any weight on it for a few days."

"Gammy, mouldy luck," cursed Ryan. "Now what? We hang around this dump?"

Karen smiled. "It's not exactly a dump, hon. And it isn't as bad as all that. Richard's going to contact a good friend of his who's a real tour guide. He said I could trust his friend. Actually," Karen laughed, "Richard said *he* could trust this friend with me!"

Ben frowned. "I have a close friend who is also a tour guide at the pyramids. Why don't I call him and arrange a private tour for us. Say, tomorrow?"

"Great on, mate!" Ryan said.

"Is your friend trustworthy?" asked Dunmoore.

"I know he does not wear a bone ring, and it will be safer for Karen if I accompany her."

"I'm game," said Karen.

Ben would pick Karen up at nine the next morning. They would meet Ben's friend, Lutar, at a restaurant out by the Giza pyramids, have a small meal and ask questions in private.

Ben strolled to the door of the suite. "Stay out of trouble until tomorrow, yes?"

When he left, Ryan said, "I know something that will keep us out of trouble. Room service. I'm starving!"

"What else is new," said Lucas, chuckling.

Maya cleared her throat. "I do not want to offend, but...I am not convinced that having Karen and Ben check out the pyramids tomorrow is a wise course of action. We know nothing about this Lutar."

"True, Maya," said Dunmoore, "but I think I speak for all of us when I say that it is the best option."

"As you will," Maya said softly.

But Lucas observed she remained quiet the rest of the afternoon.

They ordered room service and went over the plan for the pyramid tour. Karen would specifically ask to see the pyramid of Chephren, the second pyramid of the three pyramids of Giza, and the one closest to the Sphinx.

"In the margins of Jafar Moboto's journal, the part he sent to the elder Dr. Habib, is a drawing of the Sphinx and three pyramids, with a star in the middle structure." Dunmoore pointed to the crude sketch. "I believe Des's grandfather drew a map of the pyramid."

At some point, Karen would try to steer the conversation to hidden treasure and jewels. She would also have to be on the watch for any reference to The Hands of Allah or other significant religious relic, as well as to a giant asp or snake.

"Based upon our experience in Russia and Japan," said Dunmoore, "I would wager the asp is made of stone or marble." He turned to Karen. "If the opportunity arises to make a map of the pyramid and note the location of the relic or asp, so much the better."

After getting all the information they could out of the tour with Lutar, Karen and Ben would return to the hotel room for a debriefing.

Dunmoore finished up with, "Whereupon, we shall travel to the pyramid, steal the relic, and travel back to Lake Windermere. We should be back in England in a day or two at the most."

The Crusaders retired for the night.

With any luck, thought Lucas, *it will be our last night in Egypt.*

Chapter Thirty-Nine

A Tour of The Pyramids

Lucas awoke to the rapping of rain on the balcony windows. Even though the curtains were open, the room was dark. The luminous numbers of the clock radio blinked 8:00 A.M. Padding past Des's bed, he grinned at how his friend slept – spread out on the bed width-wise, the bedcovers mangled. Lucas unlatched the door. A gust of wind almost forced him back into the room. Huge raindrops pelted him, but he pushed through the wind and rain to the balcony railing.

Twenty-one stories below was a mass of traffic and pedestrians. The howling wind almost drowned out the usual din of horns, engines and shouting. A sharp *crack* and flash of lightning caused Lucas to jump. Seconds later, thunder rumbled through the sky. He rushed back into the bedroom, closed the door and shook his head, sending beads of water everywhere. His sweats were plastered to him. Des sat up in bed, yawning.

"What's with the weather?" griped Lucas. "Isn't this place supposed to be a desert?"

"It is rather unusual for late April."

Lucas stripped out of his sodden sweats and pulled on jeans and a T-shirt. "And Karen has to be out in that crap today. Just great."

"At least it should cut down on the tourists at the pyramids," said Des.

"Doesn't anything ever get you down, Mr. Optimism?"

"Now that Maya's safely back, no." Des yawned again and stretched out his arms.

"Yeah, Maya. Hey, Des, does she seem different?"

Des dropped his hands to his lap. "What do you mean?"

"Quieter? Like she's not all there." Lucas sat on the edge of his friend's bed.

"I didn't notice. She's been through a lot. Maybe she's just getting reacclimated."

"You're probably right." Lucas stood. "How 'bout some breakfast? You know what Ryan would say. 'Storms make me hungry.'"

———

Ben arrived at the hotel suite at nine and left not fifteen minutes later with Karen, words of encouragement, and Dunmoore's reminder: "At the first sign that something may be amiss, get the hell out of there."

Lucas and the others hung around the hotel suite. After about an hour of pretty lousy television – *Egyptian game shows don't get the concept of "entertainment" – just a bunch of talking heads* – Lucas was antsy.

Des suggested they locate a library and check out books on the pyramids. "Maybe we'll get a clue on where to find The Hands of Allah."

Lucas, Ryan and Dunmoore jumped on that bandwagon. Doomsday Maya – as Lucas had silently dubbed her – doubted there were any libraries in Egypt with many books in English. When Des reminded Maya he could read Arabic, Maya replied in her prissiest voice that they did not want to blow their cover by being seen in Cairo by the Dark Powers.

Lucas jumped into the fray. "We don't need to get the books here, Maya. Why don't we go to the Oxford Library? It's still early morning there, so no one will see us. And the books are in English." He looked at Dunmoore. "Tell me the books are in English. In England."

"Quite," said Dunmoore. "Why don't you four go? Someone has to be here in case Karen and Ben return. Or call."

Maya elected to stay and rest, blaming her pessimistic mood on not having fully recovered from her injuries at the Temple. So, the three boys traveled to Oxford. Half an hour later, they reappeared in the hotel room, arms loaded with heavy tomes.

While leafing through the books, Des said, "There's something peculiar about the hieroglyphics on the walls of the pyramid of Chepren. They seem familiar, somehow. Do you know what they say, Professor?"

But Dunmoore did not know how to interpret the strange symbols.

"I think this one means 'drinking' and," Des paused for a moment, then continued excitedly, "this one means 'looking' and this one means 'praying'. They're in sign language!"

"How the devil do you know that?" asked Dunmoore.

"My sister, Kinisha, is deaf. I've known sign language since I was four. Some of the signs these people are making in the paintings on the pyramid walls are like the signs we make with Kinisha."

"Listen up, mates." Ryan read, "There is some controversy among scholars over whether the paintings on the walls of the pyramid of Chephren are bona...bo –"

"*Bona fide*," said Dunmoore. "Good faith, true."

"Yeah." Ryan continued reading, "One school believes that the paintings did not appear until the ninth century A.D. Previous writings about the pyramid do not contain any mention of these paintings. The other school agrees that earlier descriptions of the pyramid of Chephren do not mention the paintings, but relies upon the fact that the carbon-dating of the paintings puts them squarely back in 2500 B.C., during the Fourth Dynasty of Egyptian rulers when the pyramid was built." Ryan slammed the book shut.

Lucas whistled. "Ninth century. Looks as if the second pyramid is it, all right."

"But not even the Dark Powers can carbon-date something centuries before it was supposedly painted," Maya argued.

"A week ago," said Dunmoore, "I would have agreed wholeheartedly. But after all we've been through, I wouldn't doubt that the Dark Powers could do just that."

"They could simply be controlling the people who *did* the carbon-dating," suggested Des.

Lucas asked, "Do the hieroglyphics tell you where the relic is? You mentioned praying."

"Give me some time." Des returned to his seat on the couch.

Lucas and Ryan continued flipping through the other books, although Lucas's heart wasn't in it. He kept glancing up to see how Des was coming along. Maya retreated to her bedroom.

Almost half an hour later, Des said, "This has to be it!" He copied the hieroglyphics onto another piece of paper and wrote his translation underneath: *This Way Praying Room Hands God.* "There's an asp at the end of the paintings – not a sign language symbol – but there's also another hieroglyphic after the asp, which translates to 'Protector.'"

Lucas leaped from the couch and held out a fist. "You rock, Des!"

Des grinned and fist-bumped Lucas.

"We may have confirmation of your hunch soon enough when Karen and Ben return," said Dunmoore. "Until then, I'll be in my bedroom."

The rain and wind tapered off just before sunset, at the same time Karen and Ben, damp but smiling, returned. Dunmoore mixed three scotch-on-the-rocks and huddled with the others in the living room in front of a fire. Karen took a long, slow sip of her drink, then began.

"We met Lutar at a restaurant in Giza. Lovely man and no bone pinkie ring. I explained how I wanted to scope out the pyramid of Chephren in particular, playing up the bit about it being cursed and guarded by some fierce monster. Off we went."

At the pyramid, Lutar had told them the story about the curse and monster – a giant asp that guarded the treasures of the pyramid.

"When I asked what kind of treasures, he said he'd heard stories of gold, silver, jewels, and even a religious relic."

Lucas smiled. *I knew it!*

Karen took another sip of scotch and continued. "Lutar took us to the very place where people claimed to have seen the giant asp. It had hieroglyphics painted all over the walls. Ben copied them."

Lucas had a hard time containing his growing excitement as Karen took the paper from her backpack and laid it on the table. He nearly shouted, "That's it! It matches the pictures in Des's book!"

Dunmoore nodded and asked, "Do you know where these paintings are? Could you draw us a map showing how to get to them through the pyramid?"

"I think so. Ben and I talked about drawing a map during the tour, but we thought that might not be such a good idea under the circumstances."

"A most prudent course," commended Dunmoore.

Ben whispered to Karen, who nodded. "When we got to the place of the hieroglyphics, one tunnel was closed to the public. There were iron gates blocking the entrance. Locked."

"That's gotta be the entrance, mate," said Ryan.

"That's it, y'all." Karen leaned back on the couch and placed a hand on Ben's knee.

Lucas's brow puckered with annoyance.

"Did you run into any agents of the Dark Powers?" asked Des.

Karen nodded, a grim frown replacing her usual smile. "As we were leaving the pyramid, we ran into two local men whom Lutar knew. At least, they looked like locals to me, what with their flowing robes and all. Lutar introduced us, telling the two men about the 'monster-tour.' They laughed, but I knew they were faking."

Ben added, "They were far too interested in us. Especially Karen."

"It gave me the creeps." Karen gave a little shudder. "And then I saw the ring."

"One of the men had a pinkie ring?" asked Ryan.

Ben's eyes narrowed. "*Both* of them. If it were not for Karen, I might have strangled them then and there."

Karen smiled. "I could tell Ben was getting all riled up, so I gave 'em the ole' Southern belle, dumb blonde routine. You know, I grew up in a haunted mansion in the South and never could shake my interest in ghost stories. Especially when I had a man to protect me. Course, that's when I caressed Ben's arm and gazed into his eyes." She batted her eyes at Ben.

Lucas said, "Your Nigel-the-customs-guy routine, right?"

Karen laughed. "You got it, hon. Those two goons left thinking I wasn't smart enough to save the world from bad flirting, much less the Dark Powers."

"Good show," Dunmoore said.

Maya said in an accusing tone, "Unless they've alerted the Dark Powers to our presence."

"And how could they have done that?" Lucas asked, frowning.

Maya shrugged. "You said this Lutar was friends with the two agents of the Dark Powers. Maybe he's in on it."

Ben shook his head. "Lutar knows them only in connection with a nearby archaeological dig. They're work acquaintances, not friends."

"What's wrong with you, Maya?" asked Lucas. *'Cause you're sure as heck bugging me.*

"What do you mean?" Maya's yellow eyes widened in what Lucas thought of as feigned innocence. "We're not supposed to question anything? Lives are at stake here, remember?"

Lucas said, "I'll tell you what I remember. I –"

"Now, now," said Dunmoore.

"Now, *I* must attend to matters at the hospital. I have surgery scheduled early tomorrow morning." Ben rose from the couch and took Karen's hand. "I'll call you afterward."

Karen smiled. "Sounds wonderful."

After seeing Ben out, Karen headed for a bedroom. "As for me, I'm going to take a nap. Do y'all mind if I sleep in here?"

"Sleep as long as you like. We'll wake you when we return from the pyramids."

"Hold on there, Morgan." Karen twirled around and came back to the living room. "What do you mean when *we* return? I don't plan on being left behind, now."

"We don't want to put you at any more risk," said Dunmoore.

Ryan added, "Nasty things can happen."

"But y'all are just as much at risk. And I happen to be certified in CPR and first aid."

Dunmoore's voice took on what Lucas thought of as his "professorial airs" – *like he's dealing with a thick student.*

"Karen, all you say is true. But this isn't your battle. Not only do we not want to put you in danger, but I would rather not have to worry about you and your safety. It puts us all at risk."

Karen's face seemed to lose all expression, and she stood taller.

Uh-oh, Prof, thought Lucas, *this is how she got when I said I wouldn't wait for her at Heathrow Airport. Not fun.*

Karen spoke, quietly but forcefully. "This isn't my battle? Apparently, I'm good enough to do your scouting. You didn't seem to mind the risk I was taking then. Is it because I don't have a damn ring? Or some dead knight from the Round Table in my lineage? Do you think that makes me care one iota less about the quest? If so, then you – all of you – can shove it right up your little butts. But before you do, you take me home. *Now.*"

"No." Des jumped up from the couch and grabbed Karen's hand. "You're as much a part of this as we are."

"Gotta fight you on that, little guy," said Ryan. "What the Prof said is true. We don't want to risk her life. Or our own. It's safer with a smaller group."

Maya said with a thin-lipped smile and wide eyes that gave Lucas a shiver, "Karen is one of us now, and if she wants to help us, I want her to be there. I think Karen is here because she is meant to be here."

"That's two for and two against," Des said. "It's up to you, Lucas."

Lucas looked at Karen as he said, "I don't want to put Karen in danger."

She frowned.

Lucas continued, "But she *is* a part of our group. We need to take advantage of everything, and everyone, we've got. Karen comes with."

Karen flashed Lucas a dazzling smile. Lucas felt his face and the tips of his ears flush.

"That's it then." Dunmoore turned to Karen. "I believe you said the pyramids close at eight. I suggest we rendezvous at midnight."

———————————

Ten minutes before midnight, the Crusaders and Karen stood in a circle in the living room of their Cairo hotel suite. Then entered the whirlwind.

Chapter Forty

The Pyramid of the Asp

When Lucas opened his eyes, he saw nothing but black. He blinked. Utter darkness. And his palms itched.

"Torches, people." That was Dunmoore's voice.

Torches? thought Lucas. *Who the heck brought torches?*

Flashlights clicked on, illuminating their landing site in the upper third of the pyramid of Chephren. It was cool and dry. Lucas scratched his palms.

Karen whispered, "There are the hieroglyphics. The passageway should be to the right." The beam from her "torch" lit up a curved entryway leading to a long passage. A thick iron gate blocked the entrance, with a gap at the bottom that only a snake could squeeze through.

And a small snake at that, Lucas thought. A wild hope rose in him.

Dunmoore examined the gate lock. "Doesn't appear to be any alarm system built into it. A simple key lock." Dunmoore turned to the others. "I suggest you three open it."

"Why don't we just travel past it?" asked Ryan.

"And if we get separated, what then?" replied Dunmoore. "I'd like to think we'd have some chance of escape from the asp."

Lucas said, "Yeah, no instant replay of the scene in the Temple." He looked at Maya.

Maya frowned, then her eyes widened and she nodded in agreement.

The three boys placed their hands on the gold fountain pen. A green beam shot into the keyhole. Seconds later, the gate sprung open. No alarm sounded.

"Remember, if any of us gets separated, come back through the gates and turn left. Follow that passage down to the entrance of the pyramid. Wait for the others outside. All right then, let's move!" Dunmoore strode past the gate.

They walked quickly but quietly, keeping steady beams on the walls. Within a few minutes, they hit a T-intersection. "Which way do we turn?" asked Karen.

"Look!" Des pointed. On a wall were two hieroglyphics: One was two open hands holding a crescent moon and five-pointed star. The other was an asp.

"The Hands of Allah!" said Lucas. He felt his heart begin to beat faster, like when he first trotted onto the track with his teammates before a meet began.

Then came the hissing.

Lucas turned in the direction of the whispery noise. Nothing could have prepared him for the sight of the asp. It was enormous – as big as the dragon at the cathedral – and covered with blood-red scales. When it opened its mouth, two pointed teeth dripped liquid onto the smooth stone floor, where it turned to steam with a soft, sizzling sound.

The only thought that sprang to Lucas's mind was, *that thing ain't fitting under the gate.* The hideous creature slithered toward them.

"Back to the gate!" Dunmoore shoved Karen and the others. They ran, Dunmoore shouting the travel spell in Middle English. "Memorize it!"

As Lucas repeated the strange words, he heard the others whispering them as well. And he heard the terror in their voices. *Ignore it,* the little voice ordered. *Keep your mind on the spell.* But he couldn't ignore the scratching slither of the asp closing in. He hit the open gates.

Quickly forming a circle, Lucas and the others repeated the spell. The asp was almost upon them, its mouth glaringly open, spitting venom as it lunged. The Crusaders vanished.

———

The asp flew headfirst into the wall opposite the gates. The creature rose slowly from a heap on the floor of the pyramid and looked around in pain and anger. There was no one there. But the asp sensed the rings were still in the pyramid. It let out a scream of frustration, eerily reminiscent of the late General Zheng's cries at the temple. The freakish serpent looked back at the now ungated passage, looked to the left, looked to the right. And went left to seek its prey.

———

Lucas and the others reappeared in a whirlwind outside a large room. The entrance was about four feet wide and five feet high, and painted at its top was a huge asp hieroglyphic – red with fangs bared. Other hieroglyphics flanked the asp, but Lucas didn't recognize the symbols.

Flashlight beams cruised around inside the room. On a wall about twenty feet in front of them was a painting of The Hands of Allah – in gold – above a small opening, about two feet square. A white light emanated from within.

"The Hands of Allah!" Karen whispered.

"I most certainly would hope so," said Dunmoore. "I had you repeat the spell to take us to the area in the Chephren pyramid at Giza that contains the relic."

Ryan said, "You Brits aren't so daft after all."

"Best to leave politics to another...." The sentence died in Dunmoore's throat.

Lucas closed his eyes and tilted his head, straining. There it was. The faint but unmistakable sound of slithering – like fingernails tracing a pattern on sandpaper. It sent shivers down his spine.

"The asp!" Maya's face paled considerably.

In the darkness, broken only by the faint beams of the flashlights, she looked almost translucent. *Weird,* thought Lucas. *Scary weird.*

Dunmoore urged, "Inside, quickly."

"Wait! We don't know what the hieroglyphics say." Lucas grabbed Dunmoore's arm.

"But we can see the Hands! And hear the asp!" Maya's voice fluttered with fear.

"We don't have time to try to decipher them." Dunmoore loosened Lucas's grasp. "We have to risk it." He stepped through the entrance.

The smooth floor of rock crumbled beneath them, pitching them into a long shaft of wood and stone.

———

Their screams ricocheted back up the shaft, echoing throughout the pyramid and halting the asp in its tracks. It raised its loathsome head and listened. It sniffed the air once, twice, then turned and slithered down into the bowels of the pyramid, unrelenting in its pursuit of the intruders. The tracks it left criss-crossed the previous ones, like those of skiers schussing down a mountainside. But these tracks emitted a faint orange light, as if from some kind of supernatural radioactivity. Or an ancient evil.

———

Lucas tumbled and slid for what seemed like forever, but was really only seconds. He and the others came to rest at the bottom of the great pyramid of Chephren, inside a secret funerary chamber. Once again, Lucas found himself imprisoned by total darkness. Two flashlight beams rescued him. He took stock.

No one had suffered any major injury. Dunmoore had borne the brunt of the fall, having landed first and absorbing the weight of the others who tumbled over atop him, cracking a rib in the process. But for that discomfort, he seemed okay to Lucas.

"The next time I say 'we have to risk it,' Luke, punch me in the jaw, what?"

"Deal, Prof," replied Lucas, gingerly checking himself for broken bones.

"If he doesn't, I will, Morgan." Karen took a kerchief from her jean pocket and tied it around her scraped, bleeding hand.

Lucas caressed the sword hilt at his side, then spied his rattler hat several feet away. As he went to retrieve it, he heard Maya emit a high-pitched, muffled scream. Lucas turned.

Two mummies held Maya in a suffocating chokehold. Other mummies appeared from behind the first two, staggering from deep within the chamber. Awakened from their centuries-long sleep by the Crusaders' trespass onto sacred ground, the mummies attacked – animated by the sorcery that had enslaved them there to guard their pharaoh against all invaders.

Through the haze of fear that seeped into his mind, Lucas heard Dunmoore calling to the horde of rag-clad zombies. Lucas glanced over. Dunmoore held the bone pinkie ring high. But the mummies' onslaught continued.

They're not agents of the Dark Powers, thought Lucas. *Oh, jeez.*

Suddenly, Des gave a loud tribal yell – courtesy of Modetta Khan – and leapt onto the mummies strangling Maya.

Lucas snapped out of his stupor. "No, Des! We need you for the rings!"

But it was too late. The mummies engulfed Des. His small body disappeared from view.

"No, damn it, no!" Lucas screamed. Hefting the sword over his head, he brought it down on the group of mummies. Bandaged heads and limbs flew through the air! Lucas again brought the sword above his head and again brought it down on the mummies. *God, don't let me hit Des or Maya*, he silently prayed. Mummy parts crumbled beneath the sword. Lucas cut a swath through the pack and managed to free Des.

"Use anything to knock off their limbs!" Lucas shouted. "Use any –"

Mummy hands around his throat choked off his words and pulled him backward, knocking the sword from his hand. He gagged on the rancid smell of the mummified arm, now clamped over his nose and mouth. The stench of four-thousand-year-old rotting flesh! The world began to spin and grow dark. The ring burned, startling him. He clawed at the mummy's arm, ripping it free from his mouth. He took in the stale dry air in heaving gulps.

Until another mummy's arm took the place of the first. And another mummy's arm clamped over that one, and another. They were methodically suffocating him. He felt his strength ebbing, the darkness growing. As if from a great distance, he heard screaming and dull thuds as the other Crusaders counter-attacked, ripping legs from torsos, arms from chests, heads from necks. The last light of consciousness flickered weakly as he struggled for one more breath.

Suddenly, the sounds grew near again, and the chamber grew bright and hot. He fell to the floor only to be dragged forward. By live, human arms! Karen. He struggled to say something, but could only retch out bits of rags and dried flesh.

"Don't try to say anything right now, hon," Karen crooned in her soft drawl. She sat him against one of the chamber walls and stroked his forehead. "You're going to be just fine."

Lucas heard coughing and turned.

Dunmoore spoke in a soothing tone as he held Maya's head. Maya took in great, ragged breaths. Her face was very pale, almost light blue. For a moment, Lucas thought she was someone else, with a green sheen to her hair. He closed his eyes and shook his head. When he opened them, she was Maya again.

Lucas looked to the source of the light and heat. Des and Ryan held aloft fiery torches, waving them at the mummies, driving them back into the depths of the chamber. Mummies lay on the floor, bandages aflame. Their burning limbs jerked once, twice, then lay still.

"They're afraid of fire." Lucas croaked out. "Someone really did bring torches."

"Those aren't torches, hon. They're mummy limbs." Karen shuddered. "Ryan's idea. Thank God."

Lucas looked again. Ryan's "torch" was an arm. Des held a fiery leg. Each time a limb's firepower diminished, the boys would pick up another limb and light it. *"Night of the Living Dead,"* said the little voice in his head. Lucas nodded, both repulsed and fascinated.

"Ryan! Des!" Dunmoore called. "They're all right. Back up so we can form the circle and get the hell out of here!"

"Don't you mean get the hell out of hell?" Lucas asked with a weak smile.

Dunmoore grinned. "It looks like near-death hasn't blessed you with great wit."

Karen helped Lucas to his feet, while Dunmoore supported Maya.

"Here's your sword." Des held out the weapon.

Lucas took the sword and nodded at Ryan. "I owe you one."

"IRA training comes in handy, eh?" Ryan coolly replied. "Theft. Handguns. Arson. Don't forget your hat, mate."

Lucas jammed the rattler hat on his head, rubbing the rattles for luck.

"We better get moving, y'all," warned Karen. "I think we've overstayed our visit."

The mummies were slowly advancing yet again.

Dunmoore suggested, "What say we have the spell bring us *inside* the sacred room of the Hands of Allah?"

Six hands joined in a circle. Ryan threw his flaming limb onto a nearby pile of mummy remains, keeping the other creatures at bay. Des held his, just in case.

The Crusaders vanished.

Chapter Forty-One

Choosing Poorly

When the Crusaders landed inside the room of the Hands of Allah, no beasties appeared – bandaged or otherwise. It was just the six of them again. Des extinguished a fiery mummy arm and tossed it on the ground. With a scowl, he wiped his hands on his jeans.

Lucas said, "You think touching those walking corpses stinks? Try chewing on 'em."

"Please, don't," said Maya, her voice small.

For a few seconds, Lucas thought she had that green tint about her again. He blinked. *It's gotta be the lighting.* He looked around.

The room turned out to be twenty feet deep, twice as long, and not much more than six feet high. Standing tall, Dunmoore's head almost brushed the pitted ceiling. The small cavern had a strong scent to it – not the faint musty smell of cellars and attics that the rest of the pyramid seemed to have. *What is it?* thought Lucas. *Pine?*

Karen must have smelled it, too. "Eucalyptus, right?"

"Yes," said Dunmoore. "With something else...I can't put my finger on it."

Lucas inhaled, then scrunched up his nose. "Rotten eggs."

"Sulfur," corrected Des.

Ryan said, "Who gives a slag's arse? Check this place out."

Each of three walls had a huge hieroglyphic of The Hands of Allah – one painted in gold, one in silver, and one in bronze. The asp hieroglyphic was painted on the ceiling, again in red. But now they saw that there were *three* marble altars – one green, one white, one black – and a small opening behind each altar, from which emanated different colors of light.

Maya followed Lucas to the green marble altar with the silver hieroglyphic. Lucas peered into the turquoise-lit opening. The light came from a silver pendant, embedded with two open hands holding a crescent moon and five-pointed star, a ring with some type of symbol rested on the middle finger of one of the hands. The pendant dangled from a silver chain.

"The Hands of Allah!" whispered Lucas.

"Yes," said Maya, licking her lips.

Like a cat cornering a mouse, thought Lucas. He saw a hunger in her eyes.

"The Hands of Allah!" echoed Des.

Ryan shouted, "Savage!"

Lucas turned. *Oh jeez.*

Behind the white marble altar, Ryan and Karen had found a pendant made of gold, hanging from a gold chain and emitting a bright white light.

Des and Dunmoore had likewise discovered a pendant, although theirs was a bronze medallion, which hung on a copper chain. It gave off a rose-colored light from behind the altar of ebony marble.

"Y'all, please tell me there are not *three* pendants?"

Dunmoore sighed. "I wish I could. It appears to be the Holy Grail situation, again."

"What did you do then?" Maya asked.

Lucas stared at her. *She was there. How could she not remember?*

"Maybe these hieroglyphics will help." Des pointed with his flashlight at the symbols painted on the ceiling around the asp. "I wish I had brought one of those books. Hey! Maybe we could travel back – "

"There's no time, not with that asp about," said Dunmoore.

Lucas touched Maya's arm and whispered, "At the Cathedral, you remember what –"

"No time to blather over these daft paintings. And it's not like in Russia with all those bleedin' grails. These are all in one place." Ryan pointed at each opening in turn. "Easy pickings. We just grab all three and sort it out with the wizard." Ryan strode behind the white altar and reached into the opening.

Des said, "Wait. It says something about death for...he who chooses...poorly."

"Death can kiss me arse." Ryan walked back to the others, dangling the golden pendant by its chain. "Grab the other two and–"

Karen and Maya screamed. Scores of scorpions poured from the empty opening behind the white altar. They buzzed and clicked, clicked and buzzed, scurrying down the wall and over the altar, poisonous stingers raised high.

Des shouted, "Stand still and they can't see you!"

"That's not scorpions! That's the T-Rex from *Jurassic Park*!" said Lucas.

At any other time, it would have been funny – a story to tell Rocky and Jason. Now, however, Lucas wished he *were* confronting an extinct dinosaur, not actual scorpions. But he stood stock-still anyway, separated once again from the others. That's when he noticed that the scorpions gave Dunmoore a wide berth. Not one came near him.

"H-h-hey, Prof," Lucas called.

"*Noooo!*" Karen – looking as white as Maya after the attack by the mummies – ran toward the entrance. Dunmoore grabbed her around the waist just as she was about to fall headlong into the chasm of the mummies. But her movement riled a hitchhiking scorpion, its stinger poised to strike. Karen screamed. Dunmoore swiftly kicked the offending insect off her ankle and smashed it beneath his boot.

The buzzing and clicking grew louder. The puny vermin seemed to be an avenging sort. Except. Lucas noticed again that the scorpions scrupulously left Dunmoore alone, and now that Karen was with him, the scorpions left her alone, too. Unlike the mummies, these creatures *were* agents of the Dark Powers. Lucas was sure of it.

He said, "Prof, it's gotta be the ninja's ring"; his voice barely above a whisper, his eyes on the angry scorpions surrounding him.

"Great God!" Dunmoore dug in his pocket for the pinkie ring, then held up his left hand, the ring between his thumb and forefinger. "I command thee!" he yelled. The scorpions turned as one toward Dunmoore.

Dunmoore helped Karen over to a wall. The scorpions clicked their way over to them. Slowly, Dunmoore turned and walked toward the chasm. The scorpions buzzed and clicked, turned and followed.

"What now?" Dunmoore spoke so softly that Lucas had to strain to hear him. "What have we here?"

Lucas looked in the direction of Dunmoore's glance. *Yes!* It was the mummified arm near the entrance, only inches from the precipice. *Yes, Prof!*

Like the mythical Pied Piper, Dunmoore made his way to the mummy arm, followed by the scorpions. Lifting the arm, he placed the ninja's ring on what was left of the mummy's pinkie. Now only a foot from the chasm, Dunmoore waited for the scorpions to surround him. He held the mummified arm out to his left. The scorpions scurried left. He held the arm out to his right. The scorpions did an about face and scurried right. Dunmoore turned back to his awestruck companions.

Lucas crossed his fingers as Dunmoore tossed the mummified arm into the chasm.

The arm and the ring disappeared into the black shaft. Scuttling one by one after the ring, the scorpions leaped into the darkness. When the last creature dove into the void, Karen collapsed. Lucas reached her first and knelt beside her.

"She's not going to die, is she, Prof?"

"Not if I have anything to say about it." Dunmoore grasped Karen's ankle in his hands, examining it gently. "I can't see the wound."

Karen raised her head and gave them a goofy smile. "I wasn't stung. I must have fainted. Sorry."

"We're just glad you're okay." Lucas put a hand to her forehead. Cold and clammy.

"How do you feel? Are you up to getting out of here?" Dunmoore asked.

"I feel like dog doo-doo," Karen replied. "When do we go?"

"As soon as we determine which pendant to take." Dunmoore turned to Ryan. "This time, my young Irish friend, let's not be so impetuous, what?"

A blushing Ryan, head bowed, mumbled, "Aye."

"Have you been able to decipher any more hieroglyphics, Des?"

"I was kind of preoccupied for a while there, Professor."

Dunmoore smiled and clapped a hand on Des's shoulder. "Point taken. Well, shall we have another go at it? At least we've got the odds narrowed to fifty-fifty."

Lucas turned back into the room. Where there were *three* Hands of Allah again.

"What in God's name is going on here?" said an exasperated Dunmoore.

Ryan tossed his golden pendant to the ground. "You can't trust anyone. Even God." But he clutched his Celtic cross in one hand as he said it.

Trust? That's it. That has to be it. "There is something we can trust." Lucas saw all heads swivel toward him.

"Any suggestion would be heartily welcomed right now, Luke," said Dunmoore.

Ryan added, "Yeah, mate. And I mean right damn now."

"Shouldn't we seal up that hole in the ground first?," asked Lucas. "So nothing can come back up?"

Maya and Karen shuddered. Lucas wasn't so keen on the prospect of more mummies or scorpions emerging from the depths of the pyramid, either. His idea was to concentrate the power of the rings on the sword to close the chasm. The three boys put their rings together and pointed the sword toward the gaping abyss. Beams of light flew from the sword and crisscrossed over the rift, like a needle repairing a mend in a skirt. In less than a minute, the chasm was gone. The entrance to the sacred room was firm ground once again.

"Excellent, Luke, most excellent! Now, what about the pendant?"

Lucas flashed a grin to Dunmoore. This felt almost as good as when he was picked for starter high jump his freshman year. No, this was better. He said, "We use the rings. We trust the rings. I'm pretty sure they'll lead us to the real Hands of Allah."

"I don't know," said Maya. "What if the next...thing is worse?"

"Nothing could be worse than those scorpions. Ugh." Karen shuddered. "Lucas is right. Y'all need to trust the rings. And can you please hurry?"

The three boys moved quickly to the center of the room. Maya stayed put, clinging to Karen's arm. Lucas nodded to her, but she looked away. *Weirder and weirder*, thought Lucas, continuing to stare at Maya.

"Don't go daft on us now, mate," said Ryan.

"What? Oh, sorry." Lucas placed his ring hand on top of Des and Ryan's. Dunmoore told them the Middle English words. They repeated the words in unison, asking the rings to lead them to the authentic, the one and only, the true Hands of Allah.

A powerful emerald light rose from the rings and propelled the boys forward into the room. The glow faded. The boys stood in front of the white marble altar. Again.

"What kind of crappy game is this?" Ryan said, drawing his hand away.

Maya whined, "I knew it wouldn't work. Let's get out of here!"

"No, look," said Des, pointing. "The pendant is silver now!"

He was right. The Hands of Allah that hung in the opening behind the white altar was now silver. And a turquoise glow surrounded it, not the white light from before. Lucas looked at the other two pendants. The gold pendant now rested where the bronze one had been, behind the black altar. And the bronze pendant nestled in the opening behind the green altar.

"If this is someone's idea of a trick, I don't like it one bit," Karen said.

Lucas turned to Dunmoore. "What do you think, Prof?"

"Is it an artifice of the Dark Powers or the real thing? Blast it!" Dunmoore pounded the wall, then rubbed his bruised hand.

Lucas first heard it – the whispering, faint but unmistakable. "Shut up! Listen."

It was the knights. Their ancestors. All whispering, "Trust the rings."

Lucas said, "I told you. We have to trust the rings."

"I think it's some trick by m'lor – Mordred. I want to go. *Now*," said Maya.

Des shook his head emphatically. "Lucas is right. Kismet. Destiny. We have to have faith."

Dunmoore chuckled, but to Lucas it sounded sad. *Defeated, that's what he is. Don't give up on us, yet, Prof.*

Dunmoore tapped his Rolex as he said, "Kismet. Unmei. Destiny. Faith." He held the watch to his ear. "I haven't had much faith in my lifetime. Now or never seems appropriate." He began to wind the watch stem. "In any event, I'm fresh out of ideas."

Karen urged, "Go ahead, Des. It's your religion. Your faith."

Des walked slowly behind the white marble altar. He started to reach into the opening and hesitated, but only for a few seconds, then thrust his hand inside. When he turned around, he held the glowing pendant tightly in his grasp. "This is it. I can feel it."

Out of the opening came...nothing. No scorpions, no snakes, nothing. Realizing he had been holding his breath, Lucas let it out and grinned.

Karen tapped Des on the shoulder. "May I?"

Lucas saw that Des wore what his mom would call a blissful smile. *Like he's seen God or something,* said the little voice. Lucas shrugged and thought, *Maybe he did.*

"It's beautiful!" cooed Karen. She handed the pendant to Ryan, somewhat reluctantly, Lucas noticed.

"Hypnotic. If you believe in that crap, that is." Ryan passed the pendant to Lucas, holding onto it longer than normal.

Lucas grinned again. He could feel the richness of the pendant, its purity. "I guess I believe in that crap, Ryan. It's like you could get lost in it." Even though he hated to give it up, he handed the relic to Dunmoore.

Dunmoore's face lit up as much as the others' had. Just as he started to place the relic into Maya's outstretched, eager hands, there came a voice from the entranceway.

"Wonderful, my dears. You've done well. Now be a good boy, Morgan, and hand it to me, or you'll have no hands left. Yours or Allah's." Joanna Richards stood in the room with a .357 Magnum trained on Dunmoore's hands – and the pendant.

Chapter Forty-Two

Revenge is Bitter

Until being trapped in that cavern by an agent of the Dark Powers, Lucas hadn't realized the full meaning of "love is blind." That when you discover someone you love is a traitor to all you hold dear, your first thought is to deny it. For Dunmoore greeted his fiancée not with outrage, but with delighted confusion. "Joanna! Whatever are you doing here? However did you find us?"

"Your little trick with Hadrian's Wall was rather clever, but not sharp enough." Joanna motioned with her gun to Dunmoore. "Hand over the relic or I *will* shoot you."

A shot rang out. The gun flew from Joanna's hands as she screeched in pain, blood streaming from her hand, and Ryan's handgun aimed at her chest. "You bastard!"

"Actually, me mother and father married *before* I was born," said Ryan. "At least you've got a hand left. Which is more than you were going to leave the Prof." Ryan motioned with his head. "Get her gun, Lucas."

While Lucas retrieved the handgun, Dunmoore crammed the pendant into his pants pocket and rushed to Joanna with a handkerchief.

Joanna backed away, crying, "Don't touch me!"

"Don't be a bloody fool, Joanna." Dunmoore grabbed her shoulders. "Let me bind your wound so you don't bleed all over the place. It isn't you we're after."

Looking away from her fiancé, she held out her hand and allowed him to fashion the handkerchief into a kind of tourniquet.

Dunmoore asked, "Are you in much pain? Can you stand it for a while longer?"

"It hurts. Hurts like hell."

Dunmoore turned to the others. "I'd like to take her back with us."

"She's a traitor, Morgan," said Karen, glowering at Joanna.

Lucas agreed. "Look at her ring, Prof. She's one of them!"

Joanna crossed her arms to her chest in a feeble attempt to hide the bone pinkie ring on her good hand. She refused to look at Dunmoore.

Maya's eyes narrowed. "We should leave her here."

"Please. She cannot do us any more harm. Ryan's seen to that." Dunmoore nodded at the gangly Irish teen.

Ryan kept his gun on Joanna. "I don't know why you'd want to help a rat like her, Prof." He shrugged. "But it's your life."

Dunmoore turned to Joanna. "There's someone who can help you. Heal you."

Joanna barked out a harsh laugh. "Merlin? Then you will have truly lost, Morgan."

"What do you mean?"

"Forget it, Prof," said Lucas. "Let's just get out of here."

"Maybe we *should* listen to what she has to say?" said Maya, with that odd half-smirk again on her face.

Lucas stared at her. *First, she can't wait to leave — without the relic. Now, she wants to stay?* Joanna's words cut off his thoughts.

"You may have retrieved all three relics, but once you leave here, the Dark Powers will know. Mordred will have them disperse for a time. Only to reunite. They'll overpower your ineffectual Merlin, *again*, and be as strong as ever. You will have won nothing but a little time. Your fathers' deaths will have been in vain." Joanna turned to Dunmoore. "You are so close to destroying them, my love."

"Why would you want to help us destroy them?" asked Dunmoore.

"It's a trap, you muppet," said Ryan. "And you better shut yours, slag-hag."

Joanna clutched Dunmoore's arm and stared into his eyes. "I'm tired of all the evil, Morgan. But Mordred will have me killed, unless we kill him first. I know where his fortress is. My ring will take me there. Will take *us* there."

"Will the man who killed my father be there?" asked Maya.

Joanna nodded. "You can take revenge upon the man who left you fatherless and your mother a grieving widow."

"Don't listen to her, Maya," ordered Des. "She's evil. She's lying!"

"Am I, Desmondo?" asked Joanna in a gentle voice. "Wouldn't you like to avenge your father's death? The same man who killed Maya's father also killed yours. Left him broken and crushed in the streets of Morocco. You weren't even fourteen. And what of your sisters? Fatherless before they were teenagers."

Ryan pointed the gun at Joanna's head. "Shut your mouth or I'll shut it for you. Your limo man didn't kill my father. We aren't biting."

Joanna gave Ryan the once-over, then curtly nodded. "You're right. The man who killed their fathers did not kill yours."

Ryan snorted, giving Lucas an "I told you so" look. But Lucas saw the thin cruel smile etched on Joanna's face. He cringed, not wanting to hear what she was going to say.

"*Your* father was killed by another agent. Or should I say, *set up* by another agent?"

"That's a lie! My father died..." Ryan did not finish the sentence.

"Your father died how?" asked Joanna, the malicious smile still upon her lips. "Tell them, brave boy." She looked at the others. "His father died in prison. Convicted of bombing a school bus, killing innocent children."

Lucas stared at Ryan. *Jeez, no wonder the guy's got such a chip.*

Ryan cocked the pistol and gave the agent a hard look.

Joanna said softly, "He *didn't* kill those children."

The pistol lowered slightly.

"One of his IRA comrades placed the bomb on the school bus and made it look like your father had done it. That man was an agent of the Dark Powers. His testimony sent your father to prison, where he died. And left you and your family to bear the shame. Your mother. Your sisters. But you're not *biting?*"

Ryan whispered, "That's a lie," as he furiously rubbed his Celtic cross between the fingers of his free hand.

Lucas knew Ryan was a goner. Ryan believed Joanna. *Wanted* to believe Joanna. As did Maya and Des...and Dunmoore.

Joanna turned to Lucas. "Didn't you ever wonder how your father, a brilliant architect, died in such a freakish construction accident? He was *pushed* into the hole, and the crane was toppled onto him, courtesy of two who serve Mordred."

Sadness and anger roiled inside Lucas. He knew she told the truth. And he hated her.

Joanna played her advantage like a card shark. "I can take you to them. To Mordred. You can kill them and avenge your fathers' deaths. For yourselves. For your families."

Lucas felt his ring sear his flesh. He stared at it. The ring had begun to darken, to blacken. He heard Don Vasquez whisper, "Destiny, Lucas. Not revenge." A calm swept over him, extinguishing his fear and anger. Opening his eyes, he realized the others had been hypnotized by Joanna's smooth voice, by her truth and lies.

"No!" he shouted. "That isn't why we're here!"

"She's right, Luke. What good will it do to reunite the relics if the Dark Powers escape? Let's finish them off for good." Dunmoore moved swiftly, grasping Joanna's left hand. He removed her ring of bone and placed it on his left pinkie. "It can take us to the Dark Powers. We can end this once and for all."

"We must move quickly," urged Joanna. "Surprise is crucial." She walked calmly out of the room, followed by Dunmoore, Maya, Des and Ryan.

Lucas felt lost. He turned to Karen. "What do we do? This is all wrong!" The panic rose like bile in his throat.

"I know, hon. But you need to convince them of that. And quickly."

Lucas and Karen ran from the room, racing after the others down the corridor. Lucas called out, "Remember what Merlin said? Why did we come on the quest? What were we trying to accomplish? Not revenge. Remember why the others failed? They sought revenge, glory!"

He caught up to Ryan and swung him around. "Our fathers are dead. It doesn't matter why or how. Not now. We're here for the living. Remember what happened back in the temple? When you quit believing? We have to be united against the Dark Powers!"

Ryan shoved Lucas hard, knocking the rattler hat to the packed dirt floor. Suddenly, he stopped and cocked his head. Lucas heard it, too. It was Gawain's voice.

"Do not bow to pride, Ryan. Your father was an honorable man. Do not blacken that honor today. Listen to your heart. Trust the ring."

Ryan's ring had turned an ugly black – the color of evil. Ryan grabbed Lucas's hand. That ring once again glowed a beautiful emerald green.

Closing his eyes, Ryan massaged his temples, a grimace on his face. When he opened his eyes, they shone clear and lucid. He grinned. "You saved *me* this time, mate. We're even."

Lucas slapped his rattler hat on his head and clapped Ryan on the shoulder. "Screw even. We gotta get to the others."

They dashed down the corridor. Ryan jerked Des and Maya to a halt, shouting, "The slag is one of them! Look at your rings! See what your hate's doing to your rings!"

Des's ring was the same ugly black color as Ryan's had been – a vicious, swirling cloud of evil. Des gasped.

Lucas glanced at Maya's hand, but she quickly hid it behind her back. Lucas thought he caught a glimpse of silver. Maya bowed her head.

"I almost became one of them, didn't I?" a shaken Des asked.

"Could never happen, little guy," said Ryan, hugging Des's shoulder.

Karen screamed.

Then, Lucas heard the hissing. The asp!

Ryan turned and assumed his shooter's stance, firing all of his bullets down the corridor. The asp screamed a high-pitched wail at each hit, but continued its relentless slithering up the corridor, fangs bared.

"The sword!" Lucas yelled. The three boys placed their hands on the sword and aimed it at the asp. Only weak beams of light shot from the sword, but where they hit, they burned, causing the asp to scream in pain. Still, the creature continued its measured advance. This time, it would not be denied.

"The rings haven't recovered yet!" shouted Lucas. Ryan's ring had turned seafoam green, on its way to emerald. Des's ring gave off only a dim blue luster. "We need more power." Lucas turned to Maya. "Put your hand in."

Maya shook her head. Her eyes bulged with terror.

She's useless. Worse than useless. Lucas yelled up the corridor. "Prof! We need the pendant!"

But Joanna was tugging at Dunmoore's sleeve, pleading with him to, "Think of your father, Morgan. Think of what they did to your father. They set the asp upon him. He died a horrible, torturous death. Avenge him!"

Dunmoore did not respond to Joanna or Lucas. He seemed dazed and disoriented.

What the heck is wrong, Prof? thought Lucas. It hit him. *The ring.* He shouted to the others, "He's wearing the ring!"

Karen stared at Lucas, frowning. Then her eyes grew wide, and she turned and ran up the corridor. Hitting Joanna hard in the back, Karen sent her sprawling to the floor, then tore the pendant from the bewildered Dunmoore and dragged him back down the corridor.

Maya screamed!

The asp was almost upon them; the sword's power was depleted.

Tossing the pendant to Lucas, Karen threw herself into the head of the creature. It hit her full force in the chest with its fangs. Screaming in agony, Karen fell to the floor. The asp rose up, ready to strike again!

In a flash, the three boys held the Hands of Allah, and a brilliant turquoise light shot from the pendant, vaporizing the asp. All that remained of the monster was the familiar, stomach-curdling stench.

Lucas had no more than a moment's respite from the terror in the pyramid when he heard Joanna's screams – accompanied by multiple hissing sounds. He looked up the corridor. *Oh, Holy Jeez!* An army of normal-size asps slithered toward them.

"Form a circle, quickly," Lucas ordered. He pulled the still-hypnotized Dunmoore into the circle, and they knelt to accommodate Karen, who moaned with pain. They began to chant.

"Don't leave me!" Joanna ran toward them. Asps now wrapped themselves around her legs. Two squirmed in and around her hair. "For God's sake, don't leave me here!"

"Too late to think of God now, you mingin' slag," said Ryan.

The wind tunnel took them away.

Chapter Forty-Three

B

Out of Reach

The damp, cold air off Lake Windermere never felt so welcoming or smelled so wonderful. The mist hung heavy as ever, but Lucas sensed something was wrong. *No wind-man. No tingling. And where's Merlin?* Lucas's pulse raced. He heard Karen's moans, soft and weak. He yelled for Merlin. The others soon joined him. Still, Merlin did not appear. "Where is he?" screamed Lucas.

Des said in a calm voice, "Let's put our rings together."

Maya knelt by Karen as the three boys huddled together, their rings glowing a brilliant emerald green. The sky darkened, and the wind-man sighed. The tingling began. Dunmoore stood apart from the others, a dazed look in his eye, the bone ring still on his pinkie. Suddenly, Merlin's image appeared in the gnarled oak tree.

"Ah, my Crusaders return. What news have you?" The wizard paused and cocked his head slightly. "Something is not right."

Lucas rushed to the oak-Merlin. "Karen is badly injured. The asp got her."

"Heal her, Merlin, sir," pleaded Ryan. "Like you healed me."

"Bring her to me," Merlin commanded.

The boys carried Karen to the wizard and laid her on the forest floor. Merlin moved his arms over the wounds on Karen's chest, then slowly around the rest of her body. The lightest blue seemed to glow all over her. Her breathing became more even, and her groans became fewer and fewer, until they ceased altogether.

"You did it!" Lucas leaped in the air, pumping his right fist.

Merlin's steel-blue eyes took in Maya, then Dunmoore. "Something is amiss."

Lucas didn't understand until Des shouted, "The ring! Dunmoore has Joanna's ring!"

With a high-pitched battle cry, Maya tackled Dunmoore and ripped the ring from his finger, then strode back to Merlin, a strange grin on her face.

Des ran to Maya with wide eyes. "Are you okay?"

Merlin's bushy eyebrows arched. He stared at Maya, then shook his head and looked at the others. "The relic? Have you brought The Hands of Allah?"

"Here it is." Des pulled the silver pendant from his pants pocket.

Maya screamed again, grabbing the pendant and Des. She held one of his arms behind his back, a knife to his throat.

"Maya, what in heaven's name," said Dunmoore, only just coming out of his stupor.

"Fools! I am Miatsu. I serve the Dark One. Maya is with *him*." She shifted Des abruptly to her left and screamed at Ryan, who had leveled his handgun at her. "Drop it or I slice his throat, then rip his heart out! Not even your Merlin could save him then."

"You're lying!" Ryan looked to Merlin. "She's lying, right?"

"And what of your precious Maya?" sneered Miatsu. "Tell them, old man!"

Merlin sighed. "She is correct, Master Casey. I cannot save Mistress Hosokawa. Not if she is with...Mordred."

"Drop the gun, Ryan. Now!" Lucas ordered.

Ryan flinched and turned to Lucas, a scowl on his face. Then, he nodded and placed the gun on the ground.

Lucas turned to the false Maya. "What do you want?"

"You accompany me to my lord and master's castle. In return for the relics and your rings, you save your friends' lives. And your own."

Dunmoore asked, "Why should we trust you? Mordred will kill us all once he has the rings and relics. He's tried many a time before."

Miatsu gave a high-pitched cackle. "Idiots! It was not you he was after, it was the rings. Once he has them, you are no threat to him. He is a man of honor."

The sky darkened and lightning flashed. "Tell your vile master that he shall not take possession of these relics!" Merlin's voice thundered. His image began to fade. Before he disappeared, he whispered, "Crusaders. Use your hands to see."

"AAIIEEE!" howled Miatsu, turning Des about this way and that, using him as a shield against any potential attack by the sorcerer.

When Miatsu stopped gyrating, Lucas saw that Des was bleeding from under his chin. "You're hurt!" Lucas started toward him.

"Away!" Miatsu screamed.

"I'm okay," Des replied. "It's just a nick." But his voice sounded shaky.

Dunmoore put out his hands. "Let's all calm down. Miss...did you say *Miatsu*? You can see that we are unable to provide your master with the Holy Grail or Eye of Buddha."

Miatsu narrowed her eyes.

"But if Mordred would settle for The Hands of Allah and the rings, then we'll agree to the exchange."

"No bloody way, Prof!" Ryan exclaimed. "Don't be a mentaller!"

"We have no choice," replied Dunmoore. "Their lives are at stake."

Miatsu nodded her head at Ryan and Lucas. "You two, over here."

The two boys walked slowly to Des and Miatsu. Dunmoore moved to join them when Miatsu yelled, "Not you! You have no ring. You stay here."

"The boys cannot travel without me."

"The Dark One said only three were needed."

"Yes, but they do not know the language. The traveling spell must be spoken in Middle English."

Miatsu pressed the knife to Des's neck and whispered, "Does he speak the truth?"

"Yes."

Miatsu grunted. "All right. You join them. No tricks."

Lucas, Ryan and Dunmoore formed a half-circle and put their right hands toward Des and Miatsu. Dunmoore explained that the ring hands had to touch, and Miatsu allowed Des to put his right hand on top of the others'. Miatsu then placed her right hand on top. Her left hand held the knife tight to Des's throat.

"Good luck, y'all," Karen whispered from under the oak tree.

"Where are we to go?" asked Dunmoore.

"Throne room. Fortress of Shadows. Transylvania."

Dunmoore muttered something in Middle English. He took a deep breath. "All right, boys, repeat after me."

In a rush of wind, they arrived *outside* the Fortress of Shadows. Before Miatsu could blink, Dunmoore wrested the knife from her and plunged it into her heart. With one soft, "Aaiiee," she fell to the ground, the blood pooling around her. Her face transformed from Maya's to that of an older Japanese woman with green streaks in her black hair.

"Jaysus, Mary and Joseph," whispered Ryan.

"Thanks, Professor," croaked Des, one hand tight to his bleeding neck.

Dunmoore tore the pendant and the silver ring from Miatsu's dead fingers. "We've got to get inside and save Maya."

"But we don't know where she is. The fortress is huge." Lucas stared at the massive monument to evil. It seemed impenetrable: The black marble towers in back faced an enormous drop from a cliff into a roiling river below. The front towers peered down the mountain slopes. If the horseshoe of jagged, smoke-gray boulders did not deter intruders, the boiling moat did.

"We've got to get out of sight, Luke." Dunmoore tapped his Rolex.

"What about near those boulders?" Lucas pointed down the slope.

In seconds, they stood behind the boulders, sheltered from view of the castle's inhabitants.

"Now, Luke, how do you propose we ascertain where Maya is within the fortress?" asked Dunmoore, holding his watch to his ear.

Like I should know? thought Lucas. Frustration and anger bubbled inside him. "Jeez, Prof! The damn watch doesn't work. Get a new one, will ya?"

Dunmoore stared open-mouthed, then lowered his arm. "It was my father's. His favorite. But, I suppose you are correct. It's useless." He slipped the watch off his wrist and dropped it to the ground, where it sank quickly in the snow.

Lucas's gut ached with guilt. "I-I didn't know," he stammered.

Dunmoore clapped him on the back. "To the task at hand, Luke. Any ideas how to find Maya?"

Lucas gave a glum nod. "I think Merlin gave us a clue. Use your hands to see."

"Do you think he meant the rings?" Des examined his hands.

Lucas shook his head. "He would have said *rings*, not hands."

"How can we see with our hands?" asked Ryan.

Lucas glanced at the pendant dangling from Dunmoore's fingers. "The Hands of Allah."

Dunmoore held it up for examination. "I suspect you boys will still have to use the rings."

The teens put their ring hands on the pendant. It emitted a turquoise glow for a brief few seconds, but nothing else.

"Maybe we should concentrate on Maya?" suggested Des.

Lucas closed his eyes and thought of Maya. *Achingly beautiful, clever Maya. Come on, Maya. Show yourself.*

"Oh my lord," whispered Dunmoore.

Lucas opened his eyes. Above their heads hung a three-dimensional hologram. Maya lay bound and suspended in a net over a watery pit, accompanied by a slightly older woman, also bound and gagged. An enormous Amazon warrior and a tall ninja guarded both. Underneath the net lurked yellow-eyed crocodiles. White and black crocodiles.

"Maya!" screamed Des.

Maya opened her eyes wide and whispered. The hologram dissolved.

Chapter Forty-Four

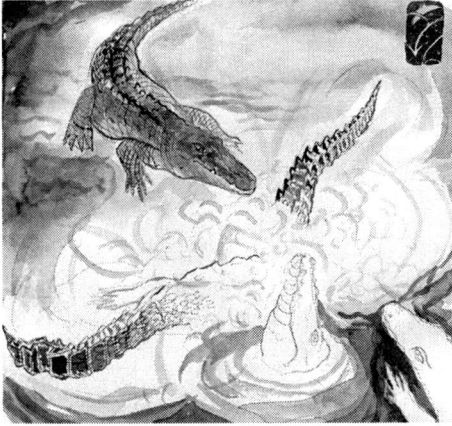

Of Mordred and Morgan

The Crusaders chanted the spell to bring them into the lagoon dungeon. They landed *atop* the ninja. In the resulting scramble to right themselves, the woman warrior attacked with a fierce battle cry. Dunmoore managed to get one shot off before his gun was ripped from his hand – along with strips of his skin from the warrior's ten-inch metal nails. But that one shot was enough to do damage to the evil Nailom.

She looked at the gaping hole in her left shoulder, blood pouring from it. With an expression of astonishment and rage, she lunged at Dunmoore, only to be hit mid-leap by turquoise laser beams from the relic. Nailom exploded into a million pieces, then dissolved into nothingness.

Lucas had little time to contemplate this oddity, however, for Dunmoore immediately shouted, "Behind you!"

With a ferocious kick, the ninja struck Ryan in the middle of the back, sending him sprawling, the relic clattering across the dungeon floor to the very edge of the embankment, just out of reach of the curious crocodiles.

Des dove for the pendant, but was knocked away by a karate chop. He sprawled in the dirt cradling his injured shoulder. Dunmoore's attempt at tackling the ninja met with a similar fate: A swinging kick caught the Professor at chest level, knocking him to the ground, where he lay gasping for air.

The ninja turned and faced his remaining adversary.

Lucas's heart pounded as he looked from the ninja to the pendant, then back to the ninja. Who tilted his head and roared with laughter.

Lucas charged.

While he may not have seemed a formidable opponent, the ninja was unaware of Lucas's capabilities as a high jumper. Lucas neared the cliff's edge. The ninja made a flying kick, but Lucas leaped higher and arched his back, completely avoiding the ninja, who tumbled into the lagoon and into the jaws of the reptiles. His screams merged with the sounds of splashing and chomping, until they ceased altogether.

Lucas grabbed the pendant and secured it around his neck, then turned to the others.

"Good show, Luke," gasped Dunmoore.

"I thought you were a goner, mate," said Ryan, still partially bent over from the ninja's attack. One side of his face was scraped raw.

Lucas helped Des to his feet. "Let's get Maya and scram."

He looked up at the two prisoners, helpless in the net stretched above the lagoon. "Do you think the net will hold us all?"

"Don't risk it," said Dunmoore. "You three travel quickly to the net, then back to the ground. Even if the net breaks, keep your ring hands together and you'll be fine. Oh..." Dunmoore dug in his pocket and took out a silver ring. "...Give this to Maya."

The three teens memorized and chanted the spell to bring them to the net above the lagoon. In a second, they were huddled over her and her companion. Suddenly, the sagging mesh broke.

"To the left of the lagoon!" Dunmoore shouted it again in Middle English.

Just as they were about to drop into the watery pit, they disappeared – and reappeared on the *opposite* side of the lagoon!

"Be there in a sec, Prof," Lucas yelled, then gasped.

A man with long dark hair, dressed all in black save for a purple cape, stood on the opposite shore. Scores of warriors stood behind him. Next to the man in black stood Dunmoore, held captive by another man with pointy gold canines. The longhaired man wore around his neck two silver rings on a silver chain. He bowed to the teens.

"Hail, Crusaders! Welcome to our humble abode!"

"Mordred!" whispered Lucas.

"What a dilemma we seem to have!" Mordred's voice floated across the cavern.

Ryan screamed, "You've got the problem, scum! We've got the relic and the rings!" He puffed out his chest, then winced.

"Quite true, quite true." Mordred twirled the chain. "But we've got dear Professor Dunmoore. Oh, and two of the rings."

Lucas looked at their rings, all of which cast a faint greenish glow, except Maya's. "Damn! He's got Maya's ring."

Maya whispered, "And Elaine's. She's one of us."

The older woman smiled through cracked, bloody lips and missing teeth. "Elaine LaCroix. *A votre service.*"

Lucas stared. "Elaine LaCroix?"

Ryan yelled across the lagoon. "We only need three rings to travel, Mordred. So screw you!"

"And leave your leader behind? Tsk, tsk, Professor." Mordred shook his head. "Only at times like this do you know who your true friends are." Mordred nodded to Vassalar.

Vassalar tilted Dunmoore's neck toward him and sank his teeth into the flesh.

Dunmoore screamed.

This cannot be happening! Lucas shouted, "No! Don't! What do you want?"

"Enough," said Mordred. Vassalar lifted his head and licked the blood from his lips. Drops of blood trickled from the two holes in Dunmoore's neck.

Suddenly, a turquoise laser beam shot across the lagoon, striking Mordred in the chest. The warriors gasped, but Mordred remained standing, unharmed. He smiled. "Ah, the benefits of immortality." His smile disappeared. "Enough of these games! Give us The Hands of Allah and your rings. In return, we will spare your lives. All your lives."

"Don't!" Dunmoore screamed.

Vassalar flashed a pointy-tooth grin. "Ah, he prefers to be my lunch."

"No!" shouted Lucas. "We'll do as you say."

Mordred stroked his chin, considering. "Leave him, Vassalar."

With a snarl, Vassalar released Dunmoore, who swayed next to Mordred. The Dark One called out, "You see? Our word is good. Come, let us commence the exchange. Say the spell."

As the teens put their ring hands together, Dunmoore screamed, "It's a trap!" and tore the chain from around Mordred's neck. Dunmoore leaped over the embankment and into the water.

"Get him!" Mordred bellowed.

But not one of the warriors took a step toward what would undoubtedly be death by reptile.

Dunmoore got thirty feet before the first crocodile reached him. As the jaws snapped open, Dunmoore hurled the chain and rings into the air.

"Prof! No!" With a strangled cry, Lucas jumped and caught the silver circles. Then watched in horror as the crocodiles dragged Dunmoore to a watery grave.

"Kill them! GET THOSE RINGS!" Mordred's face turned as purple as his cape with rage.

Amid the war screams and the hailstorm of arrows, lances and bullets, the teens spelled themselves back to Lake Windermere.

Without their friend and mentor.

Chapter Forty-Five

Destiny Fulfilled

The wind tunnel dumped them at the base of the gnarled oak, narrowly missing Karen, who had been pacing around the magical tree since they had departed with the Maya imposter.

"Thank God, you're back!" Karen rushed to the group and began hugging them. "Oh, lord, Maya, honey, are you okay?" Maya nodded and tried to smile through her split, swollen lips, then collapsed in Karen's arms.

"We've got to get Merlin. Fast!" Lucas wasted no time in getting the Crusaders to hold ring hands. All five rings emitted a deep, pulsing, green glow. A heavy mist descended, the wind-man sighed through the trees, and the tingling ran through Lucas's body.

Merlin's image appeared on the oak – his smile beamed, his blue eyes shone. "I dared not hope you would return, but you have. What joyous news have you?"

"Not now, sir. We need your help in healing Maya." Lucas looked around. "And Des and Ryan. And Elaine. Elaine LaCroix. Another Crusader."

"The Mink?" Merlin's bushy eyebrows raised high on his wrinkled forehead. He nodded and bent his image over Maya, now in Karen's arms on the ground. As he began to move his arms over her body, Maya opened her one good eye and murmured, "Leave the shoulder, sir." A light blue glow surrounded the young Asian girl, except for her left shoulder. When it vanished, Maya looked as beautiful and healthy as the day Lucas first met her. She opened her cat-yellow eyes and smiled, revealing white even teeth and smooth red lips.

Maya held one of Elaine's hands – red and blistered – as Merlin worked his magic. Miraculously, the bruises, burns and scrapes disappeared, and the bone-breaks knitted whole.

"Welcome, little Mink, welcome," said Merlin.

Merlin next moved his arms over Des's body, and the same blue glow performed its healing magic – mending his broken arm and repairing the damage done to his right knee, where a bullet had passed through during the attack at the fortress.

"You're next, Ryan," said Lucas.

Ryan nodded and stepped to the tree. He closed his eyes. When Merlin had finished, Ryan's back was no longer bruised and sore, his face was unscathed, and the two arrows which had pierced him – one in the left arm, one in the calf – lay broken on the ground, the damage they had wrought now reversed.

Merlin turned to Lucas. "Master Moreno?"

"I'm fine, sir. Lucky, I guess."

Merlin gazed at the mortals gathered around him. "I sense Professor Dunmoore is no longer with us?"

"What?" asked Karen. She put her hand to her mouth. "Oh, my God, where's Morgan?"

"Gone," choked out Lucas, wiping away the tears that had finally come.

Ryan said in a flat tone, "Dead." He took deep breaths.

"All for us. All for nothing," sobbed Des, not trying to hide his sorrow.

"What do you mean?," questioned Merlin. "Did you not retrieve The Hands of Allah?"

"We have it." Lucas took the pendant from around his neck.

The wizard furrowed his lined brow even further. "Why do you say 'all for nothing?'"

"Because we gave the Dark Powers too much lead time," replied Ryan. "That slag said they'd get away once they knew we had all three relics. And now the Prof...the bastards!"

"Do not despair, my Crusaders," said the wizard. "Professor Dunmoore's death has not been in vain. The Dark Powers are destroyed. Give me The Hands of Allah, Master Moreno."

Lucas placed the pendant in the aura of Merlin's image. The relic dangled in the air, joined by the Holy Grail and Eye of Buddha.

"Watch," commanded Merlin.

A colorful light started to twirl about the three holy relics. It grew larger and more colorful, and twirled faster and faster until it became a spinning ball of light. Suddenly, the ball broke up into tens of thousands of beams of light – a myriad of colors. They shot off in all directions – shooting beams filling the sky! Then, they vanished.

Lucas watched in awe, then looked to Merlin, who again commanded, "Wait." Within a minute, the beams of colored light again filled the sky, joining together to form a ball of light. Merlin uttered an incantation.

Inside the ball, a hologram of the Fortress of Shadows appeared. The fortress spun around and around, then dissolved to the lagoon dungeon. Warriors lay in heaps on the ground. Mordred stood screaming, ripping his hair out. Suddenly, he began to convulse, and his body emitted a blood-red glow. In a blinding flash of light, Mordred dissolved into a dark pool of slime. The hologram vanished.

The ball of light slowly dissipated over the three relics, leaving only a faint glow about them. And then, nothing.

"What happened?" whispered Lucas.

"The reuniting of the relics destroyed the dominion of the Dark Powers. Each beam of light sought out anyone wearing the ring of bone, instantly electrocuting them – stopping their hearts. The Dark Powers and their agents are no more."

"But Mordred? That was no shake-and-bake," said Ryan.

"The reuniting of the relics broke the spell of immortality. Hundreds of years of evil are now reduced to a vile pool."

"No more evil!" cheered Ryan. "That was savage!"

Lucas joined in the whooping and hollering until Merlin's somber voice stopped him mid-whoop.

"Yes...and no, Master Casey. Yes, you destroyed the Dark Powers. No, there is still evil."

"But you just said they destroyed the Dark Powers," argued Karen.

"There will always be evil, Mistress Chapman, as long as there is man. But, Mordred and his Dark Powers were a great evil, the greatest there has ever been, and they have been destroyed. It will take centuries – perhaps never again if man is fortunate – for there to be *such* evil in your world."

"What about the Prof? Why did he have to die?" asked Lucas. The joy he had felt just seconds ago lay buried beneath an avalanche of sorrow.

"I think he suspected he might, hon." Karen took a letter from her pocket. "He asked me to read this to you if....Shall I?"

My Dear Crusaders:

Our time together is nearly over. But while your lives are just beginning, I have had the sense these past few days that my time on Earth is nearing an end. And I have learned from all of you to trust my feelings.

*What we have achieved, what **you** have achieved, is nothing short of miraculous.*

*I realize now that **life** is the true miracle. Your persistence, your dedication, your **faith**, and your love of life have taught me that lesson. Had I only met you earlier. Perhaps I would not have wasted so much of myself, of my life, on revenge. But that is neither here nor there. I have a few last words for my Crusaders.*

Karen. I believe my being out-voted at the hotel will prove to be extremely fortunate for us, and the Quest. Thank you for your belief in modern-day miracles.

Karen smiled, took a deep breath, then continued to read.

Ryan. You have brought great honor to your family. Do not concern yourself about the school treasury. That has been taken care of. You take care of yourself. You are meant for great things, Ryan. Honorable endeavors.

Lucas watched Ryan turn away to wipe the tears from his eyes, the Celtic cross held tight in one hand.

Maya. You are a true Samurai. A warrior princess. Shin'ichi would be very proud.

"And Lancelot of you," Maya choked out between her soft sobs.

Des. We would never have made it without your brains and your computer wizardry. You take care of yourself and your sisters. I know you'll surpass even Bill Gates one day.

"It isn't fair." Des's shoulders heaved with his weeping. Maya hugged him.

*Luke. Thank you. You believed. And you made me believe. You made me see what was important: The measure of a man's life is not how long he lives, but **how** he lives. Any man would be proud to have you for a son.* **Lucas.**

With great fondness,
Morgan Dunmoore.

Lucas wiped the tears from his eyes and said to the sky, "It's *Luke*."

Merlin placed one hand on Lucas's shoulder and one on Des's. "Professor Dunmoore's time in this world is over. But he is not alone. The others will be there to welcome him to the next world. His father will be there for him. Cry for your loss, but not for him."

Lucas looked into Merlin's eyes and *knew* the wisdom of what he said. Then, he felt a weight on his shoulder. Merlin's hand – not his aura – on his shoulder. "Merlin! You're real! I mean, you're free!"

An excited babbling began. Merlin finally commanded their attention by creating a huge thunderclap in the sky. The Crusaders fell silent.

"I am no longer imprisoned. Your success in the quest released me from Vivienne's enchantment."

"Did you know this would happen?" Lucas asked.

"I believed it would be one result of the success of the crusade, yes."

V.L. Hoyt

"But why didn't you tell us earlier?"

"Remember what I told you before you undertook the last part of the quest, Master Moreno?"

Lucas nodded. "You told us to remember why we had joined the crusade. To remember why the others had failed."

"And why did you join the crusade?"

"To save our families," answered Lucas.

"And save the world from the Dark Powers," added Maya.

"And why did the ones who came before you fail?" asked Merlin.

"Because they wanted revenge," said Des.

"And glory," added Ryan.

Elaine said, "Riches."

"*That* is why I did not tell you. Because to succeed in the quest, your purpose, your motive, had to be pure." Merlin looked at each of the Crusaders in turn. "To save others, to save the world. That was the purity of spirit required for success. Anything else – revenge, glory, my freedom – would only have deterred you from the true nature of the quest."

"Now what?" asked Ryan.

"What do you mean, Master Casey?"

"What do we do now? Where do we go? What do we tell people?"

"And what about Professor Dunmoore?" asked Maya, sadness again creeping into her voice.

Lucas added, "And his mother? I don't want her to go through what she went through when the Prof's dad disappeared."

"I shall take care of Professor Dunmoore. His mother shall receive a telegram notifying her of his death while on a mission for the British government." Merlin looked at Lucas. "It will surely cause great grief for his mother. But at least she will know."

"What about the rest of us?" asked Des.

"The rest of you." Merlin placed his chin in his hand and closed his eyes. After a few moments, he looked up. "Your work here is finished. You are free to go wherever you like, as you always have been. Free to continue your life as you desire."

"That's it?" asked Ryan.

"Do you not desire to return to your families?"

Lucas said, "It's just...I think what Ryan's getting at is, after all that's happened, to simply go home and act like *nothing* happened, to go back to our old lives seems, well, anticlimactic."

"Boring," said Ryan.

"How else would you have it? Is that not the reason you undertook the quest? To preserve your – to use Master Moreno's words – *old lives?*"

No one responded.

"Even the original Round Table knights led routine lives after a battle or crusade. You would not truly want to have such activity as you have had over the past few days every day for the rest of your lives, would you?"

"No, sir!" said Des, shaking his head so much that his glasses slid down his nose and almost off his face.

"That is as it should be. As for acting as if this did not occur: That is up to each of you, individually, to decide. You may tell whomever you desire. Only," Merlin paused. "In this day and age, I imagine most, if not all, of the people to whom you relate your tale will find it incredulous. People are not as open to the wonders of magic and nature as they were centuries past."

Lucas shrugged. "So, that's it, then. I guess we need to figure out how to get home, since we need three of us to travel."

"I would so like to travel," Elaine said. "From what Maya tells me, it is magical."

Merlin said, "And so you shall. But you need not three to travel any longer."

"You mean that we can travel on our own?" Maya asked.

"Savage!" exclaimed Ryan.

Wonder and delight bubbled up in Lucas, again. *Traveling anywhere I want, anytime I want. What a way to go!* Lucas caressed his ring.

"You misunderstand. Now that the crusade is accomplished, the power of the rings is depleted."

Among them all, Elaine's sigh was the deepest. She looked longingly at her ring.

"Except for one last trip." Merlin smiled. "Each of your rings will take you on a final journey to wherever you wish to go. And then the ring will simply be...a ring."

Though disappointed, Lucas accepted the news as he had accepted everything else thrown at him on the quest – with a great amount of grace and a minimum of grumbling.

They planned their final trips.

Ryan was heading back to the Aran Isles. He would tell his family that he took the money in order to join up with the IRA in Northern Ireland and then had a change of heart. "I'm not so keen on violent uprisings anymore. Maybe it's time to start changing the world peacefully."

Lucas smiled. *The new and improved Ryan Casey.*

Maya was returning to school in London. "I need time to decompress." Maya began to toss her hair back, then caught herself and smiled sheepishly. "I want to learn more about the world. The way it was. The way it is." She stroked the coiled serpent brand on her shoulder.

And the Ice Princess is melted. Lucas grinned.

Des was going to Morocco to surprise his family. "I miss them. And, I have some interesting ideas for a computer game."

"I'll bet you do!" Lucas laughed, then turned to Karen. "What about you? How will you get back to Egypt?"

Karen smiled, "After what we've just been through, Egypt isn't high on my list of places to go right now. I'll catch a bus back to my cousins' house. And, I think I might just invite Dr. Aba Ben Habib to the States for a holiday."

Lucas scowled. *She's not much older than you,* said the little voice. *Give it some time.* Lucas smiled. *Right for once, buddy. There's always time.*

"What about you, Elaine?" asked Maya. "You're welcome to stay with me."

"*Non, merci.* I need time alone to think. To plan my future." Elaine gave a shy smile to Merlin. "I think my days as cat burglar are *fini.* Even one life is *trop précieux* to squander."

Lucas would "travel" to Disney World to play with his band. He missed his best friends. And Shadow. And surprisingly, he no longer grieved so terribly for his father. Lucas took from his pocket Dunmoore's watch. The Rolex that had been Alfred Dunmoore's favorite. The watch that Lucas had retrieved from a mound of snow. He slipped the Rolex on his wrist, tapped it, held it to his ear, and grinned. He knew the spirit of the Quest, and of his father and the Prof, would always be alive within him.

Lucas asked, "What about you, sir? What are you going to do?"

"Why, guard the relics. And who knows? I may call upon you Crusaders again in the future." With a smile, Merlin raised his arms high above his head and disappeared in a shimmering mist.

"Did he just say what I think he said?" asked Des.

"Let's just go before he gets any ideas." Lucas laughed, clapping Des on the back.

The Crusaders began the long walk to the Spenser cabin to gather their belongings and "travel" one last time – home.

Chapter Forty-Six

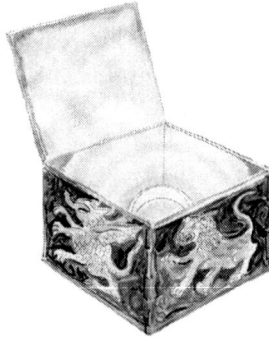

Home is Where the Heart Is

A little more than a week after boarding the plane to England, Lucas ended up where he started out – unpacking his bags in his bedroom in Texas, Shadow at his side. Lucas's band had played well at Disney World, but hardly anyone cared, because over the last three days, incredible events had taken place. The Israelis and Palestinians had signed a peace accord. A cease-fire had been called in Iraq. Many of the tribes in Africa had laid down their weapons and signed non-violence pacts. The strongest of the Colombian drug cartels had collapsed after the death of its leader. And he was not the only one who sustained a sudden coronary.

A number of world leaders' lives came to an untimely – some would say not soon enough – end, including several Ayatollahs, leaders of the Khmer Rouge, commanders of the IRA, several members of the English Parliament and heads of many of the world's governments. Numerous members of the Italian and American Mafias and the Japanese Yakuza died mysteriously, along with leaders of the larger gangs throughout the U.S., and most of the high-ranking Ku Klux Klansmen.

Political commentators, reporters and analysts were having a field day – some of their colleagues having succumbed as well – with the astounding number of individuals, both famous and infamous, who had expired on the same day at the same time. Some hinted at assassinations by the CIA and FBI. Some hinted at collaboration between various countries' secret services. Some believed it was a plague. Many opined it was the retribution of God upon the evil men and women of the world. Lucas knew the truth.

He knelt next to Shadow and rubbed the dog's fur for the hundredth time since he'd gotten home. "If only they knew, boy. If only they knew."

"Knew what?" His mom appeared in the doorway to his room.

Lucas bolted up, his mind whirling. "Uh, um, oh! If only you guys knew how much I missed you. Stupid, huh?"

"Not at all. We missed you, too, sweetie." Sandra Moreno stood on her tiptoes to kiss her son's cheek. "All unpacked?"

"Pretty much. I'm just gonna check my e-mail." Lucas started up his computer. He could feel his mom watching him. He glanced over his shoulder.

Sandra stood there with arms crossed, her head cocked to one side.

"Anything wrong, Mom?"

"No. It's just...you seem different."

Does she know anything? He cleared his throat. "Different, how?"

"More confident. More grown up." Sandra chuckled and shook her head. "Ignore me. It's just the ravings of a doting mother. Dinner's ready, honey." She walked to the door and turned. "It will be nice to have a man around the house, again."

Lucas found three e-mails waiting for him – from Des, Maya and Karen. *I'll get 'em after dinner.*

He took the ring and chain from around his neck and unclasped the chain from the ring. Holding the ring for a moment tight in his palm, he closed his eyes, remembering. Then, he placed the ring in the rosewood box, the box on top of his dresser.

Before closing the lid he said, "It certainly was an adventure, wasn't it?"

The ring did nothing.

"We really did it. Together, we really made a difference, didn't we?"

The ring did nothing.

"All and all, though, I'm kind of glad to be back, aren't you?"

The ring did nothing.

Lucas shrugged his shoulders and closed the lid. "So, you're only a ring. At least now, I won't have to worry about any more crusades."

Shadow barked and jumped up on the dresser, his front paws not quite reaching the top. He barked again.

"What is it, boy?" Lucas nudged Shadow away and opened the box, again.

The ring glowed.

"Oh, jeez," he whispered.

The glow faded.

A big smile spread across his face. "What the heck? There's always time for an adventure." He gently closed the box lid. "*After* dinner. Come on, boy."

Chapter Forty-Seven

V

From the Ashes

Deep within the Fortress of Shadows, Vassalar stepped from behind one of the rock formations supporting the lagoon cave and surveyed the gruesome scene. Bodies of warriors littered the ground, each corpse wearing a carved ring on their left pinkie. Stepping over the twin informants, Hugin and Munin, Vassalar stopped at the edge of the embankment and opened his hand. On his palm sat his ring of bone. He tossed the ivory circle into the watery pit.

Crouching over the viscous remains of his late master, Vassalar dipped two fingers into the ooze and licked them. He extracted a small crystal vial from his pocket and filled it with the black substance – pure distilled evil. He left the lagoon and made his way through the dungeon corridors to the throne room, his footsteps the only sound of life within the castle.

Holding the vial aloft, he vowed, "Out of death, a new beginning has arisen. In time, evil again shall rule."

Alone, he assumed his place on the Throne of Darkness.

The End

LaVergne, TN USA
13 October 2010
200618LV00003B/79/P